THE WORKS OF TOBIAS SMOLLETT

The Life and Adventures of Sir Launcelot Greaves

THE WORKS OF TOBIAS SMOLLETT

Alexander Pettit, General Editor
University of North Texas

O M Brack Jr., Textual Editor
Arizona State University

Jim Springer Borck, Technical Editor
Louisiana State University

*This edition includes all of the works by which Tobias Smollett was best known
in his own day and by which he most deserves to be remembered.
The edition conforms to the highest standards of textual and editorial scholarship.
Individual volumes provide carefully prepared texts together with biographical
and historical introductions and extensive explanatory notes.*

Launcelot Greaves, by Kirkwood after Rowlandson.
(Henry E. Huntington Library and Art Gallery)

The Life and Adventures of Sir Launcelot Greaves

TOBIAS SMOLLETT

Introduction and Notes by

ROBERT FOLKENFLIK

The Text Edited by

BARBARA LANING FITZPATRICK

The University of Georgia Press
Athens and London

© 2002 by the University of Georgia Press

Athens, Georgia 30602

All rights reserved

Set in 10/13 Janson Text by G&S Typesetters, Inc.

Printed and bound by Maple-Vail

The paper in this book meets the guidelines for

permanence and durability of the Committee on

Production Guidelines for Book Longevity of the

Council on Library Resources.

Printed in the United States of America

06 05 04 03 02 c 5 4 3 2 1

Library of Congress Cataloging-in-Publication Data

Smollett, Tobias George, 1721–1771.

The life and adventures of Sir Launcelot Greaves / Tobias Smollett;

introduction and notes by Robert Folkenflik;

the text edited by Barbara Laning Fitzpatrick.

p.   cm.—(The Works of Tobias Smollett)

Includes bibliographical references and index.

ISBN 0-8203-2307-1 (alk. paper)

1. Knights and knighthood—Fiction.   2. Quests (Expeditions)—Fiction.

3. Mentally ill—Fiction.   I. Title.

PR3694 .L3 2001

823'.6—dc21   2001034724

British Library Cataloging-in-Publication Data available

CONTENTS

List of Illustrations
ix

Preface
xi

Acknowledgments
xiii

List of Abbreviations
xv

Introduction
xvii

The Life and Adventures of Sir Launcelot Greaves
I

Notes to the Text
199

Textual Commentary
255

List of Emendations
271

Textual Notes
277

Word-Division
279

Historical Collation
285

Contents

Publication Dates
301

Bibliographical Descriptions
303

Index
307

ILLUSTRATIONS

A nthony Walker illustrated *Sir Launcelot Greaves* for number 2 (February 1760) and number 9 (August 1760) of the *British Magazine*, which published the first edition of the novel in twenty-five installments. William Walker, Charles Grignion, and William Blake provided engravings after Thomas Stothard for the 1782 edition published in the *Novelist's Magazine* (vol. 9, no. 4). John Kirkwood's engraving, after Thomas Rowlandson, was included in volume 5 of *Miscellaneous Works of Tobias Smollet [sic]* (London, 1790); the engravings after Richard Corbauld by Joseph Saunders and William Hawkins appeared in the 1793 (London) edition of the novel. George Cruikshank illustrated *Sir Launcelot Greaves* for the *Novelist's Library* (vol. 10, no. 2). Titles within brackets have been supplied by the general editor.

Launcelot Greaves, by Kirkwood after Rowlandson
FRONTISPIECE

Title page of first (book) edition, vol. 1, 1762
2

Sir Launcelot Greaves and his Squire, Timothy Crabshaw,
by Anthony Walker
8

[The Entrance of Sir Launcelot and Timothy Crabshaw],
by William Walker after Stothard
10

The Alarm of Crowe and Fillet at the Appearance of Sir Launcelot,
by Cruikshank
11

M^r· Greaves returning Darnel his sword after disarming him,
by Saunders after Corbauld
37

Captn· Crowe, terrified at Clarke and the Misanthrope,
by Hawkins after Corbauld
55

Sr. L. Greaves and his Squire T. Crabshaw at a Country Election,
by Anthony Walker
68

[The Election], by Blake after Stothard
74

Title page of first (book) edition, vol. 2, 1762
99

[Sir Launcelot and the Inn-keeper], by William Walker after Stothard
123

Dawdle's Victory over Captn Crowe, by Cruikshank
148

[The Conjuror], by Grignion after Stothard
171

PREFACE

No annotated edition of *Sir Launcelot Greaves* existed before the second half of the twentieth century. Two have been published recently, one prepared by David Evans (Oxford: Oxford University Press, 1973), the other by Peter Wagner (London: Penguin, 1988). Suitably for their purposes, these editions contain brief introductions and spare notes. The present edition features a more accurate text and more ambitious textual and critical apparatus.

The introduction follows the pattern established in the earlier volumes of *The Works of Tobias Smollett* by setting Smollett's achievement in this novel within the context of his career and by discussing the novel's form, the history of its composition and publication, and its major themes. I show that *Sir Launcelot Greaves*, despite its reputation as one of Smollett's least impressive novels, has had its champions from the time of its publication. Its status as the first illustrated serial novel and Smollett's only serial novel also brings up issues not previously examined in detail. This is the first edition to look closely at the work of Anthony Walker, the illustrator, and to consider the implications of the engravings that he prepared for the novel's original appearance in the *British Magazine*. A fresh consideration of Smollett's use of *Don Quixote*, the most commonly noted feature of the novel, calls attention to a subtlety and an originality for which Smollett is not generally credited.

As is customary in scholarly editions, the notes to the text will often point to topics suggested by the word or phrase glossed; but I have annotated the text, not the subjects. Notes are cross-referenced both to the text and to relevant instances in Smollett's other works. Smollett's extensive use of proverbial materials, an analogue to Cervantes's method in *Don Quixote*, often requires explanation; and Smollett's linguistic virtuosity, especially in his use of nautical slang, has led to the identification of antedates to first uses recorded in the *Oxford English Dictionary*. The annotations identify some sources that have never been recognized, including some that have proved elusive to earlier editors. I have identified some probable targets of Smollett's satire, such as Sir Joshua Vanneck and Charles Churchill's friend Robert Lloyd; and I have traced previously unrecognized allusions to Homer, Virgil, Shakespeare, Churchill, Lloyd, Thomas Otway, and Jonathan Swift. The anti-Semitic stereotyping of Mr. Isaac Vanderpelft, here considered as part of the novel's larger political context, receives more attention than it did in earlier editions.

I am indebted to Evans's and Wagner's editions and to Roger A. Hambridge, "An Annotated Edition of Tobias Smollett's *Life and Adventures of Sir Launcelot Greaves* (1760–1761)" (Ph.D. diss., University of California, Los Angeles, 1977). In considering Smollett's text, I have benefited as well from Richard L. Lettis, "A Study of Smollett's *Sir Launcelot Greaves*" (Ph.D. diss., Yale University, 1957), and Barbara Laning Fitzpatrick, "The Text of Tobias Smollett's *Life and Adventures of Sir Launcelot Greaves*, the First Serialized Novel" (Ph.D. diss., Duke University, 1987). A number of more general studies have proved essential to my work: Lewis Mansfield Knapp's edition of *The Letters of Tobias Smollett* (Oxford: Clarendon Press, 1970) and his *Tobias Smollett: Doctor of Men and Manners* (Princeton: Princeton University Press, 1949); Paul-Gabriel Boucé's *The Novels of Tobias Smollett* (London: Longman, 1976); James G. Basker's *Tobias Smollett: Critic and Journalist* (Newark: University of Delaware Press, 1988); George M. Kahrl's *Tobias Smollett: Traveler-Novelist* (Chicago: University of Chicago Press, 1945); and Robert D. Mayo's *The English Novel in the Magazines: 1740–1815* (Evanston, Ill.: Northwestern University Press, 1962). I have made use of Hambridge's tracing of Smollett's legal terminology to Giles Jacob's *New Law-Dictionary* (1729).

Many of the numerous proverbs replicated in *Sir Launcelot Greaves* are listed in Archer Taylor, "Proverbial Materials in Tobias Smollett, *The Adventures of Sir Launcelot Greaves*," *Southern Folklore Quarterly* 21 (1957): 85–92; but Taylor does not notice all the proverbs, nor does he explain any of them. In my notes to the text, I have indicated all instances in which the proverbs in question appear in Taylor. Whenever possible, references to the proverbs cite, by number, Morris Tilley, *A Dictionary of the Proverbs in England in the Sixteenth and Seventeenth Centuries* (Ann Arbor: University of Michigan Press, 1950), and, by page, *The Oxford Dictionary of English Proverbs*, 3d ed., rev. F. P. Wilson (Oxford: Clarendon Press, 1970).

Translations are my own unless otherwise noted. I have generally made reference to the Loeb editions for Latin works and to *The Riverside Shakespeare*, ed. G. Blakemore Evans et al. (Boston: Houghton Mifflin, 1974), for quotations from and allusions to Shakespeare. While it has not proven possible to identify the edition or editions that Smollett himself used, I have checked eighteenth-century editions and determined that sometimes Smollett's seeming misquotations follow the texts of the best editions of his time.

ACKNOWLEDGMENTS

O M Brack Jr. first asked me to undertake this edition many years and a few presses ago. During the years of its preparation, many friends and colleagues have helped in a variety of ways. I am grateful to Brian Allen, James G. Basker, Ann Bermingham, Albert Braunmuller, Homer Brown, W. B. Carnochan, Anne and Alan Coren, the late Robert Adams Day, Frank Felsenstein, Barbara Laning Fitzpatrick, Byron Gassman, J. Paul Hunter, Richard Kroll, Wolfgang Mieder, Ronald Paulson, Roy Porter, Daniel Punday, John Richetti, G. S. Rousseau, Patrick Sinclair, and Elaine Smyth. Special thanks go to the former general editor of *The Works of Tobias Smollett*, Jerry Beasley, and to his successor, Alexander Pettit. The Research and Travel Committee of the School of Humanities, University of California, Irvine, made possible my research trips to London. Deans Terry Parsons and Spencer Olin and my chairs, Michael Clark and Brook Thomas, supported this work. I also obtained research aid through the associate dean of graduate studies, James Calderwood, and through the Pregraduate Mentorship Program. For assistance of various kinds, I am grateful to my students Georgina Dodge, Carlos Fernandez, Maria Ianetta, Allison Kroll, Joy Lee, Lewis Long, Jesse Loren, Indhushree Rajan, Joel Reed, Priya Shah, San Truong, and Ruth Warkentin. Jason Denman checked references, and Marie O'Connor proofread the annotations. Oliver Berghof and Christina Chang read page proofs.

Martin Battestin kindly sent me an offprint of his article on Smollett's translation of *Don Quixote*. Roger Hambridge and Barbara Laning Fitzpatrick made their dissertations available to me, and Guilland Sutherland made available the chapter on the illustrations of *Sir Launcelot Greaves* from her dissertation.

One debt requires some explanation. Through the offices of G. S. Rousseau, I agreed to take on Roger Hambridge as collaborator following the completion of his dissertation. When the edition came under the auspices of the University of Georgia Press, I offered either to formalize the collaboration with Hambridge or to let him edit the volume on his own; but the general editor asked me to continue, and Hambridge decided not to participate. I mention this because an inaccurate reference to the intended collaboration found its way into Mary Wagoner's useful Smollett bibliography (New York: Garland, 1984). My debt to Hambridge, as to the other editors, is indicated in the notes, although my emphases differ markedly from his.

I am indebted to the staffs of the libraries at the University of California,

Irvine. Jackie Dooley, Pamela La Zarr, Cathy Palmer, and Eddie Yeghiayan were particularly helpful. I am indebted as well to the staffs of the British Library; the William Andrews Clark Memorial Library, UCLA; the National Library of Australia; and the Henry E. Huntington Library.

Most of all I am grateful to my family—my wife, Vivian, my daughter, Nora, and my son, David—for their support in so many ways over the years. Nora's death in 1995 makes the completion of this volume a far less happy event than it otherwise would have been. Here, as elsewhere, I wish to remember her.

Robert Folkenflik

ABBREVIATIONS

Adventures of an Atom	Tobias Smollett, *The History and Adventures of an Atom*, ed. Robert Adams Day (Athens: University of Georgia Press, 1989)
Basker	James G. Basker, *Tobias Smollett: Critic and Journalist* (Newark: University of Delaware Press; London: Associated University Presses, 1988)
Complete History	Tobias Smollett, *A Complete History of England*, 4 vols. (London, 1757–58)
Continuation	Tobias Smollett, *Continuation of the Complete History of England*, 5 vols. (London, 1760–65)
Don Quixote	Tobias Smollett, trans., *The History and Adventures of the Renowned Don Quixote* (London, 1755)
Evans	Tobias Smollett, *The Life and Adventures of Sir Launcelot Greaves*, ed. David Evans (London: Oxford University Press, 1973)
Falconer	William Falconer, *An Universal Dictionary of the Marine*, 4th ed. (London, 1780)
Hambridge	Roger A. Hambridge, "An Annotated Edition of Tobias Smollett's *Life and Adventures of Sir Launcelot Greaves* (1760–1761)" (Ph.D. diss., University of California, Los Angeles, 1977)
Hogarth's Graphic Works	William Hogarth, *Hogarth's Graphic Works*, rev. ed., ed. Ronald Paulson (London: Print Room, 1989)
Humphry Clinker	Tobias Smollett, *The Expedition of Humphry Clinker*, ed. Thomas R. Preston (Athens: University of Georgia Press, 1990)
James	Robert James, *A Medicinal Dictionary*, 3 vols. (London, 1743–45)
Johnson, *Dictionary*	Samuel Johnson, *A Dictionary of the English Language*, 2 vols. (London, 1755)
Jowitt and Walsh	William Allen Jowitt and Clifford Walsh, *Dictionary of English Law*, 2 vols. (London: Sweet and Maxwell, 1959)

Kahrl George M. Kahrl, *Tobias Smollett: Traveler-Novelist* (Chicago: University of Chicago Press, 1945)

Knapp Lewis Mansfield Knapp, *Tobias Smollett: Doctor of Men and Manners* (Princeton: Princeton University Press, 1949)

Letters *The Letters of Tobias Smollett*, ed. Lewis M. Knapp (Oxford: Clarendon Press, 1970)

NLD Giles Jacob, *A New Law Dictionary*, 7th ed. (London, 1756)

ODEP *Oxford Dictionary of English Proverbs*, 3d ed., rev. F. P. Wilson (Oxford: Clarendon Press, 1970)

OED *Oxford English Dictionary*

Poems, Plays, and "The Briton" Tobias Smollett, *Poems, Plays, and "The Briton,"* ed. Byron Gassman (Athens: University of Georgia Press, 1993)

Present State Tobias Smollett, ed., *The Present State of All Nations*, 8 vols. (London, 1768–69)

Ray John Ray, *A Collection of English Proverbs*, 2d ed. (Cambridge, 1678)

Taylor Archer Taylor, "Proverbial Materials in Tobias Smollett, *The Adventures of Sir Launcelot Greaves,*" *Southern Folklore Quarterly* 21 (1957): 85–92

Tilley Morris Tilley, *A Dictionary of the Proverbs in England in the Sixteenth and Seventeenth Centuries* (Ann Arbor: University of Michigan Press, 1950)

INTRODUCTION

Tobias Smollett's fourth novel, *The Life and Adventures of Sir Launcelot Greaves*, first appeared serially in twenty-five consecutive issues of the *British Magazine; or, Monthly Repository for Gentlemen and Ladies*, a new venture in which Smollett had a controlling interest. The magazine's inaugural issue, published 1 January 1760, printed Smollett's first chapter; the novel concluded in volume 2, number 12, published 1 January 1762. It was the longest work of original fiction yet to appear in an English periodical, and it was the first serially published novel ever to be illustrated. No doubt because Smollett himself aggressively promoted the magazine, *Sir Launcelot Greaves* was fairly well received upon its initial appearance. Three one-volume Irish editions appeared in the 1760s; a second English edition, in two volumes, was published in March 1762. No other editions were published during Smollett's lifetime. Although *Sir Launcelot Greaves* has never achieved the critical status of Smollett's most widely read novels, *The Adventures of Roderick Random* (1748) and *The Expedition of Humphry Clinker* (1771), it has always had its share of admirers.

BIOGRAPHICAL BACKGROUND

In 1760, when he began to publish the *British Magazine*, Smollett was thirty-eight years old and an important presence on the English literary scene.[1] He had founded the *Critical Review* in 1756, serving as its editor and, for a time, as its principal contributor.[2] He had finished *A Complete History of England* (1757–58) and had begun the *Continuation* (1760–65) that would extend that work from 1748 to the beginning of 1765. In addition to the three novels of his youth—*The Adventures of Roderick Random* (1748), *The Adventures of Peregrine Pickle* (1751), and *The Adventures of Ferdinand Count Fathom* (1753)—he had written poems and comic and tragic dramas and had prepared translations of *Don Quixote* (1755) and Alain René Le Sage's *Gil Blas* (1748, dated 1749) and *The Devil upon Crutches* (1750). The only British novelists whose works appeared in more editions than Smollett's in the period 1750 to 1759 were Daniel Defoe, Henry Fielding, and Samuel Richardson.[3]

The title page of Smollett's new periodical promised coverage of the "Political State of Europe and America, the Transactions of the Powers at War, and the Connections, whether Natural or Politic, that subsist among the several States upon the Continent." In addition to providing a continuing account of the Seven Years' War, the *British Magazine* would also publish fiction, essays, music, poetry, and book reviews and discuss new works of art, scientific and practical discoveries, and current events. The magazine was a success. James G. Basker gives an intentionally conservative estimate of three thousand copies sold monthly, but Barbara Laning Fitzpatrick may be nearer the mark in suggesting five thousand.[4]

Smollett's first year with the *British Magazine* was punctuated by legal problems resulting from a negative review that Smollett had published in the *Critical Review* for May 1758. A suit for libel by the author of the pamphlet in question, Adm. Charles Knowles, against Smollett and his printer resulted in Smollett's arrest for libel in June 1760 and his conviction five months later.[5] Ironically, the judge in the case was William Murray, Lord Mansfield, a fellow Scot whom Smollett had praised in chapter 3 of *Sir Launcelot Greaves* as an impressive parliamentary orator. On or about 28 November 1760, midway through the serial publication of *Sir Launcelot Greaves*, Smollett was conveyed to the King's Bench Prison, where he remained for nearly three months. Certainly his time in prison influenced the setting of chapters 20 and 21 of *Sir Launcelot Greaves;* it may also have furnished him with the models for some of his characters.

Smollett's legal problems did not change his work habits. His release from jail in February 1761 was followed by proposals for a new translation of Voltaire, the first volumes of which issued from the press in March and April 1761. The edition comprised thirty-five volumes by 1765. In 1761, the fourth volume of the *Continuation of the Complete History of England* was published, making it the best source for Smollett's thinking about politics and history at the time he was writing *Sir Launcelot Greaves*. In May 1762, two months after *Sir Launcelot Greaves* appeared in book form, Smollett began yet another periodical, the *Briton*, established to defend the policies of John Stuart, third earl of Bute, George III's first prime minister.

Already tubercular and in poor health generally, Smollett would survive less than a decade after the publication of *Sir Launcelot Greaves*. His literary output, however, did not diminish during this period. *Travels through France and Italy* (1766) chronicles the extended trip that Smollett and his wife began in 1763, following the death of their fifteen-year-old daughter. *The Present State of All Nations*, a historical compendium, appeared in weekly numbers during 1768 and 1769 and was reissued in eight volumes during the latter year. Smollett's corrosive political satire *The History and Adventures of an Atom* was published anonymously in 1769.

Smollett and his wife settled in Italy in 1768, hoping for an improvement in his health. His sole novel of this period, *Humphry Clinker*, was probably completed at Il Giardino, the Smolletts' villa in Leghorn, in 1770. Arguably Smollett's masterpiece, the novel was published in June 1771. Smollett died shortly thereafter, on 17 September 1771. His *Ode to Independence* and his translation of François de Salignac de la Mothe-Fénelon's *Adventures of Telemachus* appeared posthumously, in 1773 and 1776, respectively.

COMPOSITION, PRINTING, AND RECEPTION

At about 89,600 words, *Sir Launcelot Greaves* is the shortest of Smollett's novels.[6] Its structure is unusually regular for Smollett. After experimenting with a variety of chapter lengths in the early part of the novel, he settled down to compose in chapters of 3,000 to 4,000 words—the longest chapters in all his novels. But details concerning the composition of *Sir Launcelot Greaves* are difficult to ascertain. No manuscript exists, nor is there any direct reference to the writing of the novel in Smollett's letters. In his brief memoir of Smollett, Sir Walter Scott asserts that part of *Sir Launcelot Greaves* was written while Smollett was visiting his friend George Home in Paxton, just above the Scottish border, after his arrest for libel but before his trial. Scott claims as well that Smollett spent an hour or less on each chapter, with the timing of the mail providing his deadline, and that he did not bother to proofread his work.[7] Scott's claim has been persuasively called into question by Lewis M. Knapp; but, along with an earlier misleading comment in the *Westminster Magazine* (1775) suggesting that Smollett wrote *Sir Launcelot Greaves* in prison, it has contributed to the devaluing of the novel.[8] Scott was probably being unfair, but it is true that Smollett worked quickly. He may have had the story in mind from the time when he was translating *Don Quixote*, but there is no firm evidence indicating that he started it much before the first number of the *British Magazine*; nor, with one important exception discussed below, is there any real indication that he drafted the individual chapters much in advance of their first appearance. Probably a few chapters, perhaps more, were completed during Smollett's months in the King's Bench Prison.

A number of critics and recent editors, sometimes influenced by Scott's questionable anecdote, have cited the repetitions and errors in the book as proof that Smollett wrote more quickly and carelessly than he should have done. David Evans, for example, produces as evidence of careless workmanship the repeated allusions to the ghost scene from *Hamlet*, the differing descriptions of Greaves's mother by Tom Clarke and Mrs. Oakely, and the shift from Sir Launcelot's knowledge of Aurelia's London relations in chapter 16 to his surprise at Dolly's "revelation" about her family in chapter 24.[9] One could add that a few curious repetitions of names suggest a lack of attentiveness as well: Aurelia travels as Miss Meadows, and Sir Launcelot's nearest relative is Sir Reginald Meadows; Miss Cowslip is the dam of Sir Launcelot's horse, and Dolly Cowslip is the illegitimate daughter of Sir Launcelot's deceased uncle Jonathan. But not only is an inexactitude with respect to certain sorts of details (for example, onomastic) fairly common in eighteenth-century fiction, but, more locally, a confusion regarding names is evident in *Ferdinand Count Fathom* and *Humphry Clinker*—a fact for which one finds no explanation as convenient as Scott's remarks on Smollett's composition of his serial novel. Infelicities of this sort do not so much condemn *Sir Launcelot Greaves* for sloppiness as identify it as a product of its time and its author.

Furthermore, although serial publication may possibly have led to a somewhat higher level of improvisation than was usual for Smollett, *Sir Launcelot Greaves* actually displays the most linkage and preparation of any novel he had written to date. The individual chapters, as Robert D. Mayo has put it, frequently open and close "with a formal flourish."[10] They are also apt to be complete structural units containing either a single episode or a series of closely related episodes. Perhaps Smollett's linkage of chapters owed something to Fielding's *Tom Jones* (1749), a work he liked to depreciate in the 1750s but eventually came to respect. The chapter headings, like Fielding's, sometimes call attention to structure. Chapter 5 explicitly ends the "*recapitulation*" of the history preceding the novel's main story line. Chapters 23 and 24 refer to the "*Catastrophe*" and the untying of the "*Knot*," standard terms in neo-Aristotelian considerations of form, although Smollett's plot is hardly Aristotelian. It is a careful plot, however, and *Sir Launcelot Greaves* is arguably the most thoughtfully constructed of the original serial novels of the eighteenth century.

Several previously unremarked details suggest foresight rather than oversight in the composition of Smollett's narrative. One significant and overlooked detail is the color—black—of Sir Launcelot's armor. This detail is both verbal and pictorial. Interestingly, Anthony Walker's engraving of Sir Launcelot gets the color of his armor right, although the illustration appears in the second installment of the original serial run of the novel in the *British Magazine*, three months before the fifth chapter reveals that Sir Launcelot's armor is "lacquered black" (44). Since black armor is infrequent both in actuality and in art, the detail is striking; yet it has been overlooked, probably because Walker's two engravings for the novel have themselves received little attention. While it is possible that Walker decided to give Sir Launcelot black armor and Smollett followed suit after seeing the results, this seems unlikely. Smollett was interested in art, and he characteristically exerted strict control over his writing projects. Further evidence of Smollett's role manifests itself in the other detail appearing in Smollett's description and in Walker's illustration: the crescent moon on Sir Launcelot's shield. And Walker certainly read enough of Smollett's text in advance to obtain such visual details as Timothy Crabshaw's form and physiognomy, the crescent displayed on his cap, and his set of bandoleers, all described in chapter 2. The conclusion to be drawn is either that chapter 5 existed in manuscript early on or that Smollett told Walker of his intentions before executing them. Since the first five chapters clearly form a unit, it is likely that Smollett had completed at least that much of the novel before he began publishing it.

Other linked details suggest premeditation. In chapter 2, Captain Crowe shrewdly sizes up Ferret as a "shew-man or a conjuror" (14), a hit that leads to abuse but not denial on Ferret's part. In chapter 6, when Clarke and Fillet play a practical joke on Crowe, Ferret's greatcoat is found to conceal, "together with divers nostrums, a small vial of liquid phosphorus" (5); but it is not until chapter 10 that Ferret reveals himself to be a quack doctor, synonymous with the mountebank and showman. Since Smollett took his own antagonist, John Shebbeare (a quack in politics as well as medicine), as his satirical target in creating the character of Ferret, he had probably had the development of chapter 10 in mind from the outset.

There has been much more enthusiasm for the novel over the years than Fred W. Boege's standard account of its reception suggests,[11] although some of the praise is from dubious sources. Initially, both the serial and the book publication were ushered in by favorable notices, some of which were connected with, if not orchestrated by, Smollett himself.[12] The difference from the response to *Ferdinand Count Fathom* is striking: the earlier novel was the subject of only one contemporary review and has remained the most neglected of Smollett's novels.

A particularly friendly puff appeared in the *Public Ledger* for 16 February 1760, shortly after the publication of the second installment of *Sir Launcelot Greaves*. The occasion is an imaginary "Wow-wow," the gathering of a miscellaneous crowd at a pub to read newspapers and hear gossip. One of the group, an "Oxford scholar," takes from his pocket "a new magazine":

> He then read the adventures of Sir Launcelot Greaves to the entire satisfaction
> of the audience, which being finished, he threw the pamphlet on the table: that
> piece gentleman, says he, is written in the very spirit and manner of Cervantes,

there is a great knowledge of human nature, and evident marks of the master in almost every sentence; and from the plan, the humour, and the execution, I can venture to say that it dropt from the pen of ingenious Dr ———. Everyone was pleased with the performance, and I was particularly gratified in hearing all the sensible part of the company give orders for the British Magazine.[13]

The *British Magazine* itself was not above such huckstering. A letter, printed in April 1760 and signed "S. R.," claims that "the adventures of Sir Launcelot Greaves promise a rich fund of entertainment."[14] An odd puff appeared in the same issue in the form of a verse rebus, or word puzzle:

> The weapon erst us'd much by combating knight,
> And what was in doubt till the end of the fight:
> With what to his horses the coachman will bawl,
> And letter, which dog's we peculiarly call,
> Then guess, from the house, whence will tumble the rain,
> It may help you some part of this book to explain.

The answer, the careful reader would have discerned, was the novel's title: Launce lot G r eaves.[15]

Smollett's enemies were at work as well. An anonymous pamphlet published in March 1760, *The Battle of the Reviews*, attacks the *Critical Review*, dubbing Smollett "Sawney Mac Smallhead" and using the character of Sir Launcelot's "squire," Timothy Crabshaw, to satirize the new project of the *British Magazine*. The pamphlet says nothing specific about *Sir Launcelot Greaves* itself, the third chapter of which appeared that month, although it mentions Shebbeare's antagonism toward Smollett, exacerbated by the depiction of Ferret.[16] The author may possibly have been Shebbeare himself.

Some of the earliest praise of *Sir Launcelot Greaves* appears in the Belgian *Journal encyclopédique* (1761), which finds the hero's actions as a quixotic redresser of wrongs more "raisonnable" than those of the original Don because he does not mistake a windmill for a giant or a "grosse paysanne" (fat peasant) for his Dulcinea. The anonymous reviewer goes on to claim that "every reader, a friend of his country and of humanity will interest himself from the first in favor of the modern chevalier."[17] In Dublin, immediately following completion of the serial run of *Sir Launcelot Greaves*, the publisher James Hoey Jr. made the novel the most advertised of his reprints of Smollett. In the *Dublin Journal* (30 January 1762), Hoey wrote that *Sir Launcelot Greaves* "is the best of this Author's Performances in the Novel way."[18]

But when the London bookseller John Coote issued his two-volume edition in March 1762, it generated little notice in the form of reviews, perhaps not surprisingly, given the earlier serial appearance. As Basker has suggested, the decision to publish first in the *British Magazine* may have "preempted criticism."[19] William Rider's *An Historical and Critical Account of the Living Authors of Great Britain* (1762), which provides the first biographical account of Smollett, does not mention *Sir Launcelot Greaves*. Smollett's rival, the *Monthly Review*, noticed it, but only in a brief announcement of its appearance in book form, and only then to declare it "better than the common Novels, but unworthy the pen of Dr. Smollett."[20] This view would prove durable.

The *Critical Review*, not surprisingly, was both kinder and more voluble. Almost three pages of the number for May 1762 are devoted to a review of the novel, probably not by Smollett. Having praised Smollett, along with Laurence Sterne and Henry Fielding, for creating fictional personages who are original and "complete" conceptions, the reviewer finds that the novel's "two principal characters," Sir Launcelot and Timothy Crabshaw, "seem to be formed on those of the admirable Cervantes. . . . They resemble without imitating, and remind us of what imparted exquisite enjoyment, without diminishing their own novelty." These remarks are followed by praise for the portraits of Crowe, Ferret, and Oakely as "truly characteristical, and demonstrative of the genuine humor, satirical talents, and benevolent heart of the writer." Crowe, the reviewer says, is a particular triumph—a tar of "as extraordinary a cast" as any in Smollett's fiction.[21]

A highly favorable account of *Sir Launcelot Greaves* appeared the same month in the *Library*, although it differed in its judgment of Crowe:

> Sir Launcelot Greaves is a kind of English Quixote, and his adventures are conducted with much humour. There are many characters well drawn, many diverting incidents, and many fine strokes of genius, nature, and passion. The author has introduced certain persons too often, and especially captain Crowe, whose appearance is sometimes disgusting, and whose sea jargon is absolutely unintelligible to a land reader; but on the whole, the performance has considerable merit.[22]

The following year brought a much less discerning set of observations in the form of a fan letter from an American, Richard Smith. The letter praises *Peregrine Pickle* and some of Smollett's other novels but adds, ingenuously, "as to Lancelot Greaves many here are pleased to say that you Lent your Name upon that Occasion to a Mercenary Bookseller."[23] Smith seems only to mean that *Sir Launcelot Greaves* did not represent Smollett at his best. In 1764, Francis Vernon, Lord Orwell, devoted his *Letter to the Right Honourable Lord*

Orwell . . . and to Philip Thicknesse, Esq. to the portrayal in chapter 20 of
the King's Bench Prison, which, to Vernon's astonishment, Smollett had
presented in a favorable light. Thicknesse, the letter's intended corecipient,
took up the same theme two years later, joking that Smollett in the *Travels
through France and Italy* made a year in Paris or Nice sound less pleasurable
than the equivalent time in the King's Bench.[24] Later in the decade, the pseu-
donymous "Jeoffry Wagstaffe," one of Hoey's writers at the *Dublin Mercury*,
offered a broader but not uncritical assessment in a representation of a group
of fictional characters trying to cross the river of Dulness: "Sir Launcelot
Greaves appeared in tolerable spirits, tho under the weight of Don Quixote's
armour which he stole."[25] "Wagstaffe" placed Sir Launcelot in good company.
Richardson's Clarissa attempts the crossing too, and she fares worse than
Smollett's hero.

James Beattie, the influential critic and Smollett's fellow Scot, commented
on *Sir Launcelot Greaves* twice in the next two decades. In "An Essay on Laughter, and Ludicrous Composition" (1776), Beattie judiciously noted that "Sir
Launcelot Greaves is of Don Quixote's Kindred, but a rather different character. Smollett's design was not to expose him to ridicule but rather to recommend him to our pity and admiration. He has therefore given him youth,
strength, and beauty, as well as courage, and dignity of mind, has mounted
him on a generous steed, and arrayed him in an elegant suit of armour."[26]
Writing in 1783, Beattie ran counter to most commentators by preferring *Ferdinand Count Fathom* and *Sir Launcelot Greaves* to *Roderick Random* and *Humphry Clinker*. Smollett's two most neglected works, he wrote, "deserve to be
mentioned with more respect. . . . *Sir Launcelot Greaves*, though still more
improbable [than *Ferdinand Count Fathom*], has great merit; and is truly original in the execution, not-withstanding that the hint is borrowed from *Don
Quixote*."[27]

Although a critic writing in 1794 expressed a commonplace when he or she
proclaimed *Sir Launcelot Greaves* "romantick, but extravagant,"[28] the novel
continued to have its admirers in Smollett's own century. The publisher Joseph Wenman thought enough of *Sir Launcelot Greaves* to reprint it in 1780 as
the first volume of his *Entertaining Museum: or, Complete Circulating Library*;
the fact that Wenman published the novel again in 1783 suggests that sales of
his first edition were not sluggish.[29] Another inexpensive edition appeared in
James Harrison's popular *Novelist's Magazine* in 1782; the number was evidently reissued in 1787.[30] Some readers recorded their approval of the novel.
In 1791, for example, the bookseller James Lackington commented favorably
on its language and "incidents."[31] Francis Garden, Lord Gardenstone, in the

Bee and a few months later in his *Miscellanies in Prose and Verse* (both 1792), praised some episodes from the novel, including "the night scene in Bedlam" (chapter 23), "the ruin of captain Clewlin and his family" (chapter 21), and "the oration of Sir Launcelot to an election mob" (chapter 9). Gardenstone warmed especially to Smollett's handling of "the miserable farce of representation in parliament" (chapters 9 and 10).[32] A few years later, Robert Anderson, Smollett's earliest serious biographer, found *Sir Launcelot Greaves* hastily but often "delightfully" written.[33] The specific terms of Anderson's assessment were pillaged from earlier sources; nevertheless, the position taken by a biographer seeking to establish a more-or-less official view of his subject is telling.

The subsequent reception of *Sir Launcelot Greaves* may be briefly summarized. *Sir Launcelot Greaves* fared poorly with the influential early-nineteenth-century anthologists Anna Laetitia Barbauld, William Mudford, and Alexander Chalmers; in 1821 Scott was only slightly more generous in his appraisal.[34] Succeeding generations of Victorian and Edwardian critics did little to rehabilitate the novel, although George Saintsbury, in the introduction to his 1895 edition of Smollett's novels, called *Sir Launcelot Greaves* a "rather unjustly depreciated book" that deserved "a very much higher rank than has been generally allowed it."[35] A better understanding of the book, if not a higher ranking for it among Smollett's novels, awaited such developments as Lewis Knapp's biography of Smollett (1949), Robert Mayo's account of serial fictions in *The English Novel in the Magazines* (1962), and Ronald Paulson's *Satire and the Novel in Eighteenth-Century England* (1967), which characterized *Sir Launcelot Greaves* as the "most thoughtful if not most successful" of Smollett's novels before *Humphry Clinker*.[36] Paul-Gabriel Boucé, in his influential study of Smollett (1971; translated 1976), found much to admire in the novel.[37] So, at the end of the twentieth century, did Jerry C. Beasley, who sounded a bit like Saintsbury when he regretted that "like *Ferdinand Count Fathom*, [*Sir Launcelot Greaves*] has always merited more praise than it has received from readers whose numbers have always been fewer than it has deserved."[38]

FORM, CHARACTER, AND THEMES

Evans rightly claims that the titular character holds together the narrative of *Sir Launcelot Greaves*.[39] Smollett's own theory of the novel suggests that this role is a matter of design. The dedication to *Ferdinand Count Fathom* shows that Smollett considered his narrative designs to be unified in a simple and quite particular way. "A Novel is a large diffused picture," he wrote, comprehending the characters of life, disposed in different groupes, and exhibited in various attitudes, for the purposes of an uniform plan, and general occurrence, to which every individual figure is subservient. But this plan cannot be executed with propriety, probability or success, without a principal personage to attract the attention, unite the incidents, unwind the clue of the labyrinth, and at last close the scene by virtue of his own importance.[40]

In *Sir Launcelot Greaves*, that "principal personage" is the hero, as it is in each of the novels preceding it. The reader first encounters Sir Launcelot in chapter 2, when he enters the Black Lion Inn carrying the nearly drowned Timothy Crabshaw over his shoulder, perhaps a rough remembrance of Orlando's pietà-like entrance with old Adam in *As You Like It*. Sir Launcelot and Crabshaw join the static "groupe" of the seafarer Captain Crowe; the malcontent Ferret; the attorney Tom Clarke; Fillet, a surgeon; and Dolly Cowslip, the landlady's daughter. The grouping is not random but is instead evidence of a "uniform plan" for the novel. The principal characters introduced at the Black Lion all have prior links to Sir Launcelot: Tom Clarke, the son of old Everhard Greaves's steward, is Sir Launcelot's godson and Crowe's nephew, for example; and Crabshaw had helped to handle the hounds at Greavesbury Hall during fox hunts. These connections will help shape Smollett's plot.

The initial grouping allows Smollett to highlight certain important characteristics. Tom Clarke identifies himself as the most normal of the group, when he is not speaking in legal jargon (although Smollett will later put Clarke's legal knowledge to good use). Captain Crowe, a memorable eccentric, is the last in Smollett's series of fictional seadogs. The reader sees early on that Crowe is quite literally out of his element, for his language is sailor's slang spouted at uncomprehending landlubbers. In transferring sea traits to land, Crowe follows the lead of Commodore Trunnion, Peregrine Pickle's grotesque uncle. Smollett's main villain, Ferret, who vigorously attacks the government at every turn, has even more comic vitality, though he bears a relation to the darkly misanthropic Cadwallader Crabtree, Peregrine's partner in a series of London swindles. Timothy Crabshaw, soon to become Sir Launcelot's "squire," is a north-country naturalization of Sancho Panza, more hard-bitten than the original.[41] These characteristics will recur meaningfully in the "different groupes" that Smollett will present throughout the novel.

The "principal personage" himself, biding his "madness," is more nearly a paragon than any of Smollett's heroes, and his given name recalls England's heroic past.[42] He is also the most serious (not to say humorless) of them all, for, as the reader learns in chapter 2, he sees himself as "coadjutor to the law" (17). While his name is typical of Smollett heroes in that a romantic given name is undercut by a homely family name, "Launcelot" and "Greaves" also suggest metonyms for the knight-errant's weapon and armor, since "greaves," as is mentioned in the novel itself, are shin protectors.[43]

And of course the novel's major theme of madness centers on Sir Launcelot, although it expands to take in the whole of society. Smollett's young hero seems a variant of Thomas Gray's elegist "mutt'ring his wayward fancies" and "cross'd in hopeless love."[44] He is represented as hereditarily odd: his mother was "very whimsical" and "a little touched or so" (21); a great-great-uncle was a lunatic suicide (43). His early years had been marked by shyness and awkwardness, and his preference for the stable rather than company recalls Lemuel Gulliver's sort of reclusiveness. The rector who examines Greaves at his father's request comes to the exasperated conclusion that he will prove "either a mirrour of wisdom, or a monument of folly" (21). Even his charity seems singular: "he made the guineas fly in such a manner, as looked more like madness than generosity" (22).

While Tom Clarke, who narrates Sir Launcelot's early life, calls his actions "disorder" (38) or "pranks" (35), they have nothing in common with the picaresque practical jokes played on Captain Crowe and Timothy Crabshaw by Fillet and Ferret in this novel or with those that fill Smollett's earlier fictions. After Sir Launcelot rescues Aurelia Darnel from going over a precipice in a runaway coach and then falls in love with her only to receive a letter breaking off their pledged affection, the Greavesburyans think him "a little disordered in his brain, his grief was so wild, and his passion so impetuous" (35). They attribute this condition to Aurelia's having been spirited away by her guardian; and it is not until chapter 13 that we learn of the letter of dismissal, until chapter 15 that Aurelia denies knowing of it, and until the last chapter that Anthony Darnel's ruse in sending it is explained.

The central trope signifying both Sir Launcelot's madness and his role as (in Tom Clarke's words) "the general redresser of grievances" (40) is knight-errantry. Indeed, Smollett's narrator will later reveal that Tom "laid it down as a maxim, that knight-errantry and madness were synonimous terms" (100). Sir Launcelot is inducted into his role by a knight (probably out of his mind, according to Tom) and two attendants. As part of the ceremony, all four cavort "as if they had been mad" (44). When Sir Launcelot explains to the company at the inn why he is riding about the country dressed in outdated armor, his exchange with Ferret, the keynote of the novel, represents Smollett's own position on his adaptation of the Quixote fiction. Interestingly, however, it is the skeptical attack by Ferret just preceding this moment that has shaped much of the negative reception of the novel from its day to our own. Ferret protests,

> What! . . . you set up for a modern Don Quixote?—The scheme is rather too stale and extravagant.—What was an humorous romance, and well-timed satire in Spain, near two hundred years ago, will make but a sorry jest, and appear equally insipid and absurd, when really acted from affectation, at this time a-day, in a country like England. (15)

Sir Launcelot's response shows him to be a close student of the Quixote character:

> He that from affectation imitates the extravagances recorded of Don Quixote, is an imposter equally wicked and contemptible. He that counterfeits madness . . . not only debases his own soul, but acts as a traytor to heaven, by denying the divinity that is within him.—I am neither an affected imitator of Don Quixote, nor, as I trust in heaven, visited by that spirit of lunacy so admirably displayed in the fictitious character exhibited by the inimitable Cervantes. (15)

Sir Launcelot goes on to say that he does not confuse giants with windmills, inns with castles, or the people before him with characters from *Amadis de Gaul*. Sir Launcelot, and by implication his creator, denies the imitation of Don Quixote, and yet Smollett wants it both ways. Sir Launcelot's insistence that he can "reason without prejudice, can endure contradiction, and . . . even bear impertinent censure without passion or resentment" (15) leads to another exchange with Ferret that rouses the hero's passionate resentment and actually scares the assembled company. Thus the modern critic's typical notion that Sir Launcelot is not mad at all—Robert D. Mayo regards him as possessed of a kind of "super-sanity"[45]—needs qualification. Sir Launcelot sometimes proves to be less sane than he wants to appear, especially when he insists on his own sanity.

Smollett's narrative plays a number of variations on the theme of madness. This theme provides the link that accounts for the frequent allusions to *Hamlet* in the novel, though not all of these focus on the theme itself. Several episodes show Sir Launcelot turning from sanity to madness or behaving madly. When Crowe intends to turn knight-errant, Sir Launcelot attempts to bring him to his senses by overstating the knight's necessity to put himself in danger against overwhelming odds. But as their discussion grows more heated, Crowe winds up insulting Aurelia, and Sir Launcelot rashly challenges him to combat. Later, when Sir Launcelot providentially or coincidentally comes upon Aurelia, and she disabuses him of the notion that she has broken off their promises to one another, he represents himself as "a poor, forlorn, wandering lunatic" (117). When he hears of her guardian's oppressions, he responds with gestures familiar as representations of madness on the stage (here reminiscent of *Othello*): "He bit his nether lip, rolled his eyes around, started from his seat" (118).

The most dramatic change in Sir Launcelot's behavior comes about relatively late in the novel through a series of recognitions that help to restore him fully to sanity. His combat with Sycamore (paralleled by a subsidiary battle between Crowe and Dawdle) occurs after that character, a "childish romantic" (139), sends a knightly challenge, to which Sir Launcelot replies "in a very composed and solemn accent" by asking for an explanation "without disguise, or any such ridiculous ceremony" (143). He initially refuses to fight for Aurelia both because such an action would constrain her choice of lover if he were to win and because he considers such combat against "my own reason" and "the laws of my country" (143). When the two do fight, the victorious Sir Launcelot warns Sycamore, whom he does not discourage from paying court to Aurelia, that any underhanded methods will lead him "to demand an account of your conduct, not in the character of a lunatic knight-errant, but as a plain English gentleman, jealous of his honour, and resolute in his purpose" (150). Ultimately, Sir Launcelot reverts to the role of the modern man of honor and bases his actions on reason and law.

On a number of other occasions, however, the folly of his actions is brought painfully home to him. At one point his knight-errantry leads him to hurry off to save a threatened traveler (who turns out to be Timothy Crabshaw) and thus to abandon Aurelia, whom he has just rescued from highwaymen. In this instance he acts without thought, imagining himself "some hero of romance mounted upon a winged steed" (119). Only later does he recognize that this action has once again caused him to lose Aurelia. Still later, in one of the most effective scenes in the novel, Sir Launcelot is incarcerated by his enemies in a private madhouse; and although he does not know who is at fault for putting him there, the event causes him to repent "of his knight-errantry as a frolic which might have very serious consequences, with respect to his future life and fortune" (176). Even after this moment of clarification, the recognition of Aurelia's voice in the madhouse drives him to a "thousand extravagancies," including a threat that anyone entering his cell might expect to meet "with the fate of Lychas, whom Hercules in his frenzy destroyed" (181)—a last allusion to heroic madness, as expressed earlier in allusions to Othello, Orlando, Hamlet, and the elder Brutus.

The lessons that he learns do finally have meaning. When in the terminal chapter Sycamore and Dawdle decamp for the Continent to avoid Sir Launcelot, who has gone "in quest" of them, the determined hero was "not now so much of a knight-errant, as to leave Aurelia to the care of Providence, and pursue the traitors to the farthest extremities of the earth" (190). Instead he turns to writs of outlawry in a court of law. Despite the uncertainty of English justice, the law, not the lance, is the resort of the modern English gentleman. The ideals that Sir Launcelot had earlier espoused are not so much repudiated as adapted.

Sir Launcelot Greaves is altogether faithful to *Don Quixote* in that it represents others besides its hero as touched with lunacy. While Timothy claims of Sir Launcelot "thof he be creazy, I an't, that I an't" (45), he protests too much, for not only does he become Sir Launcelot's squire, but those around him consider it "insanity" for him to take as his horse the vicious Gilbert (46). Later in the novel, even Sir Launcelot believes Timothy's "brain was disordered" (121). Sir Launcelot's father is also represented as being in danger of derangement: when Sir Launcelot wounds Aurelia's villainous guardian in a duel, his concern that his father will "run distracted" (36), not the more palpable fear of prosecution, makes him decide to leave England and Aurelia. And Mrs. Oakely has been driven out of her wits by Justice Gobble's cruelties and by her experiences in jail. Before the end of the novel, we encounter a whole asylum of deluded inmates; and in their midst we find Aurelia, who has been falsely represented as mad in order that her uncle might confine her. Launcelot is there too, ironically not on account of his putative madness but as part of the same uncle's plot. Despite this fraud, he cannot convince the doctor of his sanity.

Much earlier, in the chapter entitled "*In which the reader will perceive that in some cases madness is catching*," Crowe claims, "I think for my part one half of the nation is mad—and the other not very sound" (50). Yet Smollett's essential point, most successfully carried out in the sections on parliamentary campaigning (chapters 9 and 10), is that Sir Launcelot's supposed madness is often good sense and that the usual practices constitute evidence of madness. The Whigs and Tories attack Sir Launcelot for his moderation and independence, truly quixotic things for which to stand in modern England. But there are limits to how far Smollett is willing to indulge the attack on contemporary political practice. When Ferret claims that the ministry "is mad, or worse than mad" (17), Sir Launcelot's opposition is decisive, and Ferret's voicing of such a position is itself significant.

The popular representation of madness derived from earlier traditions. Smollett was certainly up to date on current theories of insanity, as he had reviewed William Battie's *Treatise on Madness* (from which the asylum doctor's analysis of Sir Launcelot is drawn verbatim) and John Monro's *Remarks on Dr. Battie's Treatise on Madness* for the *Critical Review* in 1758.[46] Many of Sir Launcelot's symptoms of love madness, however, could as easily have been derived from Robert Burton's *Anatomy of Melancholy* (1621) and even older authorities. An interest in madness is also characteristic of a number of fictions of Smollett's own time. Samuel Johnson's *Rasselas* appeared the year before *Sir Launcelot Greaves* began to issue in monthly installments, and almost simultaneously Sterne produced the first volumes of *Tristram Shandy*—"shandy" meaning "crack-brained." Johnson's Imlac agrees with Captain Crowe about the British people, even if he frames the point more philosophically: "Perhaps if we speak with rigorous exactness, no human mind is in its right state."[47] The theme appears satirically in Smollett's *Humphry Clinker*. Matthew Bramble, excoriating the combination of social climbing and frenzied activity in London, declares that, "in a word, the whole nation seems to be running out of their wits."[48]

The knight-errantry at the center of Smollett's concern with madness relates to the novel's form as well as its theme. Paul-Gabriel Boucé rightly sees the design of *Sir Launcelot Greaves* as a circular journey, in part a parody of knightly questing, expressed at times in mock-epic gestures and ending with a restoration of both social and mental stability for the hero.[49] Formally, however, the novel also possesses the episodic quality associated with versions of the antiromance and with the picaresque. These characteristics perhaps facilitated Smollett's renewed attempt to examine the nature of evil and the problems of injustice in the world. But instead of the revenger of personal mistreatment exemplified in the heroes of his first two novels, Sir Launcelot is an idealistic redresser of social wrongs. Generically, the work represents both a reversal of the picaresque impulses that Smollett had followed earlier and a movement toward the antiromance, the genre of *Don Quixote* itself. Whereas the picaresque gives us what Claudio Guillen calls "half-outsiders,"[50] Sir Launcelot will reassert his place as an "English gentleman" (150) at the end of the novel. He is indeed always a gentleman, unlike Roderick Random and Peregrine Pickle. Like Matthew Bramble in *Humphry Clinker*, Sir Launcelot ultimately accepts his role in society.

This novel, that is, represents for Smollett a new structuring of the relations

between self and society. In *Roderick Random* and *Peregrine Pickle*, social ills
lead to revenge structures. In *Sir Launcelot Greaves*, they drive the hero to
distraction; but instead of seeking revenge he sets up as a kind of vigilante to
right wrongs that result from the corruption of good laws by bad men. The
closeness of Smollett's intention to that of the heroic satirist depicted by Alexander Pope in *The First Satire of the Second Book of Horace Imitated* is clear:

> What? arm'd for *Virtue* when I point the Pen,
> Brand the bold Front of shameless, guilty Men,
> Dash the proud Gamester in his gilded Car,
> Bare the mean Heart that lurks beneath a Star;
> Can there be wanting to defend Her Cause,
> Lights of the Church, or Guardians of the Laws? [51]

If we can hardly imagine Pope in armor, we ought to recognize the chivalric
terms that he, unlike Horace in the original, uses to describe his role as poet.
Pope's representation of the satirist as redresser of wrongs may suggest one of
the ways in which Smollett, his admirer and kindred satiric spirit, devised such
a character as Sir Launcelot, who will actually use a lance rather than a pen to
accomplish the same ends.

　　Smollett's satire in *Sir Launcelot Greaves*, in this sense like the satire of Pope
and Jonathan Swift, often focuses with more or less good humor on the de-
basement of language. The novel provides an extensive range of voices and
idioms, but it displays chiefly three kinds of linguistic corruption: dialect
(Yorkshire especially and northern England generally); jargon (legal, medical,
nautical); and those comic infelicities that would soon become known as malapropisms (associated with the two Gobbles and Dolly). While Smollett's representation of Yorkshire dialect is not always consistent, it effectively imitates
phonetic pronunciation and is intelligible to the reader. The novel's first three
chapters provide abundant instances of the professional jargons of the "social
triumvirate" that Smollett introduces in the opening paragraphs of the novel
(3). Smollett's medical practice, his naval experiences, and his legal entangle-
ments had prepared him for the linguistic demands of the surgeon, Mr. Fillet;
the seaman, Captain Crowe; and the attorney, Tom Clarke. Later, the language of the ignorant and malicious Justice Gobble indicts Gobble himself,
not just through his misuse of legal terminology but through his comic man-
gling of common diction, which looks back to Dogberry in *As You Like It* and
Mrs. Slipslop in Fielding's *Joseph Andrews* (1742), and forward to Smollett's
own Win Jenkins and Tabitha Bramble in *Humphry Clinker* and Mrs. Mala-
prop in Richard Brinsley Sheridan's *The Rivals* (1775). All these effects are

ingenious, and indeed the language of *Sir Launcelot Greaves*, especially the sea slang and the malapropisms, has always been considered one of its genuine triumphs.

INFLUENCES

Pope provided one of several influences upon, or sources for, *Sir Launcelot Greaves*. Others declare themselves as well. Smollett's menagerie of eccentrics and his general employment of humors characters for his satire link the novel at least indirectly to the plays of Ben Jonson. Ferret is both a sham astrologer, reminiscent of Jonson's Alchemist, and a mountebank, reminiscent of Volpone. As in Jonson we have the biter bit, though not so fiercely as in the conclusions of Jonson's harsh comedies. Ferret's great mountebank speech in chapter 10, a high point in the novel, is seen by Sir Launcelot as excessive; but in a recognizably Jonsonian manner it articulates a broad cultural indictment with which Smollett was largely in agreement. "The kingdom," says Ferret, "is full of mountebanks, empirics, and quacks. We have quacks in religion, quacks in physic, quacks in law, quacks in politics, quacks in patriotism, quacks in government" (77). Smollett loved verbal excess, as Jonson did; and like Jonson he sometimes made a grotesque poetry of the language he used to characterize his eccentrics and villains, who are often caricatures. We may think, for example, of the moment in *Sir Launcelot Greaves* when Crowe wakes Dawdle to challenge him to a duel, and Dawdle, perceiving "the head of Crowe, so swelled and swathed, so livid, hideous, and griesly," takes him for a ghost (142).

Le Sage's *Le Diable boiteux*, which Smollett translated as *The Devil upon Crutches* in 1750, is another source for *Sir Launcelot Greaves;* the pathetic story of Donna Emerenciana provides a close parallel to Aurelia's incarceration in the madhouse by her guardian.[52] Still another important influence is *Tom Jones*, which Smollett had once angrily dismissed as a plagiarism of his *Roderick Random*.[53] In an interesting reversal of Fielding's supposed thefts from that novel, Smollett appears to borrow a number of plot elements from Fielding. These center on the love between Aurelia and Sir Launcelot and begin with the implicit comparison in chapter 3 to Fielding's introduction of Sophia Western in book 4, chapter 2 of *Tom Jones*. Sir Launcelot's rescue of Aurelia from runaway horses in chapters 3 and 4 advances their love and parallels an incident in book 4, chapter 13 of *Tom Jones*. In Smollett as in Fielding, both the hero's pursuit of his lover and his discovery of her through finding her pocketbook are important devices. Smollett is probably indebted to Fielding for the narrator's hints concerning chapter linkage and the language of the chapter headings themselves; for several mock-heroic touches (in chapters 10, 19, and 20); and for some characteristic rhetoric: "The reader," says Smollett's narrator in describing a tense (but funny) early moment involving Crowe and Greaves,

> may have seen the physiognomy of a stockholder at Jonathan's when the rebels were at Derby, or the features of a bard when accosted by a bailiff, or the countenance of an alderman when his banker stops payment; if he has seen either of these phænomena, he may conceive the appearance that was now exhibited by the visage of the ferocious captain, when the naked sword of Sir Launcelot glanced before his eyes. . . . (105)

The direct address to the reader, the multiplication of examples, the suspension of the narrative, and the conditional construction are all characteristic of Fielding. Evans says that in a general way "*Launcelot Greaves* reminds us of Fielding's kind of satire precisely because of the appeal its satire makes to a background of general and ideal values," though in *Sir Launcelot Greaves* the hero and not the narrator voices them.[54] It is worth considering that Fielding's play *Don Quixote in England* (1734) served as an intermediary source for Smollett in his use of the Quixote fiction. The electioneering scenes of that play (1.8, 1.9, 2.2–3), featuring an attempt to put up Don Quixote as a candidate, anticipate chapters 9 and 10 in Smollett's novel. In terms of structure and style, Fielding's presence in *Sir Launcelot Greaves* is unmistakable.

Fielding and Smollett alike were significantly influenced by a nonliterary source: the works of William Hogarth. This artist, whom Smollett compliments explicitly in *Sir Launcelot Greaves* and often mentions in his other novels, appealed to Smollett's broad and informed interest in the graphic arts and to his highly pictorial sense of the novel as a form.[55] In *Sir Launcelot Greaves* the two chapters on the parliamentary campaign are related in important ways to Hogarth's series *Four Prints of an Election* (1755–58). Certainly, Smollett knew the series well, and he probably wrote the review of *A Poetical Description of Mr. Hogarth's Election Prints* that appeared in the *Critical Review* in 1759.[56] Of the four engravings in Hogarth's series, the most relevant to *Sir Launcelot Greaves* is *The Polling*, in which "Dr." John Shebbeare, the original of Ferret, appears prominently.[57] There are still broader connections, for while Hogarth depicts an election in Oxfordshire and Smollett locates his scene in Nottinghamshire, the tension between Tories and Whigs is represented as much the same, and the satiric purposes are identical. Both men despised political posturing and corruption. Smollett's election chapters do not directly allude to any one of Hogarth's scenes, but they surely derived some of their pictorial vigor from his example.

There is further evidence of the importance of Hogarth in the background of Smollett's novel. The account of the private madhouse probably owes something to the madhouse setting in the last scene of *The Rake's Progress*. Smollett's episode and Hogarth's engraving (1735) feature similar madmen: two inmates who believe themselves to be the pope and a king, another who is trying to find the longitude so as to revolutionize navigation at sea, and another who is a religious fanatic (in Smollett, as usual, a Methodist). These characters are familiar stereotypes of madness, and since they are not seen but only heard by the hero as he sits in his own cell, the satire is more verbal than visual. Nevertheless, the Hogarthian elements are conspicuous. Still another work by Hogarth has been claimed as influential in this novel. In exhorting Crabshaw when on his way to be hanged at Tyburn to "appear in the cart with a nosegay in one hand, and the Whole Duty of Man in the other" (172), Ferret may allude to scene 11 of Hogarth's *Industry and Idleness* (1747), though instead of holding his nosegay (a traditional accoutrement of the condemned), Hogarth's Tom Idle wears it, and he carries a different book in both hands.[58]

The most important influence at work in *Sir Launcelot Greaves* is of course Cervantes's *Don Quixote*, which, more broadly speaking, influenced the eighteenth-century British novel more than any other single work of fiction. Smollett not only produced his own English version of *Don Quixote* in 1755, but he also refers to the work in almost all his novels. New editions of translations by Charles Jarvis (1742) and by Peter Motteux and John Ozell (1719) appeared in the two years following Smollett's; and George Kelly and Charles Henry Wilmot would produce translations in the late 1760s. Smollett seems to have been aware of other translations, but it was probably his own that inspired him to write *Sir Launcelot Greaves*, even though the difference between his hero and Quixote is considerable.

Smollett's is a loving translation, now regarded by many as the one closest in spirit to the original.[59] In the "Life of Cervantes" that he prefixed to his translation, Smollett characterized Quixote's "ludicrous solemnity and self-importance," which he hoped to capture without turning him into a "dry philosopher, or debasing him to . . . an ordinary madman."[60] Earlier, Smollett had given a thumbnail account of the broad historical importance of the Quixote fiction in his preface to *Roderick Random*. As a result of romances, he wrote, "the world actually began to be infected with the spirit of knight-errantry, when Cervantes, by an inimitable piece of ridicule, reformed the taste of mankind, representing chivalry in the right point of view, and converting romance to purposes far more useful and entertaining, by making it assume the sock, and point out the follies of ordinary life."[61] Smollett recognized both the satiric basis of the portrayal of the original Quixote and the authorial sensibility that informed it. It seems accurate to say, then, that in *Sir Launcelot Greaves*, Smollett drew equally on *Don Quixote* and on his own interpretation of Cervantes's masterpiece.

Smollett was mindful of the delicate relations between the Quixote and his author, as he himself described them in the "Life of Cervantes": "Notwithstanding all the shafts of ridicule which he hath so successfully leveled against the absurdities of the Spanish Romance, we can plainly perceive from his own writings, that he himself had a turn for chivalry: his life was a chain of extraordinary adventures, his temper was altogether heroic, and his actions were, without doubt, influenced by the most romantic notions of honour."[62] Smollett might have seen something of himself in this portrait. Without intending praise, John Shebbeare taxed him in print with being a kind of Quixote. In an attack on the *Critical Review*, Shebbeare addressed its editor and principal contributor, claiming that "*Don Quixote* runs strangely in this Author's Head." "Like a true Champion," he continued, like "the Knight of *La Mancha*," Smollett had arrived with his magazine "to rescue the Charms of Literature from the avaritious Hands of the hireling Necromancers in the *Monthly Review*. What an advantage it is in a Critic to have transcribed *Don Quixote*, tho' it may prove a great *Loss* to the Bookseller who *hired* him."[63] However clearly Smollett may have understood that he was indeed something of a Quixote figure, Shebbeare's attack probably provided the germ of the Ferret-Greaves opposition within *Sir Launcelot Greaves*.

From the beginning, *Don Quixote* was enormously popular both in Great Britain and on the Continent, inspiring many imitations and even spurious continuations. A putative fifth volume of the work, *Histoire de l'admirable Don Quichotte de la Manche*, attributed to Françoise Filleau de Saint-Martin, appeared in 1695; there was even a "sixth" volume, the *Continuation de l'histoire de l'admirable Don Quichotte*, attributed to Robert Challe and published in 1713. As I have noted, Fielding's later play, *Don Quixote in England*, reintroduced Cervantes's hero for its own purposes. A number of works in France and England based their heroes or heroines on the Quixote, among them Charles Sorrel's *Le Berger extravagant* (1627) and Pierre Carlet de Chamblain de Marivaux's *Pharsamond* (1737), which was later subtitled *Le Don Quichotte moderne*. The best-known examples published in England during Smollett's life are *Joseph Andrews* and Charlotte Lennox's *The Female Quixote* (1752). Quixote fictions in other genres included Samuel Butler's poem *Hudibras*

(1663–78) and the comedy *Angelica; or Quixote in Petticoats* (1758), an anonymous adaptation of Lennox's novel.

The debate in chapter 2 between Sir Launcelot and Ferret sets up the terms of Smollett's adaptation of *Don Quixote* and establishes on the part of the characters themselves a self-consciousness about Cervantes's original conception. This awareness functions at a metaliterary level not at all characteristic of other English Quixote fictions. Neither Lennox's Arabella nor Richard Graves's Parson Wildgoose in *The Spiritual Quixote* (1773) nor, for that matter, Fielding's Parson Adams recognizes any kinship with such a fictional model. Smollett carefully underscores the metaliterary level of his narrative: Timothy is called Sancho Panza by the haberdasher's apprentices masquerading as soldiers, who dub his master "Don Quicksot" (103); and Dawdle explicitly refers to Sampson Carrasco's stratagem against Quixote to convince Sycamore that he can defeat Sir Launcelot in combat (139). Smollett also introduces many episodes or actions that explicitly echo *Don Quixote*. For example, Sir Launcelot, like Quixote, leaves battles with his inferiors to his squire, which leads Crabshaw to absorb a drubbing at the hands of soldiers. Dawdle's use of a bean-filled bladder in combat with Crowe (to make the latter's horse shy) recalls a similar trick in *Don Quixote* (part 2, book 1, chapter 11).

Alexander Welsh identifies the two major themes of "quixotic heroism" as "the quest for justice and the endurance of practical jokes."[64] Both are relevant to *Sir Launcelot Greaves;* and the former theme, which Welsh regards as the theme of realism itself, appears in the novel with unusual urgency. In Smollett's version of the latter theme, the practical jokes are endured not by the hero but by others. Far from being the satiric butt, Sir Launcelot is consistently presented as heroic, even though he frequently suffers from a distracted state that leads him to act strangely. Sir Launcelot's fundamental if sometimes dormant sanity represents a significant departure from Cervantes, for Don Quixote is truly crazy. In his depiction of the insanity that is everywhere around his hero, however, Smollett is very close to his Cervantean model; we may remember that Sancho, the curate, Cardenio, and others are characterized as mad. If Sir Launcelot, unlike Quixote, is young and driven to his follies specifically by love instead of by books, then there is still direct precedent for him in the lovesick Cardenio, portrayed by Cervantes as driven mad by the seeming faithlessness of his adored Lucinda. Sir Launcelot is an authentic knight, of course. Both his name and his armor—like his title—signify that he is so; and, though explicitly aware of the follies of Quixote, he shares with him a true belief in the ideals of chivalry. By appropriating the name "Sir Launcelot" from English folk tradition and Arthurian myth, Smollett actually imparted to his hero a national significance as a visionary and moral crusader. In this he evoked his model, for Cervantes made Don Quixote a synthesis of late Renaissance Spanish idealism and cultural folly.

A number of other connections to *Don Quixote* are readily apparent. Timothy Crabshaw is like Sancho in his lower-class origins, his absorption of blows, and his love of proverbs. Smollett the translator claims that he tried to keep his rendering of the original Sancho "from degenerating into mere proverbial phlegm,"[65] but both Sancho and Timothy often string together proverbs in a way that makes them virtuosi of this particular mannerism. Although Greaves's appearance "armed cap-a-pie" (12) is part of a pattern of allusions to *Hamlet*, this description centrally echoes *Don Quixote* (e.g., part 1, book 4, chapter 5) and directly refers to Cervantes's knight. There is, additionally, the matter of Smollett's jocular use of "Dulcinea" for "sweetheart," common to all his novels but of particular resonance in *Sir Launcelot Greaves*, where the heroine is indeed loved by a Quixote figure—although, unlike Cervantes's tavern maid, she is not undercut by any disparity between the ideal and her person. The villain Sycamore's styling himself the knight of the Griffin may owe something to Quixote's claim that "the Griffin" would be a suitable name for a knight (part 1, book 3, chapter 5).

SIR LAUNCELOT GREAVES AND CONTEMPORARY POLITICS

Paul Langford's assertion that "Sir Launcelot Greaves was plainly a Tory" expresses orthodoxy on the subject of the novel's political stance as well as a durable perspective on the politics of Smollett himself.[66] Neither Sir Launcelot nor Smollett would have warmed to the claim, however. Smollett, who wrote the *Ode to Independence* in 1766, prided himself in a letter of 1763 on his "Independancy" and claimed that he had "neither Pension nor Place, nor . . . Disposition which can stoop to Sollicit either."[67] In chapter 9 of *Sir Launcelot Greaves*, entitled "*Which may serve to shew, that true patriotism is of no party*," Sir Launcelot decries the bumpkin Sir Valentine Quickset, Tory candidate for Parliament, as one who "mistakes rusticity for independence" (73)—a shrewd observation, for independence was frequently a Tory position (or pose) rather than a nonaligned stance, while Tory partisans were historically associated with the "country" or landed interests. Smollett presents his version of the independent man in *Sir Launcelot Greaves* when the hero is attacked for his appeal to the freeholders' "independency" and for his counsel that they should follow a "doctrine of moderation" (75): "The Whigs and the Tories joined against this intruder, who being neither, was treated like a monster, or chimæra in politics" (76). Clearly, this chapter criticizes both Whigs and Tories, but the terms in which it does so will need a closer examination.

Although there is no doubt that Smollett's assertion of his personal independence was in a sense disingenuous,[68] more to the present point is that this claim and others like it represent a strain of cultural and personal mythmaking in which Smollett seemed to believe and that he seems to have imparted to Sir Launcelot Greaves. In a 1758 letter to his friend John Moore, Smollett commented on his treatment of contemporary politics in *A Complete History of England:*

> Whatever may be its defects, I protest before God I have, as far as in me lay, adhered to Truth without espousing any faction, though I own I sat down to write with a warm side to those principles in which I was educated. But in the Course of my Inquiries, the whig ministers and their abettors turned out such a Set of sordid Knaves, that I could not help stigmatising them for their want of Integrity and Sentiment.[69]

Smollett would again attack a "sordid knave" in *Sir Launcelot Greaves* (75). Probably on both occasions he had in mind Thomas Pelham-Holles, first duke of Newcastle, first lord of the treasury from 1754 to 1756 and again from 1757 to 1761.[70] Newcastle's increasingly anachronistic belief in a Europe defined by a weak France and a strong alliance of Britain and Austria (the so-called "Old System"), as well as his questionable habits of patronage and his acquiescence in George II's favoritism toward his native Hanover, made Newcastle a favorite target of Smollett. Smollett's careful summation of the preoccupations of George II in the *Continuation of the Complete History of England* clarifies the issues:

> The circumstances that chiefly marked his public character, were a predilection for his native country, and a close attention to the political interests of the Germanic body: points and principles to which he adhered with the most invincible fortitude; and, if ever the blood and treasure of Great Britain were sacrificed to these considerations, we ought not so much to blame the prince who acted from the dictates of natural affection, as we should detest a succession of ve[na]l m[iniste]rs, all of whom in their turns devoted themselves soul and body, to the gratification of this passion, or partiality, so prejudicial to the true interest of their country.[71]

This analysis, although certainly anti-Hanoverian, avoids accusing the king of malfeasance while attacking his ministers for allowing him to drain the resources of Great Britain. The strategy is consistent with opposition polemics earlier in the century, when writers associated with the *Craftsman* had hammered away at king's minister Sir Robert Walpole while simultaneously declaring their "independence" from the Tory opposition. The stance is also characteristic of Tory attacks on the Seven Years' War prior to the publication of *Sir Launcelot Greaves*. "Independence" had become a partisan posture characterized by its denial of partisanship.

The Seven Years' War of 1756–63, of which the *British Magazine* had promised to keep its readers apprised, was preceded by a series of English defeats at the hands of the French in 1754 and 1755 and, in 1756, by the Convention of Westminster, a treaty with Frederick II (the Great) of Prussia that was intended to ensure Hanoverian neutrality but that succeeded mainly in scuttling the Old System and pushing France and Austria into alliance with one another. The ensuing controversy precipitated Newcastle's resignation in November 1756; the duke was succeeded by Pitt, who came to power as secretary of state for the southern department, with a wide jurisdiction that included the British colonies. The position was an important one, and Pitt, who had forced Newcastle's hand, was now more than first among equals.[72]

At the time, Smollett seems to have seen Pitt as his kind of "independent": one who was willing to benefit from the support of the traditional Tory element in Parliament and also to negotiate with the opposition led by the earl of Bute. Initially, Pitt's ascendancy did not reverse the course of English military failures. George II's son the duke of Cumberland was ignominiously defeated at Hastenbeck in 1757 and was subsequently bound by treaty to disband his forces. In 1758, there followed a series of failures in Brittany. By 1760, however, the nation's spirits had been buoyed up by the great successes in Europe of combined British and German armies under Ferdinand, duke of Brunswick; by Robert Clive's smashing victory over the French in India; by the naval capture of French holdings in the Caribbean; by the taking of Senegal in West Africa; by Gen. James Wolfe's defeat of Gen. Louis Joseph de Montcalm to capture Quebec; and by Gen. Jeffrey Amherst's conquest of Montreal. In this year of triumphs, Pitt was considered the savior of the country.[73]

In discussing the outset of the Seven Years' War in the fourth volume of the *Continuation*, Smollett indicates that he favored only the colonial war, not the war on the Continent, which was fought, as he saw it, for the benefit of Hanover. He is severe about the latter conflict:

> The management of a mighty kingdom was consigned into the hands of a motley administration, ministers without knowledge, and men without integrity, whose

councils were timid, weak, and wavering; whose folly and extravagance exposed the nation to ridicule and contempt; by whose ignorance and presumption it was reduced to the verge of ruin. The kingdom was engaged in a quarrel truly national, and commenced a necessary war on national principles; but that war was starved, and the chief strength of the nation transferred to the continent of Europe, in order to maintain an unnecessary war, in favor of a family whose pride and ambition can be equalled by nothing but its insolence and ingratitude.[74]

Sir Launcelot does not bother with the distinction that concerned his creator. His statement on the war in the February 1760 installment of Smollett's novel reflects the high tide of Smollett's infatuation with Pitt but does not question the validity of the Continental campaign. "We are," says Sir Launcelot, "involved in a just and necessary war, which has been maintained on truly British principles, prosecuted with vigour, and crowned with success; . . . our taxes are easy, in proportion to our wealth; . . . our conquests are equally glorious and important; . . . our commerce flourishes, our people are happy, and our enemies reduced to despair" (18).[75] This defense is put forward in opposition to Ferret's thoroughgoing attack on the government. Borrowing the familiar language of Hanoverian apologetics, Sir Launcelot proclaims the war "just and necessary" (18). This stance is at odds with Smollett's typical position, which is usually closer to that of Ferret in chapters 2 and 9 on the matter of Hanover as well as on taxes and governmental corruption. We may ask why this is the case.

It is at least possible that Smollett, with a judgment hanging over his head following his conviction in the Knowles libel suit, did not want to risk offending the government. But the changing circumstances of the war undoubtedly played a larger role in Sir Launcelot's rhetoric. Archibald S. Foord notes that "in 1760 the war-time coalition enjoyed the general support of all factions and great popularity in the country."[76] When Smollett wrote Sir Launcelot's words, he may actually have believed them himself.[77] If so, he did not believe them for long.

Smollett's hatred of Newcastle was unwavering, but his attitude toward Pitt was shifting and complex. While he continued to attack Newcastle's subsidies, in the *Continuation* he praised Pitt and described the war in terms recognizable in Sir Launcelot's utterances. But one cannot miss an underlying skepticism that distinguishes Smollett's stance from Sir Launcelot's:

England, for the first time, saw a minister of state in full possession of popularity; the faithful servant of the crown; the universal darling of the people. . . . The people confiding in the integrity and abilities of their own minister, and elevated by the repeated sounds of triumph, became enamoured of the war, and granted such liberal subsidies for its support, as no other minister would have presumed to ask, as no other nation believed they could afford. Nor did they murmur at seeing great part of their treasure diverted into foreign channels; nor did they seem to bestow a serious thought on the accumulating load of the national debt, which already exceeded the immense sum of one hundred millions.[78]

The people, Smollett says in a telling summary locution, "were intoxicated with victory."[79]

Probably by the time he wrote the *Continuation*, Smollett was growing disenchanted with Pitt. Still, he could find important points of agreement with him. Both men opposed a standing army, and both favored a national militia. Pitt, "in the face of unwearied opposition" and "discouraged by the jealousy of a c[our]t,"[80] had fought valiantly (and successfully) in Parliament to change government policy on military preparedness. The real and fictive alliances become intertwined here. In chapter 2 of *Sir Launcelot Greaves*, Ferret rails against a standing army and mercenaries, as Smollett himself might have done, but also against the militia, which Smollett supported. And, in turn, Ferret's views on the standing army and the conduct of the war recall those of his model, John Shebbeare, whose antiwar pamphlet, *A Fifth Letter to the People of England* (1758), Smollett probably reviewed for the *Critical Review*. The review indicates that to some extent its author shared Shebbeare's ideas, particularly those concerning the army: like Smollett (but not like Ferret), for example, Shebbeare favored a militia.[81] Considering the enmity between the two men, it must have pained Smollett to say anything kind about Shebbeare. But for all that, he found himself agreeing at times with a scurrilous pamphleteer whom he loathed—and thus of course with Ferret, whom he hoped readers of *Sir Launcelot Greaves* would find reprehensible.

Ferret's harangues against the government sound at times like both Smollett and Shebbeare. Ferret reviles the allegiance to Hanover and attacks Newcastle (implicitly but conventionally) as a "Germanized m[iniste]r" (77); he mocks the notion of the balance of power authorized by the Old System and claims that the Protestant religion is not of importance to the allies, who are really not allies at all (78). When (in the words of the narrator) Sir Launcelot condemns Ferret for his "scurrility," he judges his language and his character, not his politics; even a scoundrel may say just things, Greaves understands, and indeed Ferret's speech does contain some "melancholy truths" (79). Smollett's assessment of Shebbeare in his review of the *Fifth Letter* is much the same; in it, Smollett attacks Shebbeare as a reprobate while acknowledging the accuracy of some of his remarks on politics. The representation of the self-styled "doctor" Shebbeare as the mountebank Ferret thus extends the passionate but qualified critique that Smollett initiated in his review of the *Fifth Letter*. In the earlier piece, characterizing Shebbeare as "our political quack" and his writings as "a railing harangue," Smollett had quoted Shebbeare's assertion that the lifeblood of England was being transfused into Germany. "Miserable state!" he apostrophized; "Nevertheless [Shebbeare] says, take but his two shilling remedy, he offers to the public from mere disinterested motives, and all will be well."[82] The "Elixir of Long Life" that Ferret offers to his hearers in chapter 10 of *Sir Launcelot Greaves* (78) is a clear echo of Smollett's remark in the review upon Shebbeare's "remedy" for current public ills.

The criticism of politics in that chapter also revolves around other issues of character connected to Smollett's ideological positions. He makes a Jew, the rich stockjobber Mr. Isaac Vanderpelft, the scapegoat symbol of Whiggism. Although Sir Launcelot presents himself as independent of party and attacks the ignorance of the Tory foxhunter, Sir Valentine Quickset, he finds the Whig worse: "Such a man" as Sir Valentine "may be dangerous," he says, but he "is neither so mischievous nor so detestable as the wretch who knowingly betrays his trust, and sues to be the hireling and prostitute of a weak and worthless minister; a sordid knave, without honour or principle, who belongs to no family whose example can reproach him with degeneracy" (73, 75). Here Smollett falls back on his characteristic rhetoric, while the oblique reference to Newcastle renews a familiar theme of his political writings. His characterization of Vanderpelft may also air some of his belated feelings about the Jewish Naturalization Bill of 1753, which Newcastle had enthusiastically endorsed. In the *Continuation*, Smollett denounces this measure as "a law so odious to the people in general, that it was soon repealed, at the request of that m[iniste]r by whom it had been chiefly patronized."[83]

Chapter 9 offers further hints about Smollett, Newcastle, and Vanderpelft. G. S. Rousseau and Roger A. Hambridge have demonstrated that the election in that chapter, which pits Vanderpelft against Quickset, recalls the 1754 election in Newark, in which Lord William Manners, a foxhunting Tory, opposed the Whig (but not Jewish) Sir Job Stanton Charlton.[84] They observe that the lord of the manor of Newark was Newcastle himself, Vanderpelft's patron in the novel. Although Rousseau and Hambridge note that most characteristics of Vanderpelft do not fit their claim, they nominate the Jewish financier Sampson Gideon (meaning Gideon's father, Samson) as the original of Smollett's character. Smollett disliked Samson Gideon, but the choice of name for his Whig candidate suggests that he was not limiting his attack to one target. His early satire *Reproof* (1747) contains an attack on the elder Gideon, along with Henry Lascelles and Sir Joshua Vanneck, in which the three are cast as "a triumvirate of contractors" benefiting from the destruction of their country.[85] No positive identification with any historical person seems possible, but the third of this triumvirate, Vanneck, is closest in surname to Vanderpelft and, like him, bears a biblical first name. Vanneck was an intimate of Newcastle just prior to the publication of *Sir Launcelot Greaves*, and he had advised the duke on French affairs.[86] Sir Joshua was not Jewish, nor, because he was foreign born, could he have served in Parliament. Like Gideon and Lascelles in *Reproof*, however, and like Vanderpelft in the novel (17), he is stigmatized as a "contractor," that is, as a supplier of goods to the army. If we accept Newark as the real-life setting for the scene in chapter 9, Smollett appears to have made Newcastle, whose support for the Jewish Naturalization Bill was such a fiasco, back one of his Jewish supporters (whether a composite of Smollett's old enemies the Jewish Gideon and the gentile Vanneck or a mere stereotype) as the candidate for Parliament in his own district.

Although the major domestic political event during the two years when Smollett was writing *Sir Launcelot Greaves* was the death of George II and the accession of George III, the three central chapters concerning politics (chapters 3, 9, and 10) all appeared before the old king's death. Ironically, Sir Launcelot's defense of the government prior to that event would not have been welcome to George III or to Bute, whose ministry Smollett would support in the *Briton*. George III later pensioned Shebbeare, but Smollett received nothing. In *Sir Launcelot Greaves*, Smollett may have intended to ingratiate himself with the government or at least with Pitt, whom the new king came to loathe before his accession. But he may actually have managed only to commit a lasting offense against those who were most likely to have rewarded him. Whatever the truth of these matters, *Sir Launcelot Greaves* is more than just an interlude in Smollett's prolonged engagement with the government's conduct of the war. It is, in fact, a remarkably full expression of the broad range of his political thought during the troubled period of its composition.

ANTHONY WALKER AND THE ILLUSTRATIONS

Appropriately, Smollett chose a Yorkshire artist to illustrate his story of a Yorkshire knight. In the estimation of Hanns Hammelmann, the foremost authority on eighteenth-century English book illustration, Anthony Walker (1726–65) was "one of the most gifted" of midcentury engravers.[87] As a young man Walker was bound apprentice to the master engraver John Tinney; his first signed work appeared in Thomas Kitchen's *English Atlas* in 1749, and he illustrated books regularly from this time. Walker's two illustrations for *Sir Launcelot Greaves* marked at least the second occasion on which he engraved for Smollett. The second and third (of four) plates in the first volume of the octavo edition of the *Complete History* (1758) were engraved by him, the latter from a design by Francis Hayman, whose work he engraved on several other occasions.[88] These two plates, *The Landing of Julius Caesar* and *The Druids, or the Conversion of the Britons to Christianity*, were the only full-page illustrations in the entire work (both were foldouts). Walker also engraved portrait vignettes of William Wallace (volume 3) and Robert Devereux, second earl of Essex (volume 6).

Walker was a delicate draftsman. He often produced his own designs for his engravings, although he was better known for such reproductive engravings as Isaac Oliver's *Edward Herbert, First Baron Herbert of Cherbury*, included in Horace Walpole's Strawberry Hill Press edition of Herbert's autobiography.[89] The Herbert engraving may have served as a model for the deservedly famous landscape portrait, *Brooke Boothby* (1781), by Joseph Wright, better known as Wright of Derby.[90] As a designer and draftsman, says Hammelmann, Walker at his best was the equal of any of his English contemporaries; if anything his technique may have been too delicate and fastidious, for it included "a great deal of preliminary etching" and "an almost invariable habit of filling every part of the pictorial surface," which led him into aesthetic difficulties.[91]

Walker's previous work had prepared him for *Sir Launcelot Greaves*. While one could argue that his elegant, French-influenced designs might not have been an ideal match for Smollett's very English satire, Walker had drawn and engraved illustrations similar in format for William Somervile's *Hobbinol* (1740), a mock-heroic account of rural games in Gloucestershire, and for a revised and expanded version (1757) of *The Chace* (1735), Somervile's Miltonic poem on the pleasures of hunting. The actual identification of Walker as the illustrator of *Sir Launcelot Greaves* is based on his signing the first engraving (see plate 3). The second engraving is unsigned (see plate 8) but is almost certainly by the same hand, as it bears comparison to an engraving for *Hobbinol*. The attribution of the second engraving to Walker has not been challenged.[92]

The illustrations that Walker provided for *Sir Launcelot Greaves* are not entirely faithful to Smollett's narrative. His first plate gives Sir Launcelot some of the elegance of the figures of Hayman; but the scene it depicts, Sir Launcelot mounted on his horse receiving his helmet from his standing squire (plate 3), does not appear in the novel. It is difficult to determine whether

Walker had any models for this illustration or the other. The numerous book illustrations of *Don Quixote* turn up some possibilities, although none seems to have been Walker's model.[93] Far more like both illustrations by Walker are the second and third plates by J. Mynde after Hogarth in Zachary Grey's edition of Samuel Butler's *Hudibras* (1744), a forerunner of *Sir Launcelot Greaves* as an English version of *Don Quixote*.[94] As in Walker's two engravings, the first depicts the hero and his servant alone with their horses, though here both are mounted; the second depicts Hudibras and Ralpho mounted, with Hudibras haranguing a crowd. A tree appears in the central foreground. Although the treatment is tonally different, this configuration is exactly that of Sir Launcelot and Timothy in Walker's second plate. Neither Walker nor Smollett was a subscriber to this important scholarly edition of *Hudibras*, but it was well known and is thus plausible as a source for the illustrations to *Sir Launcelot Greaves*. As has already been suggested, Walker had his own precedent for the second plate. The illustration opposite page 21 in *Hobbinol* shows a crowd watching a wrestling contest, with a boy in a tree to the left. In Walker's more impressive illustration of the electioneering scene in chapter 9 of *Sir Launcelot Greaves*, three boys are in a tree in the center foreground, while Sir Launcclot, below them, harangues the crowd (plate 8).

Walker's first plate may not refer directly to a particular scene, but the interplay between the sweet face of Sir Launcelot and the grimacing features of Crabshaw captures the overall spirit of the novel. Sir Launcelot wears black lacquered armor, suggesting (as noted earlier) Smollett's forethought in designing the narrative and Walker's knowledge of that design. Crescents appear on Sir Launcelot's shield and on Timothy's cap, which, more comic than military, is rather unlike the marine's cap called for by the text. This illustration appears opposite the first page of chapter 2, "*In which the hero of these adventures makes his first appearance*" (9), whereas in the text of that chapter Smollett introduces Sir Launcelot not on a field of action but at the door of the Black Lion Inn, carrying the nearly drowned Crabshaw in his arms. The scene occurs entirely indoors. Yet Walker did provide an effective visual representation of the hero, mounted and in armor, with his face fully visible and his servant, Timothy, passing a crested helmet to him. Hoey features the illustration as the frontispiece to the second Dublin edition (1762, dated 1763).

It is not entirely clear why, when readying *Sir Launcelot Greaves* for publication in the *British Magazine*, Smollett decided to request drawings from Walker, who had a lesser reputation than illustrators whom he had used previously, such as Hayman, Grignion, and Ravenet. Why were there only two illustrations, and why were they not included in the first book edition of the novel, especially when, as Hoey, at least, realized, the first of the two would have functioned so well as a frontispiece? Smollett was presumably not dissatisfied with Walker's illustrations; if he had been, he could easily have hired someone else to furnish others. It seems almost certain that he requested only the illustrations that Walker provided. Their omission from the book edition is the more curious since Sterne at about the same time obtained engravings from Hogarth for the publication of the second edition—the first London edition—of *Tristram Shandy*. Smollett was more interested in book illustration than Sterne was; he had engaged Hayman to design twenty-eight plates for his translation of *Don Quixote* and, earlier, to provide the two frontispieces for the second edition of *Roderick Random*. Basker, evaluating such evidence as exists about Smollett's decisions concerning the illustrations for *Sir Launcelot Greaves*, is unable to account for them completely but does argue that the illustrations may have been intended mainly "to stimulate interest in the novel they accompanied. If so, the fact that they ceased after the ninth installment may indicate that the novel was succeeding well enough for [Smollett] to drop the illustrations and save the extra cost they entailed." [95]

There is another possible explanation, equally plausible. Perhaps Smollett's intention was not to illustrate the first original "illustrated" serial novel at all but only to adorn his magazine. During its first year, the *British Magazine* was illustrated liberally, and Walker prepared at least three of the engravings besides those for *Sir Launcelot Greaves*: *The Interment of the POINTED SERPENT, One of the Chiefs of the NATCHES*, in the March issue (facing page 137); *His Royal Highness Edward Duke of York*, in the April issue (facing page 241); and *Laurence Shirley, Earl Ferrers*, in the May issue (facing page 520). Thus, starting in February with the second installment of *Sir Launcelot Greaves*, Walker contributed plates for four months in a row, then one in August (with chapter 9 of the novel), and none after that. The number of small figures and full-page illustrations included in the magazine remained about the same throughout the two years of the novel's run (two small figures each year; twenty-six full-page illustrations in 1760 and twenty-three in 1761), while the number of foldout illustrations, clearly the most expensive, fell from twenty-six in 1760 to one in 1761. In the extra issue for April 1760, Butler Clowes began contributing signed work; he would become the most prolific of Smollett's engravers. From October 1760 through May 1761, Alexander Bannerman engraved five signed full-page prints, mainly portraits, whereas Clowes specialized in coats of arms. The move away from foldout illustrations suggests that a project begun ambitiously yielded to budgetary restraints.

Later editions of *Sir Launcelot Greaves* included engravings by William

Walker, William Blake, and Charles Grignion after Thomas Stothard (1782; see plates 4, 9, 11, and 13); John Kirkwood after Thomas Rowlandson (1790; see plate 1); and Joseph Saunders and William Hawkins after Richard Corbauld (1793; see plates 6 and 7). The illustrations by Luke Clennell (1810) and George Cruikshank (1832; see plate 12) are among the most noteworthy from the nineteenth century.[96] To be illustrated by artists of this caliber is unusually fortunate. It is appropriate, too, as is the fact that Smollett was associated with the first effort to illustrate an original serial novel. Smollett expressed his interest in art and artists throughout his writings. In the dedication to *Ferdinand Count Fathom*, his metaphorical description of the novel as picture crystallizes his conception of narrative design. The satire in all his work has strong roots in pictorial caricature, and the *Adventures of an Atom* often relies on the political prints of the day.[97] His attention to art in the *British Magazine* is among the most striking features of this periodical, and he has been identified as the "chief art critic" of the *Critical Review*.[98] Smollett's decision to illustrate the serially published *Sir Launcelot Greaves* is of historical importance; more broadly, it is part of the attraction that this most unusual work—this story of an English knight-errant redressing wrongs in an eighteenth-century England at war—offers its modern readers.

Notes

1. The standard biography is Knapp; see also Paul-Gabriel Boucé, *The Novels of Tobias Smollett* (London: Longman, 1976), chap. 1.
2. See Basker, 39–40, 132–33.
3. See James Raven, *British Fiction 1750–1770: A Chronological Check-List of Prose Fiction in Britain and Ireland* (Newark: University of Delaware Press, 1987), 15.
4. Basker, 207; Barbara Laning Fitzpatrick, "The Text of Tobias Smollett's *Life and Adventures of Sir Launcelot Greaves*, the First Serialized Novel" (Ph.D. diss., Duke University, 1987), 57.
5. See Smollett, review of Adm. Charles Knowles, *The Conduct of Admiral Knowles on the Late Expedition Set in a True Light*, *Critical Review* 5 (1758): 438–39. See also Lewis M. Knapp, "Rex versus Smollett: More Data on the Smollett-Knowles Libel Case," *Modern Philology* 41 (1944): 221–27; and Knapp, 230–36.
6. For the publication of *Sir Launcelot Greaves* in relation to Smollett's life, see Knapp, 228–45; for the novel and the *British Magazine*, see Basker, 201–8. For the novel's publishing history, see Albert Smith, "*Sir Launcelot Greaves:* A Bibliographical Survey of Eighteenth-Century Editions," *Library*, 5th ser., 32 (1977): 214–37; and see Barbara Laning Fitzpatrick, Textual Commentary, 255–58.

7. Sir Walter Scott, "Prefatory Memoir," in vol. 1 of *The Novels of Tobias Smollett, M.D.* (London: Hurst, Robinson and Co., 1821), xxiii.

8. Knapp agrees with Scott that Smollett was in Scotland around this time; see 228–29. See also *Westminster Magazine* 3 (1775): 227.

9. Evans, ix. David K. Jeffrey claims that Sir Launcelot's close examination of Dolly's face in chapter 15 prefigures the realization that Dolly is Sir Launcelot's uncle's illegitimate daughter; see "'Premeditation' in *Sir Launcelot Greaves*," *American Notes and Queries* 1 (1978): 186–87.

10. Robert D. Mayo, *The English Novel in the Magazines: 1740–1815* (Evanston, Ill.: Northwestern University Press, 1962), 281.

11. See Fred W. Boege, *Smollett's Reputation as a Novelist* (Princeton: Princeton University Press, 1947), esp. 23–24.

12. For Smollett's role in the marketing of the *Complete History of England* and the *Continuation*, see O M Brack Jr., "Tobias Smollett Puffs His Histories," in *Writers, Books, and Trade: An Eighteenth-Century English Miscellany for William B. Todd*, ed. O M Brack Jr. (New York: AMS Press, 1994), esp. 267–69.

13. Reprinted in *Tobias Smollett: The Critical Heritage*, ed. Lionel Kelly (London: Routledge and Kegan Paul, 1987), 159. This puff has been attributed to Goldsmith, plausibly but on little evidence; see Arthur Friedman's introduction to Goldsmith's essays from the *Public Ledger*, in vol. 3 of the *Collected Works of Oliver Goldsmith*, ed. Arthur Friedman (Oxford: Clarendon Press, 1966), 156.

14. *British Magazine* 1 (1760): 181. The letter may have been by Samuel Richardson, with whom Smollett was then corresponding; Basker, 192–93, is suitably cautious about the possibility.

15. *British Magazine* 1 (1760): 216. The answer appeared the next month; see *British Magazine* 1 (1760): 268.

16. *The Battle of the Reviews* (London, 1760). Some passages are reprinted in *Tobias Smollett: The Critical Heritage*, ed. Kelly, 162–69.

17. *Journal Encyclopédique* 4 (1761): 101 ("tout Lecteur, ami de la Patrie & de l'humanité, s'intéresse d'abord en faveur du Chevalier moderne"). Smollett reprinted essays from this periodical in the *Critical Review*, which in turn praised the *British Magazine* and published excerpts in translation from *Sir Launcelot Greaves*; see Basker, 18–19, 103–4, 209–10.

18. For Hoey, see Richard Cargill Cole, *Irish Booksellers and Writers 1740–1800* (London: Mansell Publishing, 1986), 78. Dublin reprints were often unauthorized, but Cole suggests that the Dublin edition of *Sir Launcelot Greaves* may have been legitimate. See also Fitzpatrick in the Textual Commentary, 258.

19. Basker, 208.

20. *Monthly Review* 26 (1762): 391.

21. *Critical Review* 13 (1762): 428.

22. *Library* 2 (1762): 262.

23. Smith to Smollett, 26 February 1763, reprinted in *Tobias Smollett: The Critical Heritage*, ed. Kelly, 177–78. The letter does not appear in *Letters*.

24. For an extensive quotation from Vernon's *Letter*, see Knapp, 234–35, n. 55. Thicknesse's quip is from his *Observations*, 90. Thicknesse, too, had spent time in the King's Bench.

25. "Wagstaffe," *Batchelor* 42, no. 1 (1769): 167; the writer may have been Robert Jephson. Cole, *Irish Booksellers*, 78, gives the original date of the essay as 27 December 1766.

26. James Beattie, *Essays* (Edinburgh, 1776), 350–51. Beattie might have had Anthony Walker's frontispiece to the second number of the *British Magazine* in mind.

27. Beattie, "On Fable and Romance," in vol. 2 of James Beattie, *Dissertations Moral and Critical* (London, 1783), 317.

28. "Dr. Tobias Smollet [*sic*]," *Biographical Magazine* 1 (1794): n.p.

29. See Fitzpatrick, "The Text of Tobias Smollett's *Life and Adventures of Sir Launcelot Greaves*," 140–41.

30. See Fitzpatrick, "The Text of Tobias Smollett's *Life and Adventures of Sir Launcelot Greaves*," 139–40; for the popularity of the *Novelist's Magazine*, see Mayo, *The English Novel in the Magazines*, 364.

31. James Lackington, *Memoirs of the Forty-Five First Years of the Life of J. Lackington*, [12th ed.] (London: Lackington, Allen and Co., 1803), 327; the book was first published in 1791.

32. Francis Garden, Lord Gardenstone, *Miscellanies in Prose and Verse* (Edinburgh, 1792), 194–95; see also *Tobias Smollett: The Critical Heritage*, ed. Kelly, 257–58.

33. Robert Anderson, "The Life of Smollett," in vol. 1 of *The Miscellaneous Works of Tobias Smollett, M.D.*, ed. Robert Anderson, 2d ed., enlarged (Edinburgh: Mundell and Son, 1800), lxiv. Anderson omits this opinion from earlier versions of his biography in vol. 10 of *A Complete Edition of the Poets of Great Britain*, ed. Robert Anderson (London and Edinburgh, 1794), 939–48, and vol. 1 of the first edition of *The Miscellaneous Works* (Edinburgh, 1796), xiii–lxvi.

34. See vol. 30 of *The British Novelists*, ed. Anna Laetitia Barbauld (London: Rivington, 1810), v; vol. 2 of *The British Novelists*, ed. William Mudford (London: Clarke, 1810), i; vol. 15 of *Works of the English Poets*, ed. Alexander Chalmers (London: Johnson, 1810), 548; and Scott, "Prefatory Memoir," xiii–xxv.

35. George Saintsbury, introduction to *Sir Launcelot Greaves*, in vol. 10 of *The Works of Tobias Smollett*, ed. George Saintsbury (London: Gibbings; Philadelphia: Lippincott, 1895), xi.

36. See Knapp, 221–47; Mayo, *The English Novel in the Magazines*, 276–82; and Ronald Paulson, *Satire and the Novel in Eighteenth-Century England* (New Haven: Yale University Press, 1967), 199.

37. See Boucé, *The Novels of Tobias Smollett*, 174–90.

38. Jerry C. Beasley, *Tobias Smollett: Novelist* (Athens: University of Georgia Press, 1998), 183.

39. See Evans, xv.

40. Tobias Smollett, *Ferdinand Count Fathom*, ed. Jerry C. Beasley (Athens: University of Georgia Press, 1988), 4.

41. Crabshaw probably owes his hump and protuberant belly to Samuel Butler's description of Hudibras in an earlier English adaptation of *Don Quixote*. See *Hudibras* 1.1.287–96, 1:36–37 in Zachary Grey's edition (London, 1744).

42. Although some critics have supposed a relation to Malory's Sir Lancelot or to the Lancelot of more general legend, it seems unlikely that Smollett modeled his character on the adulterer of the Arthurian tales in any significant way. See, for example, John Skinner, *Constructions of Smollett: A Study of Genre and Gender* (Newark: University of Delaware Press, 1996), 152.

43. Harry Levin observes that "a greave—like a *quijote*—happens to be a piece of leg iron"; "The Quixote Principle: Cervantes and Other Novelists," in *The Interpretation of Narrative: Theory and Practice*, ed. Morton W. Bloomfield (Cambridge, Mass.: Harvard University Press, 1970), 54.

44. Thomas Gray, *Elegy Written in a Country Churchyard*, ll. 106, 108.

45. Mayo, *The English Novel in the Magazines*, 285.

46. For Battie in *Sir Launcelot Greaves*, see Richard A. Hunter and Ida Macalpine, "Smollett's Reading in Psychiatry," *Modern Language Review* 51 (1956): 409–11.

47. Samuel Johnson, *The History of Rasselas, Prince of Abyssinia*, in *Rasselas and Other Tales*, ed. Gwin Kolb (New Haven: Yale University Press, 1990), 150.

48. *Humphry Clinker*, 88.

49. See Boucé, *The Novels of Tobias Smollett*, 190.

50. Claudio Guillen, *Literature as a System: Essays toward a Theory of Literary History* (Princeton: Princeton University Press, 1971), 100.

51. Alexander Pope, *The First Satire of the Second Book of Horace Imitated*, ll. 105–10.

52. See Tobias Smollett, trans., *The Devil upon Crutches*, bk. 1, chap. 9.

53. See Tobias Smollett, *A Faithful Narrative of the base and inhuman Arts that were lately practised upon the Brain of Habbakkuk Hilding* (London, 1752), 22.

54. Evans, xvii.

55. For Hogarth and *Sir Launcelot Greaves*, see Basker, 205–6; Beasley, *Tobias Smollett*, 163, 168–72, 174–75, 182; and Pamela Cantrell, "Writing the Picture: Fielding, Smollett, and Hogarthian Pictorialism," *Studies in Eighteenth-Century Culture* 24 (1995): 80–84. Earlier, in *Peregrine Pickle*, Smollett had satirized Hogarth as Pallet; see Ronald Paulson, "Smollett and Hogarth: The Identity of Pallet," *Studies in English Literature 1500–1900* (1964): 357–59. Smollett succinctly summarized his more mature view of the artist: "Hogarth is an inimitable original with respect to invention, humour, and expression" (*Present State*, 2:230).

56. See *Critical Review* 7 (1759): 274–75. Paulson attributes the poem to John Smith; see *Hogarth's Graphic Works*, 163.

57. See *Hogarth's Graphic Works*, plate 3, Cat. 200 and 200a, 394–95. Evans, xi, also notes connections with Hogarth's Election series, especially *The Polling* and *Chairing the Member*.

58. For this scene and Hogarth's series, see Evans, 231; see also *Hogarth's Graphic Works*, 137, 360.

59. Martin C. Battestin has disproved the claim that Smollett was a plagiarist and an

incompetent translator; see "The Authorship of Smollett's *Don Quixote*," *Studies in Bibliography* 50 (1997): 295–321. For the old accusation against Smollett, see Carmine R. Linsalata, *Smollett's Hoax: Don Quixote in England* (Stanford: Stanford University Press, 1956; New York: AMS Press, 1967).

60. Tobias Smollett, "Life of Cervantes," in *Don Quixote*, 1:xxi.

61. Tobias Smollett, preface to *The Adventures of Roderick Random*, ed. Paul-Gabriel Boucé (Oxford: Oxford University Press, 1979), xxxiv. To "assume the sock" is to act in a comedy. Classical comic actors wore light footware (socks).

62. Smollett, "Life of Cervantes," ix.

63. John Shebbeare, *The Occasional Critic; or The Decrees of the Scotch Tribunal in the Critical Review Rejudged* (London, 1757), 9.

64. Alexander Welsh, *Reflections on the Hero as Quixote* (Princeton: Princeton University Press, 1981), 3, 6.

65. Smollett, "Life of Cervantes," xxi.

66. Paul Langford, *Public Life and the Propertied Englishman, 1689–1798* (Oxford: Clarendon Press, 1991), 368; see also G. S. Rousseau and Roger A. Hambridge, "Smollett and Politics: Originals for the Election Scene in *Sir Launcelot Greaves*," *English Language Notes* 14 (1976): 32–37. For revisionist studies of Smollett's own politics, see, for example, Donald J. Greene, "Smollett the Historian: A Reappraisal," in *Tobias Smollett: Bicentennial Essays Presented to Lewis M. Knapp*, ed. G. S. Rousseau and Paul-Gabriel Boucé (New York: Oxford University Press, 1971), 25–26; Robin Fabel, "The Patriotic Briton: Smollett and English Politics," *Eighteenth-Century Studies* 8 (1974): 100–114; and Robert Adams Day, introduction to *Adventures of an Atom*, xxxii–xxxviii.

67. Smollett to Richard Smith, 8 May 1763 (*Letters*, 113).

68. In December 1762, a few months prior to writing the letter in which he made his self-defining claims, Smollett had angled for an ambassadorial post in Marseilles; see Smollett to John Home, 27 December 1762 (*Letters*, 111). Smollett was vigorously partisan in the latter stages of his career, most notably in the *Briton* (1762–63), which promoted the policies of Bute's ministry.

69. 2 January 1758 (*Letters*, 65). Smollett also made public statements about his impartiality; see Brack, "Tobias Smollett Puffs His Histories," 269, 277, 278, 280.

70. See also Smollett's dedication of the *Complete History* to Pitt, in which he disclaims "sordid motives" of his own (A2r).

71. *Continuation*, 4:113.

72. See, for example, Reed Browning, *The Duke of Newcastle* (New Haven: Yale University Press, 1975), 244–45.

73. For Pitt and the Seven Years' War, see, for example, Richard Middleton, *The Bells of Victory: The Pitt-Newcastle Ministry and the Conduct of the Seven Years' War, 1757–1762* (Cambridge: Cambridge University Press, 1985).

74. *Continuation*, 4:114.

75. For similar rhetoric in proposals for the *Continuation*, see Brack, "Tobias Smollett Puffs His Histories," 274–77; for George II on the "just and necessary measures"

taken in declaring war, see the broadside *His Majesty's Declaration of War against the French King* (London, 1756), 1, 2.

76. Foord, *His Majesty's Opposition 1714–1830* (Oxford: Clarendon Press, 1964), 303.

77. Again, proposals for the *Continuation* were similarly upbeat; see Brack, "Tobias Smollett Puffs His Histories," 277–79.

78. *Continuation*, 4:116–17.

79. *Continuation*, 4:117.

80. *Continuation*, 4:116.

81. Smollett also praised Israel Mauduit's antiwar pamphlet, *Considerations on the Present German War* (1760), and adopted Mauduit's position in the *Continuation* (4: 155). This pamphlet did not appear until after the publication of chapter 2 of *Sir Launcelot Greaves*, but Smollett echoes it in chapters 9 and 10 (published in August and September). Smollett paraphrased Mauduit's argument in *Adventures of an Atom*; see 56 and 184, n. 623.

82. *Critical Review* 3 (1757): 275.

83. *Continuation*, 4:115; see also *Continuation*, 1:144–45, 1:184; and *Adventures of an Atom*, 14. And see Ian Campbell Ross, "Smollett and the Jew Bill of 1753," *American Notes and Queries* 16 (1977): 54–56.

84. G. S. Rousseau and Roger A. Hambridge, "On Ministers and Measures: Smollett, Shebbeare, and the Portrait of Ferret in *Sir Launcelot Greaves*," *Etudes Anglaises* 32 (1979): 185–91.

85. *Poems, Plays, and "The Briton,"* 42, ll. 126–28, and Smollett's note to l. 126; see also 448, n. 21. Evans observes that Vanderpelft's name may allude to George Vandeput, a candidate for Westminster in 1750 whom Smollett discusses in *Continuation* (1:75, 101–2); see Evans, 222. Even if final biographical identification is not possible, it is clear that the surname suggests a Dutch origin, characteristic of many English Jews, and a stereotypical interest in money.

86. See Browning, *The Duke of Newcastle*, 229.

87. See Hanns Hammelmann, "Anthony Walker," in *Book Illustrators in Eighteenth-Century England* (New Haven: Yale University Press, 1975), 96–101; and Hanns Hammelmann, "Anthony Walker: A Gifted Engraver and Illustrator," *Connoisseur* 168 (1968): 167–74.

88. For the engravings from Hayman, see Brian Allen, *Francis Hayman* (New Haven: Yale University Press, 1987), 190–91.

89. For Walpole's praise of Walker, see vol. 15 of *Horace Walpole's Correspondence*, ed. W. S. Lewis (New Haven: Yale University Press, 1951), 97.

90. See Judy Edgerton, *Wright of Derby* (London: Tate Gallery Publications, 1990), 117.

91. Hammelmann, *Book Illustrators*, 98.

92. In his otherwise scrupulous bibliographical essay, Albert Smith mistakenly assigns both plates to "Charles Walker"; see *"Sir Launcelot Greaves:* A Bibliographical Survey," 221.

93. For illustrations of *Don Quixote*, see Johannes Hartau, *Don Quixote in der Kunst:*

Wandlungen einer Symbolfigur (Berlin: Gebr. Mann Verlag, 1987). For various an-
tecedents, see Guilland Sutherland, "Illustrated Editions of Tobias Smollett's
Novels: A Checklist and Commentary" (Ph.D. diss., University of Edinburgh,
1974), 99–127, 236–48, and plates 140–65.

94. These are called plates 1 and 2 in Grey's *Hudibras* because the frontispiece portrait
is not included in the numbering. My findings corroborate Sutherland's ("Illustrated Editions," 105–6) on the possibility of the small Hogarth *Hudibras* engravings as models for Walker; but I think the link may be through Mynde's engravings
of the Hogarth prints, which are from a later date than Hogarth's own.

95. Basker, 203.

96. For fuller consideration of these artists' illustrations for *Sir Launcelot Greaves*, see
Sutherland, "Illustrated Editions." For the Blake illustrations specifically, see Robert N. Essick, *William Blake's Commercial Book Illustrations: A Catalogue and Study
of the Plates Engraved by Blake after Designs by Other Artists* (Oxford: Clarendon
Press, 1991), 31–32.

97. Robert Adams Day's edition of *Adventures of an Atom* reproduces many relevant
prints; see also Day, "*Ut Pictura Poesis*? Smollett, Satire, and the Graphic Arts,"
Studies in Eighteenth-Century Culture 10 (1981): 297–312.

98. See Basker, esp. 110–18.

The Life and Adventures of Sir Launcelot Greaves

THE
ADVENTURES
OF
Sir Launcelot Greaves.

By the Author of RODERICK RANDOM.

In TWO VOLUMES.

VOL. I.

LONDON:

Printed for J. COOTE, in Pater-Noster-Row.

M.DCC.LXII.

Title page of first (book) edition, vol. 1, 1762.
(Collection of Robert and Vivian Folkenflik)

CHAPTER I.

In which certain personages of this delightful history
are introduced to the reader's acquaintance.

It was on the great northern road[1] from York to London, about the beginning of the month October, and the hour of eight in the evening, that four travellers were by a violent shower of rain driven for shelter into a little public house on the side of the highway, distinguished by a sign which was said to exhibit the figure of a black lion.[2] The kitchen, in which they assembled, was the only room for entertainment in the house, paved with red bricks, remarkably clean, furnished with three or four Windsor chairs,[3] adorned with shining plates of pewter and copper sauce-pans nicely scoured, that even dazzled the eyes of the beholder; while a chearful fire of sea-coal[4] blazed in the chimney. Three of the travellers, who arrived on horseback, having seen their cattle properly accommodated in the stable, agreed to pass the time, until the weather should clear up, over a bowl of rumbo,[5] which was accordingly prepared: but the fourth, refusing to join their company, took his station at the opposite side of the chimney, and called for a pint of two-penny,[6] with which he indulged himself apart. At a little distance, on his left hand, there was another groupe, consisting of the landlady a decent widow, her two daughters, the elder of whom seemed to be about the age of fifteen, and a country lad, who served both as waiter and ostler.

The social triumvirate was composed of Mr. Fillet, a country practitioner in surgery and midwifery, Capt. Crowe, and his nephew Mr. Thomas Clarke, an attorney. Fillet was a man of some education, and a great deal of experience, shrewd, sly, and sensible. Capt. Crowe had commanded a merchant-ship in the Mediterranean-trade for many years, and saved some money by dint of frugality and traffick. He was an excellent seaman, brave, active, friendly in his way, and scrupulously honest; but as little acquainted with the world as a sucking child; whimsical, impatient, and so impetuous that he could not help breaking in upon the conversation, whatever it might be, with repeated interruptions, that seemed to burst from him by involuntary impulse: when he himself attempted to speak, he never finished his period; but made such a number of abrupt transitions, that his discourse seemed to be an unconnected series of unfinished sentences, the meaning of which it was not easy to decypher. His nephew, Tom Clarke, was a young fellow whose goodness of heart even the exercise of his profession had not been able to corrupt. Before strangers he never owned himself an attorney, without blushing,[7] though he had no reason to blush for his own practice; for he constantly refused to engage in the cause of any client whose character was equivocal, and was never known to act with such industry as when concerned for the widow and the orphan, or any other object that sued *in forma pauperis*.[8] Indeed he was so replete with human kindness, that as often as an affecting story or circumstance was told in his hearing, it overflowed at his eyes. Being of a warm complexion, he was very susceptible of passion, and somewhat libertine in his amours. In other respects, he piqued himself on understanding the practice of the courts, and in private company he took pleasure in *laying down the law;* but he was an indifferent orator, and tediously circumstantial in his explanations: his stature was rather diminutive; but, upon the whole, he had some title to the character of a pretty, dapper, little fellow. The solitary guest had something very forbidding in his aspect, which was contracted by an habitual frown. His eyes were small and red, and so deep set in the sockets, that each appeared like the unextinguished snuff of a farthing-candle, gleaming through the horn of a dark lanthorn.[9] His nostrils were elevated in scorn, as if his sense of smelling had been perpetually offended by some unsavoury odour; and he looked as if he wanted to shrink within himself, from the impertinence of society. He wore a black periwig as straight as the pinions of a raven, and this was covered with an hat flapped, and fastened to his head by a speckled handkerchief tied under his chin. He was wrapped in a great coat of brown frize,[10] under which he seemed to conceal a small bundle. His name was Ferret,[11] and his character distinguished by three peculiarities. He was never seen to smile: he was never heard to speak in praise of any person whatsoever; and he was never known to give a direct answer to any question that was asked: but seemed, on all occasions, to be actuated by the most perverse spirit of contradiction.

Capt. Crowe, having remarked that it was squally weather, asked how far it was to the next market-town; and understanding that the distance was not less than six miles, said he had a good mind to come to an anchor for the night, if so be as he could have a tolerable *berth* in this here harbour. Mr. Fillet, perceiving by his stile that he was a sea-faring gentleman, observed that their landlady was not used to lodge such company; and expressed some surprize, that he who had no doubt endured so many storms and hardships at sea, should think much of travelling five or six miles a-horseback by moon-light. "For my part," said he, "I ride in all weathers, and at all hours, without minding cold, wet, wind, or darkness. My constitution is so case-hardened, that I believe I could live all the year at Spitzbergen.[12] With respect to this road,

I know every foot of it so exactly, that I'll engage to travel forty miles upon it blindfold, without making one false step; and if you have faith enough to put yourselves under my auspices, I will conduct you safe to an elegant inn, where you will meet with the best accommodation." "Thank you, brother, (replied the Captain): we are much beholden to you for your courteous offer; but, howsomever, you must not think I mind foul weather more than my neighbours. I have worked hard aloft and alow[13] in many a taught gale[14]—but this here is the case, d'ye see; we have run down a long day's reckoning: our beasts have had a hard spell; and as for my own hap, brother, I doubt my bottom-planks have lost some of their sheathing,[15] being as how I a'n't used to that kind of scrubbing."

The Doctor, who had practised on board a man of war in his youth, and was perfectly well acquainted with the captain's dialect, assured him, that if his bottom was damaged, he would *new-pay*[16] it with an excellent salve, which he always carried about with him, to guard against such accidents on the road: but Tom Clarke, who seemed to have cast the eyes of affection upon the landlady's eldest daughter, Dolly, objected to their proceeding farther without rest and refreshment, as they had already travelled fifty miles since morning; and he was sure his uncle must be fatigued both in mind and body, from vexation as well as from a hard exercise, to which he had not been accustomed. Fillet then desisted, saying, he was sorry to find the Captain had any cause for vexation; but he hoped it was not an incurable evil. This expression was accompanied with a look of curiosity, which Mr. Clarke was glad of an occasion to gratify; for, as we have hinted above, he was a very communicative gentleman, and the affair which now lay upon his stomach interested him nearly. "I'll assure you, Sir, (said he) this here gentleman, captain Crowe, who is my mother's own brother, has been cruelly used by some of his relations. He bears as good a character as any captain of a ship on the Royal Exchange,[17] and has undergone a variety of hardships at sea. What d'ye think, now, of his bursting all his sinews, and making his eyes start out of his head, in pulling his ship off a rock, whereby he saved to his owners—" Here he was interrupted by the Captain, who exclaimed, "Belay, Tom, belay:—prithee, don't veer out such a deal of jaw. Clap a stopper upon thy cable, and bring thyself up,[18] my lad.— What a deal of stuff thou hast pumped up concerning bursting, and starting, and pulling ships, Laud have mercy on us!——Look ye here, brother—look ye here——mind these poor crippled joints: two fingers on the starboard, and three on the larboard[19] hand: crooked, d'ye see, like the knees of a bilander[20]—I'll tell you what, brother, you seem to be a——ship deep laden—rich cargoe—current setting into the bay—hard gale—lee shore[21]—all hands in the boat—tow round the headland [22]—self pulling for dear blood, against the whole crew.——Snap go the finger-braces—crack went the eye-blocks.— Bounce day-light [23]—flash starlight—down I foundered, dark as hell—— whizz went my ears, and my head spun like a whirligig.——That don't sig- nify—I'm a Yorkshire boy, as the saying is [24]—all my life at sea, brother, by reason of an old grandmother and maiden aunt, a couple of old stinking—— kept me these forty years out of my grandfather's estate.—Hearing as how they had taken their departure, came ashore, hired horses, and clapped on all my canvas, [25] steering to the northward, to take possession of my——But it don't signify talking—these two old piratical—had held a palaver with a law- yer—an attorney, Tom, d'ye mind me, an attorney—and by his assistance hove me out of my inheritance:—that is all, brother,—hove me out of five hundred pounds a year—that's all——what signifies—but such windfalls we don't every day pick up along shore.——Fill about, [26] brother——yes, by the Lord! those two smuggling harridans, with the assistance of an attorney—an attorney, Tom—hove me out of five hundred a year." "Yes, indeed, Sir, (added Mr. Clarke) those two malicious old women docked the intail, and left the estate to an alien." [27]

Here Mr. Ferret thought proper to intermingle in the conversation with a "*Pish*, what, do'st talk of docking the intail? Do'st not know that by the Statute Westm. 2, 13 Ed. I. the will and intention of the donor [28] must be fulfilled, and the tenant in *tail* shall not alien after issue had, or before?" "Give me leave, Sir, (replied Tom) I presume you are a practitioner in the law. Now you know, that in the case of a contingent *remainder*, [29] the intail may be destroyed by levying a fine, and suffering a recovery; or otherwise destroying the particular estate, before the contingency happens. If *feoffees*, who possess an estate only during the life of a son, where divers *remainders* are limited over, make a *feoff- ment* in fee [30] to him, by the *feoffment* all the future *remainders* are destroyed. Indeed, a person in *remainder* may have a writ of Intrusion, [31] if any do intrude after the death of a tenant for life; and the writ *ex gravi querela* lies [32] to execute a devise in *remainder*, after the death of tenant in tail without issue—" "Spoke like a true disciple of Geber," [33] cried Ferret. "No, Sir, (replied Mr. Clarke) counsellor Caper [34] is in the conveyancing-way [35]—I was clerk to serjeant Croaker." [36] "Ay, now you may set up for yourself; (resumed the other) for you can prate as unintelligibly as the best of them."

"Perhaps (said Tom) I do not make myself understood: if so be as how that is the case, let us change the position; and suppose that this here case is a *tail after a possibility of issue extinct*. [37] If a tenant in *tail*, after possibility, make a *feoffment* of his land, he in reversion [38] may enter for the forfeiture. Then we must make a distinction between *general tail* and *special tail*.[39] It is the word *body* that makes the *intail:*—there must be *body* in the *tail*, devised to heirs male or female, otherwise it is a fee-simple, because it is not limited of what *body*. Thus a corporation cannot be seized in *tail*. For example: here is a young woman—What is your name, my dear?" "Dolly," answered the daughter, with a curtsy. "Here's Dolly—I seize Dolly *in tail*—Dolly, I seize you in *tail*."—"Sha't then," cried Dolly, pouting. "I am seized of land in fee—I settle on Dolly in *tail*."—Dolly, who did not comprehend the nature of the illustration, understood him in a literal sense, and in a whimpering tone exclaimed, "Sha't then, I tell thee, cursed tuoad!" Tom, however, was so transported with his subject, that he took no notice of poor Dolly's mistake; but proceeded in his harangue upon the different kinds of *tails*, *remainders*, and *seisins*,[40] when he was interrupted by a noise that alarmed the whole company. The rain had been succeeded by a storm of wind, that howled around the house with the most savage impetuosity; and the heavens were overcast in such a manner, that not one star appeared, so that all without was darkness and uproar. This aggravated the horrour of divers loud screams, which even the noise of the blast could not exclude from the astonished ears of our travellers. Capt. Crowe called out, "Avast,[41] avast": Tom Clarke sat silent, staring wildly, with his mouth still open: the surgeon himself seemed startled, and Ferret's countenance betrayed evident marks of confusion. The ostler moved nearer the chimney, and the good woman of the house, with her two daughters, crept close to the company.

After some pause, the Captain starting up, "These (said he) be signals of distress. Some poor souls in danger of foundering.—Let us bear up a-head,[42] and see if we can give them any assistance." The landlady begged him, for Christ's sake, not to think of going out; for it was a spirit that would lead him astray into fens and rivers, and certainly do him a mischief. Crowe seemed to be staggered by this remonstrance, which his nephew reinforced, observing, that it might be a stratagem of rogues to decoy them into the fields, that they might rob them under cloud of night. Thus exhorted, he resumed his seat; and Mr. Ferret began to make very severe strictures upon the folly and fear of those who believed and trembled at the visitation of spirits, ghosts, and goblins. He said, he would engage with twelve pennyworth of phosphorus to frighten a whole parish out of their senses: then he expatiated on the pusillanimity of the nation[43] in general; ridiculed the militia,[44] censured the government; and dropped some hints about a change of hands,[45] which the Captain could not, and the Doctor would not comprehend. Tom Clarke, from the freedom of his discourse, concluded he was a ministerial spy, and communi-

Sir Launcelot Greaves and his Squire, Timothy Crabshaw,
by Anthony Walker. (Collection of James G. Basker)

cated his opinion to his uncle in a whisper, while this misanthrope continued to pour forth his invectives with a fluency peculiar to himself. The truth is, Mr. Ferret had been a party-writer,[46] not from principle, but employment, and had felt the rod of power; in order to avoid a second exertion of which, he now found it convenient to sculk about in the country: for he had received intimation of a warrant from the secretary of state,[47] who wanted to be better acquainted with his person. Notwithstanding the ticklish nature of his situation, it was become so habitual to him to think and speak in a certain manner, that even before strangers, whose principles and connexions he could not possibly know, he hardly ever opened his mouth, without uttering some direct or implied sarcasm against the government. He had already proceeded a considerable way in demonstrating, that the nation was bankrupt and beggared, and that those who stood at the helm were steering full into the gulph of inevitable destruction;[48] when his lecture was suddenly suspended by a violent knocking at the door, which threatened the whole house with immediate demolition. Capt. Crowe, believing they should be instantly boarded, unsheathed his hanger, and stood in a posture of defence. Mr. Fillet armed himself with the poker, which happened to be red-hot: the ostler pulled down a rusty firelock, that hung by the roof, over a flitch of bacon. Tom Clarke, perceiving the landlady and her children distracted with terror, conducted them, out of meer compassion, below stairs into the cellar; and as for Mr. Ferret, he prudently withdrew into an adjoining pantry. But as a personage of great importance in this entertaining history was forced to remain some time at the door, before he could gain admittance, so must the reader wait with patience for the next chapter, in which he will see the cause of this disturbance explained much to his comfort and edification.

CHAPTER II.

In which the hero of these adventures makes
his first appearance on the stage of action.

The outward door of the Black Lion had already sustained two dreadful shocks; but at the third it flew open, and in stalked an apparition, that smote the hearts of our travellers with fear and trepidation. It was the figure

[The Entrance of Sir Launcelot and Timothy Crabshaw], by William Walker after Stothard. (Rare Book and Manuscript Library, Columbia University)

The Alarm of Crowe and Fillet at the Appearance of Sir Launcelot, by Cruikshank.
(Richard W. Meirs Collection of George Cruikshank,
Department of Rare Books and Special Collections,
Princeton University Library)

of a man armed cap-a-pie,[1] bearing on his shoulder a bundle[2] dropping with water, which afterwards appeared to be the body of a man that seemed to have been drowned, and fished up from the bottom of the neighbouring river.[3] Having deposited his burthen carefully on the floor, he addressed himself to the company in these words: "Be not surprised, good people, at this unusual appearance, which I shall take an opportunity to explain; and forgive the rude and boisterous manner in which I have demanded, and indeed forced admittance. The violence of my intrusion was the effect of necessity. In crossing the river, my squire and his horse were swept away by the stream; and with some difficulty I have been able to drag him ashore, though I am afraid my assistance reached him too late: for, since I brought him to land, he has given no signs of life." Here he was interrupted by a groan, which issued from the chest of the squire, and terrified the spectators as much as it comforted the master. After some recollection, Mr. Fillet began to undress the body, which was laid in a blanket on the floor, and rolled from side to side by his direction. A considerable quantity of water being discharged from the mouth of this unfortunate squire, he uttered a hideous roar, and, opening his eyes, stared wildly around: then the surgeon undertook for his recovery; and his master went forth with the ostler in quest of the horses, which he had left by the side of the river. His back was no sooner turned than Ferret, who had been peeping from behind the pantry-door, ventured to rejoin the company; pronouncing with a smile, or rather grin of contempt, "Hey day! what precious mummery is this? What, are we to have the farce of Hamlet's ghost?"[4] "Adzooks, (cried the Captain) my kinsman Tom has dropped a-stern—hope in God a-has not bulged to, and gone to bottom."[5] "Pish, (exclaimed the misanthrope) there's no danger: the young lawyer is only seizing Dolly in tail."

Certain it is, Dolly squeaked at that instant in the cellar; and Clarke appearing soon after in some confusion, declared she had been frightened by a flash of lightning: but this assertion was not confirmed by the young lady herself, who eyed him with a sullen regard, indicating displeasure, though not indifference; and when questioned by her mother, replied, "A-doan't maind what a-says, so a-doan't, vor all his goalden jacket, then."

In the mean time the surgeon had performed the operation of phlebotomy[6] on the squire, who was lifted into a chair, and supported by the landlady for that purpose; but he had not as yet given any sign of having retrieved the use of his senses. And here Mr. Fillet could not help contemplating, with surprize, the strange figure and accoutrements of his patient, who seemed in age to be turned of fifty. His stature was below the middle size: he was thick, squat, and brawny, with a small protuberance on one shoulder, and a prominent belly,[7] which, in consequence of the water he had swallowed, now strutted out beyond its usual dimensions. His forehead was remarkably convex, and so very low, that his black bushy hair descended within an inch of his nose: but this did not conceal the wrinkles of his front, which were manifold. His small glimmering eyes resembled those of the Hampshire porker,[8] that turns up the soil with his projecting snout. His cheeks were shrivelled and puckered at the corners, like the seams of a regimental coat as it comes from the hands of the contractor:[9] his nose bore a strong analogy in shape to a tennis-ball, and in colour to a mulberry; for all the water of the river had not been able to quench the natural fire of that feature. His upper jaw was furnished with two long white sharp-pointed teeth or fangs, such as the reader may have observed in the chaps of a wolf, or full-grown mastiff, and an anatomist would describe as a preternatural elongation of the *dentes canini*.[10] His chin was so long, so peaked and incurvated, as to form in profile with his impending forehead the exact resemblance of a moon in the first quarter.[11] With respect to his equipage, he had a leathern cap upon his head, faced like those worn by the marines, and exhibiting in embroidery the figure of a crescent.[12] His coat was of white cloth, faced with black, and cut in a very antique fashion; and, in lieu of a waistcoat, he wore a buff jerkin.[13] His feet were cased in loose buskins,[14] which, though they rose almost to his knee, could not hide that curvature known by the appellation of bandy legs. A large string of bandaliers[15] garnished a broad belt that graced his shoulders, from whence depended an instrument of war, which was something between a back-sword and a cutlass;[16] and a case of pistols were stuck in his girdle. Such was the figure which the whole company now surveyed with admiration. After some pause, he seemed to recover his recollection. He rolled his eyes around, and, attentively surveying every individual, exclaimed, in a strange tone, "Bodikins![17] where's Gilbert?" This interrogation did not savour much of sanity, especially when accompanied with a wild stare, which is generally interpreted as a sure sign of a disturbed understanding: nevertheless the surgeon endeavoured to assist his recollection. "Come, (said he) have a good heart.—How do'st do, friend?" "Do! (replied the squire) do as well as I can:—that's a lie too: I might have done better. I had no business to be here." "You ought to thank God and your master (resumed the surgeon) for the providential escape you have had." "Thank my master! (cried the squire) thank the devil! Go and teach your grannum to crack filberds.[18] I know who I'm bound to pray for, and who I ought to curse the longest day I have to live."

Here the Captain interposing, "Nay, brother, (said he) you are bound to pray for this here gentleman as your sheet-anchor: [19] for, if so be as he had not cleared your stowage of the water you had taken in at your upper works, and lightened your veins, d'ye see, by taking away some of your blood, adad! [20] you had driven before the gale, and never been brought up in this world again, d'ye see." "What, then you would persuade me (replied the patient) that the only way to save my life was to shed my precious blood? Look ye, friend, it shall not be lost blood to me.—I take you all to witness, that there surgeon, or apothecary, or farrier,[21] or dog-doctor, or whatsoever he may be, has robbed me of the balsam of life:—he has not left so much blood in my body as would fatten a starved flea.—O! that there was a lawyer here to serve him with a *siserari*." [22] Then fixing his eyes upon Ferret, he proceeded: "An't you a limb of the law, friend?—No, I cry you mercy, you look more like a shew-man or a conjurer."——Ferret, nettled at this address, answered, "It would be well for you that I could conjure a little common sense into that numbscull of yours." "If I want that commodity, (rejoined the squire) I must go to another market, I trow.—You legerdemain men be more like to conjure the money from our pockets, than sense into our sculls.—Vor my own part, I was once cheated of vorty good shillings by one of your broother cups and balls." [23] In all probability he would have descended to particulars, had not he been seized with a return of his nausea, which obliged him to call for a bumper of brandy. This remedy being swallowed, the tumult in his stomach subsided. He desired he might be put to-bed without delay, and that half a dozen eggs and a pound of bacon might, in a couple of hours, be dressed for his supper.

He was accordingly led off the scene by the landlady and her daughter; and Mr. Ferret had just time to observe the fellow was a composition, in which he did not know whether knave or fool most predominated, when the master returned from the stable. He had taken off his helmet, and now displayed a very engaging countenance. His age did not seem to exceed thirty: he was tall, and seemingly robust; his face long and oval, his nose aquiline, his mouth furnished with a set of elegant teeth white as the drifted snow; his complexion clear, and his aspect noble. His chesnut hair loosely flowed in short natural curls; and his grey eyes shone with such vivacity, as plainly shewed that his reason was a little discomposed. Such an appearance prepossessed the greater part of the company in his favour: he bowed round with the most polite and affable address; enquired about his squire, and, being informed of the pains Mr. Fillet had taken for his recovery, insisted upon that gentleman's accepting an handsome gratuity: then, in consideration of the cold bath he had under-gone, he was prevailed upon to take the post of honour; namely, the great chair fronting the fire, which was reinforced with a billet of wood for his comfort and convenience.

Perceiving his fellow-travellers either over-awed into silence by his presence, or struck dumb with admiration at his equipage, he accosted them in these words, while an agreeable smile dimpled on his cheek.

"The good company wonders, no doubt, to see a man cased in armour, such as hath been for above a whole century disused in this and every other country of Europe; and perhaps they will be still more surprised, when they hear that man profess himself a noviciate of that military order, which hath of old been distinguished in Great Britain, as well as through all Christendom, by the name of Knights Errant. Yes, gentlemen, in that painful and thorny path of toil and danger I have begun my career, a candidate for honest fame; determined, as far as in me lies, to honour and assert the efforts of virtue; to combat vice in all her forms, redress injuries, chastise oppression, protect the helpless and forlorn, relieve the indigent, exert my best endeavours in the cause of innocence and beauty, and dedicate my talents, such as they are, to the service of my country." "What! (said Ferret) you set up for a modern Don Quixote?[24]—The scheme is rather too stale and extravagant.—What was an humorous romance, and well-timed satire in Spain, near two hundred years ago,[25] will make but a sorry jest, and appear equally insipid and absurd, when really acted from affectation, at this time a-day, in a country like England."

The Knight, eying this censor with a look of disdain, replied, in a solemn lofty tone: "He that from affectation imitates the extravagances recorded of Don Quixote, is an impostor equally wicked and contemptible. He that counterfeits madness, unless he dissembles like the elder Brutus,[26] for some virtuous purpose, not only debases his own soul, but acts as a traytor to heaven, by denying the divinity that is within him.—I am neither an affected imitator of Don Quixote, nor, as I trust in heaven, visited by that spirit of lunacy so admirably displayed in the fictitious character exhibited by the inimitable Cervantes. I have not yet encountered a windmill for a giant;[27] nor mistaken this public house for a magnificent castle:[28] neither do I believe this gentleman to be the constable;[29] nor that worthy practitioner to be master Elizabat, the surgeon recorded in Amadis de Gaul; nor you to be the enchanter Alquife,[30] nor any other sage of history or romance.—I see and distinguish objects as they are discerned and described by other men. I reason without prejudice, can endure contradiction, and, as the company perceives, even bear impertinent censure without passion or resentment. I quarrel with none but the foes of virtue and decorum, against whom I have declared perpetual war, and them I will every where attack as the natural enemies of mankind." "But that war (said the cynic) may soon be brought to a conclusion, and your adventures close in Bridewell,[31] provided you meet with some determined constable, who will seize your worship as a vagrant, according to the statute."[32] "Heaven and earth![33] (cried the stranger, starting up and laying his hand to his sword) do I live to hear myself insulted with such an opprobrious epithet, and refrain from trampling into dust the insolent calumniator!"

The tone in which these words were pronounced, and the indignation that flashed from the eyes of the speaker, intimidated every individual of the society, and reduced Ferret to a temporary privation of all his faculties. His eyes retired within their sockets: his complection, which was naturally of a copper hue, now shifted to a leaden colour: his teeth began to chatter; and all his limbs were agitated by a sudden palsy. The Knight observed his condition, and resumed his seat, saying, "I was to blame: my vengeance must be reserved for very different objects.—Friend, you have nothing to fear—the sudden gust of passion is now blown over. Recollect yourself, and I will reason calmly on the observation you have made."

This was a very seasonable declaration to Mr. Ferret, who opened his eyes, and wiped his forehead, while the other proceeded in these terms. "You say I am in danger of being apprehended as a vagrant: I am not so ignorant of the laws of my country, but that I know the description of those who fall within the legal meaning of this odious term. You must give me leave to inform you, friend, that I am neither bearward,[34] fencer, stroller,[35] gipsey, mountebank, nor mendicant; nor do I practise subtle craft to deceive and impose upon the King's lieges; nor can I be held as an idle disorderly person, travelling from place to place, collecting monies by virtue of counterfeited passes, briefs, and other false pretences.—In what respect therefore am I to be deemed a vagrant? Answer boldly, without fear or scruple." To this interrogation the misanthrope replied, with a faultering accent, "If not a vagrant, you incur the penalty for riding armed in affray of the peace."[36] "But, instead of riding armed in affray of the peace, (resumed the other) I ride in preservation of the peace; and gentlemen are allowed by the law to wear armour for their defence. Some ride with blunderbusses, some with pistols, some with swords, according to their various inclinations. Mine is to wear the armour of my forefathers: perhaps I use them for exercise, in order to accustom myself to fatigue, and strengthen my constitution: perhaps I assume them for a frolick."

"But if you swagger armed and in disguise,[37] assault me on the highway, or put me in bodily fear, for the sake of the jest, the law will punish you in earnest," (cried the other). "But my intention (answered the Knight) is carefully to avoid all those occasions of offences." "Then (said Ferret) you may go un-armed, like other sober people." "Not so, (answered the Knight) as I propose to travel all times, and in all places, mine armour may guard me against the attempts of treachery: it may defend me in combat against odds, should I be assaulted by a multitude of plebeians, or have occasion to bring malefactors to justice." "What, then (exclaimed the philosopher) you intend to co-operate with the honourable fraternity of thief-takers?"[38] "I do purpose (said the youth, eying him with a look of ineffable contempt) to act as a coadjutor to the law, and even to remedy evils which the law cannot reach; to detect fraud and treason, abase insolence, mortify pride, discourage slander, disgrace im-modesty, and stigmatize ingratitude: but the infamous part of a thief-catcher's character I disclaim. I neither associate with robbers and pickpockets, know-ing them to be such, that, in being intrusted with their secrets, I may the more effectually betray them; nor shall I ever pocket the reward granted by the leg-islature to those by whom robbers are brought to conviction: but I shall always think it my duty to rid my country of that pernicious vermin, which preys upon the bowels of the commonwealth—not but that an incorporated com-pany of licensed thieves might, under proper regulations, be of service to the community."

Ferret, emboldened by the passive tameness with which the stranger bore his last reflection, began to think he had nothing of Hector[39] but his outside, and gave a loose to all the acrimony of his party rancour. Hearing the Knight mention a company of licensed thieves, "What else (cried he) is the majority of the nation? What is your standing army at home, that eat up their fellow subjects?[40] What are your mercenaries abroad, whom you hire to fight their own quarrels?[41] What is your militia,[42] that wise measure of this sagacious m——y,[43] but a larger gang of petty thieves, who steal sheep and poultry through meer idleness; and were they confronted with an enemy, would steal themselves away? What is your . . . . . but a knot of thieves,[44] who pillage the nation under colour of law, and enrich themselves with the wreck of their country? When you consider the enormous debt of an hundred millions, the intolerable load of taxes and impositions under which we groan, and the man-ner in which that burthen is yearly accumulating, to support two German elec-torates,[45] without our receiving any thing in return but the shews of triumph and shadows of conquest: I say, when you reflect on these circumstances, and at the same time behold our cities filled with bankrupts, and our country with beggars; can you be so infatuated as to deny that our m——y is mad, or worse than mad; our wealth exhausted, our people miserable, our credit blasted, and our state on the brink of perdition?[46] This prospect, indeed, will make the fainter impression, if we recollect that we ourselves are a pack of such profligate, corrupted, pusillanimous rascals, as deserve no salvation."

The stranger, raising his voice to a loud tone, replied, "Such, indeed, are the insinuations, equally false and insidious, with which the desperate emissaries of a party endeavour to poison the minds of his Majesty's subjects, in defiance of common honesty and common sense. But he must be blind to all perception, and dead to candour, who does not see and own that we are involved in a just and necessary war, which has been maintained on truly British principles,[47] prosecuted with vigour, and crowned with success; that our taxes are easy, in proportion to our wealth; that our conquests are equally glorious and important; that our commerce flourishes, our people are happy, and our enemies reduced to despair.—Is there a man who boasts a British heart, that repines at the success and prosperity of his country? Such there are, O shame to patriotism, and reproach to Great Britain! who act as the emissaries of France both in word and writing; who exaggerate our necessary burthens, magnify our dangers, extol the power of our enemies, deride our victories, extenuate our conquests, condemn the measures of our government, and scatter the seeds of dissatisfaction through the land. Such domestic traitors are doubly the objects of detestation; first, in perverting truth; and, secondly, in propagating falsehood, to the prejudice of that community of which they have professed themselves members. One of these is well known by the name of Ferret, an old, rancorous, incorrigible instrument of sedition: happy it is for him, that he has never fallen in my way; for, notwithstanding the maxims of forbearance which I have adopted, the indignation which the character of that caitiff[48] inspires, would probably impel me to some act of violence, and I should crush him like an ungrateful viper, that gnawed the bosom which warmed it into life!"

These last words were pronounced with a wildness of look, that even bordered upon frenzy. The misanthrope once more retired to the pantry for shelter, and the rest of the guests were evidently disconcerted.

Mr. Fillet, in order to change the conversation, which was likely to produce serious consequences, expressed uncommon satisfaction at the remarks which the Knight had made, signified his approbation of the honourable office he had undertaken; declared himself happy in having seen such an accomplished cavalier; and observed, that nothing was wanting to render him a compleat knight-errant, but some celebrated beauty, the mistress of his heart, whose idea might animate his breast, and strengthen his arm to the utmost exertion of valour: he added, that love was the soul of chivalry. The stranger started at this discourse. He turned his eyes on the surgeon with a fixed regard: his countenance changed: a torrent of tears gushed down his cheeks: his head sunk upon his bosom: he heaved a profound sigh; and remained in silence with all the external marks of unutterable sorrow. The company were in some measure infected by his despondence; concerning the cause of which, however, they would not venture to inquire.

By this time the landlady, having disposed of the squire, desired to know, with many curtsies, if his honour would not chuse to put off his wet garments; assuring him, that she had a very good feather-bed at his service, upon which many gentlevolks of the virst quality had lain; that the sheets were well aired; and that Dolly should warm them for his worship with a pan of coals. This hospitable offer being repeated, he seemed to wake from a trance of grief; arose from his seat, and, bowing courteously to the company, withdrew.

Captain Crowe, whose faculty of speech had been all this time absorbed in amazement, now broke into the conversation with a volley of interjections: "Split my snatch-block!— Odd's firkin!—Splice my old shoes![49]—I have sailed the salt seas, brother, since I was no higher than the Triton's taffril[50]—east, west, north, and south, as the saying is—Blacks, Indians, Moors, Morattos, and Seapoys;[51]—but, smite my timbers![52] such a man of war—" Here he was interrupted by his nephew Tom Clarke, who had disappeared at the Knight's first entrance, and now produced himself with an eagerness in his look, while the tears started in his eyes.——"Lord bless my soul! (cried he) I know that gentleman, and his servant, as well as I know my own father.—I am his own godson, uncle: he stood for me when he was a boy—yes, indeed, Sir, my father was steward to the estate—I may say I was bred up in the family of Sir Ever-hard Greaves, who has been dead these two years—this is the only son, Sir Launcelot;[53] the best-natured, worthy, generous gentleman—I care not who knows it: I love him as well as if he was my own flesh and blood——"

At this period Tom, whose heart was of the melting mood, began to sob and weep plenteously, from pure affection. Crowe, who was not very subject to these tendernesses, damned him for a chicken-hearted lubber; repeating, with much peevishness, "What do'st cry for? what do'st cry for, noddy?"[54] The surgeon, impatient to know the story of Sir Launcelot, which he had heard imperfectly recounted, begged that Mr. Clarke would compose himself, and relate it as circumstantially as his memory could retain the particulars; and Tom, wiping his eyes, promised to give him that satisfaction; which the reader, if he be so minded, may partake in the next chapter.

CHAPTER III.

Which the reader, on perusal, may wish were chapter the last.[1]

The Doctor prescribed a *repetatur* of the julep,[2] and mixed the ingredients *secundum artem;*[3] Tom Clarke hemmed thrice, to clear his pipes; while the rest of the company, including Dolly and her mother, who had by this time administred to the knight, composed themselves into earnest and hushed attention. Then the young lawyer began his narration to this effect:—"I tell ye what, gemmen,[4] I don't pretend in this here case to flourish and harangue like a——having never been called to——but what of that, d'ye see?—perhaps I may know as much as——Facts are facts, as the saying is.—I shall tell, repeat, and relate a plain story—matters of fact, d'ye see, without rhetoric, oratory, ornament, or embellishment; without repetition, tautology, circumlocution, or going about the bush: facts which I shall aver, partly on the testimony of my own knowledge, and partly from the information of responsible evidences of good repute and credit, any circumstance known to the contrary notwithstanding:—for, as the law saith, if so be as how there is *an exception* to evidence, that *exception* is in its nature but a denial of what is taken to be good by the other party, and *exceptio in non exceptis, firmat regulam,*[5] d'ye see.—— But, howsomever, in regard to this here affair, we need not be so scrupulous as if we were pleading before a judge *sedente curia*——"[6]

Ferret, whose curiosity was rather more eager than that of any other person in this audience, being provoked by this preamble, dashed the pipe he had just filled in pieces against the grate; and after having pronounced the interjection *pish,* with an acrimony of aspect altogether peculiar to himself, "If (said he) impertinence and folly were felony by the statute, there would be no want of unexceptionable evidence to hang such an eternal babbler." "Anan,[7] babbler! (cried Tom, reddening with passion, and starting up) I'd have you to know, Sir, that I can bite as well as babble; and that, if I am so minded, I can run upon the foot after my game without being in fault,[8] as the saying is; and which is more, I can shake an old fox by the collar."

How far this young lawyer might have proceeded to prove himself staunch on the person of the misanthrope, if he had not been prevented, we shall not determine; but the whole company were alarmed at his looks and expressions. Dolly's rosy cheeks assumed an ash-colour, while she ran between the disputants, crying, "Naay, naay—vor the love of God doan't then, doan't then!" But captain Crowe exerted a parental authority over his nephew, saying, "Avast, Tom, avast!——Snug's the word⁹—we'll have no boarding, d'ye see.—Haul forward thy chair again, take thy berth, and proceed with thy story in a direct course, without yawing like a Dutch yanky."¹⁰

Tom, thus tutored, recollected himself, resumed his seat, and, after some pause, plunged at once into the current of narration. "I told you before, gemmen, that the gentleman in armour was the only son of Sir Everhard Greaves, who possessed a free estate of five thousand a year in our county, and was respected by all his neighbours, as much for his personal merit as for his family fortune. With respect to his son Launcelot, whom you have seen, I can remember nothing until he returned from the university, about the age of seventeen, and then I myself was not more than ten years old. The young gemman was at that time in mourning for his mother; though God he knows, Sir Everhard had more cause to rejoice than to be afflicted at her death:—for, among friends, (here he lowered his voice, and looked round the kitchen) she was very whimsical, expensive, and ill-tempered, and, I'm afraid, a little— upon the—flighty order—a little touched or so;—but mum for that—the lady is now dead; and it is my maxim, *de mortuis nil nisi bonum*.¹¹ The young squire was even then very handsome, and looked remarkably well in his weepers:¹² but he had an aukward air and shambling gait, stooped mortally, and was so shy and silent, that he would not look a stranger in the face, nor open his mouth before company. Whenever he spied a horse or carriage at the gate, he would make his escape into the garden, and from thence into the park; where many's the good time and often he has been found sitting under a tree, with a book in his hand, reading Greek, Latin, and other foreign linguas.

"Sir Everhard himself was no great scholar, and my father had forgot his classical learning; and so the rector of the parish was desired to examine young Launcelot. It was a long time before he found an opportunity: the squire always gave him the slip.—At length the parson catched him in bed of a-morning, and, locking the door, to it they went tooth and nail. What passed betwixt them the Lord in heaven knows; but, when the Doctor came forth, he looked wild and haggard as if he had seen a ghost, his face as white as paper, and his lips trembling like an aspen-leaf. 'Parson, (said the knight) what is the matter?—how do'st find my son? I hope he won't turn out a ninny, and disgrace his family.' The Doctor, wiping the sweat from his forehead, replied, with some hesitation, 'he could not tell—he hoped the best—the squire was to be sure a very extraordinary young gentleman——' But the father urging him to give an explicit answer, he frankly declared, that, in his opinion, the son would turn out either a mirrour of wisdom, or a monument of folly: for his genius and disposition were altogether preternatural. The knight was sorely vexed at this declaration, and signified his displeasure by saying, the doctor, like a true priest, dealt in mysteries and oracles, that would admit of different and indeed contrary interpretations. He afterwards consulted my father, who had served as steward upon the estate for above thirty years, and acquired a considerable share of his favour. 'Will. Clarke, (said he, with tears in his eyes) what shall I do with this unfortunate lad? I would to God he had never been born; for I fear he will bring my grey hairs with sorrow to the grave. When I am gone, he will throw away the estate, and bring himself to infamy and ruin by keeping company with rooks [13] and beggars.— O Will! I could forgive extravagance in a young man; but it breaks my heart to see my only son give such repeated proofs of a mean spirit and sordid disposition!'

"Here the old gentleman shed a flood of tears, and not without some shadow of reason. By this time Launcelot was grown so reserved to his father, that he seldom saw him, or any of his relations, except when he was in a manner forced to appear at table, and there his bashfulness seemed every day to increase. On the other hand, he had formed some very strange connexions. Every morning he visited the stable, where he not only conversed with the grooms and helpers, but scraped acquaintance with the horses: he fed his favourites with his own hand, stroked, caressed, and rode them by turns; till at last they grew so familiar, that, even when they were a-field at grass, and saw him at a distance, they would toss their manes, whinny like so many colts at sight of the dam, and, galloping up to the place where he stood, smell him all over.—You must know that I myself, though a child, was his companion in all these excursions. He took a liking to me on account of my being his godson, and gave me more money than I knew what to do with: he had always plenty of cash for the asking, as my father was ordered to supply him liberally, the knight thinking that a command of money might help to raise his thoughts to a proper consideration of his own importance. He never could endure a common beggar, that was not either in a state of infancy or of old age: but, in other respects, he made the guineas fly in such a manner, as looked more like madness than generosity. He had no communication with your rich yeomen; but rather treated them and their families with studied contempt, because forsooth they pretended to assume the dress and manners of the gentry: [14] they kept their footmen, their saddle-horses, and chaises: their wives and daughters appeared in their jewels, their silks, and their sattins, their negligees and trollopees: [15] their clumsy shanks, like so many shins of beef, were cased in silk-hose and embroidered slippers: their raw red fingers, gross as the pipes of a chamber-organ, which had been employed in milching the cows, in twirling the mop or churn-staff, being adorned with diamonds, were taught to thrum the pandola,[16] and even to touch the keys of the harpsichord: nay, in every village they kept a rout,[17] and set up an assembly; and in one place a hog-butcher was master of the ceremonies. I have heard Mr. Greaves ridicule them for their vanity and aukward imitation; and therefore, I believe, he avoided all concerns with them, even when they endeavoured to engage his attention. It was the lower sort of people with whom he chiefly conversed, such as plough-men, ditchers, and other day-labourers. To every cottager in the parish he was a bounteous benefactor. He was, in the literal sense of the word, a careful overseer of the poor; for he went from house to house, industriously inquiring into the distresses of the people. He repaired their huts, cloathed their backs, filled their bellies, and supplied them with necessaries for exercising their industry and different occupations.

"I'll give you one instance now, as a specimen of his character. He and I, strolling one day on the side of a common, saw two boys picking hips and haws[18] from the hedges: one seemed to be about five, and the other a year older: they were both barefoot and ragged; but at the same time fat, fair, and in good condition. 'Who do you belong to?' said Mr. Greaves. 'To Mary Stile, (replied the oldest) the widow that rents one of them housen.'[19] 'And how do'st live, my boy? Thou lookest fresh and jolly,' resumed the squire. 'Lived well enough till yesterday,' answered the child. 'And pray what happened yesterday, my boy?' continued Mr. Greaves. 'Happened! (said he) why, mammy had a coople of little Welch keawes,[20] that gi'en milk enough to fill all our bellies; mammy's, and mine, and Dick's here, and my two little sisters at hoam: yesterday the squire seized the keawes for rent, God rot'un! Mammy's gone to bed sick and sulky: my two sisters be crying at hoam vor vood; and Dick and I be come hither to pick haws and bullies.'[21]—My godfather's face grew red as scarlet: he took one of the children in either hand, and leading them towards the house, found Sir Everhard talking with my father before the gate. Instead of avoiding the old gentleman, as usual, he brushed up to him with a spirit he had never shewn before, and presenting the two ragged boys, 'Surely, Sir, (said he) you will not countenance that there ruffian, your steward, in oppressing the widow and the fatherless. On pretence of distraining for the rent[22] of a cottage, he has robbed the mother of these and other poor infant-orphans of two cows, which afforded them their whole sustenance. Shall you be concerned in tearing the hard-earned morsel from the mouth of indigence? Shall your name, which has been so long mentioned as a blessing, be now detested as a curse by the poor, the helpless, and forlorn? The father of these babes was once your game-keeper, who died of a consumption caught in your service.—You see they are almost naked—I found them plucking haws and sloes,[23] in order to appease their hunger.—The wretched mother is starving in a cold cottage, distracted with the cries of other two infants, clamorous for food; and while her heart is bursting with anguish and despair, she invokes heaven to avenge the widow's cause upon the head of her unrelenting landlord!'

"This unexpected address brought tears into the eyes of the good old gentleman. 'Will Clarke, (said he to my father) how durst you abuse my authority at this rate? You who know I have been always a protector, not an oppressor of the needy and unfortunate. I charge you, go immediately and comfort this poor woman with immediate relief: instead of her own cows, let her have two of the best milch cows of my dairy: they shall graze in my parks in summer, and be foddered with my hay in winter.—She shall sit rent-free for life; and I will take care of these her poor orphans.' This was a very affecting scene. Mr. Launcelot took his father's hand and kissed it, while the tears ran down his cheeks; and Sir Everhard embraced his son with great tenderness, crying, 'My dear boy! God be praised for having given you such a feeling heart.' My father himself was moved, thof[24] a practitioner of the law, and consequently used to distresses.—He declared, that he had given no directions to distrain; and that the bailiff must have done it by his own authority.—'If that be the case, (said the young squire) let the inhuman rascal be turned out of our service.'

"Well, gemmen, all the children were immediately cloathed and fed, and the poor widow had well nigh run distracted with joy. The old knight, being of a humane temper himself, was pleased to see such proofs of his son's generosity: he was not angry at his spending his money, but at squandering away his time among the dregs of the people. For you must know, he not only made matches, portioned[25] poor maidens, and set up young couples that came together without money; but he mingled in every rustic diversion, and bore away the prize in every contest. He excelled every swain of that district in feats of strength and activity; in leaping, running, wrestling, cricket, cudgel-playing, and pitching the bar;[26] and was confessed to be, out of sight, the best dancer at all wakes[27] and holidays: happy was the country-girl who could engage the young squire as her partner! To be sure it was a comely sight for to see as how the buxom country-lasses, fresh and fragrant, and blushing like the rose, in their best apparel dight,[28] their white hose, and clean short dimity[29] petticoats, their gaudy gowns of printed cotton; their top-knots,[30] kissing-strings,[31] and stomachers,[32] bedizened with bunches of ribbons of various colours, green, pink, and yellow; to see them crowned with garlands, and assembled on May-day, to dance before squire Launcelot, as he made his morning's progress through the village. Then all the young peasants made their appearance with cockades,[33] suited to the fancies of their several sweet-hearts, and boughs of flowering hawthorn. The children sported about like flocks of frisking lambs, or the young fry swarming under the sunny bank of some meandering river. The old men and women, in their holiday-garments, stood at their doors to receive their benefactor, and poured forth blessings on him as he passed: the children welcomed him with their shrill shouts; the damsels with songs of praise; and the young men with the pipe and tabor marched before him to the May-pole, which was bedecked with flowers and bloom. There the rural dance began: a plentiful dinner, with oceans of good liquor, was bespoke at the White Hart:[34] the whole village was regaled at the squire's expence; and both the day and the night was spent in mirth and pleasure. Lord help you! he could not rest if he thought there was an aching heart in the whole parish. Every paultry cottage was in a little time converted into a pretty, snug, comfortable habitation, with a wooden porch at the door, glass casements in the windows, and a little garden behind, well stored with greens, roots, and sallads. In a word, the poor's-rate was reduced to a meer trifle,[35] and one would have thought the golden age[36] was revived in Yorkshire. But, as I told you before, the old knight could not bear to see his only son so wholly attached to these lowly pleasures, while he industriously shunned all opportunities of appearing in that superior sphere to which he was designed by nature, and by fortune. He imputed his conduct to meanness of spirit, and advised with my father touching the properest expedient to wean his affections from such low-born pursuits. My father counselled him to send the young gentleman up to London, to be entered as a student in the Temple,[37] and recommended to the superintendance of some person who knew the town, and might engage him insensibly in such amusements, and connexions, as would soon lift his ideas above the humble objects on which they had been hitherto employed. This advice appeared so salutary, that it was followed without the least hesitation. The young squire himself was perfectly well satisfied with the proposal, and in a few days set out for the great city: but there was not a dry eye in the parish at his departure, although he prevailed upon his father to pay in his absence all the pensions he had granted to those who could not live on the fruit of their own industry. In what manner he spent his time at London, it is none of my business to inquire; thof I know pretty well what kind of lives are led by gemmen of your Inns of Court.[38]—I myself once belonged to Serjeant's Inn,[39] and was perhaps as good a wit and a critick as any Templar[40] of them all. Nay, as for that matter, thof I despise vanity, I can aver with a safe conscience, that

I had once the honour to belong to the society called *the Town:* [41] we were all of us attorneys clerks, gemmen, and had our meetings at an ale-house in Butcher-row, [42] where we regulated the diversions of the theatre. [43]

"But to return from this digression: Sir Everhard Greaves did not seem to be very well pleased with the conduct of his son at London. He got notice of some irregularities and scrapes into which he had fallen; and the squire seldom wrote to his father, except to draw upon him for money, which he did so fast, that in eighteen months the old gemman lost all patience.

"At this period squire Darnel [44] chanced to die, leaving an only daughter, a minor, heiress of three thousand a year, under the guardianship of her uncle Anthony, whose brutal character all the world knows. The breath was no sooner out of his brother's body than he resolved, if possible, to succeed him in parliament as representative for the borough of Ashenton. [45] Now you must know, that this borough had been for many years a bone of contention between the families of Greaves and Darnel; and at length the difference was compromised by the interposition of friends, on condition that Sir Everhard and Squire Darnel should alternately represent the place in parliament. They agreed to this compromise for their mutual convenience; but they were never heartily reconciled. Their political principles did not tally; and their wives looked upon each other as rivals in fortune and magnificence: so that there was no intercourse between them, thof they lived in the same neighbourhood. On the contrary, in all disputes, they constantly headed the opposite parties. Sir Everhard understanding that Anthony Darnel had begun to canvass, and was putting every iron in the fire, in violation and contempt of the *pactum familiæ* [46] before mentioned, fell into a violent passion, that brought on a severe fit of the gout, by which he was disabled from giving personal attention to his own interest. My father, indeed, employed all his diligence and address, and spared neither money, time, nor constitution, till at length he drank himself into a consumption, which was the death of him. But, after all, there is a great difference between a steward and a principal. Mr. Darnel attended in *propria persona,* [47] flattered and caressed the women, feasted the electors, hired mobs, made processions, and scattered about his money in such a manner, that our friends durst hardly shew their heads in public.

"At this very crisis our young squire, to whom his father had writ an account of the transaction, arrived unexpectedly at Greavesbury-hall, [48] and had a long private conference with Sir Everhard. The news of his return spread like wildfire thro' all that part of the country: bon-fires were made, and the bells set a-ringing in several towns and steeples; and next morning above seven hundred people were assembled at the gate, with music, flags and streamers, to welcome their young squire, and accompany him to the borough of Ashenton. He set out on foot with this retinue, and entered one end of the town just as Mr. Darnel's mob had come in at the other. Both arrived about the same time at the market-place; but Mr. Darnel, mounting first into the balcony of the town-house, made a long speech to the people in favour of his own pretensions, not without some invidious reflections glanced at Sir Everhard, his competitor. We did not much mind the acclamations of his party, which we knew had been hired for the purpose: but we were in some pain for Mr. Greaves, who had not been used to speak in public. He took his turn however in the balcony, and, uncovering his head, bowed all round with the most engaging courtesy. He was dressed in a green frock trimmed with gold, and his own dark hair flowed about his ears in natural curls,[49] while his face was overspread with a blush, that improved the glow of youth to a deeper crimson, and I dare say set many a female heart a palpitating. When he made his first appearance, there was just such a humming and clapping of hands as you may have heard when the celebrated Garrick comes upon the stage in King Lear, or King Richard, or any other top character.[50] But how agreeably were we disappointed, when our young gentleman made such an oration as would not have disgraced a Pitt, an Egmont, or a Murray![51] While he spoke, all was hushed in admiration and attention—you could have almost heard a feather drop to the ground. It would have charmed you to hear with what modesty he recounted the services which his father and grandfather had done to the corporation;[52] with what eloquence he expatiated upon the shameful infraction of the treaty subsisting between the two families; and with what keen and spirited strokes of satire he retorted the sarcasms of Darnel. He no sooner concluded his harangue,[53] than there was such a burst of applause as seemed to rend the very sky. Our musick immediately struck up; our people advanced with their ensigns, and, as every man had a good cudgel, broken heads would have ensued, had not Mr. Darnel and his party thought proper to retreat with uncommon dispatch. He never offered to make another public entrance, as he saw the torrent ran so violently against him; but sat down with his loss, and withdrew his opposition, though at bottom extremely mortified and incensed. Sir Everhard was unanimously elected, and appeared to be the happiest man upon earth; for, besides the pleasure arising from his victory over this competitor, he was now fully satisfied that his son, instead of disgracing, would do honour to his family. It would have moved a heart of stone, to see with what a tender transport of paternal joy he received his dear Launcelot, after having heard of his deportment and success at Ashenton; where, by the bye, he gave a ball to the ladies, and displayed as much elegance and politeness as if he had been bred at the court of Versailles.

"This joyous season was of short duration: in a little time all the happiness

of the family was overcast by a sad incident, which hath left such an unfortunate impression upon the mind of the young gentleman, as, I am afraid, will
never be effaced. Mr. Darnel's niece and ward, the great heiress, whose name
is Aurelia,[54] was the most celebrated beauty of the whole country—if I said
the whole kingdom, or indeed all Europe, perhaps I should but barely do her
justice. I don't pretend to be a limner,[55] gemmen; nor does it become me to
delineate such excellence: but surely I may presume to repeat from the play;

> 'O! she is all that painting can express,
> Or youthful poets fancy when they love!'[56]

"At that time she might be about seventeen, tall and fair, and so exquisitely
shaped——you may talk of your Venus de Medicis,[57] your Dianas, your
Nymphs, and Galateas;[58] but if Praxiteles, and Roubillac, and Wilton,[59] were
to lay their heads together, in order to make a complete pattern of beauty,
they would hardly reach her model of perfection.—As for complexion, poets
will talk of blending the lily with the rose, and bring in a parcel of similes of
cowslips, carnations, pinks, and daisies.——There's Dolly, now, has got a very
good complexion:—indeed, she's the very picture of health and innocence.—
You are, indeed, my pretty lass;—but *parva componere magnis.*[60]——Miss Darnel is all amazing beauty, delicacy, and dignity! Then the softness and expression of her fine blue eyes; her pouting lips of coral hue; her neck, that rises like
a tower of polished alabaster between two mounts of snow.——I tell you what,
gemmen, it don't signify talking: if e'er a one of you was to meet this young
lady alone, in the midst of a heath or common, or any unfrequented place, he
would down on his knees, and think he kneeled before some supernatural being. I'll tell you more: she not only resembles an angel in beauty, but a saint in
goodness, and an hermit in humility;——so void of all pride and affectation;
so soft, and sweet, and affable, and humane! Lord! I could tell such instances
of her charity!—Sure enough, she and Sir Launcelot were formed by nature
for each other: howsoever, the cruel hand of fortune hath intervened, and
severed them for ever. Every soul that knew them both, said it was a thousand
pities but they should come together, and extinguish in their happy union the
mutual animosity of the two families, which had so often embroiled the whole
neighbourhood. Nothing was heard but the praises of miss Aurelia Darnel,
and Mr. Launcelot Greaves; and no doubt the parties were prepossessed, by
this applause, in favour of each other. At length, Mr. Greaves went one Sunday to her parish-church; but, though the greater part of the congregation
watched their looks, they could not perceive that she took the least notice of
him; or that he seemed to be struck with her appearance. He afterwards had

an opportunity of seeing her, more at leisure, at the York-assembly, during the races;[61] but this opportunity was productive of no good effect, because he had that same day quarrelled with her uncle on the turf.—An old grudge, you know, gemmen, is soon inflamed to a fresh rupture. It was thought Mr. Darnel came on purpose to shew his resentment. They differed about a bet upon Miss Cleverlegs, and, in the course of the dispute, Mr. Darnel called him a petulant boy. The young squire, who was hasty as gunpowder, told him he was man enough to chastise him for his insolence; and would do it on the spot, if he thought it would not interrupt the diversion. In all probability they would have come to points immediately, had not the gentlemen interposed; so that nothing further passed, but abundance of foul language on the part of Mr. Anthony, and a repeated defiance to single combat.

"Mr. Greaves, making a low bow, retired from the field; and in the evening danced at the assembly with a young lady from the Bishoprick,[62] seemingly in good temper and spirits, without having any words with Mr. Darnel, who was also present. But in the morning he visited that proud neighbour betimes; and they had almost reached a grove of trees on the north-side of the town, when they were suddenly overtaken by half a dozen gentlemen, who had watched their motions. It was in vain for them to dissemble their design, which could not now take effect. They gave up their pistols, and a reconciliation was patched up by the pressing remonstrances of their common friends; but Mr. Darnel's hatred still rankled at bottom, and soon broke out in the sequel. About three months after this transaction, his niece Aurelia, with her mother, having been to visit a lady in the chariot, the horses being young, and not used to the traces, were startled at the braying of a jack-ass on the common, and taking fright, ran away with the carriage like lightning. The coachman was thrown from the box, and the ladies screamed piteously for help. Mr. Greaves chanced to be a-horseback on the other side of an inclosure, when he heard their shrieks; and riding up to the hedge, knew the chariot, and saw their disaster. The horses were then running full speed in such a direction, as to drive headlong over a precipice into a stone-quarry, where they and the chariot, and the ladies, must be dashed in pieces. You may conceive, gemmen, what his thoughts were when he saw such a fine young lady, in the flower of her age, just plunging into eternity; when he saw the lovely Aurelia on the brink of being precipitated among rocks, where her delicate limbs must be mangled and tore asunder; when he perceived that, before he could ride round by the gate, the tragedy would be finished. The fence was so thick and high, flanked with a broad ditch on the outside, that he could not hope to clear it, although he was mounted on *Scipio*,[63] bred out of Miss *Cowslip*,[64] the sire

Muley,[65] and his *grandsire* the famous Arabian *Mustapha.*[66]—*Scipio* was bred by my father, who would not have taken a hundred guineas for him from any other person but the young squire.——Indeed, I have heard my poor father say—"

By this time Ferret's impatience was become so outrageous, that he exclaimed in a furious tone, "Damn your father, and his horse, and his colt into the bargain!"

Tom made no reply; but began to strip with great expedition. Captain Crowe was so choaked with passion, that he could utter nothing but disjointed sentences: he rose from his seat, brandished his horsewhip, and seizing his nephew by the collar, cried, "Odd's heartlikins![67] sirrah, I have a good mind—Devil fire your running tackle,[68] you land-lubber!—can't you steer without all this tacking hither and thither, and the Lord knows whither?—'Noint my block![69] I'd give thee a rope's end[70] for thy supper, if it wan't——"

Dolly had conceived a sneaking kindness for the young lawyer, and, thinking him in danger of being roughly handled, flew to his relief. She twisted her hand in Crowe's neckcloth without ceremony, crying, "Sha't then, I tell thee, old coger.—Who kears a vig vor thy voolish trantrums?"

While Crowe looked black in the face, and ran the risque of strangulation under the gripe of this amazon, Mr. Clarke having disengaged himself of his hat, wig, coat, and waistcoat, advanced in an elegant attitude of manual offence towards the misanthrope, who snatched up a gridiron from the chimney-corner, and Discord seemed to clap her sooty wings[71] in expectation of battle.—But as the reader may have more than once already cursed the unconscionable length of this chapter, we must postpone to the next opportunity the incidents that succeeded this denunciation of war.[72]

CHAPTER IV.

In which it appears that the Knight, when heartily
set in for sleeping, was not easily disturbed.

I n all probability the kitchen of the Black Lion, from a domestic temple of society, and good-fellowship, would have been converted into a scene or stage of sanguinary dispute, had not Pallas[1] or Discretion interposed in the person of Mr. Fillet, and with the assistance of the hostler disarmed the combatants not only of their arms, but also of their resentment. The impetuosity of Mr. Clarke was a little checked at sight of the gridiron, which Ferret brandished with uncommon dexterity; a circumstance from whence the company were, upon reflection, induced to believe, that before he plunged into the sea of politicks, he had occasionally figured in the character of that facetious droll who accompanies your itinerant physicians, under the familiar appellation of Merry-Andrew, or Jack-Pudding,[2] and on a wooden stage entertains the populace with a solo on the salt-box,[3] or a sonnata on the tongs and gridiron.[4] Be that as it may, the young lawyer seemed to be a little discomposed at the glancing of this extraordinary weapon of offence, which the fair hands of Dolly had scoured, until it shone as bright as the shield of Achilles;[5] or as the emblem of good old English fare, which hangs by a red ribbon round the neck of that thrice-honoured sage's head, in velvet bonnet cased, who presides by rotation at the genial board, distinguished by the title of the *Beef-stake Club:*[6] where the delicate rumps irresistibly attract the stranger's eye, and, while they seem to cry "Come cut me—come cut me,"[7] constrain, by wondrous sympathy, each mouth to overflow: where the obliging and humorous Jemmy B——t, the gentle Billy H——d, replete with human kindness, and the generous Johnny B——d,[8] respected and beloved by all the world, attend as the priests and ministers of Mirth, good Cheer, and Jollity, and assist with culinary art the raw, unpractised, aukward guest.

But, to return from this digressive simile: the hostler no sooner stept between those menacing antagonists than Tom Clarke very quietly resumed his cloaths, and Mr. Ferret resigned the gridiron without further question. The doctor did not find it quite so easy to release the throat of Capt. Crowe from the masculine grasp of the virago Dolly, whose fingers could not be disengaged until the honest seaman was almost at the last gasp. After some pause, during which he panted for breath, and untied his neckcloth, "Damn thee, for a brimstone galley (cried he); I was never so grappled withal since I knew a card[9] from a compass.——Adzooks! the jade has so taughtened my rigging, d'ye see, that I——Snatch my bowlings,[10] if I come athwart thy hawser,[11] I'll turn thy keel upwards—or mayhap set thee a-driving under thy bare poles[12]—I will—I will, you hell-fire, saucy——I will."

Dolly made no reply; but seeing Mr. Clarke sit down again with great composure, took her station likewise at the opposite side of the apartment. Then Mr. Fillet requested the lawyer to proceed with his story, which, after three hemms, he accordingly prosecuted in these words.

"I told you, gemmen, that Mr. Greaves was mounted on Scipio, when he saw miss Darnel and her mother in danger of being hurried over a precipice.[13] Without reflecting a moment he gave Scipio the spur, and at one spring he cleared five and twenty feet, over hedge and ditch, and every obstruction. Then he rode full speed, in order to turn the coach-horses; and, finding them quite wild and furious, endeavoured to drive against the counter of the hither horse, which he missed, and staked poor Scipio on the pole of the coach. The shock was so great, that the coach-horses made a full stop within ten yards of the quarry, and Mr. Greaves was thrown forwards towards the coach-box, which mounting with admirable dexterity, he seized the reins before the horses could recover of their fright. At that instant the coachman came running up, and loosed them from the traces with the utmost dispatch. Mr. Greaves had now time to give his attention to the ladies, who were well nigh distracted with fear. He no sooner opened the chariot-door than Aurelia, with a wildness of look, sprung into his arms; and, clasping him round the neck, fainted away. I leave you to guess, gemmen, what were his feelings at this instant. The mother was not so discomposed but that she could contribute to the recovery of her daughter, whom the young squire still supported in his embrace. At length she retrieved the use of her senses, and perceiving the situation in which she was, the blood revisited her face with a redoubled glow, while she desired him to set her down upon the turf.

"Mrs. Darnel, far from being shy or reserved in her compliments of acknowledgments, kissed Mr. Launcelot without ceremony, the tears of gratitude running down her cheeks: she called him her dear son, her generous deliverer, who, at the hazard of his own life, had saved her and her child from the most dismal fate that could be imagined. Mr. Greaves was so much transported on this occasion, that he could not help disclosing a passion, which he had hitherto industriously concealed. 'What I have done (said he) was but a common office of humanity, which I would have performed for any of my fellow-creatures: but, for the preservation of miss Aurelia Darnel, I would at any time sacrifice my life with pleasure.' The young lady did not hear this declaration unmoved: her face was again flushed, and her eyes sparkled with pleasure: nor was the youth's confession disagreeable to the good lady her mother, who at one glance perceived all the advantages of such an union between the two families.

"Mr. Greaves proposed to send the coachman to his father's stable for a pair of sober horses, that could be depended upon, to draw the ladies home to their own habitation; but they declined the offer, and chose to walk, as the distance was not great. He then insisted upon his being their conductor; and, each taking him under the arm, supported them to their own gate, where such an apparition filled all the domestics with astonishment. Mrs. Darnel, taking him by the hand, led him into the house, where she welcomed him with another affectionate embrace, and indulged him with an ambrosial kiss of Aurelia, saying, 'But for you, we had both been by this time in eternity.—Sure it was heaven that sent you as an angel to our assistance!' She kindly inquired if he had himself sustained any damage in administring that desperate remedy to which they owed their lives. She entertained him with a small collation; and, in the course of the conversation, lamented the animosity which had so long divided two neighbouring families of such influence and character. He was not slow in signifying his approbation of her remarks, and expressing the most eager desire of seeing all those unhappy differences removed: in a word, they parted with mutual satisfaction.

"Just as he advanced from the outward gate, on his return to Greavesbury-hall, he was met by Anthony Darnel on horseback, who, riding up to him with marks of surprize and resentment, saluted him with 'Your servant, Sir.—Have you any commands for me?' The other replying with an air of indifference, 'None at all,' Mr. Darnel asked, what had procured him the honour of a visit. The young gentleman, perceiving by the manner in which he spoke that the old quarrel was not yet extinguished, answered, with equal disdain, that the visit was not intended for him; and that, if he wanted to know the cause of it, he might inform himself by his own servants. 'So I shall (cried the uncle of Aurelia); and perhaps let you know my sentiments of the matter—' 'Hereafter as it may be,' said the youth; who, turning out of the avenue, walked home, and made his father acquainted with the particulars of this adventure.

"The old gentleman chid him for his rashness; but seemed pleased with the success of his attempt, and still more so, when he understood his sentiments of Aurelia, and the deportment of the ladies.

"Next day the son sent over a servant with a compliment, to enquire about their health; and the messenger, being seen by Mr. Darnel, was told that the ladies were indisposed, and did not chuse to be troubled with messages. The mother was really seized with a fever, produced by the agitation of her spirits, which every day became more and more violent, until the physicians despaired of her life. Believing that her end approached, she sent a trusty servant to Mr. Greaves, desiring that she might see him without delay; and he immediately set out with the messenger, who introduced him in the dark. He found the old lady in bed, almost exhausted, and the fair Aurelia sitting by her, overwhelmed with grief, her lovely hair in the utmost disorder, and her charming eyes inflamed with weeping. The good lady beckoning Mr. Launcelot to approach, and directing all the attendants to quit the room, except a favourite maid, from whom I learned the story, she took him by the hand, and fixing her eyes upon him with all the fondness of a mother, shed some tears in silence, while the same marks of sorrow trickled down his cheeks. After this affecting pause, 'My dear son (said she), Oh! that I could have lived to see you so indeed! you find me hastening to the goal of life—' Here the tender-hearted Aurelia, being unable to contain herself longer, broke out into a violent passion of grief, and wept aloud. The mother, waiting patiently till she had thus given vent to her anguish, calmly intreated her to resign herself submissively to the will of heaven: then turning to Mr. Launcelot, 'I had indulged (said she) a fond hope of seeing you allied to my family.—This is no time for me to insist upon the ceremonies and forms of a vain world.—Aurelia looks upon you with the eyes of tender prepossession.' No sooner had she pronounced these words than he threw himself on his knees before the young lady, and, pressing her hand to his lips, breathed the softest expressions which the most delicate love could suggest. 'I know (resumed the mother) that your passion is mutually sincere; and I should die satisfied, if I thought your union would not be opposed: but that violent man, my brother-in-law, who is Aurelia's sole guardian, will thwart her wishes with every obstacle that brutal resentment and implacable malice can contrive. Mr. Greaves, I have long admired your virtues, and am confident that I can depend upon your honour.— You shall give me your word, that, when I am gone, you will take no steps in this affair without the concurrence of your own father; and endeavour, by all fair and honourable means, to vanquish the prejudices and obtain the consent of her uncle: the rest we must leave to the dispensations of Providence.'

"The squire promised, in the most solemn and fervent manner, to obey all her injunctions, as the last dictates of a parent whom he should never cease to honour. Then she favoured them both with a great deal of salutary advice, touching their conduct before and after marriage; and presented him with a ring, as a memorial of her affection: at the same time he pulled another off his finger, and made a tender of it as a pledge of his love to Aurelia, whom her mother permitted to receive this token. Finally, he took a last farewel of the good matron, and returned to his father with the particulars of this interview.

"In two days Mrs. Darnel departed this life, and Aurelia was removed to the house of a relation, where her grief had like to have proved fatal to her constitution.

"In the mean time, the mother was no sooner committed to the earth than Mr. Greaves, mindful of her exhortations, began to take measures for a reconciliation with the guardian. He engaged several gentlemen to interpose their good offices; but they always met with the most mortifying repulse: and at last Anthony Darnel declared, that his hatred to the house of Greaves was hereditary, habitual, and unconquerable. He swore he would spend his heart's blood to perpetuate the quarrel; and that, sooner than his niece should match with young Launcelot, he would sacrifice her with his own hand. The young gentleman, finding his prejudice so rancorous and invincible, left off making further advances; and, since he found it impossible to obtain his consent, re-solved to cultivate the good graces of Aurelia, and wed her in despite of her implacable guardian. He found means to establish a literary correspondence with her, as soon as her grief was a little abated; and even to effect an interview, after her return to her own house: but he soon had reason to repent of this indulgence. The uncle entertained spies upon the young lady, who gave him an account of this meeting; in consequence of which she was suddenly hurried to some distant part of the country, which we never could discover.

"It was then we began to think Mr. Launcelot a little disordered in his brain, his grief was so wild, and his passion so impetuous. He refused all sus-tenance, neglected his person, renounced his amusements, rode out in the rain, sometimes bare headed, strolled about the fields all night, and became so peevish, that none of the domestics durst speak to him, without the hazard of broken bones. Having played these pranks for about three weeks, to the un-speakable chagrin of his father, and the astonishment of all that knew him, he suddenly grew calm, and his good-humour returned. But this, as your sea-faring people say, was a deceitful calm, that soon ushered in a dreadful storm.

"He had long sought an opportunity to tamper with some of Mr. Darnel's servants, who could inform him of the place where Aurelia was confined; but there was not one about the family who could give him that satisfaction: for the persons who accompanied her, remained as a watch upon her motions, and none of the other domestics were privy to the transaction. All attempts proving fruitless, he could no longer restrain his impatience; but throwing himself in the way of the uncle, upbraided him in such harsh terms, that a formal challenge ensued. They agreed to decide their difference without wit-nesses; and one morning, before sun-rise, met on that very common where Mr. Greaves had saved the life of Aurelia. The first pistol was fired on each side without taking effect; but Mr. Darnel's second wounded the young squire in the flank: nevertheless, having a pistol in reserve, he desired his antago-nist to ask his life. The other, instead of submitting, drew his sword; and Mr. Greaves, firing his piece in the air, followed his example. The contest then became very hot, tho' of short continuance. Darnel being disarmed at the first onset, our young squire gave him back the sword, which he was base enough to use a second time against his conqueror. Such an instance of repeated ingratitude and brutal ferocity divested Mr. Greaves of his temper and forbearance. He attacked Mr. Anthony with great fury, and at the first longe[14] ran him up to the hilt, at the same time seizing with his left hand the shell of his enemy's sword, which he broke in disdain. Mr. Darnel having fallen, the other immediately mounted his horse, which he had tied to a tree before the engagement; and riding full speed to Ashenton, sent a surgeon to Anthony's assistance. He afterwards ingenuously confessed all these particulars to his father, who was overwhelmed with consternation, for the wounds of Darnel were judged mortal; and as no person had seen the particulars of the duel, Mr. Launcelot might have been convicted of murder.[15]

"On these considerations, before a warrant could be served upon him, the old knight, by dint of the most eager intreaties, accompanied with marks of horrour and despair, prevailed upon his son to withdraw himself from the kingdom, until such time as the storm should be overblown. Had his heart been unengaged, he would have chose to travel; but at this period, when his whole soul was engrossed and so violently agitated by his passion for Aurelia, nothing but the fear of seeing the old gentleman run distracted, would have induced him to desist from the pursuit of that young lady, far less quit the kingdom where she resided. Well then, gemmen, he repaired to Harwich, where he embarked for Holland, from whence he proceeded to Brussels, where he procured a passport from the French king, by virtue of which he travelled to Marseilles, and there took a tartan[16] for Genoa. The first letter sir Everhard received from him was dated at Florence. Mean while the surgeon's prognostic was not altogether verified. Mr. Darnel did not die immediately of his wounds; but he lingered a long time, as it were in the arms of death, and even partly recovered: yet, in all probability he will never be wholly restored to the enjoyment of health; and is obliged every summer to attend the hot well at Bristol. As his wounds began to heal, his hatred to Mr. Greaves seemed to revive with augmented violence; and he is now, if possible, more than ever determined against all reconciliation. Mr. Launcelot, after having endeavoured to amuse his imagination with a succession of curious objects, in a tour of Italy, took up his residence at a town called Pisa, and there fell into a deep melancholy, from which nothing could rouse him but the news of his father's death.

"The old gentleman (God rest his soul) never held up his head after the departure of his darling Launcelot; and the dangerous condition of Darnel kept up his apprehension: this was reinforced by the obstinate silence of the youth, and certain accounts of his disordered mind, which he had received from some of those persons who take pleasure in communicating disagreeable

Mʳ· Greaves returning Darnel his sword after disarming him,
by Saunders after Corbauld. (University of Delaware Library)

tidings. A complication of all these grievances, co-operating with a severe fit of the gout and gravel,[17] produced a fever, which in a few days brought sir Everhard to his long home; after he had settled his affairs with heaven and earth, and made his peace with God and man. I'll assure you, gemmen, he made a most edifying and christian end: he died regretted by all his neighbours except Anthony, and might be said to be embalmed by the tears of the poor, to whom he was always a bounteous benefactor.

"When the son, now sir Launcelot, came home, he appeared so meagre, wan, and hollow-ey'd, that the servants hardly knew their young master. His first care was to take possession of his fortune, and settle accounts with the steward who had succeeded my father. These affairs being discussed, he spared no pains to get intelligence concerning miss Darnel; and soon learned more of that young lady than he desired to know; for it was become the common talk of the county, that a match was agreed upon between her and young squire Sycamore, a gentleman of a very great fortune. These tidings were probably confirmed under her own hand, in a letter which she wrote to Sir Launcelot. The contents were never exactly known but to the parties themselves: nevertheless, the effects were too visible; for, from that blessed moment, he spoke not one word to any living creature for the space of three days: but was seen sometimes to shed a flood of tears, and sometimes to burst out into a fit of laughing. At last he broke silence, and seemed to wake from his disorder. He became more fond than ever of the exercise of riding, and began to amuse himself again with acts of benevolence. One instance of his generosity and justice deserves to be recorded in brass or marble: you must know, gemmen, the rector of the parish was lately dead, and Sir Everhard had promised the presentation to another clergyman. In the mean time, Sir Launcelot, chancing one Sunday to ride through a lane, perceived a horse saddled and bridled feeding on the side of a fence; and casting his eyes around, beheld on the other side of the hedge an object lying extended on the ground, which he took to be the body of a murdered traveller. He forthwith alighted; and, leaping into the field, descried a man at full length wrapped in a great coat, and writhing in agony. Approaching nearer, he found it was a clergyman, in his gown and cassock. When he inquired into the case, and offered his assistance, the stranger rose up, thanked him for his courtesy, and declared that he was now very well. The knight, who thought there was something mysterious in this incident, expressed a desire to know the cause of his rolling on the grass in that manner; and the clergyman, who knew his person, made no scruple in gratifying his curiosity. 'You must know, sir,' said he, 'I serve the curacy of your own parish, for which the late incumbent payed me twenty pounds a year; but this sum being scarce sufficient to maintain my wife and children, who are five in number, I agreed to read prayers in the afternoon at another church about four miles from hence; and for this additional duty I receive ten pounds more: as I keep a horse, it was formerly an agreeable exercise rather than a toil, but of late years I have been afflicted with a rupture,[18] for which I consulted the most eminent operators in the kingdom; but I have no cause to rejoice in the effects of their advice, tho' one of them assured me I was completely cured. The malady is now more troublesome than ever, and often comes upon me so violently while I am on horseback, that I am forced to alight, and lie down upon the ground, until the cause of the disorder can for the time be reduced.'

"Sir Launcelot not only condoled with him upon his misfortune, but desired him to throw up the second cure; and he would pay him ten pounds a year out of his own pocket. 'Your generosity confounds me, good sir: (cried the clergyman) and yet I ought not to be surprised at any instance of benevolence in Sir Launcelot Greaves, but I will check the fullness of my heart. I shall only observe, that your good intention towards me can hardly take effect. The gentleman, who is to succeed the late incumbent, has given me notice to quit the premises, as he hath provided a friend of his own for the curacy.' 'What! (cried the knight) does he mean to take your bread from you, without assigning any other reason?' 'Surely, sir,' replied the ecclesiastic, 'I know of no other reason. I hope my morals are irreproachable, and that I have done my duty with a conscientious regard: I may venture an appeal to the parishioners among whom I have lived these seventeen years. After all, it is natural for every man to favour his own friends in preference to strangers. As for me, I propose to try my fortune in the great city; and I doubt not but providence will provide for me and my little ones.' To this declaration Sir Launcelot made no reply; but riding home set on foot a strict enquiry into the character of this man, whose name was Jenkins. He found that he was a reputed scholar, equally remarkable for his modesty and good life; that he visited the sick, assisted the needy, compromised disputes among his neighbours, and spent his time in such a manner as would have done honour to any christian divine. Thus informed, the knight sent for the gentleman to whom the living had been promised; and accosted him to this effect: 'Mr. Tootle, I have a favour to ask of you. The person who serves the cure of this parish, is a man of good character, beloved by the people, and has a large family. I shall be obliged to you if you will continue him in the curacy.' The other told him he was sorry he could not comply with his request, being that he had already promised the curacy to a friend of his own. 'No matter: (replied Sir Launcelot) since I have not interest with you, I will endeavour to provide for Mr. Jenkins in some other way.'

"That same afternoon he walked over to the curate's house, and told him that he had spoken in his behalf to Dr. Tootle, but the curacy was pre-engaged. The good man having made a thousand acknowledgments for the trouble his honour had taken; 'I have not interest sufficient to make you curate, (said the knight) but I can give you the living itself, and that you shall have.' So saying, he retired; leaving Mr. Jenkins incapable of uttering one syllable, so powerfully was he struck with this unexpected turn of fortune. The presentation was immediately made out; and in a few days Mr. Jenkins was put in possession of his benefice, to the inexpressible joy of the congregation. Hitherto every thing went right, and every unprejudiced person commended the knight's conduct: but, in a little time, his generosity seemed to overleap the bounds of discretion; and even in some cases might be thought tending to a breach of the king's peace. For example, he compelled, *vi et armis*,[19] a rich farmer's son to marry the daughter of a cottager, whom the young fellow had debauched. Indeed it seems there was a promise of marriage in the case, though it could not be legally ascertained. The wench took on dismally; and her parents had recourse to Sir Launcelot, who, sending for the delinquent, expostulated with him severely on the injury he had done the young woman, and exhorted him to save her life and reputation by performing his promise; in which case he (Sir Launcelot) would give her three hundred pounds to her portion. Whether the farmer thought there was something interested in this uncommon offer, or was a little elevated by the consciousness of his father's wealth; he rejected the proposal with rustic disdain, and said, if so be as how the wench would swear the child to him, he would settle it with the parish:[20] but declared, that no squire in the land should oblige him to buckle with such a cracked pitcher.[21] This resolution, however, he could not maintain: for, in less than two hours, the rector of the parish had direction to publish the banns,[22] and the ceremony was performed in due course.

"Now, though we know not precisely the nature of the arguments that were used with the farmer, we may conclude they were of the minatory species; for the young fellow could not, for some time, look any person in the face. The knight acted as the general redresser of grievances. If a woman complained to him of being ill treated by her husband, he first inquired into the foundation of the complaint; and if he found it just, catechised the defendant. If this warning had no effect, and the man proceeded to fresh acts of violence; then this judge took the execution of the law in his own hand, and horsewhipped the party. Thus he involved himself in several law-suits, that drained him of pretty large sums of money. He seemed particularly incensed at the least appearance of oppression; and supported divers poor tenants against the extortion of the landlords. Nay, he has been known to travel two hundred miles as a volunteer, to offer his assistance in the cause of a person, who he heard was by chicanery and oppression wronged of a considerable estate. He accordingly took her under his protection, relieved her distresses, and was at a vast expence in bringing the suit to a determination; which being unfavourable to his client, he resolved to bring an appeal into the house of lords, and certainly would have executed his purpose, if the gentlewoman had not died in the interim."

At this period Ferret interrupted the narrator, by observing that the said Greaves was a common nusance, and ought to be prosecuted on the statute of barretry.[23] "No, sir, (resumed Mr. Clarke) he cannot be convicted of barretry, unless he is always at variance with some person or other, a mover of suits and quarrels, who disturbs the peace under colour of law. Therefore he is in the indictment stiled, *Communis malefactor, calumniator & seminator litium.*"[24] "Prithee, truce with thy definitions, (cried Ferret) and make an end of thy long-winded story. Thou hast no title to be so tedious, until thou comest to have a coif in the court of common pleas."[25] Tom smiled contemptuous, and had just opened his mouth to proceed, when the company were disturbed by a hideous repetition of groans, that seemed to issue from the chamber in which the body of the squire was deposited. The landlady snatched the candle, and ran into the room, followed by the doctor and the rest; and this accident naturally suspended the narration. In like manner we shall conclude the chapter, that the reader may have time to breathe and digest what he has already heard.

CHAPTER V.

In which this recapitulation draws to a close.

When the landlady entered the room from whence the groaning proceeded, she found the squire lying on his back, under the dominion of the night-mare, which rode him so hard, that he not only groaned and snorted, but the sweat ran down his face in streams. The perturbation of his brain, occasioned by this pressure and the fright he had lately undergone, gave rise to a very terrible dream, in which he fancied himself apprehended for a robbery. The horror of the gallows was strong upon him, when he was suddenly awaked by a violent shock from the doctor; and the company broke in upon his view, still perverted by fear, and bedimmed by slumber. His dream was now realized by a full persuasion that he was surrounded by the constable and his gang. The first object that presented itself to his disordered view was the figure of Ferret, who might very well have passed for the finisher of the law: against him therefore the first effort of his despair was directed. He started upon the floor; and, seizing a certain utensil, that shall be nameless,[1] launched it at the misanthrope with such violence, that had not he cautiously slipped his head aside, it is supposed that actual fire would have been produced from the collision of two such hard and solid substances.[2] All future mischief was prevented by the strength and agility of captain Crowe, who, springing upon the assailant, pinioned his arms to his sides, crying, "O damn ye, if you are for running a-head,[3] I'll soon bring you to your bearings." The squire thus restrained, soon recollected himself, and gazing upon every individual in the apartment, "Wounds![4] (said he) I've had an ugly dream. I thought, for all the world, they were carrying me to Newgate;[5] and that there was Jack Ketch[6] coom to vetch me before my taim." Ferret, who was the person he had thus distinguished, eying him with a look of the most emphatic malevolence, told him, it was very natural for a knave to dream of Newgate; and that he hoped to see the day when this dream would be found a true prophecy, and the commonwealth purged of all such rogues and vagabonds: but it could not be expected that the vulgar would be honest and conscientious, while the great were distinguished by profligacy and corruption. The squire was disposed to make a practical reply to this insinuation, when Mr. Ferret prudently withdrew himself from the scene of altercation. The good woman of the house persuaded his antagonist to take out his nap, assuring him that the eggs and bacon, with a mug of excellent ale, should be forthcoming in due season. The affair being thus fortunately adjusted, the guests returned to the kitchen, and Mr. Clarke resumed his story to this effect. "You'll please to take notice, gemmen, that besides the instances I have alledged of Sir Launcelot's extravagant benevolence, I could recount a great many others of the same nature, and particularly the laudable vengeance he took of a country lawyer.—I'm sorry that any such miscreant should belong to the profession. He was clerk of the assize,[7] gemmen, in a certain town, not a great way distant, and having a blank pardon left by the judges for some criminals, whose cases were attended with favourable circumstances, he would not insert the name of one who could not procure a guinea for the fee; and the poor fellow, who had only stole an hourglass out of a shoemaker's window, was actually executed after a long respite; during which he had been permitted to go abroad, and earn his subsistence by his daily labour.

"Sir Launcelot, being informed of this barbarous act of avarice, and having some ground that bordered on the lawyer's estate, not only rendered him contemptible and infamous, by exposing him as often as they met on the grand jury,[8] but also, being vested with the property of the great tythes,[9] proved such a troublesome neighbour, sometimes by making waste among his hay and corn, sometimes by instituting suits against him for petty trespasses, that he was fairly obliged to quit his habitation, and remove into another part of the kingdom. All these avocations could not divert Sir Launcelot from the execution of a wild scheme, which has carried his extravagance to such a pitch, that I am afraid if a statute—you understand me, gemmen, were sued, the jury would—I don't choose to explain myself further on this circumstance. Be that as it may, the servants at Greavesbury-hall were not a little confounded, when their master took down from the family armoury a compleat suit of armour, which had belonged to his great grandfather, Sir Marmaduke Greaves, a great warrior, who lost his life in the service of his king. This armour being scoured, repaired, and altered so as to fit Sir Launcelot, a certain knight, whom I don't choose to name, because I believe he cannot be proved *compos mentis*,[10] came down seemingly on a visit with two attendants; and, on the eve of the festival of St. George,[11] the armour being carried into the chapel, Sir Launcelot (Lord have mercy upon us!) remained all night in that dismal place alone and without light, though it was confidently reported, all over the country, that the place was haunted by the spirit of his great great uncle, who, being lunatic, had cut his throat from ear to ear, and was found dead on the communion table."

It was observed, that while Mr. Clarke rehearsed this circumstance, his eyes began to stare, and his teeth to chatter; while Dolly, whose looks were fixed invariably on this narrator, growing pale, and hitching her joint stool[12] nearer the chimney, exclaimed in a frighten'd tone, "Moother, moother, in the neame of God, look to 'un! how a quakes! as I'm a precious saowl, a looks as if a saw soomething." Tom forced a smile, and thus proceeded:

"While Sir Launcelot tarried within the chapel, with the doors all locked, the other knight stalked round and round it on the outside, with his sword drawn, to the terror of divers persons who were present at the ceremony. As soon as day broke he opened one of the doors, and, going in to Sir Launcelot, read a book for some time, which we did suppose to be the constitutions of knight-errantry: then we heard a loud slap which ecchoed through the whole chapel, and the stranger pronounce with an audible and solemn voice, 'In the name of God, St. Michael, and St. George,[13] I dub thee knight—be faithful, bold, and fortunate.' You cannot imagine, gemmen, what an effect this strange ceremony had upon the people who were assembled. They gazed at one another in silent horror; and, when Sir Launcelot came forth completely armed, took to their heels in a body, and fled with the utmost precipitation. I myself was overturned in the crowd; and this was the case with that very individual person who now serves him as a squire. He was so frightened that he could not rise, but lay roaring in such a manner, that the knight came up, and gave him a thwack with his launce across the shoulders, which roused him with a vengeance. For my own part, I freely own I was not altogether unmoved at seeing such a figure come stalking out of a church in the grey of the morning; for it recalled to my remembrance the idea of the ghost in Hamlet, which I had seen acted in Drury-lane,[14] when I made my first trip to London; and I had not yet got rid of the impression.

"Sir Launcelot, attended by the other knight, proceeded to the stable; from whence, with his own hands, he drew forth one of his best horses, a fine mettlesome sorrel, who had got blood in him, ornamented with rich trappings. In a trice the two knights, and the other two strangers, who now appeared to be trumpeters, were mounted. Sir Launcelot's armour was lacquered black; and on his shield was represented the moon in her first quarter,[15] with the motto *impleat orbem*.[16] The trumpets having sounded a charge, the stranger pronounced with a loud voice, 'God preserve this gallant knight in all his honourable atchievements; and may he long continue to press the sides of his now adopted steed, which I denominate Bronzomarte,[17] hoping that he will rival in swiftness and spirit Bayardo, Brigliadoro,[18] or any other steed of past or present chivalry!' After another flourish of the trumpets, all four clapped spurs to their horses, Sir Launcelot couching his lance, and galloped to and fro, as if they had been mad, to the terror and astonishment of all the spectators. What should have induced our knight to choose this here man for his squire, it is not easy to determine; for, of all the servants about the house, he was the least likely either to please his master, or engage in such an undertaking. His name is Timothy Crabshaw, and he acted in the capacity of whipper-in to Sir Everhard.[19] He afterwards married the daughter of a poor cottager, by whom he has several children, and was employed about the house as a ploughman and carter. To be sure the fellow has a dry sort of humour about him: but he was universally hated among the servants for his abusive tongue and perverse disposition, which often brought him into trouble; for though the fellow is as strong as an elephant, he has no more courage naturally than a chicken—I say naturally, because, since his being a member of knight-errantry, he has done some things that appear altogether incredible and præternatural.

"Timothy kept such a bawling, after he had received the blow from Sir

Launcelot, that every body on the field thought some of his bones were broken; and his wife, with five bantlings,[20] came snivelling to the knight, who ordered her to send the husband directly to his house. Tim accordingly went thither, groaning piteously all the way, creeping along with his body bent like a Greenland canoe.[21] As soon as he entered the court, the outward door was shut; and Sir Launcelot coming down stairs with a horsewhip in his hand, asked what was the matter with him that he complained so dismally. To this question he replied, that it was as common as duck-weed[22] in his country, for a man to complain when his bones were broke. 'What should have broke your bones?' said the knight. 'I cannot guess, (answered the other) unless it was that delicate switch that your honour in your mad pranks handled so dextrously upon my carcase.' Sir Launcelot then told him there was nothing so good for a bruise as a sweat, and he had the remedy in his hand. Timothy eying the horsewhip askance, observed that there was another still more speedy; to wit, a moderate pill of lead, with a sufficient dose of gunpowder. 'No, rascal, (cried the knight) that must be reserved for your betters.' So saying, he employed the instrument so effectually, that Crabshaw soon forgot his fractured ribs, and capered about with great agility. When he had been disciplined in this manner to some purpose, the knight told him he might retire; but ordered him to return next morning, when he should have a repetition of the medicine, provided he did not find himself capable of walking in an erect posture. The gate was no sooner thrown open, than Timothy ran home with all the speed of a grey-hound, and corrected his wife, by whose advice he had pretended to be so grievously damaged in his person. No body dreamed that he would next day present himself at Greavesbury-hall; nevertheless, he was there very early in the morning, and even closetted a whole hour with Sir Launcelot. He came out making wry faces, and several times slapped himself on the forehead, crying, 'Bodikins! thof he be creazy, I an't, that I an't!' When he was asked what was the matter, he said he believed the devil had got into him, and he should never be his own man again. That same day the knight carried him to Ashenton, where he bespoke those accoutrements which he now wears; and while these were making, it was thought the poor fellow would have run distracted. He did nothing but growl, and curse, and swear to himself, run backwards and forwards between his own hutt and Greavesbury-hall, and quarrel with the horses in the stable. At length his wife and family were removed into a snug farm-house that happened to be empty, and care taken that they should be comfortably maintained.

"These precautions being taken, the knight, one morning, at day-break, mounted Bronzomarte, and Crabshaw as his squire ascended the back of a clumsy cart horse, called Gilbert. This again was looked upon as an instance of insanity in the said Crabshaw; for of all the horses in the stable, Gilbert was the most stubborn and vicious, and had often like to have done a mischief to Timothy, while he drove the cart and plough. When he was out of humour he would kick and plunge as if the devil was in him. He once thrust Crabshaw into the middle of a quickset-hedge,[23] where he was terribly torn; another time he canted him over his head into a quagmire, where he stuck with his heels up, and must have perished if people had not been passing that way; a third time he seized him in the stable with his teeth by the rim of the belly, and swung him off the ground, to the great danger of his life; and I'll be hanged if it was not owing to Gilbert that Crabshaw was now thrown into the river. Thus mounted and accoutred, the knight and his squire set out on their first excursion. They turned off from the common highway, and travelled all that day without meeting any thing worth recounting: but, in the morning of the second day, they were favoured with an adventure. The hunt was upon a common, through which they travelled, and the hounds were in full cry after a fox, when Crabshaw, prompted by his own mischievous disposition, and neglecting the order of his master, who called aloud to him to desist, rode up to the hounds, and crossed them at full gallop. The huntsman, who was not far off, running towards the squire, bestowed upon his head such a memento with his pole, as made the landschape dance before his eyes; and in a twinkling he was surrounded by all the fox-hunters, who plied their whips about his ears with infinite agility. Sir Launcelot advancing at an easy pace, instead of assisting the disastrous squire, exhorted his adversaries to punish him severely for his insolence, and they were not slow in obeying this injunction. Crabshaw, finding himself in this disagreeable situation, and that there was no succour to be expected from his master, on whose prowess he had depended, grew desperate; and, clubbing his whip, laid about him with great fury, wheeling about Gilbert, who was not idle; for he, having received some of the favours intended for his rider, both bit with his teeth, and kicked with his heels; and at last made his way through the ring that encircled him, though not before he had broke the huntsman's leg, lamed one of the best horses on the field, and killed half a score of the hounds. Crabshaw, seeing himself clear of the fray, did not tarry to take leave of his master, but made the most of his way to Greavesbury-hall, where he appeared with hardly any vestige of the human countenance, so much had he been defaced in this adventure. He did not fail to raise a great clamour against Sir Launcelot, whom he cursed as a coward in plain terms, swearing he would never serve him another day: but whether he altered his mind on cooler reflection, or was lectured by his wife, who well understood

her own interest, he rose with the cock, and went again in quest of Sir Launcelot, whom he found on the eve of a very hazardous enterprize. In the midst
of a lane the knight happened to meet with a party of about forty recruits,
commanded by a serjeant, a corporal, and a drummer, which last had his drum
slung at his back; but seeing such a strange figure mounted on a high-spirited
horse, he was seized with an inclination to divert his company. With this view
he braced his drum, and, hanging it in its proper position, began to beat a
point of war, advancing under the very nose of Bronzomarte; while the corporal exclaimed, 'Damn my eyes, who have we got here? old king Stephen,
from the horse armoury, in the tower;[24] or the fellow that rides armed at my
lord mayor's shew.'[25] The knight's steed seemed at least as well pleased with
the sound of the drum as were the recruits that followed it; and signified his
satisfaction in some curvettings and caprioles,[26] which did not at all discom-
pose the rider, who, addressing himself to the serjeant, 'Friend,' said he, 'you
ought to teach your drummer better manners. I would chastise the fellow on
the spot for his insolence, were it not out of the respect I bear to his majesty's
service.' 'Respect mine a——! (cried this ferocious commander) what, d'ye
think to frighten us with your pewter pisspot on your scull, and your lacquer'd
potlid on your arm? get out of the way and be damned, or I'll raise with my
halbert[27] such a clutter upon your target, that you'll remember it the longest
day you have to live.' At that instant, Crabshaw arriving upon Gilbert, 'So,
rascal,' said Sir Launcelot, 'you are returned. Go and beat in that scoundrel's
drum-head.'

"The squire, who saw no weapons of offence about the drummer but a
sword, which he hoped the owner durst not draw; and being resolved to exert
himself in making atonement for his desertion, advanced to execute his master's orders: but Gilbert, who liked not the noise, refused to proceed in the
ordinary way. Then the squire turning his tail to the drummer, he advanced
in a retrograde motion, and with one kick of his heels, not only broke the
drum into a thousand pieces, but laid the drummer in the mire, with such a
blow upon his hip-bone that he halted all the days of his life. The recruits,
perceiving the discomfiture of their leader, armed themselves with stones; the
serjeant raised his halbert in a posture of defence, and immediately a severe
action ensued. By this time, Crabshaw had drawn his sword, and begun to lay
about him like a devil incarnate; but, in a little time, he was saluted by a volley
of stones, one of which knocked out two of his grinders, and brought him to
the earth, where he had like to have found no quarter; for the whole company
crowded about him, with their cudgels brandished; and perhaps he owed his
preservation to their pressing so hard that they hindered one another from

using their weapons. Sir Launcelot, seeing with indignation the unworthy treatment his squire had received, and scorning to stain his launce with the blood of plebeians, instead of couching it in the rest, seized it by the middle, and fetching one blow at the serjeant, broke in twain the halbert which he had raised as a quarter-staff for his defence. The second stroke encountered his pate, which being the hardest part about him, sustained the shock without damage; but the third, lighting on his ribs, he honoured the giver with immediate prostration. The general being thus overthrown, Sir Launcelot advanced to the relief of Crabshaw, and handled his weapon so effectually, that the whole body of the enemy were disabled or routed, before one cudgel had touched the carcase of the fallen squire. As for the corporal, instead of standing by his commanding officer, he had overleaped the hedge, and run to the constable of an adjoining village for assistance. Accordingly, before Crabshaw could be properly remounted, the peace-officer arrived with his posse; and by the corporal was charged with Sir Launcelot and his squire, as two highwaymen. The constable, astonished at the martial figure of the knight, and intimidated at sight of the havock he had made, contented himself with standing at a distance, displaying the badge of his office, and reminding the knight that he represented his majesty's person. Sir Launcelot, seeing the poor man in great agitation, assured him that his design was to enforce, not violate the laws of his country; and that he and his squire would attend him to the next justice of the peace; but in the mean time, he, in his turn, charged the peace-officer with the serjeant and the drummer, who had begun the fray. The justice had been a pettifogger,[28] and was a sycophant to a nobleman in the neighbourhood, who had a post at court. He therefore thought he should oblige his patron, by shewing his respect for *the military;* and treated our knight with the most boorish insolence; but refused to admit him into his house, until he had surrendered all his weapons of offence to the constable. Sir Launcelot and his squire being found the aggressors, the justice insisted upon making out their mittimus,[29] if they did not find bail immediately; and could hardly be prevailed upon to agree that they should remain at the house of the constable, who, being a publican, undertook to keep them in safe custody, until the knight could write to his steward. Mean while he was bound over to the peace; and the serjeant with his drummer were told they had a good action against him for assault and battery, either by information or indictment.[30] They were not, however, so fond of the law as the justice seemed to be. Their sentiments had taken a turn in favour of Sir Launcelot, during the course of his examination, by which it appeared that he was really a gentleman of fashion and fortune; and they resolved to compromise the affair without the intervention of his worship.

Accordingly, the serjeant repaired to the constable's house, where the knight was lodged; and humbled himself before his honour, protesting with many oaths, that if he had known his quality he would have beaten the drummer's brains about his ears, for presuming to give his honour or his horse the least disturbance; thof the fellow, he believed, was sufficiently punished in being a cripple for life. Sir Launcelot admitted of his apologies; and taking compassion on the fellow who had suffered so severely for his folly, resolved to provide for his maintenance. Upon the representation of the parties to the justice, the warrant was next day discharged; and the knight returned to his own house, attended by the serjeant and the drummer mounted on horseback, the recruits being left to the corporal's charge.

"The halberdeer found the good effects of Sir Launcelot's liberality; and his companion being rendered unfit for his majesty's service by the heels of Gilbert, is now entertained at Greavesbury-hall, where he will probably remain for life. As for Crabshaw, his master gave him to understand, that if he did not think him pretty well chastised for his presumption and flight by the discipline he had undergone in the last two adventures, he would turn him out of his service with disgrace. Timothy said he believed it would be the greatest favour he could do him to turn him out of a service in which he knew he should be rib-roasted[31] every day, and murdered at last. In this situation were things at Greavesbury-hall about a month ago, when I crossed the country to Ferrybridge,[32] where I met my uncle: probably, this is the first incident of their second excursion; for the distance between this here house and Sir Launcelot's estate, does not exceed fourscore or ninety miles."[33]

CHAPTER VI.

In which the reader will perceive
that in some cases madness is catching.

Mr. Clarke having made an end of his narrative, the surgeon thanked him for the entertainment he had received; and Mr. Ferret shrugged up his shoulders in silent disapprobation. As for captain Crowe, who used at such pauses to pour in a broadside of dismembered remarks, linked together like chain-shot,[1] he spoke not a syllable for some time; but, lighting a fresh pipe at the candle, began to roll such voluminous clouds of smoke as in an instant filled the whole apartment, and rendered himself invisible to the whole company. Though he thus shrouded himself from their view, he did not long remain concealed from their hearing. They first heard a strange dissonant cackle, which the doctor knew to be a sea-laugh, and this was followed by an eager exclamation of "Rare pastime, strike my yards and top-masts!—I've a good mind—why shouldn't—many a losing voyage I've—smite my taffrel[2] but I wool—" By this time, he had relaxed so much in his fumigation, that the tip of his nose and one eye reappeared; and as he had drawn his wig forwards so as to cover his whole forehead, the figure that now saluted their eyes was much more ferocious and terrible than the fire-breathing chimæra[3] of the antients. Notwithstanding this dreadful appearance there was no indignation in his heart; but, on the contrary, an agreeable curiosity which he was determined to gratify. Addressing himself to Mr. Fillet, "Prithee, doctor, (said he) can'st tell, whether a man without being rated[4] a lord or a baron, or a what d'ye call um, d'ye see, mayn't take to the highway in the way of a frolick, d'ye see?—adad! for my own part, brother, I'm resolved as how to cruise a bit in the way of an arrant—if so be as I can't at once be commander, mayhap I may be bore upon the books as a petty officer or the like, d'ye see."

"Now, the Lord forbid! (cried Clarke with tears in his eyes) I'd rather see you dead than brought to such a dilemma." "Mayhap thou would'st (answered the uncle); for then, my lad, there would be some picking—aha! do'st thou tip me the traveller,[5] my boy—" Tom assured him he scorned any such mercenary views. "I am only concerned (said he) that you should take any step that might tend to the disgrace of yourself or your family; and I say again I had rather die than live to see you reckoned any otherwise than compos—"[6] "Die and be damned! you shambling, half-timber'd son of a ——— (cried the choleric Crowe) do'st talk to me of keeping reckoning and compass!—I could keep a reckoning, and box my compass,[7] long enough before thy keelstone was laid—Sam Crowe is not come here to ask thy counsel how to steer his course—" "Lord, sir, (resumed the nephew) consider what people will say— all the world will think you mad—" "Set thy heart at ease, Tom, (cried the seaman) I'll have a trip to and again in this here channel. Mad! what then? I think for my part one half of the nation is mad—and the other not very sound—I don't see why I ha'n't as good a right to be mad as another man— but, doctor, as I was saying, I'd be bound to you, if you would direct me where I can buy that same tackle[8] that an arrant must wear. As for the matter of the long pole headed with iron,[9] I'd never desire a better than a good boat-hook; and I could make a special good target[10] of that there tin sconce that holds the candle—mayhap any blacksmith will hammer me a scull-cap, d'ye see, out of an old brass kettle: and I can call my horse by the name of my ship, which was *Mufti.*" [11]

The surgeon was one of those wags who can laugh inwardly without exhibiting the least outward mark of mirth or satisfaction. He at once perceived the amusement which might be drawn from this strange disposition of the sailor, together with the most likely means which could be used to divert him from such an extravagant pursuit. He therefore tipped Clarke the wink with one side of his face, while the other was very gravely turned to the captain, whom he addressed to this effect: "It is not far from hence to Sheffield,[12] where you might be fitted compleatly in half-a-day—then you must wake[13] your armour in church or chapel, and be dubbed. As for this last ceremony, it may be performed by any person whatsoever. Don Quixote was dubbed by his landlord;[14] and there are many instances on record, of errants obliging and compelling the next person they met to cross their shoulders, and dub them knights. I myself would undertake to be your god-father; and I have interest enough to procure the keys of the parish church that stands hard by; besides, this is the eve of St. Martin, who was himself a knight-errant, and therefore a proper patron to a noviciate.[15] I wish we could borrow Sir Launcelot's armour for the occasion."

Crowe, being struck with this hint, started up, and laying his fingers on his lips to enjoin silence, walked off softly on his tiptoes, to listen at the door of our knight's apartment, and judge whether or not he was asleep. Mr. Fillet took this opportunity to tell his nephew, that it would be in vain for him to combat this humour with reason and argument: but the most effectual way of diverting him from the plan of knight-errantry would be to frighten him heartily while he should be keeping his vigil in the church, towards the accomplishment of which purpose he craved the assistance of the misanthrope as well as the nephew. Clarke seemed to relish the scheme; and observed that his uncle, though endued with courage enough to face any human danger, had at bottom a strong fund of superstition, which he seemed to have acquired, or at least improved, in the course of a sea life. Ferret, who perhaps would not have gone ten paces out of his road to save Crowe from the gallows, nevertheless, engaged as an auxiliary, meerly in hope of seeing a fellow-creature miserable; and even undertook to be the principal agent in this adventure. For this office, indeed, he was better qualified than they could have imagined: in the bundle which he kept under his great coat, there was, together with divers nostrums, a small vial of liquid phosphorus, sufficient, as he had already observed, to frighten a whole neighbourhood out of their senses. In order to concert the previous measures, without being overheard, these confederates retired with a candle and lanthorn into the stable; and their backs were scarce turned, when captain Crowe came in loaded with pieces of the knight's armour, which he had conveyed from the apartment of Sir Launcelot, whom he had left fast asleep.

Understanding that the rest of the company were gone out for a moment, he could not resist the inclination he felt of communicating his intention to the landlady, who, with her daughter, had been too much engaged in preparing Crabshaw's supper, to know the purport of their conversation. The good woman, being informed of the captain's design to remain alone all night in the church, began to oppose it with all her rhetorick. She said it was setting his Maker at defiance, and a wilful running into temptation. She assured him all the country knew that the church was haunted by spirits and hobgoblins: that lights had been seen in every corner of it; and a tall woman in white had one night appeared upon the top of the tower: that dreadful shrieks were often heard to come from the south aile, where a murdered man had been buried: that she herself had seen the cross on the top of the steeple all a-fire; and one evening as she passed a horseback close by the stile at the entrance into the church-yard, the horse stood still sweating and trembling, and had not power to proceed until she had repeated the Lord's Prayer.

These remarks made a strong impression on the imagination of Crowe, who asked in some confusion, if she had got that same prayer in print. She made no answer; but reaching the prayer-book from a shelf, and turning up the leaf, put it into his hand: then the captain, having adjusted his spectacles, began to read or rather spell aloud with equal eagerness and solemnity. He had refreshed his memory so well as to remember the whole; when the doctor, returning with his companions, gave him to understand that he had procured the key of the chancel, where he might watch his armour as well as in the body of the church; and that he was ready to conduct him to the spot. Crowe was not now quite so forward as he had appeared before to atchieve this adventure. He began to start objections with respect to the borrowed armour: he wanted to stipulate the comforts of a can of flip,[16] and a candle's end, during his vigil; and hinted something of the damage he might sustain from your malicious imps of darkness.

The doctor told him the constitutions of chivalry absolutely required that he should be left in the dark alone and fasting, to spend the night in pious meditations; but that if he had any fears which disturbed his conscience, he had much better desist, and give up all thoughts of knight-errantry, which could not consist with the least shadow of apprehension. The captain, stung by this remark, replied not a word; but gathering up the armour into a bundle, threw it on his back, and set out for the place of probation, preceded by Clarke with the lanthorn. When they arrived at the church, Fillet, who had procured the key from the sexton, who was his patient, opened the door, and conducted our novice into the middle of the chancel, where the armour was deposited. Then bidding Crowe draw his hanger, committed him to the protection of heaven, assuring him he would come back, and find him either dead or alive by day break, and perform the remaining part of the ceremony. So saying, he and the other associates shook him by the hand and took their leave, after the surgeon had tilted up the lanthorn in order to take a view of his visage, which was pale and haggard.

Before the door was locked upon him, he called aloud, "Hilloa! doctor, hip [17]—another word, d'ye see—." They forthwith returned, to know what he wanted, and found him already in a sweat. "Heark ye, brother, (said he wiping his face) I do suppose as how one may pass away the time in whistling black joke,[18] or singing black-ey'd Susan,[19] or some such sorrowful ditty." "By no means, (cried the doctor) such pastimes are neither suitable to the place, nor the occasion, which is altogether a religious exercise. If you have got any psalms by heart, you may sing a stave or two, or repeat the doxology." "Would I had Tom Laverick here, (replied our noviciate) he would sing you anthems like a sea-mew [20]—a had been a clerk ashore—many's the time and often I've given him a rope's end for singing psalms in the larboard watch [21]—would I had hired the son of a bitch to have taught me a cast of his office [22]—but it can't be holp, brother—if we can't go large, we must haul upon a wind,[23] as the saying is—if we can't sing, we must pray." The company again left him to his devotion, and returned to the public house in order to execute the essential part of their project.

CHAPTER VII.

In which the knight resumes his importance.

D octor Fillet having borrowed a couple of sheets from the landlady, dressed the misanthrope and Tom Clarke in ghostly apparel, which was reinforced by a few drops of liquid phosphorus, from Ferret's phial, rubbed on the foreheads of the two adventurers. Thus equipped they returned to the church with their conductor, who entered with them softly at an aile which was opposite to a place where the novice kept watch. They stole unperceived through the body of the church; and though it was so dark that they could not distinguish the captain with the eye, they heard the sound of his steps, as he walked backwards and forwards on the pavement with uncommon expedition, and an ejaculation now and then escape in a murmur from his lips.

The triumvirate having taken their station, with a large pew in their front, the two ghosts uncovered their heads, which, by help of the phosphorus, exhibited a pale and lambent flame extremely dismal and ghastly to the view; then Ferret, in a squeaking tone exclaimed, "Samuel Crowe! Samuel Crowe!" The captain hearing himself accosted in this manner, at such a time, and in such a place, replied, "Hilloah";[1] and turning his eyes towards the quarter whence the voice seemed to proceed, beheld the terrible apparition. This no sooner saluted his view, than his hair bristled up, his knees began to knock, and his teeth to chatter, while he cried aloud, "In the name of God, where are you bound, ho?" To this hail, the misanthrope answered, "We are the spirits of thy grandmother Jane and thy aunt Bridget."

At mention of these names, Crowe's terrors began to give way to his resentment, and he pronounced in a quick tone of surprize, mixed with indignation, "What d'ye want? what d'ye want? what d'ye want, ho?" The spirit replied, "We are sent to warn thee of thy fate." "From whence, ho?" cried the captain, whose choler had by this time well nigh triumphed over his fear. "From heaven," said the voice. "Ye lie, ye b——s[2] of hell! (did our novice exclaim) ye are damned for heaving me out of my right, five fathom and a half by the lead,[3] in burning brimstone. Don't I see the blue flames come out of your hawse-holes[4]—mayhap you may be the devil himself for aught I know—but, I trust in the Lord, d'ye see—I never disrated[5] a kinsman, d'ye see; so don't come along side of me—put about on t'other tack, d'ye see—you need not clap hard aweather,[6] for you'll soon get to hell again with a flowing sail."

So saying, he had recourse to his Pater-noster;[7] but perceiving the apparitions approach, he thundered out, "Avast—avast—sheer off, ye babes of hell, or I'll be foul of your forelights."[8] He accordingly sprung forwards with his hanger, and very probably would have set the spirits on their way to the other world, had not he fallen over a pew in the dark, and intangled himself so much among the benches, that he could not immediately recover his footing. The triumvirate took this opportunity to retire; and such was the precipitation of Ferret in his retreat, that he encountered a post, by which his right eye sustained considerable damage: a circumstance which induced him to inveigh

SIR LAUNCELOT GREAVES Ch.7. P.67.
Capt.ⁿ Crowe, terrified at Clarke and
the Misanthrope who appear as Ghosts.

Captⁿ· Crowe, terrified at Clarke and the Misanthrope,
by Hawkins after Corbauld. (University of Delaware Library)

bitterly against his own folly, as well as the impertinence of his companions who had inveigled him into such a troublesome adventure. Neither he nor Clarke could be prevailed upon to revisit the novice. The doctor himself thought his disease was desperate; and, mounting his horse, returned to his own habitation.

Ferret finding all the beds of the public house were occupied, composed himself to sleep in a windsor-chair at the chimney-corner; and Mr. Clarke, whose disposition was extremely amorous, resolved to renew his practices on the heart of Dolly. He had reconnoitred the apartments in which the bodies of the knight and his squire were deposited, and discovered close by the top of the stair-case a sort of a closet or hovel just large enough to contain a truckle-bed,[9] which, from some other particulars, he supposed to be the bed-chamber of his beloved Dolly, who had by this time retired to her repose. Full of this idea, and instigated by the dæmon of desire, Mr. Thomas crept softly up stairs; and lifting the latch of the closet-door, his heart began to palpitate with joyous expectation: but before he could breathe the gentle effusions of his love, the supposed damsel started up, and, seizing him by the collar with an Herculean gripe, uttered in the voice of Crabshaw, "It wa'n't for nothing that I dreamed of Newgate, sirrah; but I'd have thee to know, an arrant squire is not to be robbed by such a peddling[10] thief as thee—here I'll howld thee vast, an the devil were in thy doublet—help! murder! vire! help!"

It was impossible for Mr. Clarke to disengage himself, and equally impracticable to speak in his own vindication; so that here he stood trembling and half throttled, until the whole house being alarmed, the landlady and her ostler ran up stairs with a candle. When the light rendered objects visible, an equal astonishment prevailed on all sides: Crabshaw was confounded at sight of Mr. Clarke, whose person he well knew; and releasing him instantly from his grasp, "Bodikins! (cried he) I believe as how this hawse is haunted—who thought to meet with Measter Laayer Clarke at midnight and so far from hoam." The landlady could not comprehend the meaning of this rencounter; nor could Tom conceive how Crabshaw had transported himself hither from the room below, in which he saw him quietly reposed. Yet nothing was more easy than to explain this mystery: the apartment below was the chamber which the hostess and her daughter reserved for their own convenience; and this particular having been intimated to the squire while he was at supper, he had resigned the bed quietly, and been conducted hither in the absence of the company. Tom recollecting himself as well as he could, professed himself of Crabshaw's opinion, that the house was haunted, declaring that he could not well account for his being there in the dark; and leaving those that were assembled to discuss this knotty point, retired down stairs in hope of meeting with his charmer, whom accordingly he found in the kitchen just risen, and wrapped in a loose dishabillé.[11]

The noise of Crabshaw's cries had awakened and aroused his master, who, rising suddenly in the dark, snatched up his sword that lay by his bedside, and hastened to the scene of tumult, where all their mouths were opened at once to explain the cause of the disturbance, and make an apology for breaking his honour's rest. He said nothing; but taking the candle in his hand, beckoned to his squire to follow him into his apartment, resolving to arm and take horse immediately. Crabshaw understood his meaning; and while he shuffled on his cloaths, yawning hideously all the while, wished the lawyer at the devil for having visited him so unseasonably; and even cursed himself for the noise he had made, in consequence of which he foresaw he should now be obliged to forfeit his night's rest, and travel in the dark exposed to the inclemencies of the weather. "Pox rot thee, Tom Clarke, for a wicked laayer! (said he to himself) hadst thou been hanged at Bartlemey-tide,[12] I should this night have slept in peace, that I should—an I would there was a blister on this plaguy tongue of mine for making such a hollowballoo; that I do—five gallons of cold water has my poor belly been drenched with since night fell; so as my reins[13] and my liver are all one as if they were turned into ice, and my whole harslet[14] shakes and shivers like a vial of quicksilver. I have been dragged, half drowned like a rotten ewe, from the bottom of a river; and who knows but I may be next dragged quite dead from the bottom of a coal-pit—if so be as I am, I shall go to hell to be sure, for being consarned like in my own moorder; that I will: so I will: for a plague on it, I had no business with the vagaries of this crazy-peated[15] measter of mine, a pox on him, say I."

He had just finished this soliloquy as he entered the apartment of his master, who desired to know what was become of his armour. Timothy understanding that it had been left in the room when the knight undressed, began to scratch his head in great perplexity; and at last declared it as his opinion that it must have been carried off by witchcraft. Then he related his adventure with Tom Clarke, who he said was conveyed to his bedside he knew not how; and concluded, with affirming they were no better than Papishes,[16] who did not believe in witchcraft. Sir Launcelot could not help smiling at his simplicity; but assuming a peremptory air, he commanded him to fetch the armour without delay, that he might afterwards saddle the horses, in order to prosecute their journey. Timothy retired in great tribulation to the kitchen, where finding the misanthrope, whom the noise had also disturbed, and still impressed with the notion of his being a conjurer, he offered him a shilling if he would cast a figure,[17] and let him know what was become of his master's armour.

Ferret, in hope of producing more mischief, informed him without hesitation, that one of the company conveyed it into the chancel of the church, where he would now find it deposited; at the same time presenting him with the key, which Mr. Fillet had left in his custody. The squire, who was none of those who set hobgoblins at defiance, being afraid to enter the church alone at these hours, bargained with the ostler to accompany and light him with a lanthorn. Thus attended he advanced to the place, where the armour lay in a heap, and loaded it upon the back of his attendant without molestation, the lance being shouldered over the whole. In this equipage they were just going to retire, when the ostler hearing a noise at some distance, wheeled about with such velocity, that one end of the spear saluting Crabshaw's pate, the poor squire measured his length on the ground; [18] and crushing the lanthorn in his fall, the light was extinguished. The other terrified at these effects of his own sudden motion, threw down his burthen, and would have betaken himself to flight had not Crabshaw laid fast hold on his leg, that he himself might not be deserted. The sound of the pieces clattering on the pavement, roused captain Crowe from a trance or slumber in which he had lain since the apparition vanished; and he hollowed, or rather bellowed, with vast vociferation. Timothy and his friend were so intimidated by this terrific strain, that they thought no more of the armour, but ran home arm in arm, and appeared in the kitchen with all the marks of horror and consternation.

When Sir Launcelot came forth wrapped in his cloak, and demanded his arms, Crabshaw declared that the devil had them in possession; and this assertion was confirmed by the ostler, who pretended to know the devil by his roar. Ferret sat in his corner, maintaining the most mortifying silence, and enjoying the impatience of the knight, who in vain requested an explanation of this mystery. At length his eyes began to lighten, when seizing Crabshaw in one hand and the ostler in the other, he swore by heaven he would dash their souls out, and raze the house to the foundation, if they did not instantly disclose the particulars of this transaction. The good woman fell on her knees, protesting in the name of the Lord that she was innocent as the child unborn, thof she had lent the captain a Prayer Book to learn the Lord's Prayer, a lanthorn and candle to light him to the church, and a couple of clean sheets for the use of the other gentlemen. The knight was more and more puzzled by this declaration; when Mr. Clarke, coming into the kitchen, presented himself with a low obeisance to his old patron.

Sir Launcelot's anger was immediately converted into surprize. He set at liberty the squire and the ostler; and stretching out his hand to the lawyer, "My good friend Clarke, (said he) how came you hither? Can you solve this knotty point which hath involved us all in such confusion?"

Tom forthwith began a very circumstantial recapitulation of what had happened to his uncle; in what manner he had been disappointed of the estate; how he had accidentally seen his honour, been enamoured of his character, and become ambitious of following his example. Then he related the particulars of the plan which had been laid down to divert him from his design, and concluded with assuring the knight, that the captain was a very honest man, though he seemed to be a little disordered in his intellects. "I believe it (replied Sir Launcelot): madness and honesty are not incompatible—indeed I feel it by experience."

Tom proceeded to ask pardon in his uncle's name, for his having made so free with the knight's armour; and begged his honour, for the love of God, would use his authority with Crowe that he might quit all thoughts of knight-errantry, for which he was by no means qualified; for being totally ignorant of the laws of the land, he would be continually committing trespasses, and bring himself into trouble. He said in case he should prove refractory, he might be apprehended by virtue of a friendly warrant,[19] for having feloniously carried off the knight's accoutrements. "Taking away another man's moveables, (said he) and personal goods against the will of the owner, is *furtum*[20] and felony according to the statute: different indeed from robbery, which implies putting in fear on the king's highway, *in alta via regia violenter, & felonice captum & asportatum in magnum terrorem, &c.*,[21] for if the robbery be laid in the indictment as done *in quadam via pedestri*, in a foot-path, the offender will not be ousted of his clergy.[22] It must be *in alta via regia*; and your honour will please to take notice, that robberies committed on the river Thames, are adjudged as done *in alta via regia*; for the king's high-stream is all the same as the king's highway."

Sir Launcelot could not help smiling at Tom's learned investigation. He congratulated him on the progress he had made in the study of the law. He expressed his concern at the strange turn the captain had taken; and promised to use his influence in persuading him to desist from the preposterous design he had formed. The lawyer thus assured, repaired immediately to the church, accompanied by the squire, and held a parley with his uncle, who, when he understood that the knight in person desired a conference, surrendered up the arms quietly, and returned to the publick-house. Sir Launcelot received the honest seaman with his usual complacency, and perceiving great discomposure in his looks, said, he was sorry to hear he had passed such a disagreable night to so little purpose. Crowe having recruited his spirits with a bumper of brandy, thanked him for his concern, and observed that he had passed many a hard night in his time; but such another as this, he would not be bound to weather for the command of the whole British navy. "I have seen Davy Jones in the shape of a blue flame,[23] d'ye see, hopping to and fro, on the spritsail yard arm; and I've seen your Jacks o'the Lanthorn, and Wills o'the Wisp,[24] and many such spirits both by sea and land: but, to-night I've been boarded by all the devils and damn'd souls in hell, squeaking and squalling, and glimmering and glaring. Bounce, went the door—crack, went the pew—crash, came the tackle—white-sheeted ghosts dancing in one corner by the glowworm's light—black devils hobbling in another—Lord, have mercy on us! and I was hailed, Tom, I was, by my grand-mother Jane, and my aunt Bridget, d'ye see——a couple of damn'd—but they're roasting; that's one comfort, my lad."

When he had thus disburthened his conscience, Sir Launcelot introduced the subject of the new occupation at which he aspired. "I understand," said he, "that you are desirous of treading the paths of errantry, which I assure you, are thorny and troublesome. Nevertheless, as your purpose is to exercise your humanity and benevolence, so your ambition is commendable. But towards the practice of chivalry, there is something more required than the virtues of courage and generosity. A knight-errant ought to understand the sciences,[25] to be master of ethics or morality, to be well versed in theology, a compleat casuist,[26] and minutely acquainted with the laws of his country. He should not only be patient of cold, hunger, and fatigue, righteous, just, and valiant; but also chaste, religious, temperate, polite, and conversable; and have all his passions under the rein, except love, whose empire he should submissively acknowledge." He said, this was the very essence of chivalry, and no man had ever made such a profession of arms, without having first placed his affection upon some beauteous object, for whose honour, and at whose command he would chearfully encounter the most dreadful perils.

He took notice that nothing could be more irregular than the manner in which Crowe had attempted to keep his vigil: for he had never served his noviciate—he had not prepared himself with abstinence and prayer—he had not provided a qualified godfather for the ceremony of dubbing—he had no armour of his own to wake; but, on the very threshold of chivalry, which is the perfection of justice, had unjustly purloined the arms of another knight: that this was a meer mockery of a religious institution, and therefore, unpleasing in the sight of heaven; witness, the demons and hobgoblins that were permitted to disturb and torment him in his trial.

Crowe having listened to these remarks, with earnest attention, replied, after some hesitation: "I am bound to you, brother, for your kind and christian counsel—I doubt as how I've steered by a wrong chart, d'ye see—as for the matter of the sciences, to be sure, I know plain sailing and mercator;[27] and am an indifferent good seaman, thof I say it that should not say it: but as to all the rest, no better than the viol block or the geer capstan.[28] Religion I ha'n't much over-hauled; and we tars laugh at your polite conversation, thof, may-hap, we can chaunt a few ballads to keep the hands awake in the night watch; then for chastity, brother, I doubt that's not to be expected in a sailor just come a-shore, after a long voyage—sure all those poor hearts won't be damned for steering in the wake of nature. As for a sweet-heart, Bet Mizen of St. Cathe-rine's[29] would fit me to a hair—she and I are old messmates; and—what sig-nifies talking, brother, she knows already the trim of my vessel, d'ye see." He concluded with saying, "He thought he wa'n't too old to learn; and if Sir Launcelot would take him in tow, as his tender, he would stand by him all weathers, and it should not cost his consort a farthing's expence."

The knight said, he did not think himself of consequence enough to have such a pupil; but should always be ready to give him his best advice, as a speci-men of which he exhorted him to weigh all the circumstances, and deliberate calmly and leisurely, before he actually engaged in such a boisterous profes-sion, assuring him that if, at the end of three months, his resolution should continue, he would take upon himself the office of his instructor. In the mean time, he gratified the hostess for his lodging, put on his armour, took leave of the company, and mounting *Bronzomarte*, proceeded southerly, being at-tended by his squire Crabshaw, grumbling on the back of Gilbert.

CHAPTER VIII.

Which is within a hair's breadth of proving highly interesting.

Leaving captain Crowe and his nephew for the present, though they and even the misanthrope will reappear in due season, we are now obliged to attend the progress of the knight, who proceeded in a southerly direction,[1] insensible of the storm that blew, as well as of the darkness, which was hor-rible. For some time Crabshaw ejaculated curses in silence; till at length his anger gave way to his fear, which waxed so strong upon him, that he could no longer resist the desire of alleviating it, by entering into a conversation with his master. By way of introduction, he gave Gilbert the spur, directing him towards the flank of Bronzomarte, which he encountered with such a shock that the knight was almost dismounted. When sir Launcelot, with some warmth, asked the reason of this attack, the squire replied in these words: "The devil, (God bless us) mun be playing his pranks with Gilbert too, as sure as I'm a living soul!—I'se wage a teaster,[2] the foul fiend has left the seaman, and got into Gilbert, that he has—when a has passed through an ass and a horse, I'se marvel what beast a will get into next." "Probably into a mule (said the knight); in that case you will be in some danger—but I can, at any time, dispossess[3] you with a horsewhip."—"Aye, aye, (answered Timothy) your honour has a mortal good hand at giving a flap with a fox's tail,[4] as the saying is—'tis a wonderment you did not try your hand on that there wiseacre that stole your honour's harness, and wants to be an arrant with a murrain to 'un[5]—Lord help his fool's head! it becomes him as a sow doth a cart-saddle."[6] "There is no guilt in infirmity (said the knight); I punish the vicious only." "I would your honour would punish Gilbert then, (cried the squire) for 'tis the most vicious tuoad that ever I laid a leg over—but as to that same sea-faring man, what may his distemper be?" "Madness"; (answered sir Launcelot). "Bodikins, (exclaimed the squire) I doubt as how other volks are leame of the same leg[7]—but a'n't vor such small gentry as he to be mad: they mun leave that to their betters." "You seem to hint at me, Crabshaw: do you really think I am mad?" "I may say as how I have looked your honour in the mouth; and a sorry dog should I be, if I did not know your humours as well as I know e'er a beast in the steable at Greavesbury-hall." "Since you are so well acquainted with my madness, (said the knight) what opinion have you of yourself, who serve and follow a lunatic?" "I hope I han't served your honour for nothing, but I shall inherit some of your cast vagaries—when your honour is pleased to be mad, I should be very sorry to be found right in my senses. Timothy Crabshaw will never eat the bread of unthankfulness—It shall never be said of him that he was wiser than his master: as for the matter of following a madman, we may say your honour's face is made of a fiddle; every one that looks on you loves you."[8] This compliment the knight returned by saying, "If my face is a fiddle, Crabshaw, your tongue is a fiddle-stick that plays upon it—yet your music is very disagreeable—you don't keep time." "Nor you neither, measter, (cried Timothy) or we shouldn't be here wandering about under cloud of night, like sheep-stealers, or evil spirits with troubled consciences."

Here the discourse was interrupted by a sudden disaster, in consequence of which the squire uttered an inarticulate roar that startled the knight himself, who was very little subject to the sensation of fear: but his surprize was changed into vexation when he perceived Gilbert without a rider passing by, and kicking his heels with great agility. He forthwith turned his steed, and, riding back a few paces, found Crabshaw rising from the ground. When he asked what was become of his horse, he answered in a whimpering tone, "Horse! would I could once see him fairly carrion for the hounds—for my part I believe as how 'tis no horse but a devil incarnate; and yet I've been worse mounted, that I have—I'd like to have rid a horse that was foaled of an acorn."⁹

This accident happened in a hollow way, overshadowed with trees, one of which the storm had blown down, so that it lay over the road, and one of its boughs projecting horizontally, encountered the squire as he trotted along in the dark. Chancing to hitch under his long chin, he could not disengage himself; but hung suspended like a flitch of bacon, while Gilbert, pushing forward left him dangling, and, by his aukward gambols, seemed to be pleased with the joke. This capricious animal was not retaken without the personal endeavours of the knight: for Crabshaw absolutely refusing to budge a foot from his honour's side, he was obliged to alight, and fasten Bronzomarte to a tree: then they set out together, and with some difficulty found Gilbert with his neck stretched over a five-barred gate, snuffing up the morning-air. The squire, however, was not remounted, without having first undergone a severe reprehension from his master, who upbraided him with his cowardice, threatened to chastise him on the spot, and declared that he would divorce his dastardly soul from his body, should he ever be incommoded or affronted with another instance of his base-born apprehension. Though there was some risque in carrying on the altercation at this juncture, Timothy having bound up his jaws, could not withstand the inclination he had to confute his master. He therefore, in a muttering accent, protested that if the knight would give him leave, he should prove that his honour had tied a knot with his tongue which he could not untie with all his teeth. "How, caitiff, (cried sir Launcelot) presume to contend with me in argument!" "Your mouth is scarce shut, (said the other) since you declared that a man was not to be punished for madness, because it was a distemper: now I will maintain that cowardice is a distemper as well as madness; for nobody would be afraid if he could help it." "There is more logic in that remark (resumed the knight) than I expected from your clod-pate, Crabshaw: but I must explain the difference between cowardice and madness. Cowardice, tho' sometimes the effect of natural imbecility, is generally a prejudice of education, or bad habit contracted from misinformation, or misapprehension, and may certainly be cured by experience, and the exercise of reason: but this remedy cannot be applied in madness, which is a privation or disorder of reason itself." "So is cowardice, as I'm a living soul, (exclaimed the squire) don't you say a man is frightened out of his senses? for my peart, measter, I can neither see nor hear, much less argufy when I'm in such a quandary: wherefore, I believe, odds bodikins! that cowardice and madness are both distempers, and differ no more than the hot and cold fits of an ague. When it teakes your honour, you're all heat and fire and fury, Lord bless us! but when it catches poor Tim, he's cold and dead-hearted, he sheakes and shivers like an aspen-leaf, that he does." "In that case, (answered the knight) I shall not punish you for the distemper which you cannot help, but for engaging in a service exposed to perils, when you knew your own infirmity: in the same manner as a man deserves punishment, who enlists himself for a soldier, while he labours under any secret disease." "At that rate (said the squire) my bread is like to be rarely buttered o'both sides, I faith. But, I hope, as by the blessing of God, I have run mad, so I shall in good time grow valiant, under your honour's precept and example."

By this time a very disagreeable night was succeeded by a fair, bright morning, and a market-town [10] appeared at the distance of three or four miles, when Crabshaw, having no longer the fear of hobgoblins before his eyes, and being moreover cheared by the sight of a place where he hoped to meet with comfortable entertainment, began to talk big, to expatiate on the folly of being afraid, and finally set all danger at defiance; when all of a sudden he was presented with an opportunity of putting in practice those new adopted maxims. In an opening between two lanes, they perceived a gentleman's coach stopped by two highwaymen on horseback, one of whom advanced to reconnoitre and keep the coast clear, while the other exacted contribution from the travellers in the coach. He who acted as centinel, no sooner saw our adventurer appearing from the lane, than he rode up with a pistol in his hand, and ordered him to halt on pain of immediate death.

To this peremptory mandate the knight made no other reply than charging him with such impetuosity that he was unhorsed in a twinkling, and lay sprawling on the ground, seemingly sore bruised with his fall. Sir Launcelot commanding Timothy to alight and secure the prisoner, couched his launce, and rode full speed at the other highwayman, who was not a little disturbed at sight of such an apparition. Nevertheless, he fired his pistol without effect; and, clapping spurs to his horse, fled away at full gallop. The knight pursued him with all the speed that Bronzomarte could exert; but the robber being mounted on a swift hunter, kept him at a distance; and, after a chace of several miles, escaped thro' a wood so entangled with coppice, that Sir Launcelot thought proper to desist. He then, for the first time, recollected the situation in which he had left the other thief, and remembering to have heard a female shriek, as he passed by the coach-window, resolved to return with all expedition, that he might make a proffer of his service to the lady, according to the obligation of knight-errantry. But he had lost his way; and after an hour's ride, during which he traversed many a field, and circled divers hedges, he found himself in the market-town aforementioned. Here the first object that presented itself to his eyes, was Crabshaw, on foot, surrounded by a mob, tearing his hair, stamping with his feet, and roaring out in manifest distraction, "Shew me the mayor, (for the love of God) shew me the mayor!—O Gilbert, Gilbert! a murrain take thee, Gilbert! sure thou wast foaled for my destruction!"

From these exclamations, and the antic dress of the squire, the people, not without reason, concluded that the poor soul had lost his wits; and the beadle was just going to secure him,[11] when the knight interposed, and at once attracted the whole attention of the populace. Timothy, seeing his master, fell down on his knees, crying, "The thief has run away with Gilbert—you may pound me into a peaste, as the saying is:[12] but now I'se as mad as your worship; and an't afeard of the devil and all his works." Sir Launcelot desiring the beadle would forbear, was instantly obeyed by that officer, who had no inclination to put the authority of his place in competition with the power of such a figure armed at all points, mounted on a fiery steed, and ready for the combat. He ordered Crabshaw to attend him to the next inn, where he alighted; then taking him into a separate apartment, demanded an explanation of the unconnected words he had uttered. The squire was in such agitation, that with infinite difficulty, and by dint of a thousand different questions, his master learned the adventure to this effect: Crabshaw, according to Sir Launcelot's command, had alighted from his horse, and drawn his cutlass, in hope of intimidating the discomfited robber into a tame surrender, though he did not at all relish the nature of the service: but the thief was neither so much hurt, nor so tame as Timothy had imagined. He started on his feet with his pistol still in his hand; and presenting it to the squire, swore with dreadful imprecations, that he would blow his brains out in an instant. Crabshaw, unwilling to hazard the trial of this experiment, turned his back, and fled with great precipitation; while the robber, whose horse had run away, mounted Gilbert, and rode off across the country. It was at this period, that two footmen belonging to the coach, who had stayed behind to take their morning's whet, at the inn where they had lodged, came up to the assistance of the ladies, armed with blunderbusses; and the carriage proceeded, leaving Timothy alone in distraction and despair. He knew not which way to turn, and was afraid of remaining on the spot, lest the robbers should come back and revenge themselves upon him for the disappointment they had undergone. In this distress, the first thought that occurred, was to make the best of his way to the town, and demand the assistance of the civil magistrate towards the retrieval of what he had lost: a design which he executed in such a manner, as justly entailed upon him the imputation of lunacy.

While Timothy stood fronting the window, and answering the interrogations of his master, he suddenly exclaimed, "Bodikins! there's Gilbert!" and sprung into the street with incredible agility. There finding his strayed companion brought back by one of the footmen who attended the coach, he imprinted a kiss on his forehead; and hanging about his neck, with the tears in his eyes, hailed his return with the following salutation:[13] "Art thou come back, my darling? ah Gilbert, Gilbert! a pize upon thee![14] thou hadst like to have been a dear Gilbert to me! how couldst thou break the heart of thy old friend, who has known thee from a colt? seven years next grass have I fed thee and bred thee; provided thee with sweet hay, delicate corn, and fresh litter, that thou mought lie warm, dry, and comfortable. Ha'n't I curry-combed thy carcase 'till it was as sleek as a sloe, and cherished thee as the apple of mine eye? for all that thou hast played me an hundred dog's-tricks; biting, and kicking, and plunging, as if the devil was in thy body; and now thou couldst run away with a thief, and leave me to be flea'd alive by master: what canst thou say for thyself, thou cruel, hard-hearted, unchristian tuoad!" To this tender expostulation, which afforded much entertainment to the boys, Gilbert answered not one word; but seemed altogether insensible to the caresses of Timothy, who forthwith led him into the stable. On the whole, he seems to have been an unsocial animal: for it does not appear that he ever contracted any degree of intimacy, even with Bronzomarte,[15] during the whole course of their acquaintance and fellowship. On the contrary, he has been more than once known to signify his aversion by throwing out behind, and other eruptive marks of contempt for that elegant charger, who excelled him as much in personal merit, as his rider Timothy was outshone by his all-accomplished master. While the squire accommodated Gilbert in the stable, the knight sent for the footman who had brought him back; and, having presented him with a liberal acknowledgment, desired to know in what manner the horse had been retrieved.

The stranger satisfied him in this particular, by giving him to understand, that the highwayman, perceiving himself pursued across the country, plied Gilbert so severely with whip and spur, that the animal resented the usage, and being besides, perhaps, a little struck with remorse for having left his old friend Crabshaw, suddenly halted, and stood stock still, notwithstanding all

the stripes and tortures he underwent; or if he moved at all, it was in a retrograde direction. The thief, seeing all his endeavours ineffectual, and himself
in danger of being overtaken, wisely quitted his acquisition, and fled into the
bosom of a neighbouring wood.

Then the knight inquired about the situation of the lady in the coach, and
offered himself as her guard and conductor: but was told that she was already
safely lodged in the house of a gentleman at some distance from the road. He
likewise learned that she was a person disordered in her senses, under the care
and tuition of a widow lady her relation; and that in a day or two they should
pursue their journey northward to the place of her habitation. After the footman had been some time dismissed, the knight recollected that he had forgot
to ask the name of the person to whom he belonged; and began to be uneasy
at this omission, which indeed was more interesting than he could imagine:
for an explanation of this nature would, in all likelihood, have led to a discovery, that the lady in the coach was no other than Miss Aurelia Darnel, who
seeing him unexpectedly in such an equipage and attitude, as he passed the
coach, (for his helmet was off) had screamed with surprize and terror, and
fainted away. Nevertheless, when she recovered from her swoon, she concealed the real cause of her agitation, and none of her attendants were acquainted with the person of Sir Launcelot.

The circumstances of the disorder, under which she was said to labour,
shall be revealed in due course. In the mean time, our adventurer, though
unaccountably affected, never dreamed of such an occurrence; but being very
much fatigued, resolved to indemnify himself for the loss of last night's repose;
and this happened to be one of the few things in which Crabshaw felt an ambition to follow his master's example.

CHAPTER IX.

Which may serve to shew, that true patriotism is of no party.

The knight had not enjoyed his repose above two hours, when he was disturbed by such a variety of noises, as might have discomposed a brain of
the firmest texture. The rumbling of carriages, and the rattling of horses' feet
on the pavement, was intermingled with loud shouts, and the noise of fiddle,

Sr. L. Greaves and his Squire T. Crabshaw at a Country Election,
by Anthony Walker. (Collection of James G. Basker)

french-horn, and bagpipe. A loud peal was heard ringing in the church-tower, at some distance, while the inn resounded with clamour, confusion, and uproar.

Sir Launcelot being thus alarmed, started from his bed, and running to the window, beheld a cavalcade of persons well mounted, and distinguished by blue cockades.[1] They were generally attired like jockies, with gold-laced hats and buckskin breeches, and one of them bore a standard of blue silk, inscribed in white letters, LIBERTY AND THE LANDED INTEREST.[2] He who rode at their head was a jolly figure, of a florid complexion and round belly, seemingly turned of fifty, and, in all appearance, of a choleric disposition. As they approached the market-place they waved their hats, huzza'd, and cried aloud, No FOREIGN CONNECTIONS, — OLD-ENGLAND FOR EVER.[3] This acclamation, however, was not so loud or universal, but that our adventurer could distinctly hear a counter-cry from the populace, of No SLAVERY, — No POPISH PRETENDER,[4] an insinuation so ill relished by the cavaliers, that they began to ply their horsewhips among the multitude, and were, in their turn, saluted with a discharge or volley of stones, dirt, and dead cats;[5] in consequence of which some teeth were demolished, and many surtouts[6] defiled.

Our adventurer's attention was soon called off from this scene, to contemplate another procession of people on foot, adorned with bunches of orange ribbons,[7] attended by a regular band of musick, playing *God save great George our king*,[8] and headed by a thin, swarthy personage, of a sallow aspect and large goggling eyes, arched over with two thick semicircles of hair, or rather bristles, jet black, and frowzy. His apparel was very gorgeous, though his address was aukward;[9] he was accompanied by the mayor, recorder, and heads of the corporation, in their formalities. His ensigns were known by the inscription, LIBERTY OF CONSCIENCE AND THE PROTESTANT SUCCESSION;[10] and the people saluted him as he passed with repeated cheers, that seemed to prognosticate success. He had particularly ingratiated himself with the good women, who lined the street, and sent forth many ejaculatory petitions in his favour.[11]

Sir Launcelot immediately comprehended the meaning of this solemnity: he perceived it was the prelude to the election of a member to represent the county in parliament, and he was seized with an eager desire to know the names and characters of the competitors. In order to gratify this desire, he made repeated application to the bell-rope that depended from the ceiling of his apartment; but this produced nothing, except the repetition of the words "Coming, Sir," which ecchoed from three or four different corners of the house. The waiters were so distracted by a variety of calls, that they stood motionless, in the state of the schoolman's ass between two bundles of hay,[12] incapable of determining where they should first offer their attendance.

Our knight's patience was almost exhausted, when Crabshaw entered the room, in a very strange equipage: one half of his face appeared close shaved, and the other covered with lather, while the blood trickled in two rivulets from his nose, upon a barber's cloth that was tucked under his chin; he looked grim with indignation, and, under his left arm carried his cutlass, unsheathed. Where he had acquired so much of the profession of knight-errantry we shall not pretend to determine; but, certain it is, he fell on his knees before sir Launcelot, crying, with an accent of rage and distraction, "In the name of St. George for England, I beg a boon, sir knight, and thy compliance I demand, before the peacock and the ladies."[13]

Sir Launcelot, astonished at this address, replied in a lofty strain, "Valiant squire, thy boon is granted, provided it doth not contravene the laws of the land, and the constitutions of chivalry." "Then I crave leave (answered Crabshaw) to challenge and defy to mortal combat, that caitif barber who hath left me in this piteous condition; and I vow by the peacock,[14] that I will not shave my beard, until I have shaved his head from his shoulders: so may I thrive in the occupation of an arrant squire."

Before his master had time to enquire into particulars, they were joined by a decent man in boots, who was likewise a traveller, and had seen the rise and progress of Timothy's disaster. He gave the knight to understand, that Crabshaw had sent for a barber, and already undergone one half of the operation, when the operator received the long expected message from both the gentlemen, who stood candidates at the election. The double summons was no sooner intimated to him, than he threw down his bason and retired with precipitation, leaving the squire in the suds. Timothy, incensed at this desertion, followed him with equal celerity into the street, where he collared the shaver, and insisted upon being entirely trimmed, on pain of the bastinado.[15] The other finding himself thus arrested, and having no time to spare for altercation, lifted up his fist, and discharged it upon the snout of Crabshaw with such force, that the unfortunate aggressor was fain to bite the ground, while the victor hastened away, in hope of touching the double wages of corruption.

The knight being informed of these circumstances, told Timothy with a smile, that he should have liberty to defy the barber; but in the mean time, he ordered him to saddle Bronzomarte, and prepare for immediate service. While the squire was thus employed, his master engaged in conversation with the stranger, who happened to be a London dealer travelling for orders, and was well acquainted with the particulars which our adventurer wanted to know. It was from this communicative tradesman he learned, that the competitors were sir Valentine Quickset and Mr. Isaac Vanderpelft; the first a meer fox-hunter,[16] who depended for success in this election upon his interest among the high-flying gentry; the other a stock-jobber[17] and contractor,[18] of foreign extract, not without a mixture of Hebrew blood, immensely rich, who was countenanced by his grace of ———,[19] and supposed to have distributed large sums in securing a majority of votes among the yeomanry of the county, possessed of small freeholds, and copyholders,[20] a great number of which last resided in this burrough. He said these were generally dissenters[21] and weavers;[22] and that the mayor, who was himself a manufacturer, had received a very considerable order for exportation, in consequence of which, it was believed, he would support Mr. Vanderpelft with all his influence and credit.

Sir Launcelot, rouzed at this intelligence, called for his armour, which being buckled on in a hurry, he mounted his steed, attended by Crabshaw on Gilbert, and rode immediately into the midst of the multitude by which the hustings[23] were surrounded, just as sir Valentine Quickset began to harangue the people from an occasional theatre, formed of a plank supported by the upper board of the publick stocks, and an inferior rib of a wooden cage pitched also for the accommodation of petty delinquents.

Though the singular appearance of sir Launcelot at first attracted the eyes of all the spectators, yet they did not fail to yield attention to the speech of his brother knight, sir Valentine, which ran in the following strain: "Gentlemen vreehoulders of this here county, I sha'n't pretend to meake a vine vlourishing speech—I'm a plain spoken man, as you all know. I hope I shall always speak my maind without vear or vavour, as the zaying is. 'Tis the way of the Quicksets—we are no upstarts, nor vorreigners, nor have we any Jewish blood in our veins;—we have lived in this here neighbourhood time out of maind, as you all know; and possess an estate of vive thousand clear, which we spend at whoam, among you, in old English hospitality—all my vorevathers have been parliament-men, and I can prove that ne'er a one o'um gave a zingle vote for the court since the revolution.[24] Vor my own peart, I value not the ministry three skips of a louse,[25] as the zaying is,—I ne'er knew but one minister that was an honest man; and vor all the rest I care not if they were hanged as high as Haman,[26] with a pox to 'un—I am, thank God, a vree-born, true-hearted Englishman, and a loyal, thof unworthy, son of the church—vor all they have done vor H——r,[27] I'd vain know what they have done vor the church, with a vengeance—vor my oun peart, I hate all vorreigners, and vorreign measures, whereby this poor nation is broken-backed with a dismal load of debt, and taxes rise so high that the poor cannot get bread. Gentlemen vreehoulders of this county, I value no minister a vig's end, d'ye see; if you will vavour me with your votes and interest, whereby I may be returned, I'll engage one half of my estate that I never cry yea to vour shillings in the pound;[28] but will cross the ministry in every thing, as in duty bound, and as becomes an honest vreehoulder in the ould interest[29]—but, if you sell your votes and your country for hire, you will be detested in this here world, and damned in the next to all eternity: so I leave every man to his own conscience."

This eloquent oration was received by his own friends with loud peals of applause; which, however, did not discourage his competitor, who, confident of his own strength, ascended the rostrum, or, in other words, an old cask, set upright for the purpose. Having bowed all round to the audience, with a smile of gentle condescension, he told them, how ambitious he was of the honour to represent this county in parliament; and how happy he found himself in the encouragement of his friends, who had so unanimously agreed to support his pretensions. He said, over and above the qualification he possessed among them, he had fourscore thousand pounds in his pocket, which he had acquired by commerce, the support of the nation, under the present happy establishment, in defence of which he was ready to spend the last farthing. He owned himself a faithful subject to his majesty king George, sincerely attached to the protestant succession, in detestation and defiance of a popish, an abjured, and outlawed pretender;[30] and declared that he would exhaust his substance and his blood, if necessary, in maintaining the principles of the glorious revolution. "This (cried he) is the solid basis and foundation upon which I stand."

These last words had scarce proceeded from his mouth, when the head of the barrel or puncheon[31] on which he stood, being frail and infirm, gave way; so that down he went with a crash, and in a twinkling disappeared from the eyes of the astonished beholders. The fox-hunters perceiving his disaster, exclaimed, in the phrase and accent of the chace, "Stole away! stole away!"[32] and, with hideous vociferation, joined in the sylvan chorus which the hunters hollow when the hounds are at fault.

The disaster of Mr. Vanderpelft was soon repaired by the assiduity of his friends, who disengaged him from the barrel in a trice, hoisted him on the shoulders of four strong weavers, and resenting the unmannerly exultation of their antagonists, began to form themselves in order of battle. An obstinate fray would have undoubtedly ensued, had not their mutual indignation given way to their curiosity, at the motion of our knight, who had advanced into the middle between the two fronts, and waving his hand, as a signal for them to give attention, addressed himself to them with graceful demeanor, in these words: "Countrymen, friends, and fellow-citizens, you are this day assembled to determine a point of the utmost consequence to yourselves and your posterity; a point that ought to be determined by far other weapons than brutal force and factious clamour. You, the freemen of England,[33] are the basis of that excellent constitution, which hath long flourished the object of envy and admiration. To you belongs the inestimable privilege of choosing a delegate properly qualified to represent you in the high court of parliament. This is your birth-right, inherited from your ancestors, obtained by their courage, and sealed with their blood. It is not only your birth-right, which you should maintain in defiance of all danger, but also a sacred trust, to be executed with the most scrupulous care and fidelity. The person whom you trust ought not only to be endued with the most inflexible integrity, but should likewise possess a fund of knowledge that may enable him to act as a part of the legislature. He must be well acquainted with the history, the constitution, and the laws of his country: he must understand the forms of business, the extent of the royal prerogative, the privilege of parliament, the detail of government, the nature and regulation of the finances, the different branches of commerce, the politicks that prevail, and the connections that subsist among the different powers of Europe: for, on all these subjects, the deliberations of a house of commons occasionally turn: but these great purposes will never be answered by electing an illiterate savage, scarce qualified, in point of understanding, to act as a country justice of the peace, a man who has scarce ever travelled beyond the excursion of a fox-chace, whose conversation never rambles farther than his stable, his kennel, and his barn-yard; who rejects decorum as degeneracy, mistakes rusticity for independence, ascertains his courage by leaping over gates and ditches, and founds his triumph on feats of drinking; who holds his estate by a factious tenure, professes himself the blind slave of a party, without knowing the principles that gave it birth, or the motives by which it is actuated, and thinks that all patriotism consists in railing indiscriminately at ministers, and obstinately opposing every measure of the administration.[34] Such a man, with no evil intentions of his own, might be used as a dangerous tool in the hands of desperate faction, by scattering the seeds of disaffection, embarrassing the wheels of government, and reducing the whole kingdom to anarchy."

Here the knight was interrupted, by the shouts and acclamations of the Vanderpelfites, who cried aloud, "Hear him! hear him! long life to the iron-cased orator." This clamour subsiding, he prosecuted his harangue to the following effect:

"Such a man as I have described may be dangerous from ignorance, but is

[The Election], by Blake after Stothard. (Collection of Robert N. Essick)

neither so mischievous nor so detestable as the wretch who knowingly betrays his trust, and sues to be the hireling and prostitute of a weak and worthless minister; a sordid knave,[35] without honour or principle, who belongs to no family whose example can reproach him with degeneracy; who has no country to command his respect, no friends to engage his affection, no religion to regulate his morals, no conscience to restrain his iniquity, and who worships no God but mammon.[36] An insinuating miscreant, who undertakes for the dirtiest work of the vilest administration; who practises national usury,[37] receiving by wholesale the rewards of venality, and distributing the wages of corruption by retail."

In this place our adventurer's speech was drowned in the acclamations of the fox-hunters, who now triumphed in their turn, and hoicksed the speaker,[38] exclaiming, "Well opened, Jowler—to 'un, to 'un, to 'un again, Sweetlips! hey, Merry, Whitefoot!"[39] After a short interruption, he thus resumed his discourse.

"When such a caitif presents himself to you, like the devil,[40] with a temptation in his hand, avoid him as if he were in fact the devil—it is not the offering of disinterested love; for, what should induce him, who has no affections, to love you, to whose persons he is an utter stranger?[41] alas! it is not a benevolence, but a bribe. He wants to buy you at one market, that he may sell you at another. Without doubt his intention is to make an advantage of his purchase; and this aim he cannot accomplish, but by sacrificing, in some sort, your interest, your independency,[42] to the wicked designs of a minister, as he can expect no gratification for the faithful discharge of his duty. But, even if he should not find an opportunity of selling you to advantage, the crime, the shame, the infamy, will still be the same in you, who, baser than the most abandoned prostitutes, have sold yourselves and your posterity for hire—for a paultry price, to be refunded with interest by some minister, who will indemnify himself out of your own pockets: for, after all, you are bought and sold with your own money—the miserable pittance you may now receive, is no more than a pitcher full of water thrown in to moisten the sucker of that pump which will drain you to the bottom. Let me therefore advise and exhort you, my countrymen, to avoid the opposite extremes of the ignorant clown and the designing courtier, and choose a man of honesty, intelligence, and moderation, who will—"

The doctrine of moderation was a very unpopular subject in such an assembly; and, accordingly, they rejected it as one man. They began to think the stranger wanted to set up for himself,[43] a supposition that could not fail to incense both sides equally, as they were both zealously engaged in their respective causes. The Whigs and the Tories joined against this intruder, who being neither, was treated like a monster, or chimæra in politics. They hissed, they hooted, and they hollowed; they annoyed him with missiles of dirt, sticks, and stones; they cursed, they threatened and reviled, till at length his patience was exhausted.

"Ungrateful, and abandoned miscreants! (he cried) I spoke to you as men and christians, as free-born Britons and fellow-citizens: but I perceive you are a pack of venal, infamous scoundrels, and I will treat you accordingly." So saying he brandished his lance, and riding into the thickest of the concourse, laid about him with such dexterity and effect, that the multitude was immediately dispersed, and he retired without further molestation.

The same good fortune did not attend squire Crabshaw in his retreat. The ludicrous singularity of his features, and the half-mown crop of hair that bristled from one side of his countenance, invited some wags to make merry at his expence: one of them clapped a furze-bush under the tail of Gilbert, who, feeling himself thus stimulated *a posteriori*,[44] kicked and plunged and capered in such a manner, that Timothy could hardly keep the saddle. In this commotion he lost his cap and his periwig, while the rabble pelted him in such a manner, that, before he could join his master, he looked like a pillar, or rather a pillory, of mud.[45]

CHAPTER X.

Which sheweth that he who plays at bowls,
will sometimes meet with rubbers.[1]

Sir Launcelot, boiling with indignation at the venality and faction of the electors, whom he had harrangued to so little purpose, retired with the most deliberate disdain towards one of the gates of the town,[2] on the outside of which his curiosity was attracted by a concourse of people, in the midst of whom stood Mr. Ferret, mounted upon a stool, with a kind of satchel hanging round his neck, and a vial displayed in his right hand, while he held forth to the audience in a very vehement strain of elocution.[3]

Crabshaw thought himself happily delivered, when he reached the suburbs, and proceeded without halting; but his master mingled with the crowd, and heard the orator express himself to this effect: "Very likely, you may under-value me and my medicine, because I don't appear upon a stage of rotten boards, in a shabby velvet coat and tye-periwig,[4] with a foolish fellow in mot-ley,[5] to make you laugh by making wry faces: but I scorn to use these dirty arts for engaging your attention. These paultry tricks, *ad captandum vulgus*,[6] can have no effect but on ideots, and if you are ideots, I don't desire you should be my customers. Take notice, I don't address you in the stile of a mountebank, or a high German doctor;[7] and yet the kingdom is full of mountebanks, em-pirics, and quacks. We have quacks in religion, quacks in physic, quacks in law, quacks in politics, quacks in patriotism, quacks in government;[8] high German quacks that have blistered, sweated, bled, and purged the nation into an atro-phy. But this is not all: they have not only evacuated her into a consumption, but they have intoxicated her brain, until she is become delirious: she can no longer pursue her own interest; or, indeed, rightly distinguish it: like the people of Nineveh, she can hardly tell her right hand from her left;[9] but, as a changeling, is dazzled and delighted by an *ignis fatuus*, a Will o' the wisp,[10] an exhalation from the vilest materials in nature, that leads her astray through Westphalian bogs and deserts, and will one day break her neck over some barren rock, or leave her sticking in some H——n pit[11] or quagmire. For my part, if you have a mind to betray your country, I have no objection. In selling yourselves and your fellow-citizens, you only dispose of a pack of rascals who deserve to be sold—If you sell one another, why should not I sell this here Elixir of Long Life,[12] which if properly used, will protract your days till you shall have seen your country ruined? I shall not pretend to disturb your un-derstandings, which are none of the strongest, with a hotch-potch of unintel-ligible terms, such as Aristotle's four principles of generation, unformed mat-ter, privation, efficient and final causes.[13] Aristotle was a pedantic blockhead, and still more knave than fool. The same censure we may safely put on that wise-acre Dioscorides, with his faculties of simples, his seminal, specific, and principal virtues;[14] and that crazy commentator Galen, with his four elements, elementary qualities, his eight complexions, his harmonies, and discords.[15] Nor shall I expatiate on the alkahest of that mad scoundrel Paracelsus, with which he pretended to reduce flints into salt;[16] nor the *archæus* or *spiritus rector* of that visionary Van Helmont, his simple, elementary water, his *gas*, fer-ments, and transmutations;[17] nor shall I enlarge upon the salt, sulphur, and oil, the *acidum vagum*, the mercury of metals, and the volatilized vitriol of other modern chymists,[18] a pack of ignorant, conceited, knavish rascals, that puzzle your weak heads with such jargon, just as a Germanized m——r[19] throws dust in your eyes, by lugging in and ringing the changes on the balance of power, the protestant religion, and your allies on the continent; acting like the juggler[20] who picks your pockets, while he dazzles your eyes[21] and amuses your fancy with twirling his fingers, and reciting the gibberish of *hocus pocus;* for, in fact, the balance of power is a meer chimera;[22] as for the protestant religion, no body gives himself any trouble about it; and allies on the continent[23] we have none; or at least, none that would raise an hundred men to save us from perdition, unless we paid an extravagant price for their assistance. But, to return to this here Elixir of Long Life, I might embellish it with a great many high-sounding epithets; but I disdain to follow the example of every illiterate vagabond, that from idleness turns quack, and advertises his nostrum in the public papers. I am neither a felonious dry-salter returned from exile,[24] an hospital stump-turner,[25] a decayed stay-maker,[26] a bankrupt-printer,[27] or insolvent debtor, released by act of parliament.[28] I did not pretend to administer medicines, without the least tincture of letters, or suborn wretches to perjure themselves in false affidavits of cures that were never performed; nor employ a set of led-captains[29] to harrangue in my praise, at all public places. I was bred regularly to the profession of chymistry, and have tried all the processes of alchemy, and I may venture to say, that this here Elixir is, in fact, the *chrusion pepuromenon ek puros,*[30] the visible, glorious, spiritual body, from whence all other beings derive their existence, as proceeding from their father the sun, and their mother the moon; from the sun, as from a living and spiritual gold, which is meer fire; consequently, the common and universal first created mover,[31] from whence all moveable things have their distinct and particular motions; and also from the moon, as from the wife of the sun, and the common mother of all sublunary things: and for as much as man is, and must be the comprehensive end of all creatures, and the microcosm, he is counselled in the Revelations,[32] to buy gold that is thoroughly fired, or rather pure fire,[33] that he may become rich and like the sun; as on the contrary, he becomes poor, when he abuses the arsenical poison; so that his silver, by the fire, must be calcined to a *caput mortuum,*[34] which happens, when he will hold and retain the menstruum[35] out of which he partly exists, for his own property, and doth not daily offer up the same in the fire of the sun, that the woman may be cloathed with the sun,[36] and become a sun, and thereby rule over the moon; that is to say, that he may get the moon under his feet.—Now this here Elixir, sold for no more than six-pence a vial, contains the essence of the alkahest, the archæus, the catholicon,[37] the menstruum, the sun, moon, and to sum up all in one word, is the true, genuine, unadulterated, unchangeable, immaculate and specific *chrusion pepuromenon ek puros.*"

The audience were variously affected by this learned oration: some of those who favoured the pretensions of the whig candidate, were of opinion that he ought to be punished for his presumption in reflecting so scurrilously on ministers and measures. Of this sentiment was our adventurer, though he could not help admiring the courage of the orator, and owning within himself, that he had mixed some melancholy truths with his scurrility. Mr. Ferret would not have stood so long in his rostrum unmolested, had not he cunningly chosen his station immediately without the jurisdiction of the town, whose magistrates therefore could not take cognizance of his conduct; but, application was made to the constable of the other parish, while our nostrum-monger proceeded in his speech, the conclusion of which produced such an effect upon his hearers, that his whole cargo was immediately exhausted. He had just stepped down from his stool, when the constable, with his staff, arrived, and took him under his guidance. Mr. Ferret, on this occasion, attempted to interest the people in his behalf, by exhorting them to vindicate the liberty of the subject, against such an act of oppression; but finding them deaf to the tropes and figures of his elocution, he addressed himself to our knight, reminding him of his duty to protect the helpless and the injured, and earnestly soliciting his interposition.

Sir Launcelot, without making the least reply to his intreaties, resolved to see the end of this adventure; and being joined by his squire, followed the prisoner at a distance, measuring back the ground he had travelled the day before, until he reached another small borough,[38] where Ferret was housed in the common prison. While he sat a-horseback, deliberating on the next step he should take, he was accosted by the voice of Tom Clarke, who called in a whimpering tone, through a window grated with iron, "For the love of God! Sir Launcelot, do, dear Sir, be so good as to take the trouble to alight and come up stairs—I have something to communicate of consequence to the community in general, and you in particular—Pray, do, dear Sir Knight. I beg a boon in the name of St. Michael and St. George for England."

Our adventurer, not a little surprized at this address, dismounted without hesitation, and being admitted to the common jail, there found not only his old friend Tom, but also the uncle, sitting on a bench with an woolen nightcap on his head, and a pair of spectacles on his nose, reading very earnestly in a book, which he afterwards understood was intituled, "The Life and Adventures of Valentine and Orson."[39] The captain no sooner saw his great pattern enter, than he rose and received him with the salutation of "What cheer, brother?" and before the knight could answer, added these words: "You see how the land lies—here have Tom and I been fast a-shore these four and twenty hours; and this berth we have got by attempting to tow your galley, brother, from the enemy's harbour.—Adds bobs! [40] if we had this here fellow whoreson for a consort, with all our tackle in order, brother, we'd soon shew 'em the topsail, slip our cable, and down with their barricadoes. But, howsomever, it don't signify talking,—patience is a good stream-anchor, and will hold,[41] as the saying is,—but, damn my—as for the matter of my boltsprit.[42]— Hearkye, hearkye, brother, damn'd hard to engage with three at a time, one upon my bow, one upon my quarter, and one right a-head, rubbing, and drubbing, lying athwart hawse,[43] raking fore and aft, battering and grappling, and lashing and clashing—adds heart, brother; crash went the boltsprit—down came the round-top—up with the dead lights[44]—I saw nothing but the stars at noon, lost the helm of my seven senses,[45] and down I broached upon my broadside—."[46]

As Mr. Clarke rightly conceived that his uncle would need an interpreter, he began to explain these hints by giving a circumstantial detail of his own and the captain's disaster. He told Sir Launcelot, that notwithstanding all his persuasion and remonstrances, captain Crowe insisted upon appearing in the character of a knight errant; and with that view had set out from the public-house on the morning that succeeded his vigil in the church: that upon the high-way they had met with a coach, containing two ladies, one of whom seemed to be under great agitation; for, as they passed she struggled with the other, thrust out her head at the window, and said something which he could not distinctly hear; that captain Crowe was struck with admiration of her unequalled beauty; and he, (Tom) no sooner informed him who she was, than he resolved to set her at liberty, on the supposition that she was under restraint and in distress: that he accordingly unsheathed his cutlass, and riding back after the coach, commanded the driver to bring to, on pain of death: that one of the servants believing the captain to be an highwayman, presented a blunderbuss, and in all probability would have shot him on the spot, had not he (the nephew) rode up and assured them the gentleman was *non compos:* [47] that notwithstanding his intimation, all the three attacked him with the butt ends of their horse-whips, while the coach drove on, and although he laid about him with great fury, at last brought him to the ground by a stroke on the temple: that Mr. Clarke himself then interposed in defence of his kinsman, and was also severely beaten: that two of the servants, upon application to a justice of the peace, residing near the field of battle, had granted a warrant against the captain and his nephew, and without examination, committed them as idle vagrants, after having seized their horses and their money, on pretence of their being suspected for highwaymen. "But, as there was no just cause of suspicion, (added he) I am of opinion, the justice is guilty of a trespass, and may be sued for *falsum imprisonamentum*,[48] and considerable damages obtained; for, you will please to observe, Sir, no justice has a right to commit any person 'till after due examination; besides, we were not committed for an assault and battery, *auditâ querela*,[49] nor as wandering lunatics by the statute, who, to be sure, may be apprehended by a justice's warrant, and locked up and chained, if necessary, or be sent to their last legal settlement:[50] but, we were committed as vagrants, and suspected highwaymen. Now we do not fall under the description of vagrants; nor did any circumstance appear to support the suspicion of robbery; for to constitute robbery, there must be something taken; but, here nothing was taken but blows, and they were upon compulsion: even an attempt to rob, without any taking, is not felony, but a misdemeanour. To be sure there is a taking in deed, and a taking in law: but still the robber must be in possession of a thing stolen;[51] and we attempted to steal nothing, but to steal ourselves away—My uncle indeed, would have released the young lady *vi et armis*,[52] had his strength been equal to his inclination; and in so doing, I would have willingly lent my assistance, both from a desire to serve such a beautiful young creature, and also in regard to your honour, for I thought I heard her call upon your name."——

"Ha! how! what! whose name? say, speak—heaven and earth!" (cried the Knight, with marks of the most violent emotion). Clarke terrified at his looks, replied, "I beg your pardon a thousand times; I did not say positively she did speak those words: but, I apprehended she did speak them. Words, which may be taken or interpreted by law in a general, or common sense, ought not to receive a strained, or unusual construction; and ambiguous words——"[53] "Speak, or be dumb for ever! (exclaimed Sir Launcelot in a terrific tone, laying his hand on his sword) what young lady, ha! What name did she call upon?" Clarke falling on his knees, answered, not without stammering, "Miss Aurelia Darnel; to the best of my recollection, she called upon Sir Launcelot Greaves." "Sacred powers! (cried our adventurer) which way did the carriage proceed?"

When Tom told him that the coach quitted the post-road, and struck away to the right, at full speed, Sir Launcelot was seized with a pensive fit; his head sunk upon his breast, and he mused in silence for several minutes, with the most melancholy expression on his countenance: then recollecting himself, he assumed a more composed and chearful air, and asked several questions, with respect to the arms on the coach, and the liveries worn by the servants. It was in the course of this interrogation, that he discovered he had actually conversed with one of the foot-men, who had brought back Crabshaw's horse: a circumstance that filled him with anxiety and chagrin, as he had omitted to inquire the name of his master, and the place to which the coach was travelling; though, in all probability, had he made these inquiries, he would have received very little satisfaction, there being reason to think the servants were enjoined secrecy. The knight, in order to meditate on this unexpected adventure, sat down by his old friend, and entered into a reverie, which lasted about a quarter of an hour, and might have continued longer, had it not been interrupted by the voice of Crabshaw, who bawled aloud, "Look to it, my masters—as you brew you must drink[54]—this shall be a dear day's work[55] to some of you, for my part I say nothing—the braying ass eats little grass—one barber shaves not so close, but another finds a few stubble—you wanted to catch a capon, and you've stole a cat. He that takes up his lodgings in a stable, must be contented to lie upon litter.—"[56]

The knight, desirous of knowing the cause that prompted Timothy to apothegmatize in this manner, looked through the grate, and perceived the squire fairly set in the stocks, surrounded by a mob of people. When he called to him, and asked the reason of this disgraceful restraint, Crabshaw replied, "There's no cake, but there's another of the same make—who never climbed never fell—after clouds comes clear weather.[57] 'Tis all long of your honour I've met with this preferment; no deservings of my own, but the interest of my master. Sir knight, if you will flay the justice, hang the constable, release your squire, and burn the town, your name will be famous in story: but, if you are content, I am thankful. Two hours are soon spent in such good company; in the mean time look to'un jailor, there's a frog in the stocks."[58]

Sir Launcelot, incensed at this affront offered to his servant, advanced to the prison-door, but found it fast locked, and when he called to the turnkey, he was given to understand that he himself was prisoner. Enraged at this intimation, he demanded at whose suit; and was answered through the wicket, "At the suit of the king, in whose name I will hold you fast, with God's assistance."

The knight's looks now began to lighten, he rolled his eyes around, and snatching up an oaken bench, which three ordinary men could scarce have lifted from the ground,[59] he, in all likelihood, would have shattered the door in pieces, had not he been restrained by the interposition of Mr. Clarke, who intreated him to have a little patience, assuring him he would suggest a plan that would avenge him amply on the justice, without any breach of the peace. "I say, the justice (added Tom) because it must be his doing.—He is a little petulant sort of a fellow, ignorant of the law, guilty of numberless irregularities; and if properly managed, may for this here act of arbitrary power, be not only cast in a swinging sum,[60] but even turned out of the commission with disgrace.—"

This was a very seasonable hint, in consequence of which, the bench was softly replaced, and captain Crowe deposited the poker, with which he had armed himself to second the efforts of Sir Launcelot. They now, for the first time, perceived that Ferret had disappeared; and, upon inquiry, found that he was in fact the occasion of the knight's detention and the squire's disgrace.

CHAPTER XI.

Description of a modern Magistrate.

Before the knight would take any resolution for extricating himself from his present embarrassment, he desired to be better acquainted with the character and circumstances of the justice by whom he had been confined, and likewise to understand the meaning of his own detention. To be informed in this last particular, he renewed his dialogue with the turnkey, who told him, through the grate, that Ferret no sooner perceived him in the jail, without his offensive arms, which he had left below, than he desired to be carried before the justice, where he had given information against the knight, as a violator of the public peace, who strolled about the country with unlawful arms, rendering the highways unsafe, encroaching upon the freedom of elections, putting his majesty's liege subjects in fear of their lives, and, in all probability, harbouring more dangerous designs under an affected cloak of lunacy. Ferret, upon this information, had been released, and entertained as an evidence for the king; and Crabshaw was put in the stocks, as an idle stroller.[1]

Sir Launcelot, being satisfied in these particulars, addressed himself to his fellow-prisoners, and begged they would communicate what they knew respecting the worthy magistrate, who had been so premature in the execution of his office. This request was no sooner signified than a crew of naked wretches crowded around him, and, like a congregation of rooks, opened their throats all at once, in accusation of justice Gobble.[2] The knight was moved at this scene, which he could not help comparing, in his own mind, to what would appear upon a much more awful occasion, when the cries of the widow and the orphan, the injured and oppressed, would be uttered at the tribunal of an unerring Judge against the villainous and insolent authors of their calamity.

When he had, with some difficulty, quieted their clamours, and confined his interrogation to one person of a tolerably decent appearance, he learned that justice Gobble, whose father was a taylor, had for some time served as a journeyman hosier in London, where he had picked up some law-terms, by conversing with hackney-writers and attorneys' clerks of the lowest order; that, upon the death of his master, he had insinuated himself into the good graces of the widow, who took him for her husband, so that he became a person of some consideration, and saved money apace; that his pride, increasing with his substance, was reinforced by the vanity of his wife, who persuaded him to retire from business, that they might live genteelly in the country; that his father dying, and leaving a couple of houses in this town, Mr. Gobble had come down with his lady to take possession, and liked the place so well as to make a more considerable purchase in the neighbourhood; that a certain peer[3] being indebted to him a large sum in the way of his business, and either unwilling or unable to pay the money, had compounded the debt, by inserting his name in the commission; since which period his own insolence, and his wife's ostentation, had exceeded all bounds: that, in the exertion of his authority, he had committed a thousand acts of cruelty and injustice against the poorer sort of people, who were unable to call him to a proper account: that his wife domineered with a more ridiculous, though less pernicious usurpation, among the females of the place: that, in a word, she was the subject of continual mirth, and he the object of universal detestation. Our adventurer, though extremely well disposed to believe what was said to the prejudice of Gobble, would not give intire credit to this description, without first inquiring into the particulars of his conduct. He therefore asked the speaker, what was the cause of his particular complaint. "For my own part, Sir, (said he) I lived in repute, and kept a shop in this here town, well furnished with a great variety of articles. All the people in the place were my customers; but what I and many others chiefly depended upon, was the extraordinary sale at two annual customary fairs, to which all the country people in the neighbourhood resorted to lay out their money. I had employed all my stock, and even engaged my credit to procure a large assortment of goods for the Lammas-market:[4] but having given my vote, in the election of a vestry-clerk,[5] contrary to the interest of justice Gobble, he resolved to work my ruin. He suppressed the annual fairs, by which a great many people, especially publicans, earned the best part of their subsistence. The country people resorted to another town. I was overstocked with a load of perishable commodities; and found myself deprived of the best part of my home customers by the ill-nature and revenge of the justice, who employed all his influence among the common people, making use of threats and promises, to make them desert my shop, and give their custom to another person, whom he settled in the same business under my nose. Being thus disabled from making punctual payments, my commodities spoiling, and my wife breaking her heart, I grew negligent and careless, took to drinking, and my affairs went to wreck. Being one day in liquor, and provoked by the fleers and taunts of the man who had set up against me, I struck him at his own door; upon which I was carried before the justice, who treated me with such insolence, that I became desperate, and not only abused him in the execution of his office, but also made an attempt to lay violent hands upon his person.[6] You know, Sir, when a man is both drunk and desperate, he cannot be supposed to have any command of himself. I was sent hither to jail. My creditors immediately seized my effects; and, as they were not sufficient to discharge my debts, a statute of bankruptcy[7] was taken out against me: so that here I must lie, until they think proper to sign my certificate,[8] or the parliament shall please to pass an act for the relief of insolvent debtors."[9]

The next person who presented himself in the croud of accusers was a meagre figure, with a green apron, who told the knight that he had kept a public house in town for a dozen years, and enjoyed a good trade, which was in a great measure owing to a skittle-ground,[10] in which the best people of the place diverted themselves occasionally: that justice Gobble, being disobliged at his refusing to part with a gelding which he had bred for his own use, first of all shut up the skittle-ground; but finding the publican still kept his house open, he took care that he should be deprived of his licence,[11] on pretence that the number of ale-houses was too great, and that this man had been bred to another employment. The poor publican, being thus deprived of his bread, was obliged to try the stay-making business, to which he had served an apprenticeship: but being very ill-qualified for this profession, he soon fell to decay, and contracted debts, in consequence of which he was now in prison, where he had no other support but what arose from the labour of his wife, who had gone to service.

The next prisoner who preferred his complaint against the unrighteous judge was a poacher, at whose practices justice Gobble had for some years connived, so as even to screen him from punishment, in consideration of being supplied with game gratis, till at length he was disappointed by accident. His lady had invited guests to an entertainment, and bespoke a hare, which the poacher undertook to furnish. He laid his snares accordingly over night; but they were discovered, and taken away by the game-keeper of the gentleman to whom the ground belonged. All the excuses the poacher could make, proved ineffectual in appeasing the resentment of the justice and his wife, at being thus disconcerted. Measures were taken to detect the delinquent in the exercise of his illicit occupation: he was committed to safe custody; and his wife, with five bantlings,[12] was passed to her husband's settlement[13] in a different part of the country.

A stout squat fellow, rattling with chains, had just taken up the ball of accusation, when Sir Launcelot was startled with the appearance of a woman, whose looks and equipage indicated the most piteous distress. She seemed to be turned of the middle age, was of a lofty carriage, tall, thin, weather-beaten, and wretchedly attired: her eyes were inflamed with weeping, and her looks displayed that wildness and peculiarity which denote distraction. Advancing to Sir Launcelot, she fell upon her knees, and clasping her hands together, uttered the following rhapsody in the most vehement tone of affliction:

"Thrice potent, generous, and august emperor, here let my knees cleave to the earth, until thou shalt do me justice on that inhuman caitiff Gobble. Let him disgorge my substance which he hath devoured: let him restore to my widowed arms my child, my boy, the delight of my eyes, the prop of my life, the staff of my sustenance, whom he hath torn from my embrace, stolen, betrayed, sent into captivity, and murdered!—Behold these bleeding wounds upon his lovely breast! see how they mangle his lifeless coarse! Horrour! give me my child, barbarians! his head shall lie upon his Suky's bosom—she will embalm him with her tears.—Ha! plunge him in the deep! shall my boy then float in a watry tomb!—Justice, most mighty emperor! justice upon the villain who hath ruined us all!——May heaven's dreadful vengeance overtake him! may the keen storm of adversity strip him of all his leaves and fruit! may peace forsake his mind, and rest be banished from his pillow, so that all his days shall be filled with reproach and sorrow; and all his nights be haunted with horrour and remorse! may he be stung by jealousy without cause, and maddened by revenge without the means of execution! may all his offspring be blighted and consumed, like the mildewed ears of corn, except one that shall grow up to curse his old age, and bring his hoary head with sorrow to the grave, as he himself has proved a curse to me and mine!"

The rest of the prisoners, perceiving the knight extremely shocked at her misery and horrid imprecation, removed her by force from his presence, and conveyed her to another room; while our adventurer underwent a violent agitation, and could not for some minutes compose himself so well as to inquire into the nature of this wretched creature's calamity. The shop-keeper, of whom he demanded this satisfaction, gave him to understand that she was born a gentlewoman, and had been well educated: that she married a curate, who did not long survive his nuptials; and afterwards became the wife of one Oakley, a farmer, in opulent circumstances: that, after twenty years cohabitation with her husband, he sustained such losses by the distemper among the cattle, as he could not repair; and that this reverse of fortune was supposed to have hastened his death: that the widow, being a woman of spirit, determined to keep up and manage the farm, with the assistance of an only son, a very promising youth, who was already contracted in marriage with the daughter of another wealthy farmer. Thus the mother had a fair prospect of retrieving the affairs of her family, when all her hopes were dashed and destroyed by a ridiculous pique which Mrs. Gobble conceived against the young farmer's sweet-heart, Mrs. Susan Sedgemoor. This young woman chancing to be at a country assembly, where the grave-digger of the parish acted as master of the ceremonies, was called out to dance before miss Gobble, who happened to be there present also with her mother. The circumstance was construed into an unpardonable affront by the justice's lady, who abused the director, in the most opprobrious terms, for his insolence and ill-manners; and, retiring in a storm of passion, vowed revenge against the saucy minx who had presumed to vie in gentility with miss Gobble. The justice entered into her resentment. The grave-digger lost his place; and Suky's lover, young Oakely, was pressed for a soldier.[14] Before his mother could take any steps for his discharge, he was hurried away to the East Indies, by the industry and contrivance of the justice. Poor Suky wept and pined until she fell into a consumption. The forlorn widow, being thus deprived of her son, was overwhelmed with grief to such a degree, that she could no longer manage her concerns. Every thing went backward: she ran in arrears with her landlord, and the prospect of bankruptcy aggravated her affliction, while it added to her incapacity. In the midst of these disastrous circumstances, news arrived that her son Greaves had lost his life in a sea-engagement with the enemy; and these tidings almost instantly deprived her of her reason. Then the landlord seized for his rent; and she was arrested at the suit of justice Gobble, who had bought up one of her debts, in order to distress her, and now pretended that her madness was feigned.

When the name of Greaves was mentioned our adventurer started, and changed colour; and, now the story was ended, asked, with marks of eager emotion, if the name of the woman's first husband was not Wilford. When the prisoner answered in the affirmative, he rose up, and striking his breast, "Good heaven! (cried he) the very woman who watched over my infancy, and even nourished me with her milk![15]—She was my mother's humble friend.— Alas! poor Dorothy! how would your old mistress grieve to see her favourite in this miserable condition!" While he pronounced these words, to the astonishment of the hearers, a tear stole softly down each cheek. Then he desired to know if the poor lunatic had any intervals of reason; and was given to understand, that she was always quiet, and generally supposed to have the use of her senses, except when she was disturbed by some extraordinary noise, or when any person touched upon her misfortune, or mentioned the name of her oppressor, in all which cases she started out into extravagance and frenzy. They likewise imputed great part of her disorder to the want of quiet, proper food, and necessaries, with which she was but poorly supplied by the cold hand of chance charity. Our adventurer was exceedingly affected by the distress of this woman, whom he resolved to relieve; and in proportion as his commiseration was excited, his resentment rose against the miscreant, who seemed to have insinuated himself into the commission of the peace on purpose to harrass and oppress his fellow-creatures. Thus animated, he entered into consultation with Mr. Thomas Clarke concerning the steps he should take, first for their deliverance, and then for prosecuting and punishing the justice. In result of this conference, the knight called aloud for the jaylor, and demanded to see a copy of his commitment, that he might know the cause of his imprisonment, and offer bail; or, in case that should be refused, move for a writ of Habeas Corpus.[16] The jaylor told him the copy of the writ should be forthcoming; but after he had waited some time, and repeated the demand before witnesses, it was not yet produced. Mr. Clarke then, in a solemn tone, gave the jaylor to understand, that an officer, refusing to deliver a true copy of the commitment warrant, was liable to the forfeiture of one hundred pounds for the first offence; and for the second to a forfeiture of twice that sum, besides being disabled from executing his office.

Indeed, it was no easy matter to comply with Sir Launcelot's demand; for no warrant had been granted, nor was it now in the power of the justice to remedy this defect, as Mr. Ferret had taken himself away privately, without having communicated the name and designation of the prisoner. A circumstance the more mortifying to the jaylor, as he perceived the extraordinary respect which Mr. Clarke and the captain payed to the knight, and was now fully convinced that he would be dealt with according to law. Disordered with these reflections, he imparted them to the justice, who had in vain caused search to be made for Ferret, and was now extremely well inclined to set the knight and his friends at liberty, though he did not at all suspect the quality and importance of our adventurer. He could not, however, resist the temptation of displaying the authority of his office; and therefore ordered the prisoners to be brought before his tribunal, that, in the capacity of a magistrate, he might give them a severe reproof, and proper caution, with regard to their future behaviour.

They were accordingly led thro' the street in procession, guarded by the constable and his gang, followed by Crabshaw, who had by this time been released from the stocks, and surrounded by a croud of people, attracted by curiosity. When they arrived at the justice's house, they were detained for some time in the passage: then a voice was heard, commanding the constable to bring in the prisoners, and they were introduced to the hall of audience, where Mr. Gobble sat in judgment, with a crimson velvet night-cap on his head; and on his right hand appeared his lady, puffed up with the pride and insolence of her husband's office, fat, frowzy, and not over-clean, well stricken in years, without the least vestige of an agreeable feature, having a rubicond nose, ferret eyes, and imperious aspect. The justice himself was a little, affected, pert prig, who endeavoured to solemnize his countenance by assuming an air of consequence, in which pride, impudence, and folly were strangely blended. He aspired at nothing so much as the character of an able spokesman; and took all opportunities of holding forth at vestry and quarter-sessions,[17] as well as in the administration of his office in private. He would not, therefore, let slip this occasion of exciting the admiration of his hearers, and, in an authoritative tone, thus addressed our adventurer:

"The laws of this land has provided—I says, as how provision is made by the laws of this here land, in reverence to delinquems and manefactors, whereby the king's peace is upholden by we magistrates, who represents his majesty's person, better than in e'er a contagious nation under the sun: but, howsoemever, that there king's peace, and this here magistrate's authority, cannot be adequably and identically upheld, if so be as how criminals escapes unpunished. Now, friend, you must be confidentious in your own mind, as you are a notorious criminal, who have trespassed again the laws on divers occasions and importunities; if I had a mind to exercise the rigour of the law, according to the authority wherewith I am wested, you and your companions in iniquity would be sewerely punished by the statue: but we magistrates has a power to litigate the sewerity of justice, and so I am contented that you shoulds be mercifully dealt withal, and even dismissed."

To this harangue the knight replied, with solemn and deliberate accent, "If I understand your meaning aright, I am accused of being a notorious criminal; but nevertheless you are contented to let me escape with impunity. If I am a notorious criminal, it is the duty of you, as a magistrate, to bring me to condign punishment; and if you allow a criminal to escape unpunished, you are not only unworthy of a place in the commission, but become accessory to his guilt, and, to all intents and purposes, *socius criminis*.[18] With respect to your proffered mercy, I shall decline the favour; nor do I deserve any indulgence at your hands: for, depend upon it, I shall shew no mercy to you, in the steps I intend to take for bringing you to justice. I understand that you have been long hackneyed in the ways of oppression, and I have seen some living monuments of your inhumanity—of that hereafter. I myself have been detained in prison, without cause assigned. I have been treated with indignity, and insulted by jaylors and constables, led thro' the streets like a felon, as a spectacle to the multitude, obliged to dance attendance in your passage, and afterwards branded with the name of a notorious criminal.—I now demand to see the information in consequence of which I was detained in prison, the copy of the warrant of commitment or detainer, and the face of the person by whom I was accused. I insist upon a compliance with these demands, as the privileges of a British subject; and if it is refused, I shall seek redress before a higher tribunal."

The justice seemed to be not a little disturbed at this peremptory declaration; which, however, had no other effect upon his wife, but that of enraging her choler and inflaming her countenance. "Sirrah! sirrah! (cried she) do you dares to insult a worshipful magistrate on the bench?—Can you deny that you are a vagram, and a dilatory sort of a person? Han't the man with the satchel made an affidavy of it?—If I was my husband, I'd lay you fast by the heels for your resumption, and ferk you with a primineery[19] into the bargain, unless you could give a better account of yourself—I would."

Gobble, encouraged by this fillip, resumed his petulance, and proceeded in this manner:—"Heark ye, friend, I might, as Mrs. Gobble very justly observes, trounce you for your audacious behaviour; but I scorn to take such advantages: howsomever, I shall make you give an account of yourself and your companions; for I believes as how you are all in a gang, and all in a story, and perhaps you may be found one day all in a cord.—What are you, friend? What is your station and degree?" "I am a gentleman," replied the knight. "Ay, that is English for a sorry fellow (said the justice). Every idle vagabond, who has neither home nor habitation, trade nor profession, designs himself a gentleman. But I must know how you live?" "Upon my means." "What are your means?" "My estate." "Whence doth it arise?" "From inheritance." "Your estate lies in brass, and that you have inherited from nature: but do you inherit lands and tenements?" "Yes." "But they are neither here nor there, I doubt.—Come, come, friend, I shall bring you about presently." Here the examination was interrupted by the arrival of Mr. Fillet the surgeon, who chancing to pass, and seeing a croud about the door, went in to satisfy his curiosity.

CHAPTER XII.

Which shews there are more ways to kill a dog than hanging.[1]

Mr. Fillet no sooner appeared in the judgment-chamber of justice Gobble than captain Crowe, seizing him by the hand, exclaimed, "Body o'me! Doctor, thou'rt come up in the nick of time to lend us a hand in putting about.—We're a little in the stays[2] here—but howsomever we've got a good pilot, who knows the coast, and can weather the point,[3] as the saying is. As for the enemy's vessel, she has had a shot or two already a-thwart her fore-foot:[4] the next, I do suppose, will strike the hull, and then you'll see her taken all a-back."[5] The doctor, who perfectly understood his dialect, assured him he might depend upon his assistance; and advancing to the knight, accosted him in these words: "Sir Launcelot Greaves, your most humble servant.—When I saw a croud at the door, I little thought of finding you within, treated with such indignity.—Yet, I can't help being pleased with an opportunity of proving the esteem and veneration I have for your person and character:—you will do me a particular pleasure in commanding my best services."

Our adventurer thanked him for this instance of his friendship, which he told him he would use without hesitation; and desired he would procure immediate bail for him and his two friends, who had been imprisoned, contrary to law, without any cause assigned. During this short dialogue, the justice, who had heard of Sir Launcelot's family and fortune, though an utter stranger to his person, was seized with such pangs of terror and compunction, as a groveling mind may be supposed to have felt in such circumstances; and they seemed to produce the same unsavoury effects that are so humorously delineated by the inimitable Hogarth in the print of Felix on his tribunal, done in the Dutch stile.[6] Nevertheless, seeing Fillet retire to execute the knight's commands, he recollected himself so far as to tell the prisoners there was no occasion to give themselves any further trouble; for he would release them without bail or main-prize.[7] Then discarding all the insolence from his features, and assuming an aspect of the most humble adulation, he begged the knight ten thousand pardons for the freedoms he had taken, which were intirely owing to his ignorance of Sir Launcelot's quality. "Yes, I'll assure you, Sir (said the wife), my husband would have bit off his tongue, rather than say black is the white of your eye,[8] if so be he had known your capacity.—Thank God, we have been used to deal with gentlefolks, and many's the good pound we have lost by them; but what of that? Sure we know how to behave to our betters. Mr. Gobble, thanks be to God, can defy the whole world to prove that he ever said an uncivil word, or did a rude thing to a gentleman, knowing him to be a person of fortune. Indeed, as to your poor gentry and riff-raff, your tag, rag, and bobtail,[9] or such vulgar scoundrelly people, he has always behaved like a magistrate, and treated them with the rigger of authority." "In other words (said the knight), he has tyrannized over the poor, and connived at the vices of the rich: your husband is little obliged to you for this confession, woman." "Woman! (cried Mrs. Gobble, impurpled with wrath, and fixing her hands on her sides by way of defiance) I scorn your words—Marry come up,[10] woman! quotha:[11] no more a woman than your worship." Then bursting into tears, "Husband (continued she), if you had the soul of a louse, you would not suffer me to be abused at this rate: you would not sit still on the bench, and hear your spouse called such contemptible epitaphs.—Who cares for his title and his knightship? You and I, husband, knew a taylor that was made a knight:[12] but, thank God, I have noblemen to stand by me, with their privilegs and beroguetifs."

At this instant Mr. Fillet returned with his friend, a practitioner in the law, who freely offered to join in bailing our adventurer, and the other two prisoners, for any sum that should be required. The justice, perceiving the affair began to grow more and more serious, declared that he would discharge the warrants, and dismiss the prisoners. Here Mr. Clarke interposing, observed, that against the knight no warrant had been granted, nor any information sworn to; consequently, as the justice had not complied with the form of proceeding directed by statute, the imprisonment was *coram non judice*, and void.[13] "Right, Sir (said the other lawyer), if a justice commits a felon for trial, without binding over the prosecutor to the assizes, he shall be fined."[14]——"And again (cried Clarke), if a justice issues a warrant for commitment, where there is no accusation, action will lie against the justice." "Moreover (replied the stranger), if a justice of peace is guilty of any misdemeanour in his office, information[15] lies against him in *Banco Regis*,[16] where he shall be punished by fine and imprisonment." "And besides (resumed the accurate Tom), the same court will grant an information against a justice of peace, on motion, for sending even a servant to the house of correction, or common jail, without sufficient cause." "True! (exclaimed the other limb of the law) and, for contempt of law, attachment may be had against justices of peace in *Banco Regis*. A justice of peace was fined a thousand marks[17] for corrupt practices." With these words advancing to Mr. Clarke, he shook him by the hand, with the appellation of Brother, saying, "I doubt the justice has got into a cursed hovel."

Mr. Gobble himself seemed to be of the same opinion. He changed colour several times during the remarks which the lawyers had made; and now, declaring that the gentlemen were at liberty, begged, in the most humble phrase, that the company would eat a bit of mutton with him, and after dinner the affair might be amicably compromised. To this proposal our adventurer replied, in a grave and resolute tone, "If your acting in the commission as a justice of the peace concerned my own particular only, perhaps I should wave any further inquiry, and resent your insolence no other way but by silent contempt. If I thought the errors of your administration proceeded from a good intention, defeated by want of understanding, I should pity your ignorance, and, in compassion, advise you to desist from acting a part for which you are so ill qualified: but the preposterous conduct of such a man deeply affects the interest of the community, especially that part of it which, from its helpless situation, is the more intitled to our protection and assistance. I am moreover convinced, that your misconduct is not so much the consequence of an uninformed head, as the poisonous issue of a malignant heart, devoid of humanity, inflamed with pride, and rankling with revenge. The common prison of this little town is filled with the miserable objects of your cruelty and oppression. Instead of protecting the helpless, restraining the hands of violence, preserving the public tranquillity, and acting as a father to the poor, according to the intent and meaning of that institution of which you are an unworthy member, you have distressed the widow and the orphan, given a loose to all the insolence of office, embroiled your neighbours by fomenting suits and animosities, and played the tyrant among the indigent and forlorn. You have abused the authority with which you were invested, intailed a reproach upon your office, and, instead of being revered as a blessing, you are detested as a curse among your fellow-creatures. This, indeed, is generally the case of low fellows, who are thrust into the magistracy without sentiment, education, or capacity. Among other instances of your iniquity, there is now in prison an unhappy woman, infinitely your superior in the advantages of birth, sense, and education, whom you have, even without provocation, persecuted to ruin and distraction, after having illegally and inhumanly kidnapped her only child, and exposed him to violent death in a foreign land. Ah caitiff! if you were to forego all the comforts of life, distribute your means among the poor, and do the severest penance that ever priestcraft prescribed for the rest of your days, you could not attone for the ruin of that hapless family; a family through whose sides you cruelly and perfidiously stabbed the heart of an innocent young woman, to gratify the pride and diabolical malice of that wretched low-bred woman, who now sits at your right hand as the associate of your power and presumption. Oh! if such a despicable reptile shall annoy mankind with impunity, if such a contemptible miscreant shall have it in his power to do such deeds of inhumanity and oppression, what avails the law? Where is our admired constitution, the freedom, the security of the subject, the boasted humanity of the British nation? Sacred Heaven! if there was no human institution to take cognizance of such atrocious crimes, I would listen to the dictates of eternal Justice, and, arming myself with the right of nature, exterminate such villains from the face of the earth!"

These last words he pronounced in such a strain, while his eyes lightened with indignation, that Gobble and his wife underwent the most violent agitation; the constable's teeth chattered in his head, the jailer trembled, and the whole audience was overwhelmed with consternation.

After a short pause, Sir Launcelot proceeded in a milder strain: "Thank Heaven, the laws of this country have exempted me from the disagreeable task of such an execution. To them we shall have immediate recourse, in three separate actions against you for false imprisonment; and any other person who has been injured by your arbitrary and wicked proceedings, in me shall find a warm protector, until you shall be expunged from the commission with disgrace, and have made such retaliation as your circumstances will allow for the wrongs you have done the community."

In order to compleat the mortification and terror of the justice, the lawyer, whose name was Fenton, declared, that, to his certain knowledge, these actions would be reinforced with divers prosecutions for corrupt practices, which had lain dormant until some person of courage and influence should take the lead against justice Gobble, who was the more dreaded as he acted under the patronage of lord Sharpington. By this time fear had deprived the justice and his help-mate of the faculty of speech. They were indeed almost petrified with dismay, and made no effort to speak, when Mr. Fillet, in the rear of the knight, as he retired with his company, took his leave of them in these words:

"And now, Mr. Justice, to dinner with what appetite you may." [18] Our adventurer, though warmly invited to Mr. Fenton's house, repaired to a public inn, where he thought he should be more at his ease, fully determined to punish and depose Gobble from his magistracy, to effect a general jail-delivery of all the debtors whom he had found in confinement; and, in particular, to rescue poor Mrs. Oakely from the miserable circumstances in which she was involved.

In the mean time, he insisted upon entertaining his friends at dinner, during which many sallies of sea-wit and good-humour passed between captain

Crowe and doctor Fillet, which last had just returned from a neighbouring village, whither he was summoned to fish a man's yard-arm, which had snapt in the slings.[19] Their enjoyment, however, was suddenly interrupted by a loud scream from the kitchen, whither Sir Launcelot immediately sprung, with equal eagerness and agility. There he saw the landlady, who was a woman in years, embracing a man dressed in a sailor's jacket, while she exclaimed, "It is thy own flesh and blood, so sure as I'm a living soul.——Ah! poor Greaves, poor Greaves, many a poor heart has grieved for thee!" To this salutation the youth replied, "I'm sorry for that, mistress.—How does poor mother? how does Sukey Sedgemore?"

The good woman of the house could not help shedding tears at these interrogations; while Sir Launcelot, interposing, said, not without emotion, "I perceive you are the son of Mrs. Oakely.—Your mother is in a bad state of health; but in me you will find a real parent." Perceiving that the young man eyed him with astonishment, he gave him to understand, that his name was Launcelot Greaves.

Oakely no sooner heard these words pronounced, than he fell upon his knees, and seizing the knight's hand, kissed it eagerly, crying, "God for ever bless your honour: I am your name-son, sure enough—but what of that? I can earn my bread, without being beholden to any man."

When the knight raised him up, he turned to the woman of the house, saying, "I want to see mother. I'm afraid as how times are hard with her; and I have saved some money for her use." This instance of filial duty brought tears into the eyes of our adventurer, who assured him his mother should be carefully attended, and want for nothing: but that it would be very improper to see her at present, as the surprize might shock her too much, considering that she believed him dead. "Ey, indeed, (cried the landlady) we were all of the same opinion, being as the report went that poor Greaves Oakely was killed in battle." "Lord, mistress, (said Oakely) there wa'n't a word of truth in it, I'll assure you.—What, d'ye think I'd tell a lie about the matter? Hurt I was, to be sure; but that don't signify: we gave 'em as good as they brought, and so parted.—Well, if so be I can't see mother, I'll go and have some chat with Sukey.—What d'ye look so glum for? she an't married, is she?" "No, no, (replied the woman) not married; but almost heart-broken. Since thou wast gone, she has done nothing but sighed, and wept, and pined herself into a decay. I'm afraid thou ha'st come home too late to save her life."

Oakely's heart was not proof against this information. Bursting into tears, he exclaimed, "O my dear, sweet, gentle Sukey! Have I then lived to be the death of her whom I loved more than the whole world!" He would have gone instantly to her father's house; but was restrained by the knight and his company, who had now joined him in the kitchen. The young man was seated at table, and gave them to understand, that the ship to which he belonged having arrived in England, he was indulged with a month's leave to see his relations; and that he had received about fifty pounds in wages and prize-money.[20] After dinner, just as they began to deliberate upon the measures to be taken against Gobble, that gentleman arrived at the inn, and humbly craved admittance. Fillet, struck with a sudden idea, retired into another apartment with the young farmer; while the justice, being admitted to the company, declared that he came to propose terms of accommodation. He accordingly offered to ask pardon of Sir Launcelot in the public papers, and pay fifty pounds to the poor of the parish, as an attonement for his misbehaviour, provided the knight and his friends would grant him a general release. Our adventurer told him, he would willingly wave all personal concessions; but, as the case concerned the community, he insisted upon his leaving off acting in the commission, and making satisfaction to the parties he had injured and oppressed. This declaration introduced a discussion, in the course of which the justice's petulance began to revive; when Fillet, entering the room, told them he had a reconciling measure to propose, if Mr. Gobble would for a few minutes withdraw. He rose up immediately, and was shewn into the room which Fillet had prepared for his reception. While he sat musing on this untoward adventure, so big with disgrace and disappointment, young Oakely, according to the instructions he had received, appeared all at once before him, pointing to a ghastly wound, which the doctor had painted on his forehead. The apparition no sooner presented itself to the eyes of Gobble, than, taking it for granted it was the spirit of the young farmer[21] whose death he had occasioned, he roared aloud, "Lord have mercy upon us!" and fell insensible on the floor. There being found by the company, to whom Fillet had communicated his contrivance, he was conveyed to bed, where he lay some time before he recovered the perfect use of his senses. Then he earnestly desired to see the knight, and assured him he was ready to comply with his terms, inasmuch as he believed he had not long to live. Advantage was immediately taken of this salutary disposition. He bound himself not to act as a justice of the peace, in any part of Great Britain, under the penalty of five thousand pounds. He burned Mrs. Oakely's note; payed the debts of the shopkeeper; undertook to compound those of the publican, and to settle him again in business; and, finally, discharged them all from prison, paying the dues[22] out of his own pocket. These steps being taken with peculiar eagerness, he was removed to his own house, where he assured his wife he had seen a vision that prognosticated his death; and had immediate recourse to the curate of the parish for spiritual consolation.

The most interesting part of the task that now remained, was to make the widow Oakely acquainted with her good fortune, in such a manner as might least disturb her spirits, already but too much discomposed. For this purpose they chose the landlady, who, after having received proper directions how to regulate her conduct, visited her in prison that same evening. Finding her quite calm, and her reflection perfectly restored, she began with exhorting her to put her trust in Providence, which would never forsake the cause of the injured widow and fatherless: she promised to assist and befriend her on all occasions, as far as her abilities would reach: she gradually turned the conversation upon the family of the Greaves; and by degrees informed her, that Sir Launcelot, having learned her situation, was determined to extricate her from all her troubles. Perceiving her astonished, and deeply affected at this intimation, she artfully shifted the discourse, recommended resignation to the Divine Will, and observed that this circumstance seemed to be an earnest of further happiness. "O! I'm incapable of receiving more! (cried the disconsolate widow, with streaming eyes)—Yet I ought not to be surprised at any blessing that flows from that quarter.—The family of Greaves were always virtuous, humane, and benevolent.—This young gentleman's mother was my dear lady and benefactress:—he himself was suckled at these breasts.—O! he was the sweetest, comliest, best conditioned babe!—I loved not my own Greaves with greater affection—but he, alas! is now no more!" "Have patience, good neighbour, (said the landlady of the White Hart) that is more than you have any right to affirm.—All that you know of the matter is by common report, and common report is commonly false: besides, I can tell you I have seen a list of the men that were killed in admiral P——'s ship,[23] when he fought the French in the East Indies, and your son was not in the number." To this intimation she replied, after a considerable pause, "Don't, my good neighbour, don't feed me with false hope.—My poor Greaves too certainly perished in a foreign land—yet he is happy:—had he lived to see me in this condition, grief would soon have put a period to his days." "I tell you then, (cried the visitant) he is not dead. I have seen a letter that mentions his being well since the battle. You shall come along with me—you are no longer a prisoner; but shall live at my house comfortably, till your affairs are settled to your wish."

The poor widow followed her in silent astonishment, and was immediately accommodated with necessaries.

Next morning her hostess proceeded with her in the same cautious manner, until she was assured that her son had returned. Being duly prepared, she was blessed with a sight of poor Greaves, and fainted away in his arms.

We shall not dwell upon this tender scene, because it is but of a secondary concern in the history of our knight-errant: let it suffice to say, their mutual happiness was unspeakable. She was afterwards visited by Sir Launcelot, whom she no sooner beheld, than, springing forwards with all the eagerness of maternal affection, she clasped him to her breast, crying, "My dear child! my Launcelot! my pride! my darling! my kind benefactor! This is not the first time I have hugged you in these arms! O! you are the very image of Sir Everhard in his youth; but you have got the eyes, the complexion, the sweetness, and complacency of my dear and ever-honoured lady." This was not the strain of hireling praise; but the genuine tribute of esteem and admiration. As such, it could not but be agreeable to our hero, who undertook to procure Oakely's discharge, and settle him in a comfortable farm on his own estate.

In the mean time, Greaves went with a heavy heart to the house of farmer Sedgemoor, where he found Sukey, who had been prepared for his reception, in a transport of joy, though very weak, and greatly emaciated. Nevertheless, the return of her sweetheart had such an happy effect on her constitution, that in a few weeks her health was perfectly restored.

This adventure of our knight was crowned with every happy circumstance that could give pleasure to a generous mind. The prisoners were released, and reinstated in their former occupations. The justice performed his articles from fear; and afterwards turned over a new leaf from remorse. Young Oakely was married to Sukey, with whom he received a considerable portion. The new-married couple found a farm ready stocked for them on the knight's estate; and the mother enjoyed a happy retreat in the character of the housekeeper at Greavesbury-hall.

CHAPTER XIII.

In which our Knight is tantalized with a transient glimpse of felicity.

The success of our adventurer, which we have particularized in the last chapter, could not fail of inhancing his character, not only among those who knew him, but also among the people of the town to whom he was an utter stranger. The populace surrounded the house, and testified their approbation in loud huzzas. Captain Crowe was more than ever inspired with veneration for his admired patron, and more than ever determined to pursue his

THE

ADVENTURES

OF

Sir Launcelot Greaves.

By the Author of RODERICK RANDOM.

In TWO VOLUMES.

VOL. II.

LONDON:

Printed for J. COOTE, in Pater-Noster-Row.

MDCCLXII.

Title page of first (book) edition, vol. 2, 1762.
(Collection of Robert and Vivian Folkenflik)

footsteps in the road of chivalry. Fillet, and his friend the lawyer, could not help conceiving an affection, and even a profound esteem, for the exalted virtue, the person, and the accomplishments of the knight, dashed as they were with a mixture of extravagance and insanity. Even Sir Launcelot himself was elevated to an extraordinary degree of self-complacency on the fortunate issue of his adventure, and became more and more persuaded that a knight-errant's profession might be exercised, even in England, to the advantage of the community. The only person of the company who seemed unanimated with the general satisfaction was Mr. Thomas Clarke. He had, not without good reason, laid it down as a maxim, that knight-errantry and madness were synonimous terms; and that madness, though exhibited in the most advantageous and agreeable light, could not change its nature, but must continue a perversion of sense to the end of the chapter.[1] He perceived the additional impression which the brain of his uncle had sustained, from the happy manner in which the benevolence of Sir Launcelot had so lately operated; and began to fear it would be, in a little time, quite necessary to have recourse to a commission of lunacy,[2] which might not only disgrace the family of the Crowes, but also tend to invalidate the settlement which the captain had already made in favour of our young lawyer.

Perplexed with these cogitations, Mr. Clarke appealed to our adventurer's own reflection. He expatiated upon the bad consequences that would attend his uncle's perseverance in the execution of a scheme so foreign to his faculties; and intreated him, for the love of God, to divert him from his purpose, either by arguments or authority; as, of all mankind, the knight alone had gained such an ascendency over his spirit, that he would listen to his exhortations with respect and submission. Our adventurer was not so mad, but that he saw and owned the rationality of these remarks. He readily undertook to employ all his influence with Crowe to dissuade him from his extravagant design; and seized the first opportunity of being alone with the captain, to signify his sentiments on this subject. "Captain Crowe (said he), you are then determined to proceed in the course of knight-errantry?" "I am, (replied the seaman) with God's help, d'ye see, and the assistance of wind and weather—" "What; do'st thou talk of wind and weather! (cried the knight, in an elevated tone of affected transport): without the help of Heaven, indeed, we are all vanity, imbecility, weakness, and wretchedness; but if thou art resolved to embrace the life of an errant, let me not hear thee so much as whisper a doubt, a wish, an hope, or sentiment, with respect to any other obstacle, which wind or weather, fire or water, sword or famine, danger or disappointment, may throw in the way of thy career.—When the duty of thy profession calls, thou must singly rush upon innumerable hosts of armed men: thou must storm the breach in the mouth of batteries loaded with death and destruction, while, every step thou movest, thou art exposed to the horrible explosion of subterranean mines, which, being sprung, will whirl thee aloft in air, a mangled corse, to feed the fowls of heaven. Thou must leap into the abyss of dismal caves and caverns, replete with poisonous toads and hissing serpents. Thou must plunge into seas of burning sulphur: thou must launch upon the ocean in a crazy bark,[3] when the foaming billows roll mountain high, when the lightning flashes, the thunder roars, and the howling tempest blows, as if it would commix the jarring elements of air and water, earth and fire, and reduce all nature to the original anarchy of chaos. Thus involved, thou must turn thy prow full against the fury of the storm, and stem the boisterous surge to thy destined port, though at the distance of a thousand leagues—thou must—"

"Avast, avast, brother, (exclaimed the impatient Crowe) you've got into the high latitudes, d'ye see:—if so be as you spank it away[4] at that rate, adad, I can't continue in tow—we must cast off the rope, or 'ware timbers.[5]—As for your 'osts and breeches, and hurling aloft, d'ye see, your caves and caverns, whistling tuoads and serpents, burning brimstone and foaming billows, we must take our hap; I value 'em not a rotten ratline:[6]—but, as for sailing in the wind's eye, brother, you must give me leave—no offence, I hope—I pretend to be a thoroughbred seaman, d'ye see—and I'll be damned if you, or e'er an arrant that broke biscuit, ever sailed in a three-mast vessel within five points of the wind,[7] allowing for variation and lee-way.——No, no, brother, none of your tricks upon travellers—I a'n't now to learn my compass." "Tricks! (cried the knight, starting up, and laying his hand on the pummel of his sword) what! suspect my honour!"

Crowe, supposing him to be really incensed, interrupted him with great earnestness, saying, "Nay, don't—what a-pize![8]——adds-bunt-lines![9]—I did n't go to give you the lie, brother, smite my limbs: I only said as how to sail in the wind's eye was impossible—" "And I say unto thee, (resumed the knight) nothing is impossible to a true knight-errant, inspired and animated by love." "And I say unto thee, (hollowed Crowe) if so be as how love pretends to turn his hawse-holes[10] to the wind, he's no seaman, d'ye see, but a snotty-nose lubberly boy, that knows not a cat from a capstan[11]—a-don't." "He that does not believe that love is an infallible pilot, must not embark upon the voyage of chivalry; for, next to the protection of Heaven, it is from love that the knight derives all his prowess and glory. The bare name of his mistress invigorates his arm: the remembrance of her beauty infuses in his breast the most heroic sentiments of courage, while the idea of her chastity hedges him round like a charm, and renders him invulnerable to the sword of his antagonist. A knight without a mistress is a meer non-entity, or at least a monster in nature, a pilot without compass, a ship without rudder, and must be driven to and fro upon the waves of discomfiture and disgrace." "An that be all, (replied the sailor) I told you before as how I've got a sweet-heart, as true a hearted girl as ever swung in canvas.—What tho'f she may have started a hoop in rolling [12]—that signifies nothing——I'll warrant her tight as a nut-shell." [13] "She must, in your opinion, be a paragon either of beauty or virtue. Now, as you have given up the last, you must uphold her charms unequalled, and her person without a parallel." "I do, I do uphold she will sail upon a parallel, [14] as well as e'er a frigate that was rigged to the northward of fifty." [15] "At that rate she must rival the attractions of her whom I adore; but that, I say, is impossible: the perfections of my Aurelia are altogether supernatural; and as two suns cannot shine together in the same sphere with equal splendour, so I affirm, and will prove with my body, that your mistress, in comparison with mine, is as a glow-worm to the meridian sun, a rush-light to the full moon, or a stale mackarel's eye to a pearl of orient." "Hearkye, brother, you might give good words, however: an we once fall a-jawing, d'ye see, I can heave out as much bilge-water as another; and since you besmear my sweetheart Besselia, I can as well bedaub your mistress Aurelia, whom I value no more than old junk, pork-slush, [16] or stinking stockfish." [17] "Enough, enough—such blasphemy shall not pass unchastised. In consideration of our having fed from the same table, and maintained together a friendly tho' short intercourse, I will not demand the combat before you are duly prepared. Proceed to the first great town where you can be furnished with horse and harnessing, with arms offensive and defensive: provide a trusty squire, assume a motto and device—declare yourself a son of chivalry; and proclaim the excellence of her who rules your heart. I shall fetch a compass; and wheresoever we may chance to meet, let us engage with equal arms in mortal combat, that shall decide and determine this dispute."

So saying, our adventurer stalked with great solemnity into another apartment; while Crowe, being sufficiently irritated, snapped his fingers in token of defiance. Honest Crowe thought himself scurvily used by a man whom he had cultivated with such humility of veneration; and, after an incoherent ejaculation of sea-oaths, went in quest of his nephew, in order to make him acquainted with this unlucky transaction.

In the mean time Sir Launcelot, having ordered supper, retired into his own chamber, and gave a loose to the most tender emotions of his heart. He recollected all the fond ideas which had been excited in the course of his corre-

spondence with the charming Aurelia. He remembered, with horror, the cruel
letter he had received from that young lady, containing a formal renunciation
of his attachment, so unsuitable to the whole tenour of her character and conduct. He revolved the late adventure of the coach, and the declaration of Mr.
Clarke, with equal eagerness and astonishment; and was seized with the most
ardent desire of unravelling a mystery so interesting to the predominant passion of his heart.—All these mingled considerations produced a kind of ferment in the œconomy of his mind, which subsided into a profound reverie,
compounded of hope and perplexity.

From this trance he was waked by the arrival of his squire, who entered the
room with the blood trickling over his nose, and stood before him without
speaking. When the knight asked whose livery was that he wore, he replied,
"'Tis your honour's own livery:—I received it on your account, and hope as
you will quit the score." Then he proceeded to inform his master, that two
officers of the army having come into the kitchen, insisted upon having for
their supper the victuals which Sir Launcelot had bespoke; and that he, the
squire, objecting to the proposal, one of them had seized the poker, and basted
him with his own blood; that when he told them he belonged to a knight-
errant, and threatened them with the vengeance of his master, they cursed and
abused him, calling him Sancho Panza, and such dogs' names; and bade him
tell his master Don Quicksot, that, if he made any noise, they would confine
him to his cage,[18] and lie with his mistress Dulcinea.[19] "To be sure, Sir, (said
he) they thought you as great a nicompoop as your squire—trim tram, like
master, like man;[20]—but I hope as how you will give them a Rowland for their
Oliver."[21]

"Miscreant! (cried the knight) you have provoked the gentlemen with your
impertinence, and they have chastised you as you deserve. I tell thee, Crabshaw, they have saved me the trouble of punishing thee with my own hands;
and well it is for thee, sinner as thou art, that they themselves have performed
the office: for, had they complained to me of thy insolence and rusticity, by
Heaven! I would have made thee an example to all the impudent squires upon
the face of the earth. Hence then, avaunt, caitif.—Let his majesty's officers,
who are perhaps fatigued with hard duty in the service of their country, comfort themselves with the supper which was intended for me, and leave me
undisturbed to my own meditations."

Timothy did not require a repetition of this command, which he forthwith
obeyed, growling within himself, that thenceforward he should let every cuckold wear his own horns;[22] but he could not help entertaining some doubts with

respect to the courage of his master, who, he supposed, was one of those Hectors[23] who have their fighting days, but are not at all times equally prepared
for the combat.

The knight, having taken a slight repast, retired to his repose; and had for
some time enjoyed a very agreeable slumber, when he was startled by a knocking at his chamber-door. "I beg your honour's pardon, (said the landlady) but
there are two uncivil persons in the kitchen, who have well nigh turned my
whole house topsy-turvy. Not contented with laying violent hands on your
honour's supper, they want to be rude to two young ladies who are just arrived,
and have called for a post-chaise to go on. They are afraid to open their
chamber-door to get out—and the young lawyer is like to be murdered for
taking the ladies' part."

Sir Launcelot, though he refused to take notice of the insult which had been
offered to himself, no sooner heard of the distress of the ladies than he started
up, huddled on his cloaths, and, girding his sword to his loins, advanced with
a deliberate pace to the kitchen, where he perceived Thomas Clarke warmly
engaged in altercation with a couple of young men dressed in regimentals,
who, with a peculiar air of arrogance and ferocity, treated him with great insolence and contempt. Tom was endeavouring to persuade them, that, in the
constitution of England, the military was always subservient to the civil
power; and that their behaviour to a couple of helpless young women was not
only unbecoming gentlemen, but expresly contrary to the law, inasmuch as
they might be sued for an assault on an action of damages.

To this remonstrance the two heroes in red replied by a volley of dreadful
oaths, intermingled with threats, which put the lawyer in some pain for his
ears. While one thus endeavoured to intimidate honest Tom Clarke, the other
thundered at the door of the apartment to which the ladies had retired, demanding admittance, but received no other answer than a loud shriek. Our
adventurer advancing to this uncivil champion, accosted him thus in a grave
and solemn tone: "Assuredly I could not have believed, except upon the evidence of my own senses, that persons who have the appearance of gentlemen,
and bear his majesty's honourable commission in the army, could behave so
wide of the decorum due to society, of a proper respect to the laws, of that
humanity which we owe to our fellow-creatures, and that delicate regard for
the fair-sex, which ought to prevail in the breast of every gentleman, and
which in particular dignifies the character of a soldier. To whom shall that
weaker, tho' more amiable part of the creation, fly for protection, if they are
insulted and outraged by those whose more immediate duty it is to afford

them security and defence from injury and violence? What right have you, or any man upon earth, to excite riot in a public inn, which may be deemed a temple sacred to hospitality, to disturb the quiet of your fellow-guests, some of them perhaps exhausted by fatigue, some of them invaded by distemper, to interrupt the king's lieges in their course of journeying upon their lawful occasions? Above all, what motive but wanton barbarity could prompt you to violate the apartment, and terrify the tender hearts of two helpless young ladies travelling no doubt upon some cruel emergency, which compels them unattended to encounter in the night the dangers of the highway?"

"Heark ye, Don Bethlem,[24] (said the captain, strutting up and cocking his hat in the face of our adventurer) you may be as mad as e'er a straw-crowned monarch in Moor-fields,[25] for aught I care; but damme! don't you be saucy, otherwise I shall dub your worship with a good stick across your shoulders." "How! petulant boy (cried the knight) since you are so ignorant of urbanity, I will give you a lesson that you shall not easily forget." So saying, he unsheathed his sword, and called upon the soldier to draw in his defence.

The reader may have seen the physiognomy of a stockholder at Jonathan's when the rebels were at Derby,[26] or the features of a bard when accosted by a bailiff, or the countenance of an alderman when his banker stops payment; if he has seen either of these phænomena, he may conceive the appearance that was now exhibited by the visage of the ferocious captain, when the naked sword of Sir Launcelot glanced before his eyes: far from attempting to produce his own, which was of unconscionable length, he stood motionless as a statue, staring with the most ghastly look of terror and astonishment. His companion, who partook of his pannic, seeing matters brought to a very serious crisis, interposed with a crest-fallen countenance, assuring Sir Launcelot they had no intention to quarrel, and what they had done was intirely for the sake of the frolick.

"By such frolicks (cried the knight) you become nuisances to society, bring yourselves into contempt, and disgrace the corps to which you belong. I now perceive the truth of the observation, that cruelty always resides with cowardice. My contempt is changed into compassion; and as you are probably of good families, I must insist upon this young man's drawing his sword, and acquitting himself in such a manner as may screen him from the most infamous censure which an officer can undergo." "Lack a day, Sir (said the other) we are no officers, but 'prentices to two London haberdashers, travellers for orders. Captain is a good travelling name, and we have dressed ourselves like officers to procure more respect upon the road."

The knight said he was very glad, for the honour of the service, to find they were impostors; tho' they deserved to be chastised for arrogating to themselves an honourable character, which they had not spirit to sustain.

These words were scarce pronounced, when Mr. Clarke approaching one of the bravadoes, who had threatened to crop his ears, bestowed such a benediction on his jaw, as he could not receive without immediate humiliation; while Timothy Crabshaw, smarting from his broken head and his want of supper, saluted the other with a Yorkshire hug,[27] that layed him across the body of his companion. In a word, the two pseudo-officers were very roughly handled for their presumption in pretending to act characters for which they were so ill qualified.

While Clarke and Crabshaw were thus laudably employed, the two young ladies passed through the kitchen so suddenly, that the knight had only a transient glimpse of their backs, and they disappeared before he could possibly make a tender of his services. The truth is, they dreaded nothing so much as their being discovered, and took the first opportunity of gliding into the chaise, which had been for some time waiting in the passage.

Mr. Clarke was much more disconcerted than our adventurer, by their sudden escape. He ran with great eagerness to the door, and, perceiving they were flown, returned to Sir Launcelot, saying, "Lord bless my soul, Sir, didn't you see who it was?" "Hah! how! (exclaimed the knight, reddening with alarm) who was it?" "One of them (replied the lawyer) was Dolly, our old landlady's daughter at the Black Lyon.—I knew her when first she lighted, notwithstanding her being neatly dressed in a green joseph,[28] which, I'll assure you, Sir, becomes her remarkably well.—I'd never desire to see a prettier creature. As for the other, she's a very genteel woman; but whether old or young, ugly or handsome, I can't pretend to say; for she was masqued.[29]——I had just time to salute Dolly, and ask a few questions;—but all she could tell me was, that the masqued lady's name was miss Meadows; and that she, Dolly, was hired as her waiting-woman."

When the name of Meadows was mentioned, Sir Launcelot, whose spirits had been in violent commotion, became suddenly calm and serene, and he began to communicate to Clarke the dialogue which had passed between him and capt. Crowe, when the hostess, addressing herself to our errant, "Well, (said she) I have had the honour to accommodate many ladies of the first fashion at the White Hart, both young and old, proud and lowly, ordinary and handsome; but such a miracle as miss Meadows I never yet did see. Lord, let me never thrive but I think she is of something more than a human creature.— O, had your honour but set eyes on her, you would have said it was a vision from Heaven, a cherubim of beauty:—for my part, I can hardly think it was any thing but a dream:—then so meek, so mild, so good-natured and generous! I say, blessed is the young woman who tends upon such a heavenly creature:——and poor dear young lady! she seems to be under grief and affliction; for the tears stole down her lovely cheeks, and looked for all the world like orient pearl."

Sir Launcelot listened attentively to the description, which reminded him of his dear Aurelia, and, sighing bitterly, withdrew to his own apartment.

CHAPTER XIV.

Which shews, That a man cannot always sip,
When the cup is at his lip.[1]

Those who have felt the doubts, the jealousies, the resentments, the humiliations, the hopes, the despair, the impatience, and, in a word, the infinite disquiets of love, will be able to conceive the sea of agitation on which our adventurer was tossed all night long, without repose or intermission. Sometimes he resolved to employ all his industry and address in discovering the place in which Aurelia was sequestered, that he might rescue her from the supposed restraint to which she had been subjected. But, when his heart beat high with the anticipation of this exploit, he was suddenly invaded, and all his ardour checked, by the remembrance of that fatal letter, written and signed by her own hand, which had divorced him from all hope, and first unsettled his understanding. The emotions waked by this remembrance were so strong, that he leaped from the bed, and, the fire being still burning in the chimney, lighted a candle, that he might once more banquet his spleen by reading the original billet, which, together with the ring he had received from miss Darnel's mother, he kept in a small box, carefully deposited within his portmanteau. This being instantly unlocked, he unfolded the paper, and recited the contents in these words:

"Sir, Obliged as I am by the passion you profess, and the eagerness with which you endeavour to give me the most convincing proof of your regard, I feel some reluctance in making you acquainted with a circumstance, which, in all proba-

bility, you will not learn without some disquiet. But the affair is become so interesting, I am compelled to tell you, that however agreeable your proposals may
have been to those whom I thought it my duty to please by every reasonable
concession, and howsoever you may have been flattered by the seeming complacency with which I have heard your addresses, I now find it absolutely necessary
to speak in a decisive strain, to assure you, that, without sacrificing my own peace,
I cannot admit a continuation of your correspondence; and that your regard for
me will be best shewn by your desisting from a pursuit, which is altogether incon-
sistent with the happiness of

AURELIA DARNEL."

Having pronounced aloud the words that composed this dismission, he
hastily replaced the cruel scroll; and, being too well acquainted with the hand
to harbour the least doubt of its being genuine, threw himself into his bed in
a transport of despair, mingled with resentment; during the predominancy
of which, he determined to proceed in the career of adventure, and endeavour
to forget the unkindness of his mistress, amidst the avocations of knight-
errantry. Such was the resolution that governed his thoughts, when he rose in
the morning, ordered Crabshaw to saddle Bronzomarte, and demanded a bill
of his expence. Before these orders could be executed, the good woman of the
house, entering his apartment, told him, with marks of concern, that the poor
young lady, miss Meadows, had dropped her pocket-book[2] in the next chamber, where it was found by the hostess, who now presented it unopened.

Our knight, having called in Mrs. Oakely and her son as witnesses, unfolded
the book, without reading one syllable of the contents, and found in it five
bank-notes, amounting to two hundred and thirty pounds. Perceiving, at
once, that the loss of this treasure might be attended with the most embarrassing consequences to the owner, and reflecting that this was a case which
demanded the immediate interposition and assistance of chivalry, he declared,
that he himself would convey it safely into the hands of miss Meadows; and
desired to know the road she had pursued, that he might set out in quest of
her, without a moment's delay. It was not without some difficulty that this
information was obtained from the post-boy, who had been enjoined secrecy
by the lady, and even gratified with a handsome reward for his promised discretion. The same method was used to make him disgorge his trust: he undertook to conduct Sir Launcelot, who hired a post-chaise for dispatch, and immediately departed, after having directed his squire to follow his tract with the
horses.

Yet, whatever haste he made, it is absolutely necessary for the reader's satisfaction, that we should outstrip the chaise, and visit the ladies before his arrival. We shall therefore, without circumlocution, premise that miss Meadows was no other than that paragon of beauty and goodness, the all-accomplished miss Aurelia Darnel. She had, with that meekness of resignation peculiar to herself, for some years, submitted to every species of oppression which her uncle's tyranny of disposition could plan, and his unlimited power of guardianship execute, till, at length, it rose to such a pitch of despotism as she could not endure. He had projected a match between his niece and one Philip Sycamore, Esq; a young man who possessed a pretty considerable estate in the North Country; who liked Aurelia's person, but was enamoured of her fortune, and had offered to purchase Anthony's interest and alliance with certain concessions, which could not but be agreeable to a man of loose principles, who would have found it a difficult task to settle the accounts of his wardship.

According to the present estimate of matrimonial felicity, Sycamore might have found admittance as a future son-in-law in any private family of the kingdom. He was by birth a gentleman, tall, straight, and muscular, with a fair, sleek, unmeaning face, that promised more simplicity than ill-nature. His education had not been neglected, and he inherited an estate of five thousand a year. Miss Darnel, however, had penetration enough to discover and despise him as a strange composition of rapacity and profusion, absurdity and good-sense, bashfulness and impudence, self-conceit and diffidence, aukwardness and ostentation, insolence and good-nature, rashness and timidity. He was continually surrounded and preyed upon by certain vermin called led-captains[3] and buffoons, who shewed him in leading-strings like a sucking giant, rifled his pockets without ceremony, ridiculed him to his face, traduced his character, and exposed him in a thousand ludicrous attitudes for the diversion of the public; while, all the time, he knew their knavery, saw their drift, detested their morals, and despised their understanding. He was so infatuated by indolence of thought, and communication with folly, that he would have rather suffered himself to be led into a ditch with company, than be at the pains of going over a bridge alone; and involved himself in a thousand difficulties, the natural consequences of an error in the first concoction, which, though he plainly saw it, he had not resolution enough to avoid.

Such was the character of squire Sycamore, who professed himself the rival of Sir Launcelot Greaves in the good graces of miss Aurelia Darnel. He had in this pursuit persevered with more constancy and fortitude, than he ever exerted in any other instance. Being generally needy, from extravagance, he was stimulated by his wants, and animated by his vanity, which was artfully instigated by his followers, who hoped to share the spoils of his success. These motives were reinforced by the incessant and eager exhortations of Anthony Darnel, who, seeing his ward in the last year of her minority, thought there was no time to be lost in securing his own indemnification, and snatching his niece for ever from the hopes of Sir Launcelot, whom he now hated with redoubled animosity. Finding Aurelia deaf to all his remonstrances, proof against ill-usage, and resolutely averse to the proposed union with Sycamore, he endeavoured to detach her thoughts from Sir Launcelot, by forging tales to the prejudice of his constancy and moral character; and, finally, by recapitulating the proofs and instances of his distraction, which he particularized with the most malicious exaggerations.

In spite of all his arts, he found it impracticable to surmount her objections to the purposed alliance, and therefore changed his battery. Instead of transferring her to the arms of his friend, he resolved to detain her in his own power by a legal claim, which would invest him with the uncontrouled management of her affairs. This was a charge of lunacy, in consequence of which he hoped to obtain a commission, to secure a jury to his wish, and be appointed sole committee of her person, as well as steward on her estate, of which he would then be heir apparent.[4] As the first steps towards the execution of this honest scheme, he had subjected Aurelia to the superintendency and direction of an old duenna, who had been formerly the procuress of his pleasures; and hired a new set of servants, who were given to understand, at their first admission, that the young lady was disordered in her brain.

An impression of this nature is easily preserved among servants, when the master of the family thinks his interest is concerned in supporting the imposture. The melancholy produced from her confinement, and the vivacity of her resentment under ill-usage, were, by the address of Anthony, and the prepossession of his domesticks, perverted into the effects of insanity; and the same interpretation was strained upon her most indifferent words and actions. The tydings of miss Darnel's disorder were carefully circulated in whispers, and soon reached the ears of Mr. Sycamore, who was not at all pleased with the information. From his knowledge of Anthony's disposition, he suspected the truth of the report; and unwilling to see such a prize ravished, as it were, from his grasp, he, with the advice and assistance of his myrmidons,[5] resolved to set the captive at liberty, in full hope of turning the adventure to his own advantage; for he argued in this manner: "If she is in fact *compos mentis*, her gratitude will operate in my behalf, and even prudence will advise her to embrace the proffered asylum from the villany of her uncle. If she is really disordered, it will be no great difficulty to deceive her into a marriage, and then I become her trustee of course."

The plan was well conceived; but Sycamore had not discretion enough to keep his own counsel. From weakness and vanity, he blabbed the design, which in a little time was communicated to Anthony Darnel, and he took his precautions accordingly. Being infirm in his own person, and consequently unfit for opposing the violence of some desperadoes, whom he knew to be the satellites of Sycamore, he prepared a private retreat for his ward at the house of an old gentleman, the companion of his youth, whom he had imposed upon with the fiction of her being disordered in her understanding, and amused with a story of a dangerous design upon her person. Thus cautioned and instructed, the gentleman had gone with his own coach and servants to receive Aurelia and her governante at a third house, to which she had been privately removed from her uncle's habitation; and in this journey it was, that she had been so accidentally protected from the violence of the robbers by the interposition and prowess of our adventurer.

As he did not wear his helmet in that exploit, she recognized his features as he passed the coach, and, struck with the apparition, shrieked aloud. She had been assured by her guardian, that his design was to convey her to her own house; but perceiving, in the sequel, that the carriage struck off upon a different road, and finding herself in the hands of strangers, she began to dread a much more disagreeable fate, and conceive doubts and ideas that filled her tender heart with horror and affliction. When she expostulated with the duenna, she was treated like a changeling,[6] admonished to be quiet, and reminded that she was under the direction of those who would manage her with a tender regard to her own welfare, and the honour of her family. When she addressed herself to the old gentleman, who was not much subject to the emotions of humanity, and besides firmly persuaded that she was deprived of her reason, he made no answer; but laid his finger on his mouth, by way of enjoining silence.

This mysterious behaviour aggravated the fears of the poor hapless young lady; and her terrors waxed so strong, that when she saw Tom Clarke, whose face she knew, she called aloud for assistance, and even pronounced the name of his patron Sir Launcelot Greaves, which she imagined might stimulate him the more to attempt something for her deliverance.

The reader has already been informed in what manner the endeavours of Tom and his uncle miscarried. Miss Darnel's new keeper having, in the course of his journey, halted for refreshment at the Black Lyon, of which being landlord, he believed the good woman and her family were intirely devoted to his will and pleasure, Aurelia found an opportunity of speaking in private to Dolly, who had a very prepossessing appearance. She conveyed a purse of money into the hands of this young woman, telling her, while the tears trickled down her cheeks, that she was a young lady of fortune, in danger, as she apprehended, of assassination. This hint, which she communicated in a whisper, while the governante stood at the other end of the room, was sufficient to interest the compassionate Dolly in her behalf. As soon as the coach departed, she made her mother acquainted with the transaction; and as they naturally concluded that the young lady expected their assistance, they resolved to approve themselves worthy of her confidence.

Dolly having inlisted in their design a trusty countryman, one of her own professed admirers, they set out together for the house of the gentleman in which the fair prisoner was confined, and waited for her in secret at the end of a pleasant park, in which they naturally concluded she might be indulged with the privilege of taking the air. The event justified their conception: on the very first day of their watch they saw her approach, accompanied by her duenna. Dolly and her attendant immediately tied their horses to a stake, and retired into a thicket, which Aurelia did not fail to enter. Dolly forthwith appeared, and, taking her by the hand, led her to the horses, one of which she mounted in the utmost hurry and trepidation, while the countryman bound the duenna with a cord, prepared for the purpose, gagged her mouth, and tied her to a tree, where he left her to her own meditations. Then he mounted before Dolly, and thro' unfrequented paths conducted his charge to an inn on the post-road, where a chaise was ready for their reception.

As he refused to proceed farther, lest his absence from his own home should create suspicion, Aurelia rewarded him liberally; but would not part with her faithful Dolly, who, indeed, had no inclination to be discharged: such an affection and attachment had she already acquired for the amiable fugitive, though she knew neither her story, nor her true name. Aurelia thought proper to conceal both, and assumed the fictitious appellation of Meadows, until she should be better acquainted with the disposition and discretion of her new attendant. The first resolution she could take in the present flutter of her spirits, was to make the best of her way to London, where she thought she might find an asylum in the house of a female relation, married to an eminent physician, known by the name of Kawdle. In the execution of this hasty resolve, she travelled at a violent rate, from stage to stage, in a carriage drawn by four horses, without halting for necessary refreshment or repose, until she judged herself out of danger of being overtaken. As she appeared overwhelmed with grief and consternation, the good-natured Dolly endeavoured to alleviate her distress with diverting discourse; and, among other less interesting stories, entertained her with the adventures of Sir Launcelot and captain Crowe, which she had seen and heard recited while they remained at the Black Lyon: nor did she fail to introduce Mr. Thomas Clarke, in her narrative, with such a favourable representation of his person and character, as plainly discovered that her own heart had received a rude shock from the irresistible force of his qualifications.

The history of Sir Launcelot Greaves was a theme which effectually fixed the attention of Aurelia, distracted as her ideas must have been by the circumstances of her present situation. The particulars of his conduct, since the correspondence between her and him had ceased, she heard with equal concern and astonishment; for, how far soever she deemed herself detached from all possibility of future connexion with that young gentleman, she was not made of such indifferent stuff, as to learn without emotion the calamitous disorder of an accomplished youth, whose extraordinary virtues she could not but revere.

As they had deviated from the post-road, taken precautions to conceal their route, and made such progress, that they were now within one day's journey of London, the careful and affectionate Dolly seeing her dear lady quite exhausted with fatigue, used all her natural rhetorick, which was very powerful, mingled with tears that flowed from the heart, in persuading Aurelia to enjoy some repose; and so far she succeeded in the attempt, that for one night the toil of travelling was intermitted. This recess from incredible fatigue, was a pause that afforded our adventurer time to overtake them before they reached the metropolis, that vast labyrinth, in which Aurelia might have been for ever lost to his inquiry.

It was in the afternoon of the day which succeeded his departure from the White Hart, that Sir Launcelot arrived at the inn, where miss Aurelia Darnel had bespoke a dish of tea, and a post-chaise for the next stage. He had, by inquiry, traced her a considerable way, without ever dreaming who the person really was whom he thus pursued, and now he desired to speak with her attendant. Dolly was not a little surprised to see Sir Launcelot Greaves, of whose character she had conceived a very sublime idea, from the narrative of Mr. Thomas Clarke; but she was still more surprised when he gave her to understand, that he had charged himself with the pocket-book, containing the bank-notes, which miss Meadows had dropped in the house where they had been threatened with insult. Miss Darnel had not yet discovered her disaster, when her attendant, running into the apartment, presented the prize, which she had received from our adventurer, with his compliments to miss Meadows, implying a request to be admitted into her presence, that he might make a personal tender of his best services.

It is not to be supposed that the amiable Aurelia heard unmoved such a message from a person, whom her maid discovered to be the very identical Sir Launcelot Greaves, whose story she had so lately related: but as the ensuing scene requires fresh attention in the reader, we shall defer it till another opportunity, when his spirits shall be recruited from the fatigue of this chapter.

CHAPTER XV.

Exhibiting an interview, which, it is to be hoped,
will interest the curiosity of the reader.

The mind of the delicate Aurelia was strangely agitated by the intelligence which she received, with her pocket-book, from Dolly. Confounded as she was by the nature of her situation, she at once perceived that she could not, with any regard to the dictates of gratitude, refuse complying with the request of Sir Launcelot; but, in the first hurry of her emotion, she directed Dolly to beg, in her name, that she might be excused for wearing a masque at the interview which he desired, as she had particular reasons, which concerned her peace, for retaining that disguise. Our adventurer submitted to this preliminary with a good grace, as he had nothing in view but the injunctions of his order, and the duties of humanity; and he was admitted without further preamble. When he entered the room, he could not help being struck with the presence of Aurelia. Her stature was improved since he had seen her; her shape was exquisitely formed; and she received him with an air of dignity, which impressed him with a very sublime idea of her person and character. She was no less affected at sight of our adventurer, who, though cased in armour, appeared with his head uncovered; and the exercise of travelling had thrown such a glow of health and vivacity on his features, which were naturally elegant and expressive, that we will venture to say, there was not in all England a couple that excelled this amiable pair in personal beauty and accomplishments. Aurelia shone with all the fabled graces of nymph or goddess; and to Sir Launcelot might be applied what the divine poet Ariosto says of the prince Zerbino:

Natura il fece e poi ruppe la stampa.
"When Nature stamp'd him, she the dye destroy'd." [1]

Our adventurer, having made his obeisance to this supposed miss Meadows, told her, with an air of pleasantry, that altho' he thought himself highly honoured in being admitted to her presence, and allowed to pay his respects to her, as superior beings are adored, unseen; yet his pleasure would receive a very considerable addition, if she would be pleased to withdraw that invidious veil, that he might have a glimpse of the divinity which it concealed. Aurelia immediately took off her masque, saying, with a faultering accent, "I cannot be so ungrateful as to deny such a small favour to a gentleman who has laid me under the most important obligations."

The unexpected apparition of Miss Aurelia Darnel, beaming with all the emanations of ripened beauty, blushing with all the graces of the most lovely confusion, could not but produce a violent effect upon the mind of Sir Launcelot Greaves. He was, indeed, overwhelmed with a mingled transport of astonishment, admiration, affliction, and awe. The colour vanished from his cheeks, and he stood gazing upon her, in silence, with the most emphatic expression of countenance. Aurelia was infected by his disorder: she began to tremble, and the roses fluctuated on her face.—"I cannot forget (said she) that I owe my life to the courage and humanity of Sir Launcelot Greaves, and that he at the same time rescued from the most dreadful death a dear and venerable parent." "Would to heaven she still survived! (cried our adventurer with great emotion). She was the friend of my youth, the kind patroness of my felicity! my guardian angel forsook me when she expired! her last injunctions are deep engraven on my heart!"

While he pronounced these words she lifted her handkerchief to her fair eyes, and, after some pause, proceeded in a tremulous tone, "I hope, Sir—I hope you have——I should be sorry——pardon me, Sir, I cannot reflect upon such an interesting [2] subject unmoved—" Here she fetched a deep sigh, that was accompanied with a flood of tears; while the knight continued to bend his eyes upon her with the utmost eagerness of attention. Having recollected herself a little, she endeavoured to shift the conversation: "You have been abroad since I had the pleasure to see you—I hope you were agreeably amused in your travels." "No, madam, (said our hero, drooping his head) I have been unfortunate." When she, with the most enchanting sweetness of benevolence, expressed her concern to hear he had been unhappy, and her hope that his misfortunes were not past remedy; he lifted up his eyes, and fixing them upon her again with a look of tender dejection, "Cut off (said he) from the possession of what my soul held most dear, I wished for death, and was visited by distraction.—I have been abandoned by my reason—my youth is for ever blasted——"

The tender heart of Aurelia could bear no more—her knees began to totter: the lustre vanished from her eyes, and she fainted in the arms of her attendant. Sir Launcelot, aroused by this circumstance, assisted Dolly in seating her mistress on a couch, where she soon recovered, and saw the knight on his knees before her. "I am still happy (said he) in being able to move your compassion, though I have been held unworthy of your esteem." "Do me justice (she replied): my best esteem has been always inseparably connected with the character of Sir Launcelot Greaves—" "Is it possible? (cried our hero) then surely I have no reason to complain. If I have moved your compassion, and possess your esteem, I am but one degree short of supreme happiness—that, however, is a gigantic step.——O miss Darnel! when I remember that dear, that melancholy moment—" So saying, he gently touched her hand, in order to press it to his lips, and perceived on her finger the very individual ring which he had presented in her mother's presence, as an interchanged testimony of plighted faith. Starting at the well-known object, the sight of which conjured up a strange confusion of ideas, "This (said he) was once the pledge of something still more cordial than esteem." Aurelia, blushing at this remark, while her eyes lightened with unusual vivacity, replied, in a severer tone, "Sir, you best know how it lost its original signification." "By heaven! I do not, madam (exclaimed our adventurer). With me it was ever held a sacred idea throned within my heart, cherished with such fervency of regard, with such reverence of affection, as the devout anchorite more unreasonably pays to those sainted reliques that constitute the object of his adoration—" "And, like those reliques, (answered miss Darnel) I have been insensible of my votary's devotion.—A saint I must have been, or something more, to know the sentiments of your heart by inspiration." "Did I forbear (said he) to express, to repeat, to enforce the dictates of the purest passion that ever warmed the human breast, until I was denied access, and formally discarded by that cruel dismission—" "I must beg your pardon, Sir, (cried Aurelia, interrupting him hastily) I know not what you mean." "That fatal sentence, (said he) if not pronounced by your own lips, at least written by your own fair hand, which drove me out an exile for ever from the paradise of your affection." "I would not (she replied) do Sir Launcelot Greaves the injury to suppose him capable of imposition: but you talk of things to which I am an utter stranger.—I have a right, Sir, to demand of your honour, that you will not impute to me your breaking off a connection, which—I would—rather wish—had never——" "Heaven and earth! what do

I hear? (cried our impatient knight) have I not the baleful letter to produce? What else but miss Darnel's explicit and express declaration could have destroyed the sweetest hope that ever cheared my soul; could have obliged me to resign all claim to that felicity for which alone I wished to live; could have filled my bosom with unutterable sorrow and despair; could have even divested me of reason, and driven me from the society of men, a poor, forlorn, wandering lunatic, such as you see me now prostrate at your feet; all the blossoms of my youth withered, all the honours of my family decayed?"

Aurelia looking wistfully at her lover, "Sir, (said she) you overwhelm me with amazement and anxiety! you are imposed upon, if you have received any such letter: you are deceived, if you thought Aurelia Darnel could be so insensible, ungrateful, and—inconstant."

This last word she pronounced with some hesitation, and a downcast look, while her face underwent a total suffusion, and the knight's heart began to palpitate with all the violence of emotion. He eagerly imprinted a kiss upon her hand, exclaiming, in interrupted phrase, "Can it be possible?——Heaven grant—Sure this is no illusion.—O, madam!—shall I call you my Aurelia? My heart is bursting with a thousand fond thoughts and presages. You shall see that dire paper which hath been the source of all my woes——it is the constant companion of my travels.——Last night I nourished my chagrin with the perusal of its horrid contents."

Aurelia expressed great impatience to view the cruel forgery; for such she assured him it must be: but he could not gratify her desire till the arrival of his servant with the portmanteau. In the mean time, tea was called. The lovers were seated: he looked and languished; she flushed and faultered: all was doubt and delirium, fondness and flutter. Their mutual disorder communicated itself to the kind-hearted sympathizing Dolly, who had been witness to the interview, and deeply affected with the disclosure of the scene. Unspeakable was her surprize when she found her mistress miss Meadows was no other than the celebrated Aurelia Darnel, whose eulogium she had heard so eloquently pronounced by her sweet-heart Mr. Thomas Clarke; a discovery which still more endeared her lady to her affection. She had wept plentifully at the progress of their mutual explanation; and was now so disconcerted, that she scarce knew the meaning of the orders she had received. She set the kettle on the table, and placed the tea-board on the fire. Her confusion, by attracting the notice of her mistress, helped to relieve her from her own embarrassing situation. She, with her own delicate hands, rectified the mistake of Dolly; who still continued to sob, and said, "Yaw may think, my leady Darnel, as haw I 'aive yeaten hoolcheese;[3] but it y'an't soa.—I'se think, vor maai peart, as how I'aive bean bewitched." Sir Launcelot could not help smiling at the simplicity of Dolly, whose goodness of heart, and attachment, Aurelia did not fail to extol, as soon as her back was turned. It was in consequence of this commendation, that, the next time she entered the room, our adventurer, for the first time, considered her face, and seemed to be struck with her features. He asked her some questions, which she could not answer to his satisfaction, applauded her regard for her lady, and assured her of his friendship and protection. He now begged to know the cause that obliged his Aurelia to travel at such a rate, and in such an equipage; and she informed him of those particulars which we have already communicated to the reader.

Sir Launcelot glowed with resentment, when he understood how his dear Aurelia had been oppressed by her perfidious and cruel guardian. He bit his nether lip, rolled his eyes around,[4] started from his seat, and striding across the room, "I remember (said he) the dying words of her who is now a saint in heaven—'That violent man, my brother-in-law, who is Aurelia's sole guardian, will thwart her wishes with every obstacle that brutal resentment and implacable malice can contrive.'—What followed, it would ill become me to repeat: but she concluded with these words—'The rest we must leave to the dispensations of Providence.'—Was it not Providence that sent me hither, to guard and protect the injured Aurelia?" Then turning to miss Darnel, whose eyes streamed with tears, he added, "Yes, divine creature! heaven, careful of your safety, and in compassion to my sufferings, hath guided me hither, in this mysterious manner, that I might defend you from violence, and enjoy this transition from madness to deliberation, from despair to felicity." So saying, he approached this amiable mourner, this fragrant flower of beauty, glittering with the dew-drops of the morning; this sweetest, gentlest, loveliest ornament of human nature: he gazed upon her with looks of love ineffable: he sat down by her; he pressed her soft hand in his; he began to fear that all he saw was the flattering vision of a distempered brain. He looked, and sighed; and turning up his eyes to heaven, breathed, in broken murmurs, the chaste raptures of his soul. The tenderness of this communication was too painful to be long endured. Aurelia industriously interposed other subjects of discourse, that his attention might not be dangerously overcharged, and the afternoon passed insensibly away.

Though he had determined, in his own mind, never more to quit this idol of his soul, they had not yet concerted any plan of conduct, when their happiness was all at once interrupted by a repetition of cries, denoting horror; and a servant, coming in, said he believed some rogues were murdering a traveller on the highway. The supposition of such distress operated like gunpowder on the disposition of our adventurer, who, without considering the situation of Aurelia, and indeed without seeing, or being capable to think on her, or any other subject, for the time being, ran directly to the stable, and mounting the first horse which he found saddled, issued out in the twilight, having no other weapon but his sword. He rode full speed to the spot whence the cries seemed to proceed; but they sounded more remote as he advanced. Nevertheless he followed them to a considerable distance from the road, over fields, ditches, and hedges; and at last came so near, that he could plainly distinguish the voice of his own squire, Timothy Crabshaw, bellowing for mercy, with hideous vociferation. Stimulated by this recognition, he redoubled his career in the dark, till at length his horse plunged into a hole, the nature of which he could not comprehend; but he found it impracticable to disengage him. It was with some difficulty that he himself clambered over a ruined wall, and regained the open ground. Here he groped about, in the utmost impatience of anxiety, ignorant of the place, mad with vexation for the fate of his unfortunate squire, and between whiles invaded with a pang of concern for Aurelia, left among strangers, unguarded, and alarmed. In the midst of this emotion, he bethought himself of hollowing aloud, that, in case he should be in the neighbourhood of any inhabited place, he might be heard and assisted. He accordingly practised this expedient, which was not altogether without effect; for he was immediately answered by an old friend, no other than his own steed Bronzomarte, who, hearing his master's voice, neighed strenuously at a small distance. The knight, being well acquainted with the sound, heard with astonishment; and, advancing in the right direction, found his noble charger fastened to a tree. He forthwith untied and mounted him; then, laying the reins upon his neck, allowed him to chuse his own path, in which he began to travel with equal steadiness and expedition. They had not proceeded far when the knight's ears were again saluted by the cries of Crabshaw; which Bronzomarte no sooner heard than he pricked up his ears, neighed, and quickened his pace, as if he had been sensible of the squire's distress, and hastened to his relief. Sir Launcelot, notwithstanding his own disquiet, could not help observing and admiring this generous sensibility of his horse: he began to think himself some hero of romance mounted upon a winged steed,[5] inspired with reason, directed by some humane inchanter, who pitied virtue in distress. All circumstances considered, it is no wonder that the commotion in the mind of our adventurer produced some such delirium. All night he continued the chace; the voice, which was repeated at intervals, still retreating before him, till the morning began to appear in the East, when, by divers piteous groans, he was directed to the corner of a wood, where he beheld his miserable squire stretched upon the grass, and Gilbert feeding by him altogether unconcerned, the helmet and the launce suspended at the saddle-bow, and the portmanteau safely fixed upon the crupper.

The knight, riding up to Crabshaw, with equal surprize and concern, asked what had brought him there; and Timothy, after some pause, during which he surveyed his master with a rueful aspect, answered, "The devil." "One would imagine, indeed, you had some such conveyance (said Sir Launcelot). I have followed your cries since last evening I know not how, nor whither, and never could come up with you till this moment. But, say, what damage have you sustained, that you lie in that wretched posture, and groan so dismally?" "I can't guess, (replied the squire) if it bean't that mai hoole carcase is drilled into oilet hools, and my flesh pinched into a jelly."——"How! wherefore? (cried the knight)—who were the miscreants that treated you in such a barbarous manner? Do you know the ruffians?" "I know nothing at all, (answered the peevish squire) but that I was tormented by vive hoondred and vifty thousand legions of devils, and there's an end oan't." "Well, you must have a little pa-tience, Crabshaw—there's a salve for every sore."[6]——"Yaw mought as well tell ma, for every zow there's a zirreverence."[7] "For a man in your condition, methinks you talk very much at your ease.——Try if you can get up and mount Gilbert, that you may be conveyed to some place where you can have proper assistance.——So—well done—chearly—"

Timothy actually made an effort to rise; but fell down again, and uttered a dismal yell. Then his master exhorted him to take advantage of a park-wall, by which he lay, and raise himself gradually upon it. Crabshaw, eying him askance, said, by way of reproach, for his not alighting and assisting him in person, "Thatch your house with t——d, and you'll have more teachers than reachers."[8]—Having pronounced this inelegant adage, he made shift to stand upon his legs; and now, the knight lending a hand, was mounted upon Gilbert, though not without a world of oh's! and ah's! and other ejaculations of pain and impatience. As they jogged on together, our adventurer endeavoured to learn the particulars of the disaster which had befallen the squire; but all the information he could obtain, amounted to a very imperfect sketch of the ad-venture. By dint of a thousand interrogations he understood, that Crabshaw had been, in the preceding evening, encountered by three persons on horse-back with Venetian masques[9] on their faces, which he mistook for their natural features, and was terrified accordingly: that they not only presented pistols to his breast, and led his horse out of the highway; but pricked him with goads, and pinched him, from time to time, till he screamed with the torture: that he was led through unfrequented places across the country, sometimes at an easy trot, sometimes at full gallop, and tormented all night by those hideous dæmons, who vanished at day-break, and left him lying on the spot where he was found by his master. This was a mystery which our hero could by no means unriddle: it was the more unaccountable, as the squire had not been robbed of his money, horses, and baggage. He was even disposed to believe, that Crabshaw's brain was disordered, and the whole account he had given, no more than a chimera. This opinion, however, he could no longer retain, when he arrived at an inn on the post-road, and found, upon examination, that Timothy's lower extremities were covered with blood, and all the rest of his body speckled with livid marks of contusion. But he was still more chagrined when the landlord informed him, that he was thirty miles distant from the place where he had left Aurelia, and that his way lay through cross-roads, which were almost impassable at that season of the year. Alarmed at this intelligence, he gave directions that his squire should be immediately conveyed to bed in a comfortable chamber, as he complained more and more; and indeed was seized with a fever, occasioned by the fatigue, the pain, and terror he had undergone. A neighbouring apothecary being called, and giving it as his opinion that he could not for some days be in a condition to travel, his master deposited a sum of money in his hands, desiring he might be properly attended, till he should hear further. Then mounting Bronzomarte, he set out with a guide for the place he had left, not without a thousand fears and perplexities, arising from the reflection of having left the jewel of his heart with such precipitation.

CHAPTER XVI.

Which, it is to be hoped, the reader will find an agreeable medley of mirth and madness, sense and absurdity.

It was not without reason that our adventurer afflicted himself: his fears were but too prophetic. When he alighted at the inn, which he had left so abruptly the preceding evening, he ran directly to the apartment where he had been so happy in Aurelia's company; but her he saw not—all was solitary. Turning to the woman of the house, who had followed him into the room, "Where is the lady?" cried he, in a tone of impatience. Mine hostess, screwing up her features into a very demure aspect, said she saw so many ladies, she could not pretend to know who he meant. "I tell thee, woman, (exclaimed the knight, in a louder accent) thou never sawest such another—I mean that miracle of beauty—" "Very like (replied the dame, as she retired to the room-door). Husband, here's one as axes concerning a miracle of beauty; hi, hi, hi. Can you give him any information about this miracle of beauty?——Ola! hi, hi, hi." Instead of answering this question, the inn-keeper advancing, and surveying Sir Launcelot, "Friend, (said he) you are the person that carried off my horse out of the stable." "Tell not me of a horse——where is the young lady?" "Now I will tell you of the horse; and I'll make you find him too, before you and I part." "Wretched animal! how dar'st thou dally with my impatience?—Speak, or despair.—What is become of miss Meadows? Say, did she leave this place of her own accord, or was she—hah!—speak—answer, or, by the Powers above—" "I'll answer you flat—she you call miss Meadows is in very good hands—so you may make yourself easy on that score—" "Sacred Heaven! explain your meaning, miscreant, or I'll make you a dreadful example to all the insolent publicans of the realm." So saying, he seized him with one hand, and dashing him on the floor, set one foot on his belly, and kept him trembling in that prostrate attitude. The hostler and waiter flying to the assistance of their master, our adventurer unsheathed his sword, declaring he would dismiss their souls from their bodies, and exterminate the whole family[1] from the face of the earth, if they would not immediately give him the satisfaction he required.

The hostess, being by this time terrified almost out of her senses, fell on her knees before him, begging he would spare their lives, and promising to declare the whole truth. He would not, however, remove his foot from the body of her husband, until she told him, that, in less than half an hour after he had sallied out upon the supposed robbers, two chaises arrived, each drawn by four horses; that two men, armed with pistols, alighting from one of them, laid violent hands upon the young lady; and, notwithstanding her struggling and shrieking, forced her into the other carriage, in which was an infirm gentleman, who called himself her guardian: that the maid was left to the care of a third servant, to follow with a third chaise, which was got ready with all possible dispatch, while the other two proceeded at full speed on the road to London. It was by this communicative lacquey the people of the house were informed, that the old gentleman his master was squire Darnel, the young lady his niece and ward, and our adventurer a needy sharper, who wanted to make prey of her fortune. The knight, fired even almost to frenzy by this intimation, spurned the carcase of his host; and, his eye gleaming terror, rushed into the

[Sir Launcelot and the Inn-keeper], by William Walker after Stothard.
(Rare Book and Manuscript Library, Columbia University).

yard, in order to mount Bronzomarte, and pursue the ravisher, when he was diverted from his purpose by a new incident.

One of the postilions, who had driven the chaise in which Dolly was conveyed, happened to arrive at that instant; when, seeing our hero, he ran up to him cap in hand, and, presenting a letter, accosted him in these words: "Please your noble honour, if your honour be Sir Launcelot Greaves of the West Riding, here's a letter from a gentlewoman, that I promised to deliver into your honour's own hands."

The knight, snatching the letter with the utmost avidity, broke it up, and found the contents couched in these terms:

"Honoured Sir,
    The man az gi'en me leave to lat yaw knaw my dear leady is going to Loondon with her unkle squaire Darnel.——Be not conzarned, honoured sir, vor I'se teake it on mai laife, to let yaw knaw wheare we be zettled, if zo be I can vind wheare you loadge in Loondon.——The man zays yaw may put it in the pooblic prints.——I houp the bare-heir will be honest enuff to deliver this scrowl; and that your honour will pardon

                              Your umbil servant to command
                              DOROTHY COWSLIP.

P. S. Please my kaind sarvice to laayer Clarke. Squire Darnel's man is very civil vor sartain; but I'ave no thoughts on him I'll assure yaw.—Marry hap, worse ware may have a better chap,[2] as the zaying goes."

Nothing could be more seasonable than the delivery of this billet; which he had no sooner perused, than his reflection returned, and he entered into a serious deliberation with his own heart. He considered that Aurelia was by this time far beyond a possibility of being overtaken; and that by a precipitate pursuit he should only expose his own infirmities. He confided in the attachment of his mistress, and in the fidelity of her maid, who would find opportunities of communicating her sentiments, by the means of this lacquey, of whom he perceived by the letter she had already made a conquest. He therefore resolved to bridle his impatience, to proceed leisurely to London, and, instead of taking any rash step which might induce Anthony Darnel to remove his niece from that city, remain in seeming quiet until she should be settled, and her guardian returned to the country. Aurelia had mentioned to him the name of doctor Kawdle, and from him he expected, in due time, to receive the most interesting information.[3]

These reflections had an instantaneous effect upon our hero, whose rage immediately subsided, and whose visage gradually resumed its natural cast of courtesy and good humour. He forthwith gratified the postilion with such a remuneration, as sent him dancing into the kitchen, where he did not fail to extol the generosity and immense fortune of Sir Launcelot Greaves.

Our adventurer's next step was to see Bronzomarte properly accommodated; then he ordered a refreshment for himself, and retired into an apartment, where mine host with his wife and all the servants waited on him, to beseech his honour to forgive their impertinence, which was owing to their ignorance of his honour's quality, and the false information they had received from the gentleman's servant. He had too much magnanimity to retain the least resentment against such inconsiderable objects. He not only pardoned them without hesitation; but assured the landlord he would be accountable for the horse, which, however, was that same evening brought home by a countryman, who had found him pounded as it were within the walls of a ruined cottage. As the knight had been greatly fatigued, without enjoying any rest for eight and forty hours, he resolved to indulge himself with one night's repose, and then return to the place where he had left his squire indisposed: for by this time even his concern for Timothy had recurred.

On a candid scrutiny of his own heart, he found himself much less unhappy than he had been before his interview with Aurelia; for, instead of being as formerly tormented with the pangs of despairing love, which had actually unsettled his understanding, he was now happily convinced that he had inspired the tender breast of Aurelia with mutual affection; and though she was invidiously snatched from his embrace, in the midst of such endearments as had wound up his soul to extasy and transport, he did not doubt of being able to rescue her from the power of an inhuman kinsman, whose guardianship would soon of course expire; and in the mean time, he rested with the most perfect dependence on her constancy and virtue.

As he next day crossed the country, ruminating on the disaster that had befallen his squire, and could now compare circumstances coolly, he easily comprehended the whole scheme of that adventure, which was no other than an artifice of Anthony Darnel and his emissaries, to draw him from the inn where he proposed to execute his design upon the innocent Aurelia. He took it for granted, that the uncle, having been made acquainted with his niece's elopement, had followed her track by the help of such information as he received from one stage to another; and that, receiving more particulars at the White Hart touching Sir Launcelot, he had formed the scheme in which Crabshaw was an involuntary instrument towards the seduction of his master.

Amusing himself with these and other cogitations, our hero in the afternoon reached the place of his destination; and entering the inn where Timothy had been left at sick quarters, chanced to meet the apothecary retiring precipitately in a very unsavoury pickle from the chamber of his patient. When he inquired about the health of his squire, this retainer to medicine, wiping himself all the while with a napkin, answered in manifest confusion, That he apprehended him to be in a very dangerous way, from an inflammation of the *pia mater*,[4] which had produced a most furious delirium. Then he proceeded to explain, in technical terms, the method of cure he had followed; and concluded with telling him the poor squire's brain was so outrageously disordered, that he had rejected all administration, and just thrown an urinal in his face.

The knight's humanity being alarmed at this intelligence, he resolved that Crabshaw should have the benefit of further advice, and asked if there was not a physician in the place. The apothecary, after some interjections of hesitation, owned there was a doctor in the village, an odd sort of a humourist;[5] but he believed he had not much to do in the way of his profession, and was not much used to the forms of prescription. He was counted a scholar, to be sure; but as to his medical capacity,——he would not take upon him to say——"No matter, (cried Sir Launcelot) he may strike out some lucky thought for the benefit of the patient; and I desire you will call him instantly."——

While the apothecary was absent on this service, our adventurer took it in his head to question the landlord about the character of this physician, which had been so unfavourably represented, and received the following information:

"For my peart, measter, I knows nothing amiss of the doctor——he's a quiet sort of an inoffensive man; uses my house sometimes, and pays for what he has, like the rest of my customers. They says he deals very little in physic stuff, but cures his patients with fasting and water-gruel, whereby he can't expect the pothecary to be his friend. You knows, master, one must live, and let live, as the saying is. I must say, he, for the value of three guineas, set up my wife's constitution in such a manner, that I have saved within these two years, I believe, forty pounds in pothecary's bills. But what of that? Every man must eat, thof at another's expence; and I should be in a deadly hole myself, if all my customers should take it in their heads to drink nothing but water-gruel, because it is good for the constitution. Thank God, I have as good a constitution as e'er a man in England; but for all that, I and my whole family bleed and purge and take a diet-drink twice a-year, by way of serving the pothecary, who is a very honest man, and a very good neighbour."

Their conversation was interrupted by the return of the apothecary with the doctor, who had very little of the faculty in his appearance. He was dressed remarkably plain; seemed to be turned of fifty; had a careless air, and a sarcastical turn in his countenance. Before he entered the sick man's chamber, he asked some questions concerning the disease; and when the apothecary, pointing to his own head, said, "It lies all here"; the doctor, turning to Sir Launcelot, replied, "If that be all, there's nothing in it."

Upon a more particular enquiry about the symptoms, he was told that the blood was seemingly viscous, and salt upon the tongue; the urine remarkably acrosaline; and the fæces atrabilious[6] and foetid. When the doctor said he would engage to find the same phænomena in every healthy man of the three kingdoms; the apothecary added, that the patient was manifestly comatous, and moreover afflicted with griping pains and borborygmata.[7]—"A f——t for your borborygmata (cried the physician). What has been done?" To this question he replied, that venæsection[8] had been three times performed: that a vesicatory had been applied *inter scapulas*:[9] that the patient had taken occasionally of a cathartic apozem,[10] and, between whiles, alexipharmic boluses and neutral draughts.[11]—"Neutral, indeed (said the doctor); so neutral, that I'll be crucified if ever they declare either for the patient or the disease." So saying, he brushed into Crabshaw's chamber, followed by our adventurer, who was almost suffocated at his first entrance. The day was close, the window-shutters were fastened; a huge fire blazed in the chimney; thick harateen[12] curtains were close drawn round the bed, where the wretched squire lay extended under an enormous load of blankets. The nurse, who had all the exteriors of a bawd given to drink, sat stewing in this apartment, like a damned soul in some infernal bagnio: but rising, when the company entered, made her curtsies with great decorum. "Well, (said the doctor) how does your patient, nurse?" "Blessed be God for it, I hope in a fair way:—to be sure his apozem has had a blessed effect—five and twenty stools since three o'clock in the morning.—But then a'would not suffer the blisters to be put upon his thighs.—Good lack! a'has been mortally obstropolous,[13] and out of his senses all this blessed day."——"You lie, (cried the squire) I a'n't out of my seven senses,[14] thof I'm half mad with vexation."

The doctor having withdrawn the curtain, the hapless squire appeared very pale and ghastly; and having surveyed his master with a rueful aspect, addressed him in these words: "Sir knight, I beg a boon: be pleased to tie a stone about the neck of the apothecary, and a halter about the neck of the nurse, and throw the one into the next river, and the other over the next tree, and in so doing you will do a charitable deed to your fellow-creatures; for he and she do the devil's work in partnership, and have sent many a score of their betters home to him before their time." "Oh, he begins to talk sensibly. Have a good heart (said the physician). What is your disorder?" "Physick." "What do you chiefly complain of?" "The doctor." "Does your head ake?" "Yea, with impertinence." "Have you a pain in your back?" "Yes, where the blister lies." "Are you sick at stomach?" "Yes, with hunger." "Do you feel any shiverings?" "Always at sight of the apothecary." "Do you perceive any load in your bowels?" "I would the apothecary's conscience was as clear." "Are you thirsty?" "Not thirsty enough to drink barley-water." "Be pleased to look into his fauces[15] (said the apothecary): he has got a rough tongue, and a very foul mouth, I'll assure you." "I have known that the case with some limbs of the faculty, where they stood more in need of correction than of physick.—Well, my honest friend, since you have already undergone the proper purgations in due form, and say you have no other disease than the doctor, we will set you on your legs again, without further question. Here, nurse, open that window, and throw these vials into the street. Now lower the curtain, without shutting the casement, that the man may not be stifled in his own steam. In the next place, take off two thirds of these coals, and one third of these blankets.——How do'st feel now, my heart?" "I should feel heart-whole, if so be as yow would throw the noorse a'ter the bottles, and the pothecary a'ter the noorse, and oorder me a pound of chops for my dinner; for I be so hoongry, I could eat a horse behind the saddle."[16]

The apothecary, seeing what passed, retired of his own accord, holding up his hands in sign of astonishment. The nurse was dismissed in the same breath. Crabshaw rose, dressed himself without assistance, and made a hearty meal on the first eatable that presented itself to his view. The knight passed the evening with the physician, who, from his first appearance, concluded he was mad; but, in the course of the conversation, found means to resign that opinion, without adopting any other in lieu of it, and parted with him under all the impatience of curiosity. The knight, on his part, was very well entertained with the witty sarcasms and erudition of the doctor, who appeared to be a sort of cynic philosopher, tinctured with misanthropy, and at open war with the whole body of apothecaries, whom, however, it was by no means his interest to disoblige.

Next day, Crabshaw being to all appearance perfectly recovered, our adventurer reckoned with the apothecary, payed the landlord, and set out on his return for the London-road, resolving to lay aside his armour at some distance from the metropolis: for, ever since his interview with Aurelia, his fondness for chivalry had been gradually abating. As the torrent of his despair had disordered the current of his sober reflection, so now, as that despair subsided, his thoughts began to flow deliberately in their antient channel. All day long he regaled his imagination with plans of connubial happiness, formed on the possession of the incomparable Aurelia; determined to wait with patience, until the law should supersede the authority of her guardian, rather than adopt any violent expedient which might hazard the interest of his passion.

He had for some time travelled in the turnpike road, when his reverie was suddenly interrupted by a confused noise; and when he lifted up his eyes, he beheld at a little distance a rabble of men and women, variously armed with flails, pitch-forks, poles, and muskets, acting offensively against a strange figure on horseback, who, with a kind of lance, laid about him with incredible fury. Our adventurer was not so totally abandoned by the spirit of chivalry, as to see without emotion a single knight in danger of being overpowered by such a multitude of adversaries. Without staying to put on his helmet, he ordered Crabshaw to follow him in the charge against those plebeians: then couching his lance, and giving Bronzomarte the spur, he began his career with such impetuosity as overturned all that happened to be in his way; and intimidated the rabble to such a degree, that they retired before him like a flock of sheep, the greater part of them believing he was the devil *in propria persona*. He came in the very nick of time to save the life of the other errant, against whom three loaded musquets were actually levelled, at the very instant that our adventurer began his charge. The unknown knight was so sensible of the seasonable interposition, that riding up to our hero, "Brother, (said he) this is the second time you have holp me off, when I was bump ashore.—Bess Mizen, I must say, is no more than a leaky bumboat,[17] in comparison of the glorious galley you want to man. I desire that henceforth we may cruise in the same latitudes, brother; and I'll be damned if I don't stand by you as long as I have a stick standing, or can carry a rag of canvas."

By this address our knight recognized the novice captain Crowe, who had found means to accommodate himself with a very strange suit of armour. By way of helmet, he wore one of the caps used by the light horse,[18] with straps buckled under his chin, and contrived in such a manner as to conceal his whole visage, except the eyes. Instead of cuirass, mail, greaves, and the other pieces of complete armour, he was cased in a postilion's leathern jerkin, covered with thin plates of tinned iron: his buckler was a potlid, his lance a hop-pole[19] shod with iron, and a basket-hilt broad sword, like that of Hudibras,[20] depended by a broad buff belt, that girded his middle. His feet were defended by jack-boots, and his hands by the gloves of a trooper. Sir Launcelot would not lose time in examining particulars, as he perceived that some mischief had been done, and that the enemy had rallied at a distance: he therefore commanded Crowe to follow him, and rode off with great expedition; but he did not perceive that his squire was taken prisoner; nor did the captain recollect that his nephew, Tom Clarke, had been disabled and secured in the beginning of the fray. The truth is, the poor captain had been so belaboured about the pate, that it was a wonder he remembered his own name.

CHAPTER XVII.

Containing adventures of chivalry,
equally new and surprising.

The knight Sir Launcelot, and the novice Crowe, retreated with equal order and expedition to the distance of half a league from the field of battle, where the former, halting, proposed to make a lodgment in a very decent house of entertainment, distinguished by the sign of St. George of Cappadocia encountering the dragon,[1] an atchievement in which temporal and spiritual chivalry were happily reconciled. Two such figures alighting at the inn-gate, did not pass through the yard unnoticed and unadmired by the guests and attendants; some of whom fairly took to their heels, on the supposition that these outlandish creatures were the avant couriers, or heralds of a French invasion.[2] The fears and doubts, however, of those who ventured to stay were soon dispelled, when our hero accosted them in the English tongue, and with the most courteous demeanour desired to be shewn into an apartment. Had captain Crowe been the spokesman, perhaps their suspicions would not have so quickly subsided; for he was, in reality, a very extraordinary novice, not only in chivalry, but also in his external appearance, and particularly in those dialects of the English language which are used by the terrestrial animals of this kingdom. He desired the hostler to take his horse in tow, and bring him to his moorings in a safe riding. He ordered the waiter, who shewed them into a parlour, to bear-a-hand, ship his oars, mind his helm, and bring along-side a short allowance of brandy or grog,[3] that he might cant a slug into his breadroom;[4] for there was such a heaving and pitching, that he believed he should shift his ballast. The fellow understood no part of this address but the word *brandy*, at mention of which he disappeared. Then Crowe, throwing himself into an elbow-chair, "Stop my hawse-holes,[5] (cried he) I can't think what's the matter, brother; but, a-gad, my head sings and simmers like a pot of chowder.—My eye-sight yaws to and again, d'ye see:—then there's such a walloping and whushing in my hold——smite my——Lord have mercy upon us.—Here, you swab, ne'er mind a glass—hand me the noggin—."[6]

The latter part of this address was directed to the waiter, who had returned with a quartern[7] of brandy, which Crowe, snatching eagerly, started into his bread-room at one cant. Indeed there was no time to be lost, inasmuch as he seemed to be on the verge of fainting away when he swallowed this cordial, by which he was instantaneously revived. He then desired the servant to unbuckle the straps of his helmet; but this was a task which the drawer could not perform, even though assisted with the good offices of Sir Launcelot: for the head and jaws were so much swelled with the discipline they had undergone, that the straps and buckles lay buried, as it were, in pits formed by the tumefaction of the adjacent parts. Fortunately for the novice, a neighbouring surgeon passed by the door on horseback; a circumstance which the waiter, who saw him from the window, no sooner disclosed, than the knight had recourse to his assistance. This practitioner having viewed the whole figure, and more particularly the head of Crowe, in silent wonder, proceeded to feel his pulse; and then declared, that as the inflammation was very great, and going on with violence to its akme, it would be necessary to begin with copious phlebotomy, and then to empty the intestinal canal. So saying, he began to strip the arm of the captain, who perceiving his aim, "Avast, brother, (cried he) you go the wrong way to work—you may as well rummage the afterhold,[8] when the damage is in the forecastle.—I shall right again, when my jaws are unhooped."

With these words he drew a clasp-knife from his pocket, and, advancing to a glass, applied it so vigorously to the leather straps of his headpiece, that the Gordian-knot was cut,[9] without any other damage to his face than a moderate scarification, which, added to the tumefaction of features, naturally strong, and a whole week's growth of a very bushy beard, produced, on the whole, a most hideous caricatura. After all, there was a necessity for the administration of the surgeon, who found divers contusions on different parts of the skull, which even the tin-cap had not been able to protect from the weapons of the rusticks.

These being shaved, and dressed *secundum artem*,[10] and the operator dismissed with a proper acknowledgment, our knight detached one of the postboys to the field of action for intelligence, concerning Mr. Clarke and squire Timothy; and, in the interim, desired to know the particulars of Crowe's adventures since he parted from him at the White Hart. A connected relation, in plain English, was what he had little reason to expect from the novice, who, nevertheless, exerted his faculties to the uttermost for his satisfaction: he gave him to understand, that in steering his course to Birmingham,[11] where he thought of fitting himself with tackle, he had fallen in, by accident, at a public house, with an itinerant tinker, in the very act of mending a kettle: that, seeing him do his business like an able workman, he had applied to him for advice; and the tinker, after having considered the subject, had undertaken to make him such a suit of armour as neither sword nor lance should penetrate: that they adjourned to the next town, where the leather coat, the plates of tinned iron, the lance, and the broad sword, were purchased, together with a copper sauce-pan, which the artist was now at work upon, in converting it to a shield: but, in the mean time, the captain, being impatient to begin his career of chivalry, had accommodated himself with a pot-lid, and taken to the highway, notwithstanding all the intreaties, tears, and remonstrances of his nephew Tom Clarke, who could not however be prevailed upon to leave him in the dangerous voyage he had undertaken: that this being but the second day of his journal,[12] he descried five or six men on horseback, bearing up full in his teeth; upon which he threw his sails a-back, and prepared for action: that he hailed them at a considerable distance, and bad them bring-to:[13] that, when they came along-side, notwithstanding his hail, he ordered them to clew up their corses,[14] and furl their topsails, otherwise he would be foul of their quarters:[15] that, hearing this salute, they luffed[16] all at once, till their cloth shook in the wind: then he hollowed in a loud voice, that his sweet-heart Besselia Mizzen[17] wore the broad pendant[18] of beauty, to which they must strike their topsails, on pain of being sent to the bottom: that, after having eyed him for some time with astonishment, they clapped on all their sails,[19] some of them running under his stern, and others athwart his forefoot,[20] and got clear off: that, not satisfied with running a-head, they all of a sudden tacked about,[21] and one of them boarding him on the lee-quarter,[22] gave him such a drubbing about his upper works,[23] that the lights danced in his lanthorns: that he returned the salute with his hop-pole so effectually, that his aggressor broached-to[24] in the twinkling of an hand-spike;[25] and then he was engaged with all the rest of the enemy, except one who sheered off, and soon returned with a mosqueto fleet[26] of small craft, who had done him considerable damage, and, in all probability, would have made prize[27] of him, hadn't he been brought off by the knight's gallantry. He said, that in the beginning of the conflict Tom Clarke rode up to the foremost of the enemy, as he did suppose, in order to prevent hostilities; but before he got up to him, near enough to hold discourse, he was pooped with a sea[28] that almost sent him to the bottom, and then towed off he knew not whither.

Crowe had scarce finished his narration, which consisted of broken hints, and unconnected explosions of sea-terms, when a gentleman of the neighbourhood, who acted in the commission of the peace, arrived at the gate, attended by a constable, who had in custody the bodies of Thomas Clarke and Timothy Crabshaw, surrounded by five men on horseback, and an innumerable posse of men, women, and children, on foot. The captain, who always kept a good look-out, no sooner descried this cavalcade and procession than he gave notice to Sir Launcelot, and advised that they should crowd away with all the cloth they could carry.[29] Our adventurer was of another opinion, and determined at any rate to procure the enlargement of the prisoners.[30] The justice, ordering his attendants to stay without the gate, sent his compliments to Sir Launcelot Greaves, and desired to speak with him for a few minutes. He was immediately admitted, and could not help starting at sight of Crowe, who, by this time, had no remains of the human physiognomy, so much was the swelling increased and the skin discoloured. The gentleman, whose name was Mr. Elmy, having made a polite apology for the liberty he had taken, proceeded to unfold his business. He said, information had been lodged with him, as a justice of the peace, against two armed men on horseback, who had stopped five farmers on the king's highway, put them in fear and danger of their lives, and even assaulted, maimed, and wounded divers persons, contrary to the king's peace, and in violation of the statute: that, by the description, he supposed the knight and his companion to be the persons against whom the complaint had been lodged; and understanding his quality from Mr. Clarke, whom he had known in London, he was come to wait on him, and, if possible, effect an accommodation.

Our adventurer, having thanked him for the polite and obliging manner in which he proceeded, frankly told him the whole story, as it had been just related by the captain; and Mr. Elmy had no reason to doubt the truth of the narrative, as it confirmed every circumstance which Clarke had before reported. Indeed, Tom had been very communicative to this gentleman, and made him acquainted with the whole history of Sir Launcelot Greaves, as well as with the whimsical resolution of his uncle, captain Crowe. Mr. Elmy now told the knight, that the persons whom the captain had stopped were farmers, returning from a neighbouring market, a set of people naturally boorish, and at that time elevated with ale to an uncommon pitch of insolence: that one of them, in particular, called Prickle, was the most quarrelsome fellow in the whole county; and so litigious, that he had maintained above thirty law-suits, in eight and twenty of which he had been condemned in costs. He said the others might be easily influenced in the way of admonition; but there was no way of dealing with Prickle, except by the form and authority of the law: he therefore proposed to hear evidence in a judicial capacity, and, his clerk being in attendance, the court was immediately opened in the knight's apartment.

By this time Mr. Clarke had made such good use of his time in explaining the law to his audience, and displaying the great wealth and unbounded liberality of Sir Launcelot Greaves, that he had actually brought over to his sentiments the constable and the commonalty, tag, rag, and bob-tail,[31] and even staggered the majority of the farmers, who, at first, had breathed nothing but defiance and revenge. Farmer Stake, being first called to the bar, and sworn, touching the identity of Sir Launcelot Greaves and captain Crowe, declared, that the said Crowe had stopped him on the king's highway, and put him in bodily fear: that he afterwards saw the said Crowe with a pole or weapon, value three pence, breaking the king's peace, by committing assault and battery against the heads and shoulders of his majesty's liege subjects, Geoffrey Prickle, Hodge Dolt, Richard Bumpkin, Mary Fang, Catherine Rubble, and Margery Litter; and that he saw Sir Launcelot Greaves, baronet, aiding, assisting, and comforting the said Crowe, contrary to the king's peace, and against the form of the statute.

Being asked if the defendant, when he stopped them, demanded their money, or threatened violence, he answered, he could not say, inasmuch as the defendant spoke in an unknown language. Being interrogated if the defendant did not allow them to pass without using any violence, and if they did not pass unmolested, the deponent replied in the affirmative: being required to tell for what reason they returned, and if the defendant Crowe was not assaulted before he began to use his weapon, the deponent made no answer. The depositions of farmers Bumpkin and Muggins, as well as of Madge Litter and Mary Fang, were taken much to the same purpose; and his worship earnestly exhorted them to an accommodation, observing, that they themselves were in fact the aggressors, and that captain Crowe had done no more than exerted himself in his own defence.

They were all pretty well disposed to follow his advice, except farmer Prickle, who, entering the court with a bloody handkerchief about his head, declared, that the law should determine it at next 'size;[32] and in the mean time insisted, that the defendants should find immediate bail, or go to prison, or be set in the stocks. He affirmed, that they had been guilty of an *affray*, in appearing with armour and weapons not usually worn, to the terror of others, which is in itself a breach of the peace: but that they had, moreover, with force of arms, that is to say, with swords, staves, and other warlike instruments, by turns, made an assault and *affray*, to the terror and disturbance of him and divers subjects of our lord the king then and there being, and to the evil and pernicious example of the liege people of the said lord the king, and against the peace of our said lord the king, his crown, and dignity.[33]

This peasant had purchased a few law-terms at a considerable expence, and he thought he had a right to turn his knowledge to the annoyance of all his neighbours. Mr. Elmy, finding him obstinately deaf to all proposals of accommodation, held the defendants to very moderate bail, the landlord and the curate of the parish freely offering themselves as sureties. Mr. Clarke, with Timothy Crabshaw, against whom nothing appeared, were now set at liberty; when the former, advancing to his worship, gave information against Geoffrey Prickle, and declared upon oath, that he had seen him assault captain Crowe, without any provocation; and when he, the deponent, interposed to prevent further mischief, the said Prickle had likewise assaulted and wounded him the deponent, and detained him for some time in false imprisonment,[34] without warrant or authority.

In consequence of this information, which was corroborated by divers evidences, selected from the mob at the gate, the tables were turned upon farmer Prickle, who was given to understand, that he must either find bail, or be forthwith imprisoned. This *honest* boor, who was in opulent circumstances, had made such popular use of the benefits he possessed, that there was not an houseckeeper in the parish who would not have rejoiced to see him hanged. His dealings and connections however were such, that none of the other four would have refused to bail him, had not Clarke given them to understand, that, if they did, he would make them all principals and parties, and have two separate actions against each. Prickle happened to be at variance with the innkeeper, and the curate durst not disoblige the vicar, who at that very time was suing the farmer for the small tythes.[35] He offered to deposit a sum equal to the recognizance of the knight's bail; but this was rejected as an expedient contrary to the practice of the courts. He sent for the attorney of the village, to whom he had been a good customer; but the lawyer was hunting evidence in another county. The exciseman presented himself as a surety; but he not being an housekeeper, was not accepted. Divers cottagers, who depended on farmer Prickle, were successively refused, because they could not prove that they had payed scot and lot,[36] and parish taxes.

The farmer, finding himself thus forlorn, and in imminent danger of visiting the inside of a prison, was seized with a paroxysm of rage; during which he inveighed against the bench, reviled the two adventurers errant, declared that he believed, and would lay a wager of twenty guineas, that he had more money in his pocket than e'er a man in the company; and in the space of a quarter of an hour swore forty oaths, which the justice did not fail to number.

"Before we proceed to other matters, (said Mr. Elmy) I order you to pay forty shillings for the oaths you have swore; otherwise I will cause you to be set in the stocks, without further ceremony."

Prickle, throwing down a couple of guineas, with two execrations more to make up the sum, declared, that he could afford to pay for swearing as well as e'er a justice in the county; and repeated his challenge of the wager, which our adventurer now accepted, protesting, at the same time, that it was not a step taken from any motive of pride, but intirely with a view to punish an insolent plebeian, who could not otherwise be chastised without a breach of the peace. Twenty guineas being deposited on each side in the hands of Mr. Elmy, Prickle, with equal confidence and dispatch, produced a canvas bag, containing two hundred and seventy pounds, which, being spread upon the table, made a very formidable shew, that dazzled the eyes of the beholders, and induced many of them to believe he had ensured his conquest.

Our adventurer, asking if he had any thing further to offer, and being answered in the negative, drew forth, with great deliberation, a pocket-book, in which there was a considerable parcel of bank-notes, from which he selected three of one hundred pounds each, and exhibited them upon the table, to the astonishment of all present. Prickle, mad with his overthrow and loss, said it might be necessary to make him prove the notes were honestly come by; and Sir Launcelot started up, in order to take vengeance upon him for this insult; but was withheld by the arms and remonstrances of Mr. Elmy, who assured him that Prickle desired nothing so much as another broken head, to lay the foundation of a new prosecution.

The knight, calmed by this interposition, turned to the audience, saying, with the most affable deportment, "Good people, do not imagine that I intend to pocket the spoils of such a contemptible rascal. I shall beg the favour of this worthy gentleman to take up these twenty guineas, and distribute them as he shall think proper, among the poor of the parish: but, by this benefaction, I do not hold myself acquitted for the share I had in the bruises some of you have received in this unlucky fray; and therefore I give the other twenty guineas to be divided among the sufferers, to each according to the damage he or she shall appear to have sustained; and I shall consider it as an additional obligation, if Mr. Elmy will likewise superintend this retribution."

At the close of this address, the whole yard and gate-way rung with acclamation: while honest Crowe, whose generosity was not inferior even to that of the accomplished Greaves, pulled out his purse, and declared that as he had begun the engagement, he would at least go share and share alike in new caulking their seams and repairing their timbers. The knight, rather than enter into a dispute with his novice, told him he considered the twenty guineas as given by them both in conjunction, and that they would confer together on that subject hereafter.

This point being adjusted, Mr. Elmy assumed all the solemnity of the magistrate, and addressed himself to Prickle in these words: "Farmer Prickle, I am both sorry and ashamed to see a man of your years and circumstances so little respected, that you cannot find sufficient bail for forty pounds; a sure testimony that you have neither cultivated the friendship, nor deserved the goodwill of your neighbours. I have heard of your quarrels and your riots, your insolence, and litigious disposition; and often wished for an opportunity of giving you a proper taste of the law's correction. That opportunity now offers—You have in the hearing of all these people poured forth a torrent of abuse against me, both in the character of a gentleman and of a magistrate: your abusing me personally, perhaps I should have overlooked with the contempt it deserves; but I should ill vindicate the dignity of my office as magistrate, by suffering you to insult the bench with impunity. I shall therefore imprison you for contempt;[37] and you shall remain in jail, until you can find bail on the other prosecutions."

Prickle, the first transports of his anger having subsided, began to be pricked with the thorns of compunction. He was indeed exceedingly mortified at the prospect of being sent to jail so disgracefully. His countenance fell, and, after a hard internal struggle while the clerk was employed in writing the mittimus,[38] he said he hoped his worship would not send him to prison. He begged pardon of him and our adventurers for having abused them in his passion, and observed, that as he had received a broken head, and payed two and twenty guineas for his folly, he could not be said to have escaped altogether without punishment, even if the plaintiff should agree to exchange releases.

Sir Launcelot, seeing this stubborn rustic effectually humbled, became an advocate in his favour with Mr. Elmy and Tom Clarke, who forgave him at his request, and a mutual release being executed, the farmer was permitted to depart. The populace were regaled at our adventurer's expence; and the men, women, and children, who had been wounded or bruised in the battle, to the number of ten or dozen, were desired to wait upon Mr. Elmy in the morning to receive the knight's bounty. The justice was prevailed upon to spend the evening with Sir Launcelot and his two companions, for whom supper was bespoke; but the first thing the cook prepared was a poultice for Crowe's head, which was now enlarged to a monstrous exhibition. Our knight, who was all

kindness and complacency, shook Mr. Clarke by the hand, expressing his satisfaction at meeting with his old friends again, and told him softly that he had
compliments for him from Mrs. Dolly Cowslip, who now lived with his
Aurelia.

Clarke was confounded at this intelligence, and after some hesitation, "Lord
bless my soul! (cried he) I'll be shot then if the pretended miss Meadows
wa'n't the same as miss Darnel!" He then declared himself extremely glad that
poor Dolly had got into such an agreeable situation, passed many warm en-
comiums on her goodness of heart and virtuous inclinations, and concluded
with appealing to the knight whether she did not look very pretty in her green
Joseph.[39] In the mean time, he procured a plaister for his own head, and helped
to apply the poultice to that of his uncle, who was sent to bed betimes with
a moderate dose of sack-whey[40] to promote perspiration. The other three
passed the evening to their mutual satisfaction; and the justice in particular
grew enamoured of the knight's character, dashed as it was with extravagance.

Let us now leave them to the enjoyment of a sober and rational conversation; and give some account of other guests who arrived late in the evening,
and here fixed their night-quarters—But as we have already trespassed on the
reader's patience, we shall give him a short respite until the next chapter makes
its appearance.

CHAPTER XVIII.

In which the Rays of Chivalry shine with renovated Lustre.

Our hero little dreamed that he had a formidable rival in the person of the
knight who arrived about eleven at the sign of the St. George, and, by
the noise he made, gave intimation of his importance. This was no other than
squire Sycamore, who, having received advice that Miss Aurelia Darnel had
eloped from the place of her retreat, immediately took the field, in quest of
that lovely fugitive; hoping that, should he have the good fortune to find her
in her present distress, his good offices would not be rejected. He had followed
the chace so close, that, immediately after our adventurer's departure, he
alighted at the inn from whence Aurelia had been conveyed; and there he
learned the particulars which we have related above. Mr. Sycamore had a great

deal of the childish romantic in his disposition, and, in the course of his amours, is said to have always taken more pleasure in the pursuit than in the final possession. He had heard of Sir Launcelot's extravagance, by which he was in some measure infected; and he dropped an insinuation, that he could eclipse his rival even in his own lunatic sphere. This hint was not lost upon his companion, counsellor, and buffoon, the facetious Davy Dawdle, who had some humour and a great deal of mischief in his composition. He looked upon his patron as a fool, and his patron knew him to be both knave and fool: yet the two characters suited each other so well, that they could hardly exist asunder. Davy was an artful sycophant, but he did not flatter in the usual way; on the contrary, he behaved *en cavalier*,[1] and treated Sycamore, on whose bounty he subsisted, with the most sarcastic familiarity. Nevertheless, he seasoned his freedom with certain qualifying ingredients that subdued the bitterness of it, and was now become so necessary to the squire, that he had no idea of enjoyment with which Dawdle was not some how or other connected. There had been a warm dispute betwixt them about the scheme of contesting the prize with Sir Launcelot in the lists of chivalry. Sycamore had insinuated, that if he had a mind to play the fool, he could wear armour, wield a launce, and manage a charger, as well as Sir Launcelot Greaves. Dawdle snatching the hint, "I had some time ago, (said he) contrived a scheme for you, which I was afraid you had not address enough to execute—It would be no difficult matter, in imitation of the batchelor Sampson Carrasco, to go in quest of Greaves as a knight errant, defy him as a rival, and establish a compact, by which the vanquished should obey the injunctions of the victor"[2]——"That is my very idea" (cried Sycamore). "Your idea, (replied the other) had you ever an idea of your own conception?"—Thus the dispute began, and was maintained with great vehemence; until other arguments failing, the squire offered to lay a wager of twenty guineas. To this proposal Dawdle answered by the interjection *Pish!* which inflamed Sycamore to a repetition of the defiance.—"You are in the right (said Dawdle) to use such an argument, as you know is by me unanswerable. A wager of twenty guineas will at any time overthrow and confute all the logick of the most able syllogist, who has not got a shilling in his pocket."

Sycamore looked very grave at this declaration, and, after a short pause, said, "I wonder, Dawdle, what you do with all your money!" "I am surprised you should give yourself that trouble—I never ask what you do with yours."— "You have no occasion to ask: you know pretty well how it goes." "What! do you upbraid me with your favours?—'tis mighty well, Sycamore."—"Nay, Dawdle, I did not intend to affront."—"Z——s![3] affront! what d'ye mean?"— "I'll assure you, Davy, you don't know me, if you think I could be so ungenerous as to—a—to—" "I always thought, whatever faults or foibles you might have, Sycamore, that you was not deficient in generosity,—tho' to be sure it is often very absurdly displayed." "Ay, that's one of my greatest foibles: I can't refuse even a scoundrel, when I think he's in want.——Here, Dawdle, take that note."—"Not I, sir,—what d'ye mean?—what right have I to your notes?" "Nay, but Dawdle—come."—"By no means,—it looks like the abuse of good nature.—All the world knows you're good natured to a fault."—"Come, dear Davy, you shall—you must oblige me."——Thus urged, Dawdle accepted the bank note with great reluctance, and restored the idea to the right owner.

A suit of armour being brought from the garret or armoury of his ancestors, he gave orders for having the pieces scoured and furbished up; and his heart dilated with joy, when he reflected upon the superb figure he should make when cased in complete steel, and armed at all points for the combat.

When he was fitted with the other parts, Dawdle insisted on buckling on his helmet, which weighed fifteen pounds, and the head-piece being adjusted, made such a clatter about his ears with a cudgel, that his eyes had almost started from their sockets. His voice was lost within the vizor, and his friend affected not to understand his meaning when he made signs with his gauntlets, and endeavoured to close with him that he might wrest the cudgel from his hand. At length he desisted, saying, "I'll warrant the helmet sound, by its ringing"; and taking it off, found the squire in a cold sweat. He would have achieved his first exploit on the spot, had his strength permitted him to assault Dawdle; but, what with want of air, and the discipline he had undergone, he had well nigh swooned away; and before he retrieved the use of his members, he was appeased by the apologies of his companion, who protested he meant nothing more than to try if the helmet was free of cracks, and whether or not it would prove a good protection for the head it covered. His excuses were accepted: the armour was packed up, and next morning Mr. Sycamore set out from his own house, accompanied by Dawdle, who undertook to perform the part of his squire at the approaching combat. He was also attended by a servant on horseback, who had charge of the armour, and another who blowed the trumpet. They no sooner understood that our hero was housed at the George, than the trumpeter sounded a charge, which alarmed Sir Launcelot and his company, and disturbed honest captain Crowe in the middle of his first sleep. Their next step was to pen a challenge, which, when the stranger departed, was by the trumpeter delivered with great ceremony into the hands of Sir Launcelot, who read it in these words: "To the Knight of the Crescent,[4] greeting. Whereas I am informed you have the presumption to lay claim to the heart of the peerless Aurelia Darnel, I give you notice that I can admit no rivalship in the affection of that paragon of beauty; and I expect that you will either resign your pretensions, or make it appear in single combat, according to the law of arms, and the institutions of chivalry, that you are worthy to dispute her favour with him of the Griffin.[5] POLYDORE."[6]

Our adventurer was not a little surprised at this address, which, however, he pocketed in silence; and began to reflect, not without mortification, that he was treated as a lunatic by some person who wanted to amuse himself with the infirmities of his fellow creatures. Mr. Thomas Clarke, who saw the ceremony with which the letter was delivered, and the emotions with which it was read, hied him to the kitchen for intelligence, and there learned that the stranger was squire Sycamore. He forthwith comprehended the nature of the billet, and, in the apprehension that bloodshed would ensue, resolved to alarm his uncle, that he might assist in keeping the peace. He accordingly entered the apartment of the captain, who had been waked by the trumpet, and now peevishly asked the meaning of that damned piping, as if all hands were called upon deck. Clarke having imparted what he knew of the transaction, together with his own conjectures, the captain said, he did not suppose as how they would engage by candle-light; and that for his own part he should turn out in the larboard watch,[7] long enough before any signals could be hove out for forming the line. With this assurance the lawyer retired to his nest, where he did not fail to dream of Mrs. Dolly Cowslip; while Sir Launcelot passed the night awake, in ruminating on the strange challenge he had received. He had got notice that the sender was Mr. Sycamore, and hesitated with himself whether he should not punish him for his impertinence: but when he reflected on the nature of the dispute, and the serious consequences it might produce, he resolved to decline the combat, as a trial of right and merit, founded upon absurdity. Even in his maddest hours, he never adopted those maxims of knight-errantry which related to challenges. He always perceived the folly and wickedness of defying a man to mortal fight, because he did not like the colour of his beard, or the complexion of his mistress; or of deciding by homicide, whether he or his rival deserved the preference, when it was the lady's prerogative to determine which should be the happy lover. It was his opinion that chivalry was an useful institution while confined to its original purposes of protecting the innocent, assisting the friendless, and bringing the guilty to condign punishment: but he could not conceive how these laws should be answered by violating every suggestion of reason, and every precept of humanity. Captain Crowe did not examine the matter so philosophically. He took it for granted that in the morning the two knights would come to action, and slept sound on that supposition. But he rose before it was day, resolved to be some how concerned in the fray; and understanding that the stranger had a companion, set him down immediately for his own antagonist. So impatient was he to establish this secondary contest, that by day-break he entered the chamber of Dawdle, to which he was directed by the waiter, and roused him with a hilloah, that might have been heard at the distance of half a league. Dawdle, startled by this terrific sound, sprung out of bed, and stood upright on the floor, before he opened his eyes upon the object by which he had been so dreadfully alarmed. But when he beheld the head of Crowe, so swelled and swathed, so livid, hideous, and griesly, with a broad sword by his side, and a case of pistols in his girdle, he believed it was the apparition of some mur-thered man; his hair bristled up, his teeth chattered, and his knees knocked; he would have prayed, but his tongue denied its office. Crowe seeing his per-turbation, "May-hap, friend," said he, "you take me for a buccaneer: but I am no such person.—My name it is captain Crowe.—I come not for your silver nor your gold; your rigging nor your stowage; but hearing as how your friend intends to bring my friend Sir Launcelot Greaves to action, d'ye see; I desire in the way of friendship, that, while they are engaged, you and I as their sec-onds may lie board and board for a few glasses,[8] to divert one another, d'ye see." Dawdle hearing this request, began to retrieve his faculties, and throw-ing himself into the attitude of Hamlet, when the ghost appears, exclaimed in theatrical accent, "Angels and ministers of grace defend us!—Art thou a spirit of grace, or goblin damn'd?"——As he seemed to bend his eye on va-cancy,[9] the captain began to think that he really saw something preternatural, and stared wildly around. Then addressing himself to the terrified Dawdle, "Damn'd, (said he) for what should I be damn'd? if you are afeard of goblins, brother, put your trust in the Lord, and he'll prove a sheet-anchor[10] to you." The other having by this time recollected himself perfectly, continued, not-withstanding, to spout tragedy, and in the words of Macbeth pronounced,

> What man dare, I dare:
> Approach thou like the rugged Russian bear,
> The armed rhinoceros, or Hyrcanian tyger;
> Take any shape but that, and my firm nerves
> Shall never tremble. . . .[11]

" 'Ware names, Jack,[12] (cried the impatient mariner) if so be as how you'll bear a hand and rig yourself,[13] and take a short trip with me into the offing,[14] we'll overhaul this here affair in the turning of a capstan."[15]

At this juncture they were joined by Mr. Sycamore in his night-gown and slippers. Disturbed by Crowe's first salute he had sprung up; and now expressed no small astonishment at first sight of the novice's countenance. After having gazed alternately at him and Dawdle, "Who have we got here," said he, "raw head and bloody bones?"[16] When his friend, slipping on his cloaths, gave him to understand that this was a friend of Sir Launcelot Greaves, and explained the purport of his errand, he treated him with more civility. He assured him that he should have the pleasure to break a spear with Mr. Dawdle; and signified his surprise that Sir Launcelot had made no answer to his letter. It being by this time clear day-light, and Crowe extremely interested in this affair, he broke without ceremony into the knight's chamber, and told him abruptly that the enemy had brought to,[17] and waited for his coming up, in order to begin the action. "I've hailed his consort," said he, "a shambling chattering fellow: he took me first for an hobgoblin, then called me names, a tyger, a wry-nose o'ross, and a Persian bear: but egad, if I come athwart him, I'll make him look like the bear and ragged staff[18] before we part.——I wool.——"

This intimation was not received with that alacrity which the captain expected to find in our adventurer, who told him in a peremptory tone, that he had no design to come to action, and desired to be left to his repose. Crowe forthwith retired, crest-fallen; and muttered something which was never distinctly heard.

About eight in the morning Mr. Dawdle brought him a formal message from the knight of the Griffin, desiring he would appoint the lists,[19] and give security of the field. To which request he made answer in a very composed and solemn accent, "If the person who sent you thinks I have injured him, let him without disguise, or any such ridiculous ceremony, explain the nature of the wrong; and then I shall give such satisfaction as may suit my conscience and my character. If he hath bestowed his affection upon any particular object, and looks upon me as a favoured rival, I shall not wrong the lady so much as to take any step that may prejudice her choice, especially a step that contradicts my own reason as much as it would outrage the laws of my country. If he who calls himself knight of the Griffin, is really desirous of treading in the paths of true chivalry, he will not want opportunities of signalizing his valour in the cause of virtue.——Should he, notwithstanding this declaration, offer violence to me in the course of my occasions, he will always find me in a posture of defence: or, should he persist in repeating his importunities, I shall without ceremony chastise the messenger." His declining the combat was interpreted into fear by Mr. Sycamore, who now became more insolent and ferocious, on the supposition of our knight's timidity. Sir Launcelot, mean while, went to breakfast with his friends; and having put on his armour, or-

dered the horses to be brought forth. Then he payed the bill, and walking
deliberately to the gate, in presence of squire Sycamore and his attendants,
vaulted at one spring into the saddle of Bronzomarte, whose neighing and
curvetting proclaimed the joy he felt in being mounted by his accomplished
master.

Though the knight of the Griffin did not think proper to insult his rival
personally, his friend Dawdle did not fail to crack some jokes on the figure
and horsemanship of Crowe; who again declared he should be glad to fall in
with him upon the voyage: nor did Mr. Clarke's black patch [20] and rueful countenance pass unnoticed and unridiculed. As for Timothy Crabshaw, he beheld
his brother squire with the contempt of a veteran: and Gilbert payed him his
compliments with his heels at parting: but when our adventurer and his retinue were clear of the inn, Mr. Sycamore ordered his trumpeter to sound a
retreat, by way of triumph over his antagonist. Perhaps he would have contented himself with this kind of victory had not Dawdle further inflamed his
envy and ambition by launching out in praise of Sir Launcelot. He observed
that his countenance was open and manly; his joints strong knit, and his form
unexceptionable; that he trod like Hercules, and vaulted into the saddle like a
winged Mercury: [21] nay, he even hinted it was lucky for Sycamore that the
knight of the Crescent happened to be so pacifically disposed. His patron sick-
ened at these praises, and took fire at the last observation. He affected to un-
dervalue personal beauty, though the opinion of the world had been favourable to himself in that particular: he said he was at least two inches taller than
Greaves; and as to shape and air, he would make no comparisons; but with
respect to riding, he was sure he had a better seat than Sir Launcelot, and
would wager five hundred to fifty guineas, that he would unhorse him at the
first encounter. "There is no occasion for laying wagers," replied Mr. Dawdle,
"the doubt may be determined in half an hour—Sir Launcelot is not a man to
avoid you at full gallop." Sycamore, after some hesitation, declared he would
follow and provoke him to battle, on condition that Dawdle would engage
Crowe; and this condition was accepted: for though Davy had no stomach to
the tryal, he could not readily find an excuse for declining it: besides, he had
discovered the captain to be a very bad horseman, and resolved to eke out his
own scanty valour with a border of ingenuity. The servants were immediately
ordered to unpack the armour, and in a little time, Mr. Sycamore made a very
formidable appearance. But the scene that followed is too important to be
huddled in at the end of a chapter, and therefore we shall reserve it for a more
conspicuous place in these memoirs.

CHAPTER XIX.

Containing the atchievements of the knights of the Griffin and Crescent.

M r. Sycamore, alias the knight of the Griffin, so denominated from a gryphon painted on his shield, being armed at all points, and his friend Dawdle provided with a certain implement, which he flattered himself, would ensure a victory over the novice Crowe; they set out from the George, with their attendants, in all the elevation of hope, and pranced along the highway that led towards London, that being the road which our adventurer pursued. As they were extremely well mounted, and proceeded at a round pace, they, in less than two hours, came up with Sir Launcelot and his company; and Sycamore sent another formal defiance to the knight, by his trumpeter, Dawdle having, for good reasons, declined that office.

Our adventurer hearing himself thus addressed, and seeing his rival, who had passed him, posted to obstruct his progress, armed capapie,[1] with his lance in the rest; determined to give the satisfaction that was required, and desired that the regulations of the combat[2] might be established. The knight of the Griffin proposed, that the vanquished party should resign all pretensions to Miss Aurelia Darnel, in favour of the victor; that while the principals were engaged, his friend Dawdle should run a tilt with captain Crowe; that squire Crabshaw, and Mr. Sycamore's servant, should keep themselves in readiness to assist their respective masters occasionally, according to the law of arms; and that Mr. Clarke should observe the motions of the trumpeter, whose province was to sound the charge to battle.[3]

Our knight agreed to these regulations, notwithstanding the earnest and pathetic remonstrances of the young lawyer, who, with tears in his eyes, conjured all the combatants, in their turns, to refrain from an action that might be attended with bloodshed and murder; and was contrary to the laws both of God and man. In vain he endeavoured to move them by tears and intreaties, by threatning them with prosecutions in this world, and pains and penalties in the next: they persisted in their resolution, and his uncle would have begun hostilities on his carcase, had not he been prevented by Sir Launcelot, who exhorted Clarke to retire from the field, that he might not be involved in the consequences of the combat. He relished this advice so well, that he had actually moved off to some distance; but his apprehension and concern for his friends co-operating with an insatiable curiosity, detained him in sight of the engagement.

The two knights having fairly divided the ground, and the same precautions being taken by the seconds, on another part of the field, Sycamore began to be invaded with some scruples, which were probably engendered by the martial appearance, and well known character of his antagonist. The confidence which he had derived from the reluctance of Sir Launcelot, now vanished, because it plainly appeared, that the knight's backwardness was not owing to personal timidity; and he foresaw that the prosecution of this joke might be attended with very serious consequences to his own life and reputation. He, therefore, desired a parley, in which he observed his affection for Miss Darnel was of such a delicate nature, that should the discomfiture of his rival contribute to make her unhappy, his victory must render him the most miserable wretch upon earth. He proposed, therefore, that her sentiments and choice should be ascertained before they proceeded to extremity.

Sir Launcelot declared that he was much more afraid of combating Aurelia's inclination, than of opposing the knight of the Griffin in arms; and that if he had the least reason to think Mr. Sycamore, or any other person, was distinguished by her preference, he would instantly give up his suit as desperate. At the same time, he observed that Sycamore had proceeded too far to retract; that he had insulted a gentleman, and not only challenged, but even pursued him, and blocked up his passage in the public highway; outrages which he (Sir Launcelot) would not suffer to pass unpunished. Accordingly, he insisted on the combat, on pain of treating Mr. Sycamore as a craven, and a recreant. This declaration was reinforced by Dawdle, who told him that should he now decline the engagement, all the world would look upon him as an infamous poltroon.[4]

These two observations gave a necessary fillip to the courage of the challenger. The parties took their stations: the trumpet sounded to charge, and the combatants began their career with great impetuosity. Whether the gleam of Sir Launcelot's arms affrighted Mr. Sycamore's steed, or some other object had an unlucky effect on his eye-sight; certain it is he started, at about midway, and gave his rider such a violent shake as discomposed his attitude, and disabled him from using his lance to the best advantage. Had our hero continued his career, with his launce couched, in all probability Sycamore's armour would have proved but a bad defence to his carcase: but Sir Launcelot perceiving his rival's spear unrested, had just time to throw up the point of his own, when the two horses closed with such a shock, that Sycamore, already wavering in the saddle, was overthrown, and his armour crashed around him as he fell.[5]

The victor, seeing him lie without motion, alighted immediately and began to unbuckle his helmet, in which office he was assisted by the trumpeter. When the head-piece was removed, the hapless knight of the Griffin appeared in the pale livery of death, tho' he was only in a swoon, from which he soon recovered by the effect of the fresh air, and the aspersion of cold water, brought from a small pool in the neighbourhood. When he recognized his conqueror doing the offices of humanity about his person, he closed his eyes from vexation, told Sir Launcelot that his was the fortune of the day, tho' he himself owed his mischance to the fault of his own horse; and observed that this ridiculous affair would not have happened, but for the mischievous instigation of that scoundrel Dawdle, on whose ribs he threatened to revenge his mishap.

Perhaps captain Crowe might have saved him this trouble, had that wag honourably adhered to the institutions of chivalry, in his conflict with our novice: but on this occasion, his ingenuity was more commendable than his courage. He had provided at the inn a blown bladder, in which several smooth pebbles were inclosed;[6] and this he slily fixed to the head of his pole, when the captain obeyed the signal to battle. Instead of bearing the brunt of the encounter, he turned out of the straight line, so as to avoid the launce of his antagonist, and rattled his bladder with such effect, that Crowe's horse pricking up his ears, took to his heels, and fled across some ploughed land with such precipitation, that the rider was obliged to quit his spear, and lay fast hold on the mane, that he might not be thrown out of the saddle. Dawdle, who was much better mounted, seeing his condition, rode up to the unfortunate novice, and belaboured his shoulders without fear of retaliation. Mr. Clarke, seeing his kinsman so roughly handled, forgot his fears, and flew to his assistance; but, before he came up, the aggressor had retired, and now perceiving that fortune had declared against his friend and patron, very honourably abandoned him in his distress, and went off at full speed for London.

Nor was Timothy Crabshaw without his share in the noble atchievements of this propitious day. He had by this time imbibed such a tincture of errantry, that he firmly believed himself and his master equally invincible; and this belief operating upon a perverse disposition, rendered him as quarrelsome in his sphere, as his master was mild and forbearing. As he sat on horseback, in the place assigned to him and Sycamore's lacquey, he managed Gilbert in such a manner, as to invade with his heels, the posteriors of the other's horse; and this insult produced some altercation, which ended in mutual assault. The

Dawdle's Victory over Captn Crowe, by Cruikshank.
(Richard W. Meirs Collection of George Cruikshank,
Department of Rare Books and Special Collections,
Princeton University Library)

footman handled the butt-end of his horse-whip with great dexterity about the head of Crabshaw, who declared afterwards, that it sung and simmered like a kettle of cod-fish: but the squire, who understood the nature of long lashes, as having been a carter from his infancy, found means to twine his thong about the neck of his antagonist, and pull him off his horse half strangled, at the very instant his master was thrown by Sir Launcelot Greaves.

Having thus obtained the victory, he did not much regard the punctilios of chivalry; but taking it for granted he had a right to make the most of his advantage, resolved to carry off the *spolia opima*.[7] Alighting with great agility, "Brother, (cried he) I think as haw yawrs bean't a butcher's horse, a doan't carry calves[8] well—I'se make yaw knaw your churning days,[9] I wool—what, yaw look as if yaw was crow-trodden,[10] you do—now, you shall pay the score you have been running on my peate, you shall, brother."

So saying, he rifled his pockets, stripped him of his hat and coat, and took possession of his master's portmanteau. But he did not long enjoy his plunder: for the lacquey complaining to Sir Launcelot, of his having been despoiled, the knight commanded his squire to refund, not without menaces of subjecting him to the severest chastisement, for his injustice and rapacity. Timothy represented, with great vehemence, that he had won the spoils in fair battle, at the expence of his head and shoulders, which he immediately uncovered, to prove his allegation: but his remonstrance having no effect upon his master, "Wounds! (cried he) an I mun gee thee back the pig, I'se gee thee back the poke[11] also; I'm a drubbing still in thy debt."

With these words, he made a most furious attack upon the plaintiff, with his horse-whip, and before the knight could interpose, repayed the lacquey with interest. As an appurtenance to Sycamore and Dawdle, he ran the risque of another assault from the novice Crowe, who was so transported with rage, at the disagreeable trick which had been played upon him, by his fugitive antagonist, that he could not for some time pronounce an articulate sound, but a few broken interjections, the meaning of which could not be ascertained. Snatching up his pole, he ran towards the place where Mr. Sycamore sat on the grass, supported by the trumpeter, and would have finished what our adventurer had left undone, if the knight of the Crescent, with admirable dexterity, had not warded off the blow which he aimed at the knight of the Griffin, and signified his displeasure in a resolute tone: then he collared the lacquey, who was just disengaged from the chastising hand of Crabshaw, and swinging his launce with his other hand, encountered the squire's ribs by accident.

Timothy was not slow in returning the salutation, with the weapon which he still wielded: Mr. Clarke, running up to the assistance of his uncle, was opposed by the lacquey, who seemed extremely desirous of seeing the enemy revenge his quarrel, by falling foul of one another. Clarke, thus impeded, commenced hostilities against the footman, while Crowe grappled with Crabshaw; a battle-royal insued, and was maintained with great vigour, and some bloodshed on all sides, until the authority of Sir Launcelot, reinforced by some weighty remonstrances, applied to the squire, put an end to the conflict. Crabshaw immediately desisted, and ran roaring to communicate his grievances to Gilbert, who seemed to sympathize very little with his distress. The lacquey took to his heels; Mr. Clarke wiped his bloody nose, declaring he had a good mind to put the aggressor in the Crown-office;[12] and captain Crowe continued to ejaculate unconnected oaths, which, however, seemed to imply that he was almost sick of his new profession. "D——n my eyes, if you call this—start my timbers, brother—look ye, d'ye see—a lousy, lubberly, cowardly son of a—among the breakers, d'ye see—lost my steerage way[13]—split my binnacle;[14] haul away—O! damn all arrantry—give me a tight vessel, d'ye see, brother—mayhap you mayn't—snatch my—sea room[15] and a spanking gale—odds heart, I'll hold a whole year's—smite my limbs: it don't signify talking—"

Our hero consoled the novice for his disaster, by observing, that if he had got some blows, he had lost no honour. At the same time, he observed that it was very difficult, if not impossible, for a man to succeed in the paths of chivalry, who had passed the better part of his days in other occupations; and hinted that as the cause which had engaged him in this way of life no longer existed, he was determined to relinquish a profession, which, in a peculiar manner, exposed him to the most disagreeable incidents. Crowe chewed the cud upon this insinuation, while the other personages of the drama were employed in catching the horses, which had given their riders the slip. As for Mr. Sycamore, he was so bruised by his fall, that it was necessary to procure a litter for conveying him to the next town, and the servant was dispatched for this convenience; Sir Launcelot staying with him until it arrived.

When he was safely deposited in the carriage, our hero took leave of him in these terms. "I shall not insist upon your submitting to the terms, you yourself proposed before this rencounter. I give you free leave to use all your advantages, in an honourable way, for promoting your suit with the young lady, of whom you profess yourself enamoured. Should you have recourse to sinister practices, you will find Sir Launcelot Greaves ready to demand an account of your conduct, not in the character of a lunatic knight-errant, but as a plain English gentleman, jealous of his honour, and resolute in his purpose."

To this address Mr. Sycamore made no reply, but with a sullen aspect ordered the carriage to proceed; and it moved accordingly to the right, our hero's road to London, lying in the other direction. Sir Launcelot had already exchanged his armour for a riding-coat, hat, and boots; and Crowe parting with his skull-cap and leathern jerkin, regained in some respects the appearance of a human creature. Thus metamorphosed, they pursued their way in an easy pace, Mr. Clarke endeavouring to amuse them with a learned dissertation on the law, tending to demonstrate that Mr. Sycamore was, by his behaviour of that day, liable to three different actions, besides a commission of lunacy;[16] and that Dawdle might be prosecuted for having practised subtle craft, to the annoyance of his uncle, over and above an action for assault and battery; because, for why? The said Crowe having run away, as might be easily proved, before any blows were given, the said Dawdle by pursuing him even out of the high road, putting him in fear, and committing battery on his body, became, to all intents and purposes, the aggressor; and an indictment would lie in *Banco Regis*.[17]

The Captain's pride was so shocked at these observations, that he exclaimed with equal rage and impatience, "You lie, you dog, in *Bilkum Regis*—you lie, I say, you lubber, I did not run away; nor was I in fear, d'ye see. It was my son of a bitch of a horse that would not obey the helm, d'ye see, whereby I couldn't use my metal, d'ye see—As for the matter of fear, you and fear may kiss my——So don't go and heave your stink-pots[18] at my character, d'ye see, or agad I'll trim thee fore and aft with a—I wool." Tom protested he meant nothing but a little speculation, and Crowe was appeased.

In the evening they reached the town of Bugden,[19] without any farther adventure, and passed the night in great tranquility. Next morning, even after the horses were ordered to be saddled, Mr. Clarke, without ceremony, entered the apartment of Sir Launcelot, leading in a female, who proved to be the identical Mrs. Dolly Cowslip. This young woman advancing to the knight, cried, "O, Sir Launcelot! my dear leady, my dear leady"—but was hindered from proceeding by a flood of tears, which the tender-hearted lawyer mingled with a plentiful shower of sympathy.

Our adventurer starting at this exclamation, "O heavens! (cried he) where is my Aurelia? speak, where did you leave that jewel of my soul? answer me in a moment—I am all terror and impatience!" Dolly having recollected herself, told him that Mr. Darnel had lodged his niece in the new buildings by Mayfair;[20] that on the second night after their arrival, a very warm expostulation had passed between Aurelia and her uncle, who next morning dismissed Dolly, without permitting her to take leave of her mistress, and that same day moved to another part of the town, as she afterwards learned of the landlady, though she could not inform her whither they were gone. That when she was turned away, John Clump, one of the footmen, who pretended to have a kindness for her, had faithfully promised to call upon her and let her know what passed in the family; but as he did not keep his word, and she was an utter stranger in London, without friends or settlement, she had resolved to return to her mother, and travelled so far on foot since yesterday morning.

Our knight, who had expected the most dismal tidings from her lamentable preamble, was pleased to find his presaging fears disappointed; tho' he was far from being satisfied, with the dismission of Dolly, from whose attachment to his interest, joined to her influence over Mr. Clump, he had hoped to reap such intelligence as would guide him to the haven of his desires. After a minute's reflection, he saw it would be expedient to carry back Mrs. Cowslip, and lodge her at the place where Mr. Clump had promised to visit her with intelligence; for, in all probability, it was not for want of inclination that he had not kept his promise.

Dolly did not express any aversion to the scheme of returning to London, where she hoped once more to rejoin her dear lady, to whom by this time, she was attached by the strongest ties of affection; and her inclination, in this respect, was assisted by the consideration of having the company of the young lawyer, who, it plainly appeared, had made strange havock in her heart, tho' it must be owned, for the honour of this blooming damsel, that her thoughts had never once deviated from the paths of innocence and virtue. The more Sir Launcelot surveyed this agreeable maiden, the more he felt himself disposed to take care of her fortune; and from this day he began to ruminate on a scheme which was afterwards consummated in her favour—In the mean time, he laid injunctions on Mr. Clarke to conduct his addresses to Mrs. Cowslip, according to the rules of honour and decorum, as he valued his countenance and friendship. His next step was to procure a saddle-horse for Dolly, who preferred this to any other sort of carriage; and thereby gratified the wish of her admirer, who longed to see her on horseback in her green joseph.[21]

The armour, including the accoutrements of the novice and the squire, were left in the care of the inn-keeper, and Timothy Crabshaw was so metamorphosed by a plain livery-frock, that even Gilbert with difficulty recognized his person. As for the novice Crowe, his head had almost resumed its natural dimensions; but then his whole face was so covered with a livid suffusion; his nose appeared so flat, and his lips so tumified, that he might very well have passed for a Caffre or Æthiopian.[22] Every circumstance being now adjusted, they departed from Bugden in a regular cavalcade, dined at Hatfield,[23] and in the evening arrived at the Bull and Gate inn in Holborn,[24] where they established their quarters for the night.

CHAPTER XX.

In which our Hero descends into the Mansions of the Damned.[1]

The first step which Sir Launcelot took in the morning that succeeded his arrival in London, was to settle Mrs. Dolly Cowslip in lodgings at the house where John Clump had promised to visit her; as he did not doubt, that tho' the visit was delayed, it would some time or other be performed; and in that case, he might obtain some intelligence of Aurelia. Mr. Thomas Clarke was permitted to take up his habitation in the same house, on his earnestly desiring he might be intrusted with the office of conveying information and instruction between Dolly and our adventurer. The knight himself resolved to live retired until he should receive some tidings relating to miss Darnel, that would influence his conduct; but he proposed to frequent places of public resort incognito, that he might have some chance of meeting by accident with the mistress of his heart. Taking it for granted that the oddities of Crowe would help to amuse him in his hours of solitude and disappointment, he invited that original to be his guest at a small house which he determined to hire ready furnished in the neighbourhood of Golden-square.[2] The captain thanked him for his courtesy, and frankly embraced his offer; tho' he did not much approve of the knight's choice, in point of situation. He said he would recommend him to a special good upper-deck[3] hard by St. Catherine's[4] in Wapping, where he would be delighted with the prospect of the street forwards, well frequented by passengers, carts, drays, and other carriages; and having backwards, an agreeable view of alderman Parsons' great brewhouse,[5] with two hundred hogs feeding almost under the window. As a further inducement, he mentioned the vicinity of the Tower guns, which would regale his hearing on days of salutation: nor did he forget the sweet sound of mooring and unmooring ships in the river, and the pleasing objects on the other side of the Thames, displayed in the oozy docks and cabbage-gardens of Rotherhithe.[6] Sir Launcelot was not insensible to the beauties of this landscape; but, his pursuit lying another way, he contented himself with a less enchanting situation, and Crowe accompanied him out of pure friendship. At night Mr. Clarke arrived at our hero's house with tidings that were by no means agreeable. He told him that Clump had left a letter for Dolly, informing her that his master 'squire Darnel was to set out early in the morning for Yorkshire; but he could give no account of her lady, who had, the day before, been convey'd, he knew not whither, in a hackney-coach,[7] attended by his uncle and an ill-looking fellow who had much the appearance of a bailiff or turn-key; so that he feared she was in trouble.

Sir Launcelot was deeply affected by this intimation. His apprehension was even roused by a suspicion that a man of Darnel's violent temper, and unprincipled heart, might have practised upon the life of his lovely niece: but, upon recollection, he could not suppose that he had recourse to such infamous expedients, knowing, as he did, that an account of her would be demanded at his hands, and that it would be easily proved he had conveyed her from the lodging in which she resided. His first fears now gave way to another suggestion, that Anthony, in order to intimidate her into a compliance with his proposals, had trumped up a spurious claim against her, and by virtue of a writ confined her in some prison or spunging-house.[8] Possessed with this idea, he desired Mr. Clarke to search the sheriff's office in the morning, that he might know whether any such writ had been granted; and he himself resolved to make a tour of the great prisons belonging to the metropolis, to enquire if perchance she might not be confined under a borrowed name. Finally, he determined, if possible, to apprise her of his place of abode by a paragraph in all the daily papers, signifying that Sir Launcelot Greaves had arrived at his house by Golden-square.

All these resolutions were punctually executed. No such writ had been taken out in the sheriff's office; and therefore, our hero set out on his jail expedition, accompanied by Mr. Clarke, who had contracted some acquaintance with the commanding officers in these garrisons, in the course of his clerkship, and practice as an attorney. The first day they spent in prosecuting their inquiry through the Gate-house, Fleet, and Marshalsea;[9] the next they allotted to the King's-bench,[10] where they understood there was a great variety of prisoners. There they proposed to make a minute scrutiny, by the help of Mr. Norton the deputy-marshal, who was Mr. Clarke's intimate friend, and had nothing at all of the jailor either in his appearance or in his disposition, which was remarkably humane and benevolent towards all his fellow-creatures.

The knight having bespoke dinner at a tavern in the Borough,[11] was, together with captain Crowe, conducted to the prison of the King's-bench, which is situated in St. George's-fields,[12] about a mile from the end of Westminster-bridge, and appears like a neat little regular town, consisting of one street, surrounded by a very high wall, including an open piece of ground which may be termed a garden, where the prisoners take the air, and amuse themselves with a variety of diversions. Except the entrance, where the turnkeys keep watch and ward, there is nothing in the place that looks like a jail, or bears the least colour of restraint. The street is crowded with passengers. Tradesmen of all kinds here exercise their different professions. Hawkers of all sorts are admitted to call and vend their wares as in any open street of London. Here are butchers-stands, chandlers-shops, a surgery, a tap-house well frequented, and a public kitchen in which provisions are dressed for all the prisoners gratis, at the expence of the publican. Here the voice of misery never complains, and, indeed, little else is to be heard but the sounds of mirth and jollity. At the farther end of the street, on the right hand, is a little paved court leading to a separate building, consisting of twelve large apartments, called state-rooms,[13] well furnished, and fitted up for the reception of the better sort of crown-prisoners; and on the other side of the street, facing a separate division of ground, called the common side, is a range of rooms occupied by prisoners of the lowest order, who share the profits of a begging-box, and are maintained by this practice, and some established funds of charity. We ought also to observe, that the jail is provided with a neat chapel, in which a clergyman, in consideration of a certain salary, performs divine service every Sunday.

Our adventurer having searched the books, and perused the description of all the female prisoners who had been for some weeks admitted into the jail, obtained not the least intelligence of his concealed charmer, but resolved to alleviate his disappointment by the gratification of his curiosity. Under the auspices of Mr. Norton, he made a tour of the prison, and in particular visited the kitchen, where he saw a number of spits loaded with a variety of provision, consisting of butcher's meat, poultry, and game: he could not help expressing his astonishment with up-lifted hands, and congratulating himself in secret, upon his being a member of that community which had provided such a comfortable asylum for the unfortunate. His ejaculation was interrupted by a tumultuous noise in the street; and Mr. Norton declaring he was sent for to the lodge, consigned our hero to the cure of one Mr. Felton, a prisoner of a very decent appearance, who paid his compliments with a good grace, and invited the company to repose themselves in his apartment, which was large, commodious, and well furnished. When Sir Launcelot asked the cause of that uproar, he told him that it was the prelude to a boxing-match between two of the prisoners, to be decided in the ground, or garden of the place.

Capt. Crowe expressing an eager curiosity to see the battle, Mr. Felton assured him there would be no sport, as the combatants were both reckoned dunghills:[14] "But, in half an hour (said he) there will be a battle of some consequence between two of the demagogues of the place, Dr. Crabclaw and

Mr. Tapley, the first a physician, and the other a brewer. You must know, Gentlemen, that this microcosm or republic in miniature, is like the great world, split into factions.[15] Crabclaw is the leader of one party; and the other is headed by Tapley: both are men of warm and impetuous tempers; and their intrigues have embroiled the whole place, insomuch that it was dangerous to walk the street, on account of the continual skirmishes of their partizans. At length, some of the more sedate inhabitants having met and deliberated upon some remedy for these growing disorders, proposed that the dispute should be at once decided by single combat between the two chiefs, who readily agreed to the proposal. The match was accordingly made for five guineas, and this very day and hour appointed for the trial, on which considerable sums of money are depending. As for Mr. Norton, it is not proper that he should be present, or seem to countenance such violent proceedings, which, however, it is necessary to connive at, as convenient vents for the evaporation of those humours, which being confined, might accumulate and break out with greater fury, in conspiracy and rebellion."

The knight owned he could not conceive by what means such a number of licentious people, amounting, with their dependants, to above five hundred, were restrained within the bounds of any tolerable discipline, or prevented from making their escape; which they might at any time accomplish, either by stealth or open violence, as it could not be supposed that one or two turnkeys, continually employed in opening and shutting the door, could resist the efforts of a whole multitude. "Your wonder, good Sir, (said Mr. Felton) will vanish, when you consider it is hardly possible that the multitude should co-operate in the execution of such a scheme; and that the keeper perfectly well understands the maxim *divide et impera*.[16] Many prisoners are restrained by the dictates of gratitude towards the deputy-marshal, whose friendship and good offices they have experienced: some, no doubt, are actuated by motives of discretion. One party is an effectual check upon the other; and I am firmly persuaded that there are not ten prisoners within the place that would make their escape, if the doors were laid open. This is a step which no man would take, unless his fortune was altogether desperate; because it would oblige him to leave his country for life, and expose him to the most imminent risque of being retaken and treated with the utmost severity. The majority of the prisoners live in the most lively hope of being released by the assistance of their friends, the compassion of their creditors, or the favour of the legislature. Some who are cut off from all these proposals, are become naturalized to the place, knowing they cannot subsist in any other situation. I, myself, am one of these. After having resigned all my effects for the benefit of my creditors, I have been detained these nine years in prison, because one person refuses to sign my certificate.[17] I have long outlived all my friends from whom I could expect the least countenance or favour: I am grown old in confinement; and lay my account with ending my days in jail, as the mercy of the legislature in favour of insolvent debtors, is never extended to uncertified bankrupts taken in execution.[18] By dint of industry, and the most rigid oeconomy, I make shift to live independant in this retreat. To this scene my faculty of subsisting, as well as my body, is peculiarly confined. Had I an opportunity to escape, where should I go? All my views of fortune have been long blasted. I have no friends nor connexions in the world. I must, therefore, starve in some sequestred corner, or be recaptivated and confined for ever to close prison, deprived of the indulgences which I now enjoy."

Here the conversation was broke off by another uproar, which was the signal to battle between the doctor and his antagonist. The company immediately adjourned to the field, where the combatants were already undressed and the stakes deposited. The doctor seemed of the middle age and middle stature, active and alert, with an atrabiliarious[19] aspect, and a mixture of rage and disdain expressed in his countenance. The brewer was large, raw-boned, and round as a but of beer, but very fat, unwieldy, short-winded and phlegmatic. Our adventurer was not a little surprised when he beheld in the character of seconds, a male and a female, stripped naked from the waist upwards, the latter ranging on the side of the physician: but the commencement of the battle prevented his demanding of his guide an explanation of this phœnomenon. The doctor, retiring some paces backwards, threw himself into the attitude of a battering ram, and rushed upon his antagonist with great impetuosity, fore-seeing that should he have the good fortune to over-turn him in the first assault, it would not be an easy task to raise him up again and put him in a capacity of offence. But the momentum of Crabclaw's head, and the concomitant efforts of his knuckles, had no effect upon the ribs of Tapley, who stood firm as the Acroceraunian promontory:[20] and stepping forward with his projected fist, something smaller and softer than a sledge-hammer, struck the physician to the ground. In a trice, however, by the assistance of his female second, he was on his legs again, and grappling with his antagonist, endeavoured to tip him a fall; but, instead of accomplishing his purpose, he received a cross-buttock,[21] and the brewer throwing himself upon him as he fell, had well-nigh smothered him on the spot. The amazon flew to his assistance, and Tapley shewing no inclination to get up, she smote him on the temple 'till he roared. The male second hastening to the relief of his principal, made application to the eyes of the female, which were immediately surrounded with black circles; and she returned the salute with a blow which brought a double stream of blood from his nostrils, greeting him at the same time with the opprobrious appellation of a lousy son of a b——h. A combat more furious than the first would now have ensued, had not Felton interposed with an air of authority, and insisted on the man's leaving the field; an injunction which he forthwith obeyed, saying, "Well, damme, Felton, you're my friend and commander: I'll obey your order—but the b——h will be foul of me before we sleep—." Then Felton, advancing to his opponent, "Madam, (said he) I'm very sorry to see a lady of your rank and qualifications expose yourself in this manner.—For God's sake, behave with a little more decorum; if not for the sake of your own family, at least for the credit of your sex in general." "Hark ye, Felton, (said she) decorum is founded upon a delicacy of sentiment and deportment, which cannot consist with the disgraces of a jail, and the miseries of indigence.—But I see the dispute is now terminated, and the money is to be drank: if you'll dine with us you shall be welcome; if not, you may die in your sobriety, and be damned."

By this time the doctor had given out, and allowed the brewer to be the better man; yet he would not honour the festival with his presence, but retired to his chamber, exceedingly mortified at his defeat. Our hero was reconducted to Mr. Felton's apartment, where he sat some time without opening his mouth, so astonished he was at what he had seen and heard. "I perceive, Sir, (said the prisoner) you are surprised at the manner in which I accosted that unhappy woman; and perhaps you will be more surprised when you hear, that within these eighteen months, she was actually a person of fashion, and her opponent (who by the bye) is her husband, universally respected as a man of honour, and a brave officer." "I am, indeed, (cried our hero) overwhelmed with amazement and concern as well as stimulated by an eager curiosity to know the fatal causes which have produced such a deplorable reverse of character and fortune. But, I will rein my curiosity till the afternoon, if you will favour me with your company at a tavern in the neighbourhood, where I have bespoke dinner; a favour which I hope Mr. Norton will have no objection to your granting, as he himself is to be of the party.—" The prisoner thanked him for his kind invitation, and they adjourned immediately to the place, taking up the deputy-marshal in their passage through the lodge or entrance of the prison.

CHAPTER XXI.

Containing further Anecdotes relating
to the Children of Wretchedness.

Dinner being chearfully discussed, and our adventurer expressing an eager desire to know the history of the male and female who had acted as 'squires or seconds to the champions of the King's-bench, Felton gratified his curiosity to this effect:

"All that I know of Captain Clewlin,[1] previous to his committment, is, that he was commander of a sloop of war, and bore the reputation of a gallant officer; that he married the daughter of a rich merchant in the city of London against the inclination, and without the knowledge of her father, who renounced her for this act of disobedience: that the captain consoled himself for the rigour of the parent, with the possession of the lady, who was not only remarkably beautiful in person, but highly accomplished in her mind, and amiable in her disposition. Such, a few months ago, were those two persons whom you saw acting in such a vulgar capacity. When they first entered the prison they were undoubtedly the handsomest couple mine eyes ever beheld, and their appearance won universal respect even from the most brutal inhabitants of the jail. The captain having unwarily involved himself as security for a man to whom he had lain under obligations, became liable for a considerable sum; and his own father-in-law being the sole creditor of the bankrupt, took this opportunity of wreaking vengeance upon him for having espoused his daughter. He watched an opportunity until the captain had actually stept into the post-chaise with his lady, for Portsmouth, where his ship lay, and caused him to be arrested in the most public and shameful manner. Mrs. Clewlin had like to have sunk under the first transports of her grief and mortification; but these subsiding, she had recourse to personal sollicitation. She went with her only child in her arms (a lovely boy) to her father's door, and being denied admittance, kneeled down in the street, imploring his compassion in the most pathetic strain; but this hard-hearted citizen, instead of recognizing his child, and taking the poor mourner to his bosom, insulted her from the window with the most bitter reproach, saying, among other shocking expressions, 'Strumpet, take yourself away, with your brat, otherwise I shall send for the beadle, and have you to Bridewell.'[2]

"The unfortunate lady was cut to the heart by this usage, and fainted in the street; from whence she was conveyed to a public house by the charity of some passengers. She afterwards attempted to soften the barbarity of her father, by repeated letters, and by interesting some of his friends to intercede with him in her behalf; but all her endeavours proving ineffectual, she accompanied her husband to the prison of the King's-bench, where she must have felt, in the severest manner, the fatal reverse of circumstance to which she was exposed. The captain being disabled from going to sea, was superseded, and he saw all his hopes blasted in the midst of an active war,[3] at a time when he had the fairest prospects of fame and fortune. He saw himself reduced to extreme poverty, cooped up with the tender partner of his heart in a wretched hovel, amidst the refuse of mankind, and on the brink of wanting the common necessaries of life. The mind of man is ever ingenious in finding resources. He comforted his lady with vain hopes of having friends who would effect his deliverance, and repeated assurances of this kind so long, that he at length began to think they were not altogether void of foundation.

"Mrs. Clewlin, from a principle of duty, recollected all her fortitude, that she might not only bear her fate with patience, but even contributed to alleviate the woes of her husband, whom her affection had ruined. She affected to believe the suggestions of his pretended hope; she interchanged with him assurances of better fortune; her appearance exhibited a calm, while her heart was torn with anguish. She assisted him in writing letters to former friends, the last consolation of the wretched prisoner; she delivered these letters with her own hand, and underwent a thousand mortifying repulses, the most shocking circumstances of which she concealed from her husband. She performed all the menial offices in her own little family, which was maintained by pawning her apparel; and both the husband and wife, in some measure sweetened their cares, by prattling and toying with their charming little boy, on whom they doated with an enthusiasm of fondness.—Yet, even this pleasure was mingled with the most tender and melancholy regret. I have seen the mother hang over him, with the most affecting expression of this kind in her aspect, the tears contending with the smiles upon her countenance, while she exclaimed: 'Alas! my poor prisoner, little did your mother once think she should be obliged to nurse you in a jail.' The captain's paternal love was dashed with impatience—He would snatch up the boy in a transport of grief, press him to his breast, devour him as it were with kisses, throw up his eyes to heaven in the most emphatic silence; then convey the child hastily to his mother's arms, pull his hat over his eyes, stalk out into the common walk, and finding himself alone, break out into tears and lamentation.

"Ah! little did this unhappy couple know what further griefs awaited them! The small-pox broke out in the prison, and poor Tommy Clewlin was infected. As the eruption appeared unfavourable, you may conceive the consternation with which they were overwhelmed. Their distress was rendered inconceivable by indigence; for, by this time, they were so destitute that they could neither pay for common attendance, nor procure proper advice. I did, on that occasion, what I thought my duty towards my fellow-creatures.—I wrote to a physician of my acquaintance, who was humane enough to visit the poor little patient: I engaged a careful woman prisoner as a nurse, and Mr. Norton supplied them with money and necessaries. These helps were barely sufficient to preserve them from the horrors of despair, when they saw their little darling panting under the rage of a loathsome pestilential malady, during the excessive heat of the dog-days, and struggling for breath in the noxious atmosphere of a confined cabin, where they scarce had room to turn, on the most necessary occasions. The eager curiosity with which the mother eyed the doctor's looks as often as he visited the boy; the terror and trepidation of the father, while he desired to know his opinion; in a word, the whole tenour of their distress, baffled all description.

"At length the physician, for the sake of his own character, was obliged to be explicit; and returning with the captain, to the common walk, told him in my hearing, that the child could not possibly recover.—This sentence seemed to have petrified the unfortunate parent, who stood motionless, and seemingly bereft of sense. I led him to my apartment, where he sat a full hour in that state of stupefaction; then he began to groan hideously; a shower of tears burst from his eyes; he threw himself on the floor, and uttered the most piteous lamentation that ever was heard. Mean while, Mrs. Norton being made acquainted with the doctor's prognostic, visited Mrs. Clewlin, and invited her to the lodge. Her prophetic fears immediately took the alarm. 'What! (cried she, starting up with a frantic wildness in her looks) then our case is desperate—I shall lose my dear Tommy!—the poor prisoner will be released by the hand of heaven!—Death will convey him to the cold grave!'—The dying innocent hearing this exclamation, pronounced these words: 'Tommy won't leave you, my dear mamma—if death comes to take Tommy, pappa shall drive him away with his sword.' This address deprived the wretched mother of all resignation to the will of Providence. She tore her hair, dashed herself on the pavement, shrieked aloud, and was carried off in a deplorable state of distraction.

"That same evening the lovely babe expired, and the father grew frantic. He made an attempt on his own life, and being with difficulty restrained, his agitation sunk into a kind of sudden insensibility, which seemed to absorb all

sentiment, and gradually vulgarized his faculty of thinking. In order to dissi-
pate the violence of his sorrow, he continually shifted the scene from one company to another, contracted abundance of low connexions, and drowned his
cares in repeated intoxication. The unhappy lady underwent a long series of
hysterical fits and other complaints, which seemed to have a fatal effect on her
brain as well as constitution. Cordials were administred to keep up her spirits;
and she found it necessary to protract the use of them to blunt the edge of
grief, by overwhelming reflexion, and remove the sense of uneasiness arising
from a disorder in her stomach. In a word, she became an habitual dram-
drinker; and this practice exposed her to such communication as debauched
her reason, and perverted her sense of decorum and propriety. She and her
husband gave a loose to vulgar excess, in which they were enabled to indulge
by the charity and interest of some friends, who obtained half-pay for the
captain. They are now metamorphosed into the shocking creatures you have
seen; he into a riotous plebeian, and she into a ragged trull. They are both
drunk every day, quarrel and fight one with another, and often insult their
fellow-prisoners. Yet, they are not wholly abandoned by virtue and humanity.
The captain is scrupulously honest in all his dealings, and pays off his debts
punctually every quarter, as soon as he receives his half-pay. Every prisoner in
distress is welcome to share his money while it lasts; and his wife never fails,
while it is in her power, to relieve the wretched; so that their generosity, even
in this miserable disguise, is universally respected by their neighbours. Sometimes the recollection of their former rank comes over them like a qualm,
which they dispel with brandy, and then humorously rally one another on
their mutual degeneracy. She often stops me in the walk, and pointing to the
captain, says, 'My husband, tho' he's become a black-guard jail-bird, must be
allowed to be an handsome fellow still.'—On the other hand, he will frequently desire me to take notice of his rib,[4] as she chances to pass.—'Mind
that draggle-tail'd drunken drab—(he will say) what an antidote it is—yet, for
all that, Felton, she was a fine woman when I married her—Poor Bess, I have
been the ruin of her, that is certain, and deserve to be damned for bringing
her to this pass.'

"Thus they accommodate themselves to each other's infirmities, and pass
their time not without some taste of plebeian enjoyment—but, name their
child, they never fail to burst into tears, and still feel a return of the most
poignant sorrow."

Sir Launcelot Greaves did not hear this story unmoved. Tom Clarke's
cheeks were bedewed with the drops of sympathy, while with much sobbing,
he declared his opinion, that an action would lie against the lady's father.—

Captain Crowe having listened to the story, with uncommon attention, expressed his concern that an honest seaman should be so taken in stays:[5] but he
imputed all his calamities to the wife: "For why? (said he) a sea-faring man
may have a sweet-heart in every port; but he should steer clear of a wife, as he
would avoid a quick-sand—you see, brother, how this here Clewlin lags astern
in the wake of a sniveling b——; otherwise he'd never make a weft in his
ensign[6] for the loss of a child—odds heart! he could have done no more if he
had sprung a top-mast, or started a timber.—"

The knight declaring that he would take another view of the prison in the
afternoon, Mr. Felton insisted upon his doing him the honour to drink a dish
of tea in his apartment, and Sir Launcelot accepted his invitation. Thither they
accordingly repaired, after having made another circuit of the jail, and the tea-
things were produced by Mrs. Felton, when she was summoned to the door,
and in a few minutes returning, communicated something in a whisper to her
husband. He changed colour, and repaired to the stair-case, where he was
heard to talk aloud in an angry tone. When he came back he told the company
he had been teazed by a very importunate beggar. Addressing himself to our
adventurer, "You took notice (says he) of a fine lady flaunting about our walk
in all the frippery of the fashion—she was lately a gay young widow that made
a great figure at the court end of the town; she distinguished herself by her
splendid equipage, her rich liveries, her brilliant assemblies, her numerous
routs, and her elegant taste in dress and furniture. She is nearly related to some
of the best families in England, and it must be owned, mistress of many fine
accomplishments. But, being deficient in true delicacy, she endeavoured to
hide that defect by affectation. She pretended to a thousand antipathies which
did not belong to her nature. A breast of veal threw her into mortal agonies. If
she saw a spider she screamed; and at sight of a mouse she fainted away. She
could not without horror behold an entire joint of meat; and nothing but fric-
assees and other made-dishes were seen upon her table. She caused all her
floors to be lined with green bays,[7] that she might trip along them with more
ease and pleasure. Her footmen wore clogs, which were deposited in the hall,
and both they and her chairmen were laid under the strongest injunctions to
avoid porter and tobacco. Her jointure[8] amounted to eight hundred pounds
per annum, and she made shift to spend four times that sum: at length it was
mortgaged for nearly the entire value; but, far from retrenching, she seemed
to increase in extravagance until her effects were taken in execution, and her
person here deposited in safe custody. When one considers the abrupt transition she underwent from her spacious apartments to an hovel scarce eight feet
square; from sumptuous furniture to bare benches; from magnificence to

meanness; from affluence to extreme poverty; one would imagine she must have been totally overwhelmed by such a sudden gush of misery. But this was not the case: she has, in fact, no delicate feelings. She forthwith accommodated herself to the exigency of her fortune; yet, she still affects to keep state amidst the miseries of a gaol; and this affectation is truly ridiculous.—She lies abed till two o'clock in the afternoon: she maintains a female attendant for the sole purpose of dressing her person. Her cabin is the least cleanly in the whole prison; she has learned to eat bread and cheese, and drink porter; but she always appears once a day dressed in the pink of the fashion. She has found means to run in debt at the chandler's shop, the baker's, and the tap-house, tho' there is nothing got in this place but with ready money: she has even borrowed small sums from divers prisoners, who were themselves on the brink of starving. She takes pleasure in being surrounded with duns,[9] observing that by such people a person of fashion is to be distinguished. She writes circular letters[10] to her former friends and acquaintance, and by this method has raised pretty considerable contributions; for she writes in a most elegant and irresistible stile. About a fortnight ago she received a supply of twenty guineas; when, instead of paying her little goal-debts, or withdrawing any part of her apparel from pawn, she laid out the whole sum in a fashionable suit and laces; and next day borrowed of me a shilling to purchase a neck of mutton for her dinner—She seems to think her rank in life intitles her to this kind of assistance. She talks very pompously of her family and connexions, by whom, however, she has been long renounced. She has no sympathy nor compassion for the distresses of her fellow-creatures; but she is perfectly well bred; she bears a repulse the best of any woman I ever knew; and her temper has never been once ruffled since her arrival at the King's-bench—She now intreated me to lend her half a guinea, for which she said she had the most pressing occasion, and promised upon her honour it should be repaid to-morrow; but I lent a deaf ear to her request, and told her in plain terms that her honour was already bankrupt.—" Sir Launcelot thrusting his hand mechanically into his pocket, pulled out a couple of guineas, and desired Felton to accommodate her with that trifle in his own name; but he declined the proposal, and refused to touch the money. "God forbid, (said he) that I should attempt to thwart your charitable intention: but, this, my good sir, is no object—she has many resources. Neither should we number the clamorous beggar among those who really feel distress. He is generally gorg'd with bounty misapplied. The liberal hand of charity should be extended to modest want that pines in silence, encountering cold, and nakedness, and hunger, and every species of distress. Here you may find the wretch of keen sensations, blasted by accident in the blossom of his fortune, shivering in the solitary recess of indigence, disdaining to beg, and even ashamed to let his misery be known. Here you may see the parent who has known happier times, surrounded by his tender offspring, naked and forlorn, demanding food, which his circumstances cannot afford.—That man of decent appearance and melancholy aspect, who lifted his hat as you passed him in the yard, is a person of unblemished character. He was a reputable tradesman in the city, and failed through inevitable losses. A commission of bankruptcy was taken out against him by his sole creditor, a quaker, who refused to sign his certificate.[11] He has lived these three years in prison, with a wife and five small children. In a little time after his commitment, he had friends who offered to pay ten shillings in the pound of what he owed, and to give security for paying the remainder in three years, by installments. The honest quaker did not charge the bankrupt with any dishonest practices; but he rejected the proposal with the most mortifying indifference, declaring that he did not want his money. The mother repaired to his house, and kneeled before him with her five lovely children, imploring mercy with tears and exclamations. He stood this scene unmoved, and even seemed to enjoy the prospect, wearing the looks of complacency while his heart was steeled with rancour. 'Woman, (said he) these be hopeful babes, if they were duly nurtured. Go thy ways in peace; I have taken my resolution.' Her friends maintained the family for some time; but it is not in human charity to persevere: some of them died; some of them grew unfortunate; some of them fell off; and now the poor man is reduced to the extremity of indigence, from whence he has no prospect of being retrieved. The fourth part of what you would have bestowed upon the lady would make this poor man and his family sing with joy."

He had scarce pronounced these words when our hero desired the man might be called, and in a few minutes he entered the apartment with a low obeisance. "Mr. Coleby, (said the knight) I have heard how cruelly you have been used by your creditor, and beg you will accept this trifling present, if it can be of any service to you in your distress." So saying, he put five guineas into his hand. The poor man was so confounded at such an unlooked-for acquisition, that he stood motionless and silent, unable to thank the donor; and Mr. Felton conveyed him to the door, observing that his heart was too full for utterance. But, in a little time, his wife bursting into the room with her five children, looked around, and going up to Sir Launcelot, without any direction, exclaimed: "This is the angel sent by Providence to succour me and my poor innocents." Then falling at his feet, she pressed his hand and bathed it with her tears—He raised her up with that complacency which was natural to his disposition. He kissed all her children, who were remarkably handsome and neatly kept, tho' in homely apparel; and, giving her his direction, assured her she might always apply to him in her distress.

After her departure, he produced a bank-note for twenty pounds, and would have deposited it in the hands of Mr. Felton, to be distributed in charities among the objects of the place; but he desired it might be left with Mr. Norton, who was the proper person for managing his benevolence; and he promised to assist the deputy with his advice in laying it out.

CHAPTER XXII.

In which Capt. Crowe *is sublimed*[1] *into the Regions of Astrology.*

Three whole days had our adventurer prosecuted his inquiry about the amiable Aurelia, whom he sought in every place of public and of private entertainment, or resort, without obtaining the least satisfactory intelligence, when he received one evening, from the hands of a porter, who instantly vanished, the following billet: "If you would learn the particulars of Miss Darnel's fate, fail not to be in the fields by the Foundling Hospital,[2] precisely at seven o'clock this evening, when you shall be met by a person who will give you the satisfaction you desire, together with his reason for addressing you in this mysterious manner.—" Had this intimation concerned any other subject, perhaps the knight would have deliberated with himself in what manner he should take a hint so darkly communicated: but his eagerness to retrieve the jewel he had lost, divested him of all his caution; the time of assignation was already at hand; and neither the captain nor his nephew could be found to accompany him, had he been disposed to make use of their attendance. He therefore, after a moment's hesitation, repaired to the place appointed, in the utmost agitation and anxiety, lest the hour should be elapsed before his arrival.

Crowe was one of those defective spirits, who cannot subsist for any length of time on their own bottoms.[3] He wanted a familiar prop, upon which he could disburthen his cares, his doubts, and his humours: an humble friend who would endure his caprices, and with whom he could communicate, free of all reserve and restraint. Though he loved his nephew's person, and admired his parts, he considered him often as a little petulant jackanapes, who presumed upon his superior understanding; and as for Sir Launcelot, there was something in his character that overawed the seaman, and kept him at a disagreeable distance. He had, in this dilemma, cast his eyes upon Timothy Crabshaw, and admitted him to a considerable share of familiarity and fellowship. These companions had been employed in smoking a social pipe at an alehouse in the neighbourhood, when the knight made his excursion; and returning to the house about supper-time, found Mr. Clarke in waiting. The young lawyer was alarmed when he heard the hour of ten, without seeing our adventurer, who had been used to be extremely regular in his œconomy; and the captain and he supped in profound silence. Finding, upon enquiry among the servants, that the knight went out abruptly, in consequence of having received a billet, Tom began to be visited with the apprehension of a duel, and sat the best part of the night by his uncle, sweating with the expectation of seeing our hero brought home a breathless corse: but no tidings of him arriving, he, about two in the morning, repaired to his own lodging, resolved to publish a description of Sir Launcelot in the newspapers, if he should not appear next day. Crowe did not pass the time without uneasiness. He was extremely concerned at the thought of some mischief having befallen his friend and patron; and he was terrified with the apprehension, that in case Sir Launcelot was murdered, his spirit might come and give him notice of his fate. Now he had an insuperable aversion to all correspondence with the dead; and taking it for granted, that the spirit of his departed friend could not appear to him except when he should be alone, and a-bed in the dark, he determined to pass the remainder of the night without going to bed. For this purpose his first care was to visit the garret in which Timothy Crabshaw lay fast asleep, snoring with his mouth wide open. Him the captain with difficulty roused, by dint of promising to regale him with a bowl of rum punch in the kitchen, where the fire, which had been extinguished, was soon rekindled. The ingredients were fetched from a public-house in the neighbourhood; for the captain was too proud to use his interest in the knight's family, especially at these hours when all the rest of the servants had retired to their repose; and he and Timothy drank together until day-break, the conversation turning upon hobgoblins, and God's revenge against murder.[4] The cookmaid lay in a little apartment contiguous to the kitchen; and whether disturbed by these horrible tales of apparitions, or titillated by the savoury steams that issued from the punch-bowl, she made a virtue of necessity, or appetite, and dressing herself in the dark, suddenly appeared before them, to the no small perturbation of both. Timothy, in particular, was so startled, that in his endeavours to make an hasty retreat towards the chimney-corner, he overturned the table; the liquor was spilt, but the bowl was saved by falling on a heap of ashes. Mrs. Cook having reprimanded him for his foolish fear, declared she had got up betimes, in order to scour her saucepans; and the captain proposed to have the bowl replenished, if materials could be procured. This difficulty was overcome by Crabshaw; and they sat down with their new associate to discuss[5] the second edition. The knight's sudden disappearing being again brought upon the carpet, their female companion gave it as her opinion, that nothing would be so likely to bring this affair to light, as going to a cunning man,[6] whom she had lately consulted about a silver spoon that was mislaid, and who told her all the things that she ever did, and ever would happen to her through the whole course of her life.

Her two companions pricked up their ears at this intelligence; and Crowe asked if the spoon had been found? She answered in the affirmative, and said, the cunning man described to a hair the person that should be her true love, and her wedded husband: that he was a sea-faring man; that he was pretty well stricken in years; a little passionate or so; and that he went with his fingers clinched like, as it were. The captain began to sweat at this description, and mechanically thrust his hands into his pockets, while Crabshaw, pointing to him, told her he believed she had got the right sow by the ear.[7] Crowe grumbled, that may hap for all that he should not be brought up by such a grappling neither. Then he asked if this cunning man dealt with the devil, declaring, in that case he would keep clear of him: for why? because he must have sold himself to old scratch; and being a servant of the devil, how could he be a good subject to his majesty? Mrs. Cook assured him, the conjurer was a good christian; and that he gained all his knowledge by conversing with the stars and planets. Thus satisfied, the two friends resolved to consult him as soon as it should be light; and being directed to the place of his habitation, set out for it by seven in the morning. They found the house forsaken, and had already reached the end of the lane in their return, when they were accosted by an old woman, who gave them to understand, that if they had occasion for the advice of a fortune-teller, as she did suppose they had, from their stopping at the house where Dr. Grubble[8] lived, she would conduct them to a person of much more eminence in that profession; at the same time she informed them, that the said Grubble had been lately sent to Bridewell;[9] a circumstance which, with all his art, he had not been able to foresee. The captain, without any scruple, put himself and his companion under convoy of this beldame, who, thro' many windings and turnings, brought them to the door of a ruinous house, standing in a blind alley; which door having opened with a key drawn from her pocket, she introduced them into a parlour, where they saw no other furniture than a naked bench, and some frightful figures on the bare walls, drawn, or rather scrawled with charcoal. Here she left them locked in until she should give the doctor notice of their arrival; and they amused themselves with decyphering these characters and hieroglyphics. The first figure that engaged their attention, was that of a man hanging upon a gibbet, which both considered as an unfavourable omen, and each endeavoured to avert from his own person. Crabshaw observed, that the figure so suspended was cloathed in a sailor's jacket and trowsers; a truth which the captain could not deny; but on the other hand he affirmed, that the said figure exhibited the very nose and chin of Timothy, together with the hump on one shoulder. A warm dispute ensued; and being maintained with much acrimonious altercation, might have dissolved the new-cemented friendship of these two originals, had it not been interrupted by the old sybil,[10] who, coming into the parlour, intimated that the doctor waited for them above. She likewise told them that he never admitted more than one at a time. This hint occasioned a fresh contest: the captain insisted upon Crabshaw's making sail a-head, in order to look out afore; but Timothy persisted in refusing this honour, declaring he did not pretend to lead, but he would follow, as in duty bound. The old gentlewoman abridged the ceremony, by leading out Crabshaw with one hand, and locking up Crowe with the other. The former was dragged up stairs like a bear to the stake,[11] not without reluctance and terror, which did not at all abate at sight of the conjurer, with whom he was immediately shut up by his conductress; after she had told him in a whisper, that he must deposit a shilling in a little black coffin, supported by a human skull and thigh bones crossed, on a stool covered with black bays,[12] that stood in one corner of the apartment. The squire having made this offering with fear and trembling, ventured to survey the objects around him, which were very well calculated to augment his confusion. He saw divers skeletons hung by the head; the stuffed skin of a young alligator, a calf with two heads, and several snakes suspended from the cieling, with the jaws of a shark, and a starved weasle. On another funereal table he beheld two spheres, between which lay a book open, exhibiting outlandish characters, and mathematical diagrams. On one side stood an ink-standish with paper, and behind this desk appeared the conjurer himself in sable vestments, his head so overshadowed with hair, that far from contemplating his features, Timothy could distinguish nothing but a long white beard, which, for ought he knew, might have belonged to a four-legged goat, as well as to a two-legged astrologer.

This apparition, which the squire did not eye without manifest discomposure, extending a white wand, made certain evolutions over the head of Timothy, and having muttered an ejaculation, commanded him, in a hollow tone, to come forward and declare his name. Crabshaw thus adjured advanced to the altar; and whether from design or (which is more probable) from confusion, answered "Samuel Crowe." The conjuror taking up the pen, and making a few scratches on the paper, exclaimed in a terrific accent: "How! miscreant! attempt to impose upon the stars?—you look more like a *crab* than a *crow*, and was born under the sign of Cancer." The squire, almost annihilated by this exclamation, fell upon his knees, crying, "I pray yaw, my lord conjuror's worship, pardon my ignorance, and down't go to baind me oover to the Red Sea like[13]——I'se a poor Yorkshire tyke,[14] and would no more cheat the stars than I'd cheat my own vather, as the saying is—a must be a good hand at *trapping*, that catches the starns a *napping*[15]—but as your honour's worship observed, my name is Tim Crabshaw, of the East Riding, groom and squair to Sir Launcelot Greaves, baron knaight, and arrant knaight, who ran mad for a wench, as your worship's conjuration well knoweth:—the person below is captain Crowe; and we coom by Margery Cook's recommendation, to seek after my master, who is gone away, or made away, the Lord he knows how and where."

Here he was interrupted by the conjurer, who exhorted him to sit down and compose himself until he should cast a figure:[16] then he scrawled the paper, and waving his wand, repeated abundance of gibberish concerning the number, the names, the houses, and revolutions of the planets, with their conjunctions, oppositions, signs, circles, cycles, trines, and trigons.[17] When he perceived that this artifice had its proper effect in disturbing the brain of Crabshaw, he proceeded to tell him from the stars, that his name was Crabshaw, or Crabsclaw; that he was born in the East-riding of Yorkshire, of poor, yet honest parents, and had some skill in horses; that he served a gentleman, whose name began with the letter G——, which gentleman had run mad for love, and left his family; but whether he would return alive or dead the stars had not yet determined. Poor Timothy was thunderstruck to find the conjurer acquainted with all these circumstances, and begged to know if he mought be so bauld as to ax a question or two about his own fortune. The astrologer pointing to the little coffin, our squire understood the hint, and deposited another shilling. The sage had recourse to his book, erected another scheme, performed once more his airy evolutions with the wand, and having recited another mystical preamble, expounded the book of fate in these words: "You shall neither die by war nor water, by hunger or by thirst, nor be brought to the grave by old age or distemper; but, let me see—ay, the stars will have it so,——you shall be—exalted—hah!—ay, that is——hanged for horse-stealing."——"O, good my lord conjurer! (roared the squire) I'd as lief give forty shillings as be hanged."——"Peace, sirrah! (cried the other) would you

[The Conjuror], by Grignion after Stothard.
(Rare Book and Manuscript Library, Columbia University)

contradict or reverse the immutable decrees of fate? Hanging is your destiny; and hanged you shall be——and comfort yourself with the reflection, that as you are not the first, so neither will you be the last to swing on Tyburn tree."[18] This comfortable assurance composed the mind of Timothy, and in a great measure reconciled him to the prediction. He now proceeded in a whining tone, to ask whether he should suffer for the first fact?[19] whether it would be for a horse or a mare? and of what colour? that he might know when his hour was come.—The conjurer gravely answered, that he would steal a dappled gelding on a Wednesday; be cast at the Old Baily[20] on a Thursday, and suffer on a Friday; and he strenuously recommended it to him, to appear in the cart with a nosegay in one hand, and the Whole Duty of Man[21] in the other. "But if in case it should be in the winter (said the squire) when a nosegay can't be had"—"Why then (replied the conjurer) an orange will do as well." These material points being adjusted to the entire satisfaction of Timothy, he declared he would bestow another shilling to know the fortune of an old companion, who truly did not deserve so much at his hands; but he could not help loving him better than e'er a friend he had in the world. So saying, he dropped a third offering in the coffin, and desired to know the fate of his horse Gilbert. The astrologer having again consulted his art, pronounced, that Gilbert would die of the staggers,[22] and his carcase be given to the hounds; a sentence, which made a much deeper impression upon Crabshaw's mind, than did the prediction of his own untimely and disgraceful fate. He shed a plenteous shower of tears, and his grief broke forth in some passionate expressions of tenderness:—at length he told the astrologer he would go and send up the captain, who wanted to consult him about Margery Cook, because as how she had informed him that Dr. Grubble had described just such another man as the captain for her true love; and he had no great stomach to the match, if so be as the stars were not bent upon their coming together. Accordingly the squire being dismissed by the conjurer, descended to the parlour with a rueful length of face; which being perceived by the captain, he demanded "What cheer, ho?" with some signs of apprehension. Crabshaw making no return to this salute, he asked if the conjurer had taken an observation, and told him any thing? Then the other replied, he had told him more than he desired to know. "Why, an that be the case, (said the seaman) I have no occasion to go aloft this trip, brother." This evasion would not serve his turn: old Tisiphone[23] was at hand, and led him up growling into the hall of audience, which he did not examine without trepidation. Having been directed to the coffin, where he presented half a crown, in hope of rendering the fates propitious, the usual ceremony was performed; and the doctor addressed him in these words: "Approach, Raven." The captain advancing, "You an't much mistaken, brother, (said he) heave your eye into the binnacle, and box your compass;[24] you'll find I'm a Crowe, not a Raven, tho'f indeed they be both fowls of a feather,[25] as the saying is."—"I know it; (cried the conjurer) thou art a northern crow,—a sea crow; not a crow of prey, but a crow to be preyed upon:—a crow to be plucked,—to be flayed,—to be basted,—to be broiled by Margery upon the gridiron of matrimony——." The novice changing colour at this denunciation, "I do understand your signals, brother, (said he) and if it be set down in the log-book of fate, that we must grapple, why then, 'ware timbers. But as I know how the land lies, d'ye see, and the current of my inclination sets me off, I shall haul up close to the wind, and mayhap we shall clear Cape Margery. But, howsomever, we shall leave that reef in the foretopsail:—I was bound upon another voyage, d'ye see—to look and to see, and to know, if so be as how I could pick up any intelligence along shore, concerning my friend Sir Launcelot, who slipped his cable last night, and has lost company,[26] d'ye see." "What! (exclaimed the cunning man) art thou a crow, and can'st not smell carrion? If thou would'st grieve for Greaves, behold his naked carcase lies unburied to feed the kites, the crows, the gulls, the rooks, and ravens."—— "What, broach'd to?"[27] "Dead! as a boiled lobster." "Odd's heart! friend, these are the heaviest tidings I have heard these seven long years—there must have been deadly odds when he lowered his topsails—Smite my eyes! I had rather the Mufti had foundered at sea, with myself and all my generation on board—well fare thy soul, flower of the world! had honest Sam Crowe been within hail——but what signifies palavering." Here the tears of unaffected sorrow flowed plentifully down the furrows of the seaman's cheeks:—then his grief giving way to his indignation, "Hark ye, brother conjurer, (said he) you that can spy foul weather before it comes, damn your eyes! why didn't you give us warning of this here squall? Blast my limbs! I'll make you give an account of this here damned, horrid, confounded murder, d'ye see—mayhap you yourself was concerned, d'ye see.—For my own part, brother, I put my trust in God, and steer by the compass; and I value not your pawwawing,[28] and your conjuration, of a rope's end, d'ye see."—The conjurer was by no means pleased, either with the matter, or the manner of this address. He therefore began to soothe the captain's choler, by representing that he did not pretend to omniscience, which was the attribute of God alone; that human art was fallible and imperfect; and all that it could perform, was to discover certain partial circumstances of any particular object to which its inquiries were directed: that being questioned by the other man, concerning the cause of his master's disappearing, he had exercised his skill upon the subject, and found reason to believe that Sir Launcelot was assassinated; that he should think himself happy in being the instrument of bringing the murderers to justice, though he foresaw they would, of themselves, save him that trouble; for they would quarrel about dividing the spoil, and one would give information against the other.

The prospect of this satisfaction appeased the resentment, and, in some measure, mitigated the grief of captain Crowe, who took his leave without much ceremony; and being joined by Crabshaw, proceeded with a heavy heart to the house of Sir Launcelot, where they found the domestics at breakfast, without exhibiting the least symptom of concern for their absent master. Crowe had been wise enough to conceal from Crabshaw what he had learned of the knight's fate. This fatal intelligence he reserved for the ear of his nephew, Mr. Clarke, who did not fail to attend him in the forenoon.

As for the squire, he did nothing but ruminate in rueful silence upon the dappled gelding, the nosegay, and the predicted fate of Gilbert. Him he forthwith visited in the stable, and saluted with the kiss of peace. Then he bemoaned his fortune with tears, and by the sound of his own lamentation, was lulled asleep among the litter.

CHAPTER XXIII.

In which the Clouds that cover the Catastrophe begin to disperse.

We must now leave Capt. Crowe and his nephew Mr. Clarke, arguing with great vehemence about the fatal intelligence obtained from the conjurer, and penetrate at once the veil that concealed our hero. Know then, reader, that Sir Launcelot Greaves, repairing to the place described in the billet which he had received, was accosted by a person muffled in a cloak, who began to amuse him with a feigned story of Aurelia; to which while he listened with great attention, he found himself suddenly surrounded by armed men, who seized and pinioned down his arms, took away his sword, and conveyed him by force into a hackney-coach provided for the purpose. In vain he expostulated on this violence with three persons, who accompanied him in the vehicle. He could not extort one word by way of reply; and, from their gloomy aspects, he began to be apprehensive of assassination. Had the carriage passed through any frequented place, he would have endeavoured to alarm the inhabitants; but it was already clear of the town, and his conductors took care to avoid all villages and inhabited houses.

After having travelled about two miles, the coach stopped at a large iron-gate, which being opened, our adventurer was led in silence thro' a spacious house into a tolerably decent apartment, which he understood was intended for his bed-chamber. In a few minutes after his arrival, he was visited by a man of no very prepossessing appearance, who endeavoured to smoothe his countenance, which was naturally stern, welcomed our adventurer to his house; exhorted him to be of good chear; assured him he should want for nothing; and desired to know what he would choose for supper.

Sir Launcelot, in answer to this civil address, begged he would explain the nature of his confinement, and the reasons for which his arms were tied like those of the worst malefactor. The other postponed till to-morrow the explanation he demanded; but, in the mean time, unbound his fetters, and as he declined eating, left him alone to his repose. He took care, however in retiring, to double-lock the door of the room, whose windows were grated on the outside with iron.

The knight, being thus abandoned to his own meditations, began to ruminate on the present adventure with equal surprize and concern; but the more he revolved circumstances, the more was he perplexed in his conjectures. According to the state of the mind, a very subtle philosopher is often puzzled by a very plain proposition; and this was the case of our adventurer—What made the strongest impression upon his mind, was a notion that he was apprehended on suspicion of treasonable practices, by a warrant from the secretary of state, in consequence of some false malicious information; and that his prison was no other than the house of a messenger,[1] set apart for the accommodation of suspected persons. In this opinion, he comforted himself by recollecting his own conscious innocence, and reflecting that he should be intitled to the privilege of *habeas corpus*, as the act including that inestimable jewel, was happily not suspended at this juncture.[2]

Consoled by this self-assurance, he quietly resigned himself to slumber; but, before he fell asleep, he was very disagreeably undeceived in his conjecture. His ears were all at once saluted with a noise from the next room, conveyed in distinct bounces against the wainscot;[3] then an hoarse voice[4] exclaimed: "Bring up the artillery—let Brutandorf's brigade[5] advance—detach my black hussars[6] to ravage the country—let them be new-booted—take particular care of the spur-leathers—make a desert of Lusatia[7]—bombard the suburbs of Pera[8]—go, tell my brother Henry[9] to pass the Elbe at Meissen[10] with forty battalions and fifty squadrons—so ho, you major-general Donder, why don't you finish your second parallel?[11]—send hither the engineer Schittenbach[12]— I'll lay all the shoes in my shop, the breach will be practicable in four and twenty hours—don't tell me of your works[13]—you and your works may be damn'd—"

"Assuredly, (cried another voice from a different quarter) he that thinks to be saved by works is in a state of utter reprobation—I myself was a prophane weaver, and trusted to the rottenness of works—I kept my journeyman and 'prentices at constant work; and my heart was set upon the riches of this world, which was a wicked work—but now I have got a glimpse of the new-light—I feel the operations of grace—I am of the new birth—I abhor good works[14]—I detest all working but the working of the spirit—Avaunt, Satan— —O! how I thirst for communication[15] with our sister Jolly—"[16]

"The communication is already open with the Marche,[17] (said the first) but as for thee, thou caitif, who hast presumed to disparage my works, I'll have thee rammed into a mortar with a double charge of powder, and thrown into the enemy's quarters."

This dialogue operated like a train upon many other inhabitants of the place: one swore he was within three vibrations of finding the longitude,[18] when this noise confounded his calculation: a second, in broken English, complained he vas distorped in the moment of de proshection[19]—a third, in the character of his holiness, denounced interdiction, excommunication, and anathemas; and swore by St. Peter's keys,[20] they should howl ten thousand years in purgatory, without the benefit of a single mass. A fourth began to hollow in all the vociferation of a fox-hunter in the chace; and in an instant the whole house was in an uproar——The clamour, however, was of a short duration. The different chambers being opened successively, every individual was effectually silenced by the sound of one cabalistical word, which was no other than *waistcoat*:[21] a charm which at once cowed the king of P——,[22] dis-possessed the fanatic, dumbfounded the mathematician, dismayed the alche-mist, deposed the pope, and deprived the 'squire of all utterance.

Our adventurer was no longer in doubt concerning the place to which he had been conveyed; and the more he reflected on his situation, the more he was overwhelmed with the most perplexing chagrin. He could not conceive by whose means he had been immured in a mad-house; but he heartily repented of his knight-errantry, as a frolic which might have very serious consequences, with respect to his future life and fortune. After mature deliberation, he re-solved to demean himself with the utmost circumspection, well knowing that every violent transport would be interpreted into an undeniable symptom of insanity. He was not without hope of being able to move his jailor by a due administration of that which is generally more efficacious than all the flowers of elocution; but when he rose in the morning, he found his pockets had been carefully examined, and emptied of all his papers and cash.

The keeper entering, he enquired about these particulars, and was given to understand that they were all safely deposited for his use, to be forthcoming at a proper season: but, at present, as he should want for nothing, he had no occasion for money. The knight acquiesced in this declaration, and eat his breakfast in quiet. About eleven, he received a visit from the physician, who contemplated his looks with great solemnity; and, having examined his pulse, shook his head, saying, "Well, sir, how d'ye do?——come, don't be dejected—everything is for the best—you are in very good hands, sir, I assure you; and I dare say will refuse nothing that may be thought conducive to the recovery of your health.—"

"Doctor, (said our hero) if it is not an improper question to ask, I should be glad to know your opinion of my disorder——" "O! sir, as to that—(replied the physician) your disorder is a——kind of a——sir, 'tis very common in this country—a sort of a—" "Do you think my distemper is madness, doctor?"—"O Lord! sir,—not absolute madness—no—not madness—you have heard, no doubt, of what is called a weakness of the nerves, sir,—tho' that is a very inaccurate expression; for this phrase, denoting a morbid excess of sensation,[23] seems to imply that sensation itself is owing to the loose cohesion of those material particles which constitute the nervous substance, inasmuch as the quantity of every effect must be proportionable to its cause; now you'll please to take notice, sir, if the case were really what these words seem to import, all bodies, whose particles do not cohere with too great a degree of proximity, would be nervous; that is, endued with sensation—Sir, I shall order some cooling things to keep you in due temperature; and you'll do very well—sir, your humble servant."

So saying, he returned, and our adventurer could not but think it was very hard that one man should not dare to ask the most ordinary question without being reputed mad, while another should talk nonsense by the hour, and yet be esteemed as an oracle—The master of the house finding Sir Launcelot so tame and so tractable, indulged him after dinner with a walk in a little private garden, under the eye of a servant who followed him at a distance. Here he was saluted by a brother prisoner, a man seemingly turned of thirty, tall and thin, with staring eyes, a hook-nose, and a face covered with pimples.

The usual compliments having passed, the stranger, without further ceremony, asked if he would oblige him with a chew of tobacco, or could spare him a mouthful of any sort of cordial, declaring he had not tasted brandy since he came to the house—The knight assured him it was not in his power to comply with his request; and began to ask some questions relating to the character of their landlord, which the stranger represented in very unfavourable colours. He described him as a ruffian, capable of undertaking the darkest schemes of villainy. He said his house was a repository of the most flagrant iniquities: that it contained fathers kidnapped by their children, wives confined by their husbands, gentlemen of fortune sequestered by their relations, and innocent persons immured by the malice of their adversaries. He affirmed this was his own case; and asked if our hero had never heard of Dick Distich,[24] the poet and satirist. "Ben Bullock[25] and I (said he) were confident against the world in arms—did you never see his ode to me beginning with 'Fair blooming youth'?[26] We were sworn brothers, admired and praised, and quoted each other,[27] sir: we denounced war against all the world, actors, authors, and critics;[28] and having drawn the sword, threw away the scabbard—we pushed through thick and thin, hacked and hewed helter skelter, and became as formidable to the writers of the age, as the Bœotian band of Thebes.[29] My friend Bullock, indeed, was once rolled in the kennel;[30] but soon

> He vig'rous rose, and from th' effluvia strong
> Imbib'd new life, and scour'd, and stunk along.[31]

Here is a satire, which I wrote in an alehouse when I was drunk[32]—I can prove it by the evidence of the landlord and his wife: I fancy you'll own I have some right to say with my friend Horace,

> *Qui me commorit, melius non tangere clamo;*
> *Flebit et insignis toto cantabitur urbe.*[33]—

The knight, having perused the papers, declared his opinion that the verses were tolerably good; but at the same time observed that the author had reviled as ignorant dunces several persons who had writ with reputation, and were generally allowed to have genius:[34] a circumstance that would detract more from his candour, than could be allowed to his capacity.

"Damn their genius! (cried the satyrist) a pack of impertinent rascals! I tell you, sir, Ben Bullock and I had determined to crush all that were not of our own party—besides, I said before, this piece was written in drink." "Was you drunk too when it was printed and published?" "Yes, the printer shall make affidavit that I was never otherwise than drunk or maudlin, till my enemies, on pretence that my brain was turned, conveyed me to this infernal mansion—"

"They seem to have been your best friends, (said the knight) and have put the most tender interpretation on your conduct; for, waving the plea of insanity, your character must stand as that of a man who hath some small share of genius, without an atom of integrity—Of all those whom Pope lashed in his Dunciad, there was not one who did not richly deserve the imputation of dulness; and every one of them had provoked the satirist by a personal attack.[35] In this respect the English poet was much more honest than his French pattern Boileau,[36] who stigmatized several men of acknowledged genius; such as Quinault, Perrault, and the celebrated Lulli;[37] for which reason every man of a liberal turn must, in spite of all his poetical merit, despise him as a rancorous knave. If this disingenuous conduct cannot be forgiven in a writer of his superior genius, who will pardon it in you whose name is not half emerged from obscurity?"

"Heark ye, friend, (replied the bard) keep your pardon and your counsel for who ask and want it; or, if you will force them upon people, take one piece of advice in return: If you don't like your present situation, apply for a committee[38] without delay: they'll find you too much of a fool to have the least tincture of madness; and you'll be released without further scruple: in that case I shall rejoice in your deliverance; you will be freed from confinement, and I shall be happily deprived of your conversation."

So saying, he flew off at a tangent, and our knight could not help smiling at the peculiar virulence of his disposition. Sir Launcelot then endeavoured to enter into conversation with his attendant, by asking how long Mr. Distich had resided in the house; but he might as well have addressed himself to a Turkish mute: the fellow either pretended ignorance, or refused an answer to every question that was proposed. He would not even disclose the name of his landlord, nor inform him whereabouts the house was situated.

Finding himself agitated with impatience and indignation, he returned to his apartment, and the door being locked upon him, began to review, not without horror, the particulars of his fate. "How little reason (said he to himself) have we to boast of the blessings enjoyed by the British subject, if he holds them on such a precarious tenure: if a man of rank and property may be thus kidnapped even in the midst of the capital; if he may be seized by ruffians, insulted, robbed, and conveyed to such a prison as this, from which there seems to be no possibility of escape! Should I be indulged with pen, ink, and paper, and appeal to my relations, or to the magistrates of my country, my letters would be intercepted by those who superintend my confinement. Should I try to alarm the neighbourhood, my cries would be neglected as those of some unhappy lunatic under necessary correction. Should I employ the force which heaven hath lent me, I might imbrue my hands in blood, and after all find it impossible to escape through a number of successive doors, locks, bolts, and centinels. Should I endeavour to tamper with the servant, he might discover my design, and then I should be abridged of the little comfort I enjoy. People may inveigh against the Bastile in France, and the Inquisition in Portugal; [39] but I would ask if either of these be in reality so dangerous or dreadful as a private mad-house in England, [40] under the direction of a ruffian. The Bastile is a state prison, the Inquisition is a spiritual tribunal; but both are under the direction of government. It seldom, if ever, happens that a man intirely innocent is confined in either; or, if he should, he lays his account with a legal trial before established judges. But in England, the most innocent person upon earth is liable to be immured for life under the pretext of lunacy, sequestered from his wife, children, and friends, robbed of his fortune, deprived even of necessaries, and subjected to the most brutal treatment from a low-bred barbarian, who raises an ample fortune on the misery of his fellow-creatures, and may, during his whole life, practise this horrid oppression, without question or controul."

This uncomfortable reverie was interrupted by a very unexpected sound that seemed to issue from the other side of a thick party-wall. [41] It was a strain of vocal music, more plaintive than the widow'd turtle's [42] moan, more sweet and ravishing than Philomel's love-warbled song. [43] Through his ear it instant pierced into his heart; for at once he recognized it to be the voice of his adored Aurelia. Heavens! what was the agitation of his soul, when he made this discovery! how did every nerve quiver! how did his heart throb with the most violent emotion! He ran round the room in distraction, foaming like a lion in the toil—then he placed his ear close to the partition, and listened as if his whole soul was exerted in his sense of hearing. When the sound ceased to vibrate on his ear, he threw himself on the bed; he groaned with anguish; he exclaimed in broken accents; and, in all probability, his heart would have burst, had not the violence of his sorrow found vent in a flood of tears.

These first transports were succeeded by a fit of impatience, which had well-nigh deprived him of his senses in good earnest. His surprize at finding his lost Aurelia in such a place; the seeming impossibility of relieving her; and his unspeakable eagerness to contrive some scheme for profitting by the interesting discovery he had made, concurred in brewing up a second extasy, during which he acted a thousand extravagancies, which it was well for him the attendants did not observe. Perhaps it was well for the servant that he did not enter while the paroxism prevailed: had this been the case, he might have met with the fate of Lychas, whom Hercules in his frenzy destroyed.[44]

Before the cloth was laid for supper, he was calm enough to conceal the disorder of his mind: but he complained of the head-ach, and desired he might be next day visited by the physician, to whom he resolved to explain himself in such a manner, as should make an impression upon him, provided he was not altogether destitute of conscience and humanity.

CHAPTER XXIV.

The Knot that puzzles human Wisdom, the Hand of Fortune sometimes will untie familiar as her Garter.

When the doctor made his next appearance in Sir Launcelot's apartment, the knight addressed him in these words: "Sir, the practice of medicine is one of the most honourable professions exercised among the sons of men; a profession which hath been revered at all periods and in all nations, and even held sacred in the most polished ages of antiquity. The scope of it is to preserve the being, and confirm the health of our fellow-creatures; of consequence, to sustain the blessings of society, and crown life with fruition. The character of a physician, therefore, not only supposes natural sagacity, and acquired erudition, but it also implies every delicacy of sentiment, every tenderness of nature, and every virtue of humanity. That these qualities are centered in you, doctor, I would willingly believe: but it will be sufficient for my purpose, that you are possessed of common integrity. To whose concern I am indebted for your visits, you best know: but if you understand the art of medicine, you must be sensible by this time, that with respect to me your prescriptions are altogether unnecessary—come, Sir, you cannot—you don't believe that my intellects are disordered. Yet, granting me to be really under the influence of that deplorable malady, no person has a right to treat me as a lunatic,[1] or to sue out a commission, but my nearest kindred.—That you may not plead ignorance of my name and family, you shall understand that I am Sir Launcelot Greaves, of the county of York, baronet; and that my nearest relation is Sir Reginald Meadows, of Cheshire, the eldest son of my mother's sister—

that gentleman, I am sure, had no concern in seducing me by false pretences under the clouds of night into the fields, where I was surprised, overpowered, and kidnapped by armed ruffians. Had he really believed me insane, he would have proceeded according to the dictates of honour, humanity, and the laws of his country. Situated as I am, I have a right, by making application to the lord chancellor, to be tried by a jury[2] of honest men.—But of that right, I cannot avail myself, while I remain at the mercy of a brutal miscreant, in whose house I am inclosed, unless you contribute your assistance. Your assistance, there-fore, I demand, as you are a gentleman, a christian, and a fellow-subject, who, tho' every other motive should be overlooked, ought to interest himself in my case as a common concern, and concur with all your power towards the pun-ishment of those who dare commit such outrages against the liberty of your country."

The doctor seemed to be a little disconcerted; but after some recollection, resumed his air of sufficiency and importance, and assured our adventurer he would do him all the service in his power; but, in the mean time, advised him to take the potion he had prescribed.

The knight's eyes lightning with indignation, "I am now convinced, (cried he) that you are accomplice in the villainy which has been practised upon me; that you are a sordid wretch, without principle or feeling, a disgrace to the faculty, and a reproach to human nature—yes, sirrah, you are the most per-fidious of all assassins—you are the hireling minister of the worst of all vil-lains, who from motives even baser than malice, envy, and revenge, rob the innocent of all the comforts of life, brand them with the imputation of mad-ness, the most cruel species of slander, and wantonly protract their misery, by leaving them in the most shocking confinement, a prey to reflections infinitely more bitter than death—but I will be calm—do me justice at your peril. I demand the protection of the legislature—if I am refused,—remember, a day of reckoning will come—you and the rest of the miscreants who have com-bined against me, must, in order to cloak your treachery, have recourse to mur-der; an expedient which I believe you very capable of embracing, for a man of my rank and character cannot be much longer concealed——Tremble, caitif, at the thoughts of my release—in the mean time, begone, lest my just resent-ment impel me to dash out your brains upon that marble—away.—"

The honest doctor was not so firmly persuaded of his patient's lunacy as to reject his advice, which he made what haste he could to follow, when an unexpected accident intervened. That this may be properly introduced, we must return to the knight's brace of trusty friends, captain Crowe and lawyer Clarke, whom we left in sorrowful deliberation upon the fate of their patron.

Clarke's genius being rather more fruitful in resources, than that of the seaman, he suggested an advertisement, which was accordingly inserted in the daily papers; importing, that, "whereas a gentleman of considerable rank and fortune had suddenly disappeared on such a night from his house, near Golden-square,[3] in consequence of a letter delivered to him by a porter; and there is great reason to believe some violence hath been offered to his life: any person capable of giving such information as may tend to clear up this dark transaction, shall, by applying to Mr. Thomas Clarke, attorney, at his lodgings in Upper Brook-street,[4] receive proper security for the reward of one hundred guineas, to be paid to him upon his making the discovery required."

The porter who delivered the letter appeared accordingly; but could give no other information, except that it was put into his hand with a shilling, by a man muffled up in a great coat, who stopped him for the purpose, in his passing through Queen-street.[5] It was necessary that the advertisement should produce an effect upon another person, who was no other than the hackney coachman who drove our hero to the place of his imprisonment. This fellow had been enjoined secrecy, and indeed bribed to hold his tongue, by a considerable gratification, which, it was supposed, would have been effectual, as the man was a master-coachman in good circumstances, and well known to the keeper of the mad-house, by whom he had been employed on former occasions of the same nature. Perhaps his fidelity to his employer, reinforced by the hope of many future jobbs of that kind, might have been proof against the offer of fifty pounds; but double that sum was a temptation he could not resist. He no sooner read the intimation in the Daily Advertiser,[6] over his morning's pot at an alehouse, than he entered into consultation with his own thoughts, and having no reason to doubt that this was the very fare he had conveyed, he resolved to earn the reward, and abstain from all such adventures in time coming. He had the precaution, however, to take an attorney along with him to Mr. Clarke, who entered into a conditional bond; and, with the assistance of his uncle deposited the money, to be forthcoming when the conditions should be fulfilled. These previous measures being taken, the coachman declared what he knew, and discovered the house in which Sir Launcelot had been immured. He moreover accompanied our two adherents to a judge's chamber, where he made oath to the truth of his information; and a warrant was immediately granted to search the house of Bernard Shackle, and set at liberty Sir Launcelot Greaves, if there found.

Fortified with this authority, they engaged a constable with a formidable posse, and embarking them in coaches, repaired, with all possible expedition, to the house of Mr. Shackle, who did not think proper to dispute their claim, but admitted them, tho' not without betraying evident symptoms of consternation. One of the servants directing them, by his master's order, to Sir Launcelot's apartment, they hurried up stairs in a body, occasioning such a noise as did not fail to alarm the physician, who had just opened the door to retire, when he perceived their irruption. Capt. Crowe conjecturing he was guilty, from the confusion that appeared in his countenance, made no scruple of seizing him by the collar, as he endeavoured to retreat; while the tender-hearted Tom Clarke, running up to the knight with his eyes brimfull of joy and affection, forgot all the forms of distant respect, and throwing his arms around his neck, blubbered in his bosom.

Our hero did not receive this proof of his attachment unmoved. He strained him in his embrace, honoured him with the title of his deliverer, and asked him by what miracle he had discovered the place of his confinement. The lawyer began to unfold the various steps he had taken, with equal minuteness and self-complacency, when Crowe dragging the doctor still by the collar, shook his old friend by the hand, protesting he was never so overjoyed since he got clear of a Sallee Rover on the coast of Barbary;[7] and that two glasses ago[8] he would have started[9] all the money he had in the world in the hold of any man who would have shewn Sir Launcelot safe at his moorings. The knight, having made a proper return to this sincere manifestation of good will, desired him to dismiss that worthless fellow, meaning the doctor, who, finding himself released, withdrew with some precipitation.

Then our adventurer, attended by his friends, walked with a deliberate pace to the outward gate, which he found open, and getting into one of the coaches, was entertained by the way to his own house with a detail of every measure which had been pursued for his release. In his own parlour he found Mrs. Dolly Cowslip, who had been waiting with great fear and impatience for the issue of Mr. Clarke's adventure. She now fell upon her knees, and bathed the knight's hand with tears of joy; while the face of this young woman, recalling the idea of her mistress, roused his heart to strong emotion, and stimulated his mind to the immediate atchievement he had already planned. As for Crabshaw, he was not the last to signify his satisfaction at his master's return. After having kissed the hem of his garment, he repaired to the stable, where he communicated these tidings to his friend Gilbert, whom he saddled and bridled: the same office he performed for Bronzomarte: then putting on his squire-like attire and accoutrements, he mounted one, and led the other to the knight's door, before which he paraded, uttering from time to time repeated shouts, to the no small entertainment of the populace, until he received orders to house his companions. Thus commanded, he led them back to their stalls, resumed his livery, and rejoined his fellow-servants, who were resolved to celebrate the day with banquets and rejoicings.

Their master's heart was not sufficiently at ease to share in their festivity. He held a consultation with his friends in the parlour, whom he acquainted with the reasons he had to believe Miss Darnel was confined in the same house which had been his prison: a circumstance which filled them with equal pleasure and astonishment. Dolly, in particular, weeping plentifully, conjured him to deliver her dear lady without delay; nothing now remained but to concert the plan for her deliverance. As Aurelia had informed Dolly of her connection with Mrs. Kawdle,[10] at whose house she proposed to lodge, before she was overtaken on the road by her uncle, this particular was now imparted to the council, and struck a light which seemed to point out the direct way to Miss Darnel's enlargement.

Our hero, accompanied by Mrs. Cowslip, and Tom Clarke, set out immediately for the house of Dr. Kawdle, who happened to be abroad; but his wife received them with great courtesy. She was a well-bred, sensible, genteel woman, and strongly attached to Aurelia by the ties of affection as well as of consanguinity. She no sooner learned the situation of her cousin than she expressed the most impatient concern for her being set at liberty; and assured Sir Launcelot she would concur in any scheme he should propose for that purpose. There was no room for hesitation or choice; he attended her immediately to the judge, who upon proper application issued another search-warrant for Aurelia Darnel. The constable and his posse were again retained; and Sir Launcelot Greaves once more crossed the threshold of Mr. Bernard Shackle. Nor was the search-warrant the only implement of justice with which he had furnished himself for this visit. In going thither, they agreed upon the method in which they should introduce themselves gradually to Miss Darnel, that her tender nature might not be too much shocked by their sudden appearance.

When they arrived at the house therefore, and produced their credentials, in consequence of which, a female attendant was directed to shew the lady's apartment, Mrs. Dolly first entered the chamber of the accomplished Aurelia, who, lifting up her eyes, screamed aloud, and flew into the arms of her faithful Cowslip. Some minutes elapsed before Dolly could make shift to exclaim,— "Am coom to live and daai with my beloved leady!" "Dear Dolly! (cried her mistress) I cannot express the pleasure I have in seeing you again—good heaven! what solitary hours of keen affliction have I passed since we parted!— but, tell me, how did you discover the place of my retreat?—has my uncle relented?——do I owe your coming to his indulgence?"

Dolly answered in the negative; and by degrees gave her to understand that her cousin, Mrs. Kawdle, was in the next room; that lady immediately appeared, and a very tender scene of recognition passed between the two relations. It was she who, in the course of conversation, perceiving that Aurelia was perfectly composed, declared the happy tidings of the approaching deliverance. When the other eagerly insisted upon knowing to whose humanity and address she was indebted for this happy turn of fortune, her cousin declared the obligation was due to a young gentleman of Yorkshire called Sir Launcelot Greaves. At mention of that name, her face was overspread with a crimson glow, and her eyes beamed redoubled splendor,—"Cousin, (said she, with a sigh) I know not what to say—that gentleman,—Sir Launcelot Greaves was surely born—Lord bless me!—I tell you, cousin, he has been my guardian angel.—"

Mrs. Kawdle, who had maintained a correspondence with her by letters, was no stranger to the former part of the connexion subsisting between those two lovers, and had always favoured the pretensions of our hero, without being acquainted with his person. She now observed with a smile, that as Aurelia esteemed the knight her guardian angel, and he adored her as a demi-deity, nature seemed to have intended them for each other; for such sublime ideas exalted them both above the sphere of ordinary mortals. She then ventured to intimate that he was in the house, impatient to pay his respects in person. At this declaration, the colour vanished from her cheeks; which, however, soon underwent a total suffusion. Her heart panted; her bosom heaved; and her gentle frame was agitated by transports rather violent than unpleasing. She soon, however, recollected herself; and her native serenity returned; when rising from her seat, she declared she would see him in the next apartment, where he stood in the most tumultuous suspence, waiting for permission to approach her person. Here she broke in upon him, arrayed in an elegant white undress,[11] the emblem of her purity, beaming forth the emanations of amazing beauty, warmed and improved with a glow of gratitude and affection. His heart was too big for utterance; he ran towards her with rapture, and, throwing himself at her feet, imprinted a respectful kiss upon her lilly hand. "This, divine Aurelia, (cried he) is a foretaste of that ineffable bliss, which you was born to bestow!—Do I then live to see you smile again? to see you restored to liberty; your mind at ease, and your health unimpaired!" "You have lived, (said she) to see my obligations to Sir Launcelot Greaves accumulated in such a manner, that a whole life spent in acknowledgment will scarce suffice to demonstrate a due sense of his goodness." "You greatly over-rate my services, which have been rather the duties of common humanity, than the efforts of a generous passion, too noble to be thus evinced;—but let not my unseasonable transports detain you a moment longer on this detested scene—Give me leave to hand you into the coach, and commit you to the care of this good lady, attended by this honest young gentleman, who is my particular friend." So saying, he presented Mr. Thomas Clarke, who had the honour to salute the fair hand of the ever amiable Aurelia.

The ladies being safely coached under the escorte of the lawyer, Sir Launcelot assured them he should wait on them in the evening, at the house of Dr. Kawdle, whither they immediately directed their course. Our hero, who remained with the constable and his gang, enquired for Mr. Bernard Shackle, upon whose person he intended to serve a writ of conspiracy,[12] over and above a prosecution for robbery, in consequence of his having disencumbered the knight of his money and other effects, on the first night of his confinement. Mr. Shackle had discretion enough to avoid this encounter, and even to anticipate the indictment for felony, by directing one of his servants to restore the cash and papers, which our adventurer accordingly received, before he quitted the house.

In the prosecution of his search after Shackle, he chanced to enter the chamber of the bard, whom he found in dishabille,[13] writing at a table, with a bandage over one eye, and his head covered with a night-cap of bays.[14] The knight, having made an apology for his intrusion, desired to know if he could be of any service to Mr. Distich, as he was now at liberty to use the little influence he had, for the relief of his fellow sufferers.—The poet having eyed him for some time askance, "I told you, (said he) your stay in this place would be of short duration.—I have sustained a small disaster on my left eye, from the hands of a rascally cordwainer,[15] who pretends to believe himself the king of Prussia; and I am now in the very act of galling his majesty with keen iambicks.[16]—If you can help me to a roll of tobacco, and a bottle of genever,[17] so;—If you are not so inclined, your humble servant—I shall share in the joy of your deliverance."

The knight declined gratifying him in these particulars, which he apprehended might be prejudicial to his health; but offered his assistance in redressing his grievances, provided he laboured under any cruel treatment, or inconvenience. "I comprehend the full extent of your generosity: (replied the satyrist) you are willing to assist me, in every thing, except the only circumstances in which assistance is required.—God b' w' ye—If you see Ben Bullock, tell him I wish he would not dedicate any more of his works to me.—Damn the fellow; he has changed his note, and begins to snivel.—For my part, I stick to my former maxim; defy all the world, and will die hard, even if death should be preceded by damnation."

The knight finding him incorrigible, left him to the slender chance of being one day comforted by the dram-bottle; but resolved, if possible, to set on foot an accurate inquiry into the oeconomy and transactions of this private inquisition, that ample justice might be done in favour of every injured individual confined within its walls. In the afternoon, he did not fail to visit his Aurelia; and all the protestations of their mutual passion were once more interchanged. He now produced the letter, which had caused such fatal disquiet in his bosom; and Miss Darnel no sooner eyed the paper, than she recollected it was a formal dismission, which she had intended and directed for Mr. Sycamore. This the uncle had intercepted, and cunningly inclosed in another cover, addressed to Sir Launcelot Greaves, who was now astonished beyond measure to see the mystery so easily unfolded. The joy that now diffused itself in the hearts of our lovers, is more easily conceived than described; but, in order to give a stability to this mutual satisfaction, it was necessary that Aurelia should be secured from the tyranny of her uncle, whose power of guardianship would not otherwise for some months expire.

Dr. Kawdle and his lady having entered into their deliberations on this subject, it was agreed that Miss Darnel should have recourse to the protection of the lord-chancellor: [18] but such application was rendered unnecessary by the unexpected arrival of John Clump with the following letter to Mrs. Kawdle from the steward of Anthony Darnel, dated at Aurelia's house in the country. "Madam, it hath pleased God to afflict Mr. Darnel with a severe stroke of the dead palsy.[19]—He was taken yesterday, and now lies insensible, seemingly at the point of death. Among the papers in his pocket, I found the inclosed, by which it appears that my honoured young lady Miss Darnel is confined in a private mad-house. I am afraid Mr. Darnel's fate is a just judgment of God upon him for his cruelty to that excellent person. I need not exhort you, madam, to take, immediately upon the receipt of this, such measures as will be necessary for the enlargement of my poor young lady. In the mean time, I shall do the needful for the preservation of her property in this place, and send you an account of any further alteration that may happen; being very respectfully, Madam, your most obedient humble servant, Ralph Mattocks."

Clump had posted up to London with this intimation, on the wings of love, and being covered with clay from the heels to the eyes upwards, he appeared in such an unfavourable light at Dr. Kawdle's door, that the footman refused him admittance. Nevertheless, he pushed him aside, and fought his way upstairs into the dining-room, where the company was not a little astonished at such an apparition. The fellow himself was no less amazed at seeing Aurelia, and his own sweetheart Mrs. Dolly Cowslip. He forthwith fell upon his knees, and, in silence, held out the letter, which was taken by the doctor, and presented to his wife, according to the direction. She did not fail to communicate the contents, which were far from being unwelcome to the individuals who composed this little society. Mr. Clump was honoured with the approbation of his young lady, who commended him for his zeal and expedition; bestowed upon him an handsome gratuity in the mean time, and desired to see him again when he should be properly refreshed after the fatigue he had undergone.

Mr. Thomas Clarke being consulted on this occasion, gave it as his opinion, that Miss Darnel should without delay, choose another guardian for the few months that remained of her minority.[20] This opinion was confirmed by the advice of some eminent lawyers, to whom immediate recourse was had; and Dr. Kawdle, being the person pitched upon for this office, the necessary forms were executed with all possible dispatch. The first use the doctor made of his guardianship was to sign a power, constituting Mr. Ralph Mattocks his attorney *pro tempore*,[21] for managing the estate of Miss Aurelia Darnel; and this was forwarded to the steward by the hands of Clump, who set out with it for the seat of Darnel-hill, though not without a heavy heart, occasioned by some intimation he had received, concerning the connexion between his dear Dolly, and Mr. Clarke the lawyer.

CHAPTER THE LAST.

*Which, it is to be hoped, will be, on more accounts
than one, agreeable to the reader.*

Sir Launcelot having vindicated the liberty, confirmed the safety, and secured the heart of his charming Aurelia, now found leisure to unravel the conspiracy which had been executed against his person; and with that view commenced a law-suit against the owner of the house where he and his mistress had been separately confined. Mr. Shackle was, notwithstanding all the submissions and atonement which he offered to make, either in private or in public, indicted on the statute of kidnapping, tried, convicted, punished by a severe fine, and standing in the pillory. A judicial writ *ad inquirendum*[1] being executed, the prisons of his inquisition were laid open, and several innocent captives enlarged.

In the course of Shackle's trial, it appeared that the knight's confinement was a scheme executed by his rival Mr. Sycamore, according to the device of his counsellor Dawdle, who, by this contrivance, had reconciled himself to his patron, after having deserted him in the day of battle. Our hero was so incensed at the discovery of Sycamore's treachery and ingratitude, that he went in quest of him immediately, to take vengeance on his person, accompanied by Capt. Crowe, who wanted to ballance accounts with Mr. Dawdle. But those gentlemen had wisely avoided the impending storm, by retiring to the continent, on pretence of travelling for improvement.

Sir Launcelot was not now so much of a knight-errant, as to leave Aurelia to the care of Providence, and pursue the traitors to the farthest extremities of the earth. He practised a much more easy, certain, and effectual method of revenge, by instituting a process against them, which, after writs of *capias, alias, & pluries*, had been repeated, subjected them both to outlawry.[2] Mr. Sycamore and his friend being thus deprived of the benefit of the law, by their own neglect, would likewise have forfeited their goods and chattels to the king, had not they made such submissions as appeased the wrath of Sir Launcelot and Capt. Crowe; then they ventured to return, and by dint of interest obtained a reversal of the outlawry. But this grace they did not enjoy, till long after our adventurer was happily established in life.

While the knight waited impatiently for the expiration of Aurelia's minority, and, in the mean time, consoled himself with the imperfect happiness arising from her conversation, and those indulgences which the most unblemished virtue could bestow; Capt. Crowe projected another plan of vengeance against the conjurer, whose lying oracles had cost him such a world of vexation. The truth is, the captain began to be tired of idleness, and undertook this adventure to keep his hand in use. He imparted his design to Crabshaw, who had likewise suffered in spirit from the predictions of the said offender, and was extremely well disposed to assist in punishing the false prophet. He now took it for granted that he should not be hanged for stealing a horse; and thought it very hard to pay so much money for a deceitful prophecy, which, in all likelihood, would never be fulfilled.

Actuated by these motives, they set out together for the house of consultation; but they found it shut up and abandoned, and, upon inquiry in the neighbourhood, learned that the conjurer had moved his quarters that very day on which the captain had recourse to his art. This was actually the case: he knew the fate of Sir Launcelot would soon come to light, and he did not chuse to wait the consequence. He had other motives for decamping. He had run a score at the public house, which he had no mind to discharge, and wanted to disengage himself from his female associate, who knew too much of his affairs, to be kept at her proper distance. All these purposes he had answered, by retreating softly without beat of drum, while his Sybil was abroad running down prey for his devouring. He had not, however, taken his measures so cunningly, but that this old hag discovered his new lodgings, and in revenge, gave information to the publican. This creditor took out a writ accordingly; and the bailiff had just secured his person as Capt. Crowe and Timothy Crabshaw chanced to pass by the door in their way homewards, through an obscure street near the Seven Dials.[3]

The conjurer having no subterfuge left, but a great many particular reasons for avoiding an explanation with the justice, like the man between the devil and the deep sea,[4] of two evils chose the least; and beckoning to the captain, called him by his name. Crowe, thus addressed, replied with a "Hilloah!" and looking towards the place from whence he was hailed, at once recognized the negromancer.[5] Without farther hesitation he sprang across the street, and collaring Albumazar,[6] exclaimed, "Aha! old boy; is the wind in that corner?——I thought we should grapple one day——now will I bring you up by the head, tho' all the devils in hell were blowing abaft the beam."[7]

The bailiff seeing his prisoner so roughly handled before, and at the same time assaulted behind by Crabshaw, who cried, "Shew me a liar, and I'll shew you a thief—who is to be hanged now?"—I say, the bailiff, fearing he should lose the benefit of his job, began to put on his contentious face, and, declaring the doctor was his prisoner, swore he could not surrender him, without a warrant from the lord chief justice. The whole groupe adjourning into the parlour, the conjurer desired to know of Crowe, whether Sir Launcelot was found? being answered, "Ey, ey, safe enough to see you made fast in the bilboes,[8] brother"; he told the captain he had something of consequence to communicate for his advantage; and proposed that Crowe and Crabshaw should bail the action, which lay only for a debt of three pounds.

Crowe stormed, and Crabshaw grinned at this modest proposal: but when they understood that they could only be bound for his appearance, and reflected that they needed not part with him, until his body should be surrendered unto justice, they consented to give bail; and the bond being executed, conveyed him directly to the house of our adventurer. The boisterous Crowe introduced him to Sir Launcelot with such an abrupt, unconnected detail of his offence, as the knight could not understand without Timothy's annotations. These were followed by some questions put to the conjurer, who laying aside his black gown, and plucking off his white beard, exhibited to the astonished spectators, the very individual countenance of the empirical politician Ferret, who had played our hero such a slippery trick after the electioneering adventure.

"I perceive (said he) you are preparing to expostulate, and upbraid me for having given a false information against you to the country justice. I look upon mankind to be in a state of nature, a truth which Hobbes hath stumbled upon by accident. I think every man has a right to avail himself of his talents, even at the expence of his fellow-creatures; just as we see the fish, and other animals of the creation, devouring one another.⁹—I found the justice but one degree removed from ideotism, and knowing that he would commit some blunder in the execution of his office, which would lay him at your mercy, I contrived to make his folly the instrument of my escape—I was dismissed without being obliged to sign the information I had given; and you took ample vengeance for his tyranny and impertinence. I came to London, where my circumstances obliged me to live in disguise. In the character of a conjurer, I was consulted by your follower Crowe, and your 'squire Crabshaw. I did little or nothing but eccho back the intelligence they brought me, except prognosticating that Crabshaw would be hanged; a prediction to which I found myself so irresistibly impelled, that I am persuaded it was the real effect of inspiration—I am now arrested for a paultry sum of money; and, moreover, liable to be sent to Bridewell as an impostor¹⁰—let those answer for my conduct, whose cruelty and insolence have driven me to the necessity of using such subterfuges—I have been oppressed and persecuted by the government for speaking truth—your omnipotent laws have reconciled contradictions. That which is acknowleged to be truth in fact is construed falshood in law; and great reason we have to boast of a constitution founded on the basis of absurdity——But, waving these remarks, I own I am unwilling to be either imprisoned for debt, or punished for imposture—I know how far to depend upon generosity, and what is called benevolence; words to amuse the weak-minded—I build upon a surer bottom—I will bargain for your assistance—it is in my power to put twelve thousand pounds in the pocket of Samuel Crowe, that there sea-ruffian, who by his good-will would hang me to the yard's arm—"

There he was interrupted by the seaman. "Damn your rat's eyes! none of your—hang thee!—fish my topmasts! if the rope was fairly reeved¹¹ and the tackle sound, d'ye see—" Mr. Clarke, who was present, began to stare; while the knight assured Ferret, that if he was really able and willing to serve Capt. Crowe in any thing essential, he should be amply rewarded. In the mean time, he discharged the debt, and assigned him an apartment in his own house. That same day, Crowe, by the advice of Sir Launcelot and his nephew, entered into conditional articles with the Cynic, to allow him the interest of fifteen hundred pounds for life; provided, by his means, the captain should obtain possession of the estate of Hobby-hole in Yorkshire,¹² which had belonged to his grandfather, and of which he was heir of blood.

This bond being executed, Mr. Ferret discovered that he himself was the lawful husband of Bridget Maple, aunt to Samuel Crowe, by a clandestine marriage;[13] which, however, he convinced them he could prove by undeniable evidence. This being the case, she, the said Bridget Maple, alias Ferret, was a *covert femme*,[14] consequently could not transact any deed of alienation[15] without his concurrence; ergo, the docking of the intail[16] of the estate of Hobbyhole was illegal and of none effect. This was a very agreeable declaration to the whole company, who did not fail to congratulate Captain Crowe on the prospect of his being restored to his inheritance. Tom Clarke, in particular, protested, with tears in his eyes, that it gave him unspeakable joy; and his tears trickled the faster, when Crowe, with an arch look, signified that now he was pretty well victualled for life, he had some thoughts of embarking on the voyage of matrimony.

But that point of happiness to which, as the north pole, the course of these adventures hath been invariably directed, was still unattained; we mean, the indissoluble union of the accomplished Sir Launcelot Greaves and the enchanting Miss Darnel. Our hero now discovered in his mistress a thousand charms, which hitherto he had no opportunity to contemplate. He found her beauty excelled by her good sense, and her virtue superior to both. He found her untainted by that giddiness, vanity, and affectation, which distinguish the fashionable females of the present age. He found her uninfected by the rage for diversion and dissipation; for noise, tumult, gewgaws, glitter, and extravagance. He found her not only raised by understanding and taste far above the amusements of little vulgar minds; but even exalted by uncommon genius and refined reflection, so as to relish the more sublime enjoyments of rational pleasure. He found her possessed of that vigour of mind which constitutes true fortitude, and vindicates the empire of reason. He found her heart incapable of disguise or dissimulation; frank, generous, and open; susceptible of the most tender impressions; glowing with a keen sense of honour, and melting with humanity. A youth of his sensibility could not fail of being deeply affected by such attractions. The nearer he approached the centre of happiness, the more did the velocity of his passion increase. Her uncle still remained insensible, as it were, in the arms of death. Time seemed to linger in its lapse, 'till the knight was inflamed to the most eager degree of impatience. He communicated his distress to Aurelia; he pressed her with the most pathetic remonstrances to abridge the torture of his suspence. He interested Mrs. Kawdle in his behalf; and, at length, his importunity succeeded. The banns of marriage were regularly published; and the ceremony was performed in the parish church, in presence of Dr. Kawdle and his lady, Capt. Crowe, lawyer Clarke, and Mrs. Dolly Cowslip.—

The bride, instead of being disguised in tawdry stuffs of gold or silver, and sweating under a harness of diamonds, according to the elegant taste of the times, appeared in a negligee[17] of plain blue sattin, without any other jewels than her eyes, which far outshone all that ever was produced by the mines of Golconda.[18] Her hair had no other extraneous ornament, than a small sprig of artificial roses; but the dignity of her air, the elegance of her shape, the sweet-ness and sensibility of her countenance, added to such warmth of colouring, and such exquisite symmetry of features, as could not be excelled by human nature, attracted the eyes and excited the admiration of all the beholders. The effect they produced in the heart of Sir Launcelot, was such a rapture as we cannot pretend to describe. He made his appearance on this occasion, in a white coat and blue sattin vest,[19] both embroidered with silver; and all who saw him could not but own that he alone seemed worthy to possess the lady whom heaven had destined for his consort. Capt. Crowe had taken off a blue suit of cloaths strongly guarded with bars of broad gold lace, in order to hon-our the nuptials of his friend: he wore upon his head a bag-wig *a la pigeon*,[20] made by an old acquaintance in Wapping; and to his side he had girded a huge plate-hilted sword, which he had bought of a recruiting serjeant. Mr. Clarke was dressed in pompadour, with gold buttons, and his lovely Dolly, in a smart checked lutestring,[21] a present from her mistress.

The whole company dined, by invitation, at the house of Dr. Kawdle; and here it was that the two most deserving lovers on the face of the earth attained to the consummation of all earthly felicity. The captain and his nephew had a hint to retire in due time. Mrs. Kawdle conducted the amiable Aurelia, trembling, to the marriage-bed: our hero glowing with a bride-groom's ardour, claimed the husband's privilege: Hymen lighted up his brightest torch at Vir-tue's lamp, and every star shed its happiest influence on their heaven-directed union. Instructions had been already dispatched to prepare Greavesbury-hall for the reception of its new mistress; and for that place the new-married couple set out next morning, according to the plan which had been previously con-certed. Sir Launcelot and lady Greaves, accompanied by Mrs. Kawdle and attended by Dolly, travelled in their own coach drawn by six dappled horses. Dr. Kawdle, with Capt. Crowe, occupied the doctor's post-chariot, provided with four bays: Mr. Clark had the honour to bestride the loins of Bronzo-marte: Mr. Ferret was mounted upon an old hunter: Crabshaw stuck close to his friend Gilbert; and two other horsemen completed the retinue. There was not an aching heart in the whole cavalcade, except that of the young lawyer, which was by turns invaded with hot desires and chilling scruples. Tho' he was fond of Dolly to distraction, his regard to worldly reputation, and his attention to worldly interest, were continually raising up bars to a legal gratification of his love. His pride was startled at the thought of marrying the daughter of a poor country publican; and he moreover dreaded the resentment of his uncle Crowe, should he take any step of this nature without his concurrence. Many a wishful look did he cast at Dolly, the tears standing in his eyes; and many a woeful sigh did he utter.

Lady Greaves immediately perceived the situation of his heart, and, by questioning Mrs. Cowslip, discovered a mutual passion between these lovers. She consulted her dear knight on the subject; and he catechised the lawyer, who pleaded guilty. The captain being sounded, as to his opinion, declared he would be steered in that as well as every other course of life, by Sir Launcelot and his lady, whom he verily revered as beings of an order superior to the ordinary race of mankind. This favourable response being obtained from the sailor, our hero took an opportunity on the road, one day after dinner, in presence of the whole company, to accost the lawyer in these words: "My good friend Clarke, I have your happiness very much at heart—your father was an honest man, to whom my family had manifold obligations. I have had these many years a personal regard for yourself, derived from your own integrity of heart and goodness of disposition—I see you are affected, and shall be brief— Besides this regard, I am indebted to your friendship for the liberty—what shall I say?—for the inestimable happiness I now enjoy, in possessing the most excellent—But I understand that significant glance of my Aurelia—I will not offend her delicacy——The truth is, my obligation is very great, and it is time I should evince my gratitude—if the stewardship of my estate is worth your acceptance, you shall have it immediately, together with the house and farm of Cockerton in my neighbourhood. I know you have a passion for Mrs. Dolly; and believe she looks upon you with the eyes of tender prepossession—don't blush, Dolly—besides your agreeable person, which all the world must approve, you can boast of virtue, fidelity, and friendship. Your attachment to lady Greaves, neither she or I shall ever forget—if you are willing to unite your fate with Mr. Clarke, your mistress gives me leave to assure you she will stock the farm at her own expence; and we will celebrate the wedding at Greavesbury-hall—"

By this time the hearts of these grateful lovers had overflowed. Dolly was sitting on her knees bathing her lady's hand with her tears; and Mr. Clarke appeared in the same attitude by Sir Launcelot. The uncle, almost as much affected as the nephew, by the generosity of our adventurer, cried aloud, "I pray God that you and your glorious consort may have smooth seas and gentle gales whithersoever you are bound—as for my kinsman Tom, I'll give him a thousand pounds to set him fairly afloat; and if he do not prove a faithful tender to you his benefactor, I hope he will founder in this world, and be damned in that which is to come." Nothing now was wanting to the completion of their happiness, but the consent of Dolly's mother, at the Black Lyon, who they did not suppose could have any objection to such an advantageous match for her daughter: but, in this particular, they were mistaken.

In the mean time, they arrived at the village where the knight had exercised the duties of chivalry; and there he received the gratulation of Mr. Fillet, and the attorney who had offered to bail him before justice Gobble. Mutual civilities having passed, they gave him to understand, that Gobble and his wife were turned methodists.[22] All the rest of the prisoners whom he had delivered came to testify their gratitude, and were hospitably entertained. Next day, they halted at the Black Lyon, where the good woman was overjoyed to see Dolly so happily preferred: but, when Sir Launcelot unfolded the proposed marriage, she interrupted him with a scream. "Christ Jesus forbid—marry and amen! match with her own brother!"[23]

At this exclamation Dolly fainted: her lover stood with his hairs erect, and his mouth wide open; Crowe stared; while the knight and his lady expressed equal surprise and concern. When Sir Launcelot intreated Mrs. Cowslip to explain this mystery, she told him that about sixteen years ago, Mr. Clarke senior had brought Dolly, then an infant, to her house, when she and her late husband lived in another part of the country; and as she had then been lately delivered of a child which did not live, he hired her as nurse to the little foundling. He owned she was a love-begotten babe, and from time to time paid handsomely for the board of Dolly, who he desired might pass for her own daughter. In his last illness, he assured her he had taken care to provide for the child; but since his death she had received no account of any such provision. She, moreover, informed his honour, that Mr. Clarke had deposited in her hands a diamond ring and a sealed paper, never to be opened without his order, until Dolly should be demanded in marriage by the man she should like; and not then, except in presence of the clergyman of the parish. "Send for the clergyman this instant, (cried our hero, reddening, and fixing his eyes on Dolly) I hope all will yet be well."

The vicar arriving, and being made acquainted with the nature of the case, the landlady produced the paper; which being opened, appeared to be an authentic certificate, that the person, commonly known by the name of Dorothy Cowslip, was in fact Dorothea Greaves, daughter of Jonathan Greaves, esq; by a young gentlewoman who had been some years deceased. ——

"The remaining part of the mystery I myself can unfold—(exclaimed the knight, while he ran and embraced the astonished Dolly, as his kinswoman).

Jonathan Greaves was my uncle, and died before he came of age; so that he could make no settlement on his child, the fruit of a private amour founded on a promise of marriage, of which this ring was a token. Mr. Clarke, being his confident, disposed of the child, and at length finding his constitution decay, revealed the secret to my father, who, in his will, bequeathed one hundred pounds a year to this agreeable foundling: but, as they both died while I was abroad, and some of the memorandums touching this transaction probably were mislaid, I never 'till now could discover where or how my pretty cousin was situated. I shall recompence the good woman for her care and fidelity, and take pleasure in bringing this affair to a happy issue."

The lovers were now overwhelmed with transports of joy and gratitude, and every countenance was lighted up with satisfaction. From this place to the habitation of Sir Launcelot, the bells were rung in every parish, and the corporation[24] in their formalities congratulated him in every town through which he passed. About five miles from Greavesbury-hall he was met by above five thousand persons of both sexes and every age, dressed out in their gayest apparel, headed by Mr. Ralph Mattocks from Darnel-hill, and the rector from the knight's own parish. They were preceded by music of different kinds, ranged under a great variety of flags and ensigns; and the women, as well as the men, bedizened with fancy-knots and marriage-favours.[25] At the end of the avenue, a select bevy of comely virgins arrayed in white, and a separate band of choice youths, distinguished by garlands of laurel and holly interweaved, fell into the procession, and sung in chorus a rustic epithalamium[26] composed by the curate. At the gate they were received by the venerable house-keeper Mrs. Oakely, whose features were so brightened by the occasion, that with the first glance she made a conquest of the heart of captain Crowe; and this connexion was improved afterwards into a legal conjunction.

Mean while the houses of Greavesbury-hall and Darnel-hill were set open for the entertainment of all comers, and both ecchoed with the sounds of festivity. After the ceremony of giving and receiving visits had been performed by Sir Launcelot Greaves and his lady, Mr. Clarke was honoured with the hand of the agreeable Miss Dolly Greaves; and the captain was put in possession of his paternal estate. The perfect and uninterrupted felicity of the knight and his endearing consort, diffused itself through the whole adjacent country, as far as their example and influence could extend. They were admired, esteemed, and applauded by every person of taste, sentiment, and benevolence; at the same time beloved, revered, and almost adored by the common people, among whom they suffered not the merciless hand of indigence or misery to seize one single sacrifice.

Ferret, at first, seemed to enjoy his easy circumstances; but the novelty of this situation soon wore off, and all his misanthropy returned. He could not bear to see his fellow-creatures happy around him; and signified his disgust to Sir Launcelot, declaring his intention of returning to the metropolis, where he knew there would be always food sufficient for the ravenous appetite of his spleen. Before he departed, the knight made him partake of his bounty, though he could not make him taste of his happiness, which soon received a considerable addition in the birth of a son, destined to be the heir and representative of two worthy families, whose mutual animosity, the union of his parents had so happily extinguished.

NOTES TO THE TEXT

Chapter 1

1. "the great northern road": The Great North Road connected London and Edinburgh.
2. "black lion": The Black Lion Inn on Scarthing Moor near Weston, Nottinghamshire (Kahrl, 57).
3. "Windsor chairs": "Wooden chair[s] with the back formed of upright rod-like pieces, surmounted by a crosspiece, and often with arms" (*OED*).
4. "sea-coal": "Coal, so called not because found in the sea, but because brought to *London* by sea; pitcoal" (Johnson, *Dictionary*).
5. "rumbo": A strong rum-based punch. *OED* cites chapter 9 of Smollett's *Peregrine Pickle* (1751) as the first usage, though the word is first used in chapter 2 of that novel.
6. "a pint of two-penny": Ale sold at two pence per quart.
7. "without blushing": Attorneys were frequently satirized. Smollett, who had incurred great expenses from a lawsuit in 1753 and would be jailed in connection with another while writing *Sir Launcelot Greaves*, indignantly comments on the law in a letter to Alexander Hume Campbell, the opposing lawyer in the first case brought against him (*Letters*, 21–26).
8. "*in forma pauperis*": "Forma Pauperis [in the form of a pauper], is where any Person has just Cause of Suit, and is so *poor*, that he cannot bear the usual Charges of suing at Law, or in Equity"; in such cases, the suitor will be permitted to sue without fees (*NLD*). According to 11 Hen. 7, c. 12 (1495), "pauper" meant someone worth less than five pounds.
9. "the horn of a dark lanthorn": The side of a lantern (usually made of animal horn) with a device by which light can be concealed.
10. "frize": Frieze, "a kind of coarse woollen cloth" (*OED*).
11. "Ferret": The character satirizes Smollett's enemy John Shebbeare (1709–88), quack doctor and medical and political writer; see Introduction, xlii–xliii. Smollett had used this name for a character in chapter 44 of *Ferdinand Count Fathom*. See James R. Foster, "Smollett's Pamphleteering Foe Shebbeare," *PMLA* 57 (1942): 1053–1100; and G. S. Rousseau and Roger A. Hambridge, "On Ministers and Measures: Smollett, Shebbeare, and the Portrait of Ferret in *Sir Launcelot Greaves*," *Etudes Anglaises* 32 (1979): 185–91. An anonymous article published at the time of Shebbeare's death notes that Smollett "introduced [Shebbeare] in no very respectful light, under the name of Ferret" in *Sir Launcelot Greaves* ("An Account of the Life and Writings of Dr. John Shebbeare," *European Magazine* 14 [1788]: 83).

12. "Spitzbergen": Spitsbergen is an archipelago in the Arctic Ocean, about 400 miles north of the mainland of Norway.

13. "aloft and alow": Above and below deck.

14. "taught gale": That is, taut gale. *OED* cites chapter 24 of *Roderick Random* (1748).

15. "bottom-planks . . . sheathing": "Sheathing" is "a covering of thin copper plates" used to protect a ship's bottom, hence "bottom-planks," from sea worms (*The Oxford Companion to Ships and the Sea*, ed. Peter Kemp [London: Oxford University Press, 1976]).

16. "*new-pay*": To pay is to protect a ship from the effects of water by applying tallow, resin, turpentine, tar, or such materials to its bottom and sides (Falconer).

17. "the Royal Exchange": From Elizabethan times this building, called by Thomas Pennant "that concourse of all the nations of the world," served as the center of commercial London. See Pennant, *Some Account of London*, 3d ed. (London, 1793), 446.

18. "Belay. . . . Clap a stopper upon thy cable, and bring thyself up": Sailors' slang meaning "keep quiet" or "shut up." To belay is to fasten a rope around a belaying pin, or wooden peg. *OED* gives no usage as early as Smollett's for "belay" as sailors' slang. A stopper is a short, secured rope that holds another temporarily in place. To bring oneself up is to come to a mooring.

19. "starboard . . . larboard": Right and left (or "port").

20. "the knees of a bilander": The bent iron or timber joints of a Dutch or French double-masted merchant ship.

21. "lee shore": The shore that affords shelter from the wind.

22. "tow round the headland": To draw a ship with a rope on the water around a point of land jutting into the sea.

23. "finger-braces . . . eye-blocks.—Bounce day-light": Finger-braces are ropes or wire ropes at the ends of yards that hold them at angles to catch the wind. Eye-blocks are pulleys looped through eyes in the sails. "Bounce" here means to explode with a loud sound and the force of a blow (*OED*).

24. "I'm a Yorkshire boy, as the saying is": Proverbial; like "Yorkshire tyke" (see chap. 22, n. 14), it applies to a man from Yorkshire. It is not listed in Taylor, Tilley, or *ODEP*.

25. "clapped on all my canvas": Went as fast as possible; literally, raised every sail.

26. "Fill about": "To trim the sails so that the wind can fill [them]," thus, to change the ship's direction (*Oxford Companion to Ships and the Sea*, "to Fill").

27. "docked the intail, and left the estate to an alien": An entailed estate cannot be alienated or transferred to another party. Tail is "a limited Fee," or land held in possession (*NLD*).

28. "Statute Westm. 2, 13 Ed. I. . . . donor": Westminster 2, 13 Edw. I (1285) changed the interpretation of inheritance from gifts in fee simple (unlimited tenure). The donor is the party who gives the land. Smollett follows *NLD*, "*Tail*," closely at this point. For Smollett's source for many legal terms in the novel, see Roger A. Ham-

bridge, "Smollett's Legalese: Giles Jacob's *New Law-Dictionary* and *Sir Launcelot Greaves*," *Revue des Langues Vivantes* 44 (1978): 37–44.

29. "contingent *remainder*": A "Remainder is an Estate limited in Lands or Tenements, to be enjoyed after the Estate of another expired" (*NLD*). A contingent remainder is a remainder that takes effect upon the death of one who holds the remainder, which may be entailed.

30. "*feoffees . . . feoffment* in fee": A feoffee is the receiver of a feoffment, "a Gift or Grant of any Manors, Messuages, Lands or Tenements, to another in Fee, to him and his Heirs for ever, by the Delivery of Seisin and Possession of the Thing given or granted." The feoffor gives in fee simple, the donor gives in fee tail (*NLD*, "*Feoffment*").

31. "writ of Intrusion": An intrusion "is when the Ancestor dies seised of any Estate of Inheritance, expectant upon an Estate for Life, and then Tenant for Life dies, between whose Death and the Entry of the Heir, a Stranger *intrudes*" (*NLD*). The writ of intrusion, which *NLD* publishes, declares the stranger's lack of right and his obligation to render the land to the rightful heir.

32. "*ex gravi querela* lies": A writ enabling a person "to whom any lands or tenements in fee are devised by will and the heir of the divisor enters thereon" to eject the premature inheritor (*The Student's Law-Dictionary, or Compleat English Law-Expositor* [London, 1740]). "Lies" in this sense means "is admissible."

33. "true disciple of Geber": Speaker of gibberish, in this case, legal jargon. "Geber" is a European corruption of the name of the eighth-century alchemist Abu Musa Jabir ibn Haiyan, whose alchemical treatises appeared in translation throughout the eighteenth century. Shebbeare probably would have known Geber's work, given his chemical and alchemical interests. Johnson, *Dictionary*, and Smollett in *Critical Review* 1 (1756): 323 cite this (false) etymology for "gibberish." Smollett also mentions Geber in *Adventures of an Atom*, 60.

34. "Caper": To cut a caper is to dance frolicsomely and, by extension, to act fantastically.

35. "conveyancing-way": Specialty at law in deeds of conveyance and other means of conveying property from one person to another.

36. "serjeant Croaker": A serjeant is a member of an order of "barristers of superior degree" from which, until 1873, the Common Law judges were always chosen (Jowitt and Walsh). This order of barristers alone can plead in the Court of Common Pleas, though they can also practice in other courts; see *NLD*, "*Serjeant*." Goldsmith would use this surname in *The Good-Natur'd Man* (1768).

37. "*tail . . . extinct*": "Tail after Possibility of Issue extinct is where Lands and Tenements are given to a Man and his Wife in special *Tail*, and either of them dies without Issue had between them; the Survivor hath an Estate in Tail after Possibility of Issue, &c." (*NLD*). For "tail," see n. 27, above.

38. "reversion": The return of what is left of an estate to a prior possessor (Jowitt and Walsh).

39. *"general tail* and *special tail"*: Where "Lands and Tenements are given to a Man and his Wife and to the Heirs of the Body of the Man, the Husband hath an estate in general Tail," as distinct from special tail, "where no other Persons can inherit but the Issue that are begotten by him on that particular Wife" (*NLD*, "*Tail*"). The passage follows *NLD*.

40. *"seisins"*: "Seisin in the Common Law signifies Possession. To *seise* is to take Possession of a Thing" (*NLD*).

41. "Avast": The order at sea to stop or hold.

42. "bear up a-head": Sail closer to the wind.

43. "he expatiated on the pusillanimity of the nation": Shebbeare made the familiar point on several occasions. In *A Letter to the People of England on the Present Situation and Conduct of National Affairs* (London, 1755), known as the *First Letter to the People of England*, he notes, by way of analogy, that the Persians, Greeks, and Romans "debased by Corruption and Pleasure, became Pusilanimous [*sic*] in Action" (10). In *A Sixth Letter to the People of England on the Progress of National Ruin* (London, 1757), he laments the decline of England "into Sloth, Pusillanimity, and Dishonor" (5).

44. "ridiculed the militia": Pitt's Militia Bill passed in 1757. The militia offered an alternative to the standing army and consisted of regiments in each county under a local landowner; it was a defensive, thus domestic, force. The political opposition had argued for militias and against standing armies for some decades. Ferret's ridicule distorts Shebbeare's actual preference for a militia. See chap. 2, nn. 40, 42.

45. "censured the government . . . hints about a change of hands": Like some of Ferret's previous opinions, this recalls Shebbeare's *Letters to the People of England*. Evans suggests that Ferret wants the return of the Tories to power (214); but since Crowe "could not" and the doctor "would not comprehend" him, it may be that Ferret hints at a return of the Stuart line, the heirs of the deposed King James II, who fled the country in 1688. Shebbeare was generally taken to be a Jacobite, that is, a supporter of James II and his successors.

46. "party-writer": Smollett, reviewing Shebbeare's *A Fourth Letter to the People of England on the Conduct of the m — rs in Alliances, Fleets, and Armies* (London, 1756), claimed, "Dr. *Sb* — has not scrupled to declare publickly, that though he writes well against the *M — y*, he could write much better in their defence or vindication" (*Critical Review* 2 [1756]: 279). "Party" carried the implication of zealous partisanship.

47. "a warrant from the secretary of state": A general warrant for seditious libel in his *Sixth Letter* was issued against Shebbeare (and the printer and compositor of the work) on 12 January 1758. Shebbeare was fined and stood in the pillory, though shielded by a sympathetic undersheriff from the rigors of this public disgrace, and was sentenced to prison for three years. See Foster, "Smollett's Pamphleteering Foe Shebbeare," 1061–62, 1087–89.

48. "He had already proceeded a considerable way . . . into the gulph of inevitable

destruction": Summarizes Shebbeare's position in, for example, *A Third Letter to the People of England on Liberty, Taxes, and the Application of Public Money* (London, 1756), reviewed by Smollett in *Critical Review* 1 (1756): 88–90. "Those who stood at the helm" recalls Shebbeare on "the weakness of those at the helm," in *Letters on the English Nation*, written under the pseudonym Batista Angeloni (2d ed., 2 vols. [London, 1756], 1:119); see also the *First Letter*, where Shebbeare says he will "presume to examine the understanding of him who presides at the helm" (16).

Chapter 2

1. "armed cap-a-pie": Covered in armor from head to foot. Smollett's translation of *Don Quixote* presents Quixote and others as "armed cap-a-pee" (e.g., 2:85); see also chapter 68 of *Peregrine Pickle*, ed. James L. Clifford (Oxford: Oxford University Press, 1964), 341. Given the reference to *Hamlet* that follows, Shakespeare's description of old Hamlet's ghost as "armed at point exactly, cap-a-pe" (1.2.200) is pertinent.

2. "bearing on his shoulder a bundle": The first appearance of Sir Launcelot carrying Timothy Crabshaw, much admired in the nineteenth and twentieth centuries, recalls the more pathetic entrance of Orlando carrying his old servant, Adam, in *As You Like It* (2.7.166). In chapter 39 of *Ferdinand Count Fathom*, Smollett quotes part of two lines from the famous speech of Jacques (2.7.139–40) that precedes Orlando's entrance.

3. "the neighbouring river": The Trent.

4. "the farce of Hamlet's ghost": See *Hamlet* 1.4; see also chap. 5, n. 14; and chap. 18, n. 9. In *Humphry Clinker*, Smollett again alludes to the scene when Tabitha Bramble asks the great actor James Quin to "spout a little the Ghost of Gimlet" (Jery Melford to Sir Watkin Phillips, Bath, April 30, p. 51). A passage from the ghost's speech (1.5.59) appears in *Adventures of an Atom* (35). The use of the ghost provides one of many correspondences between *Sir Launcelot Greaves* and *Tom Jones* (London, 1749); see bk. 16, chap. 5 for Tom and Partridge at the playhouse.

5. "Adzooks . . . a-has not bulged to, and gone to bottom": "Adzooks" means "by God's hooks (nails)"; Crowe uses nautical slang to note Clarke's disappearance into the cellar, by analogy the bilge, or bottom of the hull of a ship.

6. "phlebotomy": Bloodletting. This minor operation was thought by medical authorities to be effective in curing or easing a variety of ailments.

7. "protuberance on one shoulder, and a prominent belly": These details suggest another naturalization of Don Quixote, Samuel Butler's Sir Hudibras, but Smollett has transferred the satiric details from the protagonist to his squire. See *Hudibras* (1663), 1.1.291–96.

8. "small glimmering eyes . . . Hampshire porker": Hampshire was famed for the fatness of its pigs. For another porcine reference to Crabshaw, see chap. 7, n. 14.

9. "contractor": A supplier of stipulated articles, especially to the government. Smollett often satirized contractors as war profiteers; see, for example, his portrait of Vanderpelft in chapter 9; and see Matthew Bramble's complaint in *Humphry Clinker* of "contractors, who have fattened, in two successive wars, on the blood of the nation; usurers, brokers, and jobbers of every kind; men of low birth, and no breeding, have found themselves suddenly translated into a state of affluence, unknown to former ages" (Matthew Bramble to Dr. Lewis, Bath, April 23, p. 36).

10. "*dentes canini*": Canine teeth.

11. "a moon in the first quarter": Suggests the face of Punch, the English puppet often represented as hunchbacked and large stomached.

12. "leathern cap . . . the figure of a crescent": Anthony Walker used the descriptions of Sir Launcelot and Crabshaw for his frontispiece to the second number of the *British Magazine*, in which this chapter appeared. See plate 3; and see Introduction, xx–xxi. The comical pointed cap in Walker's illustration does not resemble any known marine's cap.

13. "buff jerkin": A close-fitting jacket, jersey, or short coat of light, yellow-brownish leather.

14. "buskins": Half boots that normally reached the middle of the leg (Johnson, *Dictionary*).

15. "string of bandaliers": A bandoleer was actually the broad belt itself, but by transference it came to mean the cartridges hanging from it, which can be seen in two rows in Walker's engraving. This was standard gear for an infantryman.

16. "back-sword and a cutlass": A back sword had only one cutting edge; the cutlass, short, heavy, and curving, was typically a sailor's weapon (see *OED*).

17. "Bodikins": "God's dear body," a mild oath (see *OED*).

18. "Go and teach your grannum to crack filberds": "Go and teach your grandmother to crack filberts"—a dismissal of those who would give advice to those more knowledgeable than they. Compare *Don Quixote:* "You may tell such stuff to my grannam" (1:235). See also Tilley, G406–9.

19. "sheet-anchor": The largest anchor on a ship, used in emergencies.

20. "adad": Probably "by God." Like "egad," a mild oath. Compare Old Bellair's "Adod" in George Etherege, *The Man of Mode* (1676), 2.1.

21. "farrier": A person who treats and shoes horses.

22. "*siserari*": "Court Indictments from the Inferior Courts are frequently removed by *Certiorari*" to a higher court (Giles Jacob, *A Law Grammar* [London, 1749], 99). Crowe's form is a corruption.

23. "cups and balls": A toy consisting of a cup on a stem to which is attached a ball by a string; with a flick of the wrist, the player attempts to catch the ball in the cup.

24. "Don Quixote": Don Quixote's description of knight-errantry to the goatherds in *Don Quixote* (pt. 1, bk. 2, chap. 5) dwells on the heroes of the tradition rather than on the actions of the knight-errant, as Sir Launcelot has done here. See Introduction, xxxv–xxxviii, for Sir Launcelot and Don Quixote.

25. "near two hundred years ago": Part 1 of *Don Quixote* appeared in 1605, part 2 in 1615.

26. "unless he dissembles like the elder Brutus": Lucius Junius Brutus (fl. late sixth century B.C.), the putative founder of the Roman Republic who feigned madness to deceive the Tarquins and expel them from the kingship (510 B.C.).

27. "a windmill for a giant": See *Don Quixote*, pt. 1, bk. 1, chap. 8.

28. "nor mistaken this public house for a magnificent castle": See *Don Quixote*: "As our hero's imagination converted whatsoever he saw, heard or considered, into something of which he had read in books of chivalry; he no sooner perceived the inn, than his fancy represented it, as a stately castle" (1:9).

29. "the constable": See *Don Quixote*, pt. 1, bk. 1, chap. 3.

30. "Elizabat . . . Amadis de Gaul . . . Alquife": *Amadis de Gaul*, a Spanish or Portuguese romance sometimes attributed to Vasco Lobeira (d. 1403), provided Quixote's model. Quixote quarrels with the love-mad Cardenio about Elizabat in *Don Quixote* (pt. 1, bk. 3, chap. 10); in the succeeding chapter, he respectfully discusses the physician. Alquife appears in some continuations of *Amadis de Gaul*; Quixote, in pt. 2, bk. 3, chap. 2, is fooled by the Duke's presentation of someone masquerading as that magician.

31. "Bridewell": The original Bridewell was a house of correction built in 1555 on the site of a palace of Henry VIII, between Fleet Street and the Thames in London. The term came to mean prisons generally.

32. "as a vagrant, according to the statute": The statute 17 Geo. 2, c. 5 (1744) amended longstanding laws against vagrancy. Many of the specific activities cataloged by Sir Launcelot follow the language of the statute as it appears in *NLD*, "*Vagrants*."

33. "Heaven and earth": The phrase echoes *Hamlet* (1.2.142) and links Sir Launcelot to the madness of Shakespeare's character. Sir Launcelot will use it again in chapters 10 and 15.

34. "bearward": The leader of a bear that performs or that serves as the object of bearbaiting (see chap. 22, n. 11). This term and others appear specifically in the statute.

35. "stroller": Vagrant, but more specifically, an itinerant actor.

36. "riding armed in affray of the peace": Sir Launcelot's case is summed up in *NLD*: "*Affray* . . . formerly meant no more [than *affright*]; as where Persons appeared with Armour or Weapons not usually worn, to the Terror of others." See also *NLD*, "*Riding armed*."

37. "armed and in disguise": An act for continuing the law relating to the punishment of persons going armed or disguised was passed in 1758 (see *Complete History*, 3: 239, n.).

38. "thief-takers": Ferret's ironic statement is a recognition that "thief-taking" was frequently a confidence trick in which a putative private helper in locating stolen material was in league with the thieves. See, for example, *The True and Genuine Account of the Life and Actions of the Late Jonathan Wild* (London, 1725), by Daniel

Defoe, and *The Life of Mr. Jonathan Wild the Great* (London, 1743), by Henry
Fielding.

39. "Hector": In the *Iliad*, Hector was a sympathetic Trojan hero overcome by Achilles, but the term had become synonymous with "bully."

40. "your standing army at home, that eat up their fellow subjects": A standing army
was a target of opposition polemicists throughout most of the eighteenth century;
see, for example, Jonathan Swift's *Examiner* in the 1710s and Nicholas Amhurst
and Henry St. John, Viscount Bolingbroke's *Craftsman* in the late 1720s and the
1730s. Smollett claims that during George II's reign "a standing army was, by dint
of ministerial influence, ingrafted on the constitution of Great Britain" and praises
the militia in opposition to "the venal retainers of a standing army" (*Continuation*,
4:113, 116). See chap. 1, n. 44; and see n. 42, below.

41. "your mercenaries abroad, whom you hire to fight their own quarrels": Shebbeare
often spoke against the employment of German mercenaries; see, for example, *A
Second Letter to the People of England on Foreign Subsidies, Subsidiary Armies, and their
Consequences to the Nation* (London, 1755), 20; and *Third Letter*, 22. Smollett, who
opposed the continental war fought on behalf of George II's home electorate of
Hanover, also attacked the use of mercenaries on various grounds; see, for example, *Continuation*, 1:312, where, probably with Shebbeare in mind, he distinguished his position from that of "some incendiaries" who claimed that mercenaries were employed as "part of a plot."

42. "What is your militia": See chap. 1, n. 44; and see n. 40, above. Smollett was aware
of the limitations of a militia; see *Complete History*, 3:391–92.

43. "m——y": Ministry.

44. "What is your . . . . . but a knot of thieves": "Parliament" is the word Smollett
omits. In bk. 3, chapter 7 of *Gulliver's Travels*, Gulliver describes Parliament as "a
Knot of Pedlars, Pick-pockets, Highwaymen and Bullies" (*The Prose Writings of
Jonathan Swift*, rev. ed. Herbert Davis, 14 vols. [Oxford: Basil Blackwell, 1957–
68], 11:196). In a review, Smollett reports Shebbeare as saying that "the ministry
is a knot of fools" (*Critical Review* 1 [1756]: 89). Shebbeare suggests in his *Second
Letter* and elsewhere that it may be to the "private Advantage" of the parliamentarians to tax their countrymen (7).

45. "enormous debt of an hundred millions . . . two German electorates": Shebbeare
claimed that taxes had increased from the reign of William III from over £2 million to more than £10 million in wartime and £7.5 million in peacetime, and that
England had been saddled with "a national debt of Eighty Millions" (*Third Letter*,
20–21). Smollett himself judged the national debt in 1759 to be over £100 million.
The two electorates are Hanover and Prussia.

46. "our m——y is mad . . . and our state on the brink of perdition": Shebbeare's
vitriolic *Sixth Letter* contains similar attacks on the ministry.

47. "British principles": As opposed to German principles, implicitly.

48. "caitiff": Originally a captive or prisoner; hence, a villain. The word was old-fashioned in the eighteenth century.
49. "Split my snatch-block!—Odd's firkin!—Splice my old shoes!": Nautical swearing. While "odd's firkin" ("God's little keg") is a mild oath, the other phrases are roughly equivalent formulaic oaths of surprise or disbelief: "may my pulley-case be split, my anchor blocks joined together (if this should be so)."
50. "Triton's taffril": Here, the rail capping the stern of the ship *Triton* (with the suggestion of the posteriors of Triton, son of Neptune). See Falconer, "Taffarel."
51. "Morattos, and Seapoys": The Mahrattas were Hindu warriors of central and southwestern India; the sepoys, from a word meaning "horseman" or "soldier," were natives of India who served as troops for European, especially British, forces. Smollett uses obsolete forms, the former antedating the examples in *OED*.
52. "smite my timbers": "Smite my ship's ribs (if this should be so)."
53. "Sir Everhard Greaves . . . Sir Launcelot": Harry Levin notes that Smollett was indebted to *Don Quixote* "even to the point of the heroic agnomen—inasmuch as a greave, like a quijote, happens to be a piece of leg armor" ("The Quixotic Principle: Cervantes and Other Novelists," in *The Interpretation of Narrative: Theory and Practice*, ed. Morton W. Bloomfield [Cambridge: Harvard University Press, 1970], 54). Sir Everhard's forename and surname thus reinforce one another. For "greaves" as armor in this novel, see chapter 16, 129. While there is no reason to believe that the name "Greaves" depends additionally on real names, John Greaves was an eighteenth-century Hampshire mathematician, and Hambridge notes that one George Burton Greaves lived in Yorkshire in the early nineteenth century (24). In *Humphry Clinker*, Ferdinand Count Fathom appears using the alias Grieve (Matthew Bramble to Dr. Lewis, Harrigate, June 26). Quixote mentions Sir Launcelot in *Don Quixote* (pt. 1, bk. 2, chap. 5).
54. "noddy": Fool, simpleton.

Chapter 3

1. *"Which the reader . . . may wish were chapter the last"*: Probably because of its length; this is the longest chapter of the book.
2. *"repetatur* of the julep": Repeated doses of a medicinal drink "usually prepared of delicate and sweet Ingredients, or at least with sugar" (James, "Julap").
3. *"secundum artem"*: According to the rules of his art.
4. "gemmen": Gentlemen; singular "gemman."
5. *"exceptio . . . firmat regulam"*: "The exception, amongst cases which are not excepted, proves the rule." The Latin maxim has become proverbial in English. See also Tilley, E213a; *ODEP*, 234. The language in this passage follows *NLD*, "Exception."

6. *"sedente curia"*: Seated in court.

7. "Anan": "Anon; say you so?" See also *Peregrine Pickle* (chapter 93): "This reply converted the looks of the inquirer into a stare of infinite stolidity, accompanied with the word, *Anan!* which he pronounced in a tone of fear and astonishment" (581).

8. "being in fault": In hunting, to lose or be off the scent or track (*OED*).

9. "Snug's the word": Keep silent.

10. "yawing like a Dutch yanky": To yaw is to deviate from one's course, as through bad steering. Although the origin and meaning are obscure, a yanky is evidently a small, hard-to-steer Dutch ship. This passage provides the earliest example in *OED* of this meaning.

11. *"de mortuis nil nisi bonum"*: "Of the dead speak nothing but good." See Tilley, D123; *ODEP*, 611.

12. "weepers": Mourning badges usually consisting of "a strip of white linen or muslin formerly worn on the cuff of a man's sleeve" (*OED*).

13. "rooks": Swindlers.

14. "assume the dress and manners of the gentry": This phrase suggests a residual interest in the sumptuary laws that distinguished social classes by proscribing certain forms of dress. See also Matthew Bramble, who inveighs against the "luxury" of traders, brokers, and attorneys who keep footmen and whose wives and daughters "appear in the richest stuffs, bespangled with diamonds" (*Humphry Clinker*, Matthew Bramble to Dr. Lewis, London, May 29, p. 87). And see John Sekora, *Luxury: The Concept in Western Thought from Eden to Smollett* (Baltimore: Johns Hopkins University Press, 1977), esp. 23.

15. "negligees and trollopees": Informal, loose-fitting gowns. "Trollopee" derives from "trollope," meaning something that hangs loosely.

16. "thrum the pandola": Strum or play the pandora or bandore, an ancient stringed instrument that by the eighteenth century had become lute-like and was used as a bass to the cithern. *OED* quotes this passage under "pandora."

17. "rout": "A large evening party" (*OED*).

18. "hips and haws": The fruits of the wild rose and the hawthorn.

19. "housen": An older plural of "house," surviving as dialect.

20. "keawes": Cows.

21. "bullies": Wild plums.

22. "distraining for the rent": Seizing possessions (here the cows) until payment is received.

23. "sloes": Fruits of the blackthorn.

24. "thof": Though; another obsolete term surviving in the period as dialect.

25. "portioned": Dowered.

26. "pitching the bar": A popular sport in which contestants throw a long, heavy rod.

27. "wakes": Parish festivals observed "on the feast of the patron saint of the church" (*OED*).

28. "dight": Dressed.

29. "dimity": "A stout cotton fabric, woven with raised stripes or fancy figures, usually employed undyed for beds and bedroom hangings, and sometimes for garments" (*OED*).

30. "top-knots": "Knot[s] or bow[s] of ribbon worn on the top of the head by ladies towards the end of the 17th and in the 18th century" (*OED*).

31. "kissing-strings": "A woman's bonnet- or cap-strings tied under the chin with the ends hanging loose" (*OED*).

32. "stomachers": Stiff coverings of the chest worn under the lacing of the bodice. Among fashionable women these might be highly ornamental.

33. "cockades": Each consists of "a ribbon, knot of ribbons, rosette, or the like, worn in the hat as a badge of office or party, or as part of a livery dress" (*OED*), though here for festive show. For the cockade as party badge, see chap. 9, n. 1.

34. "White Hart": A popular name for an inn or pub since the reign of Richard II. On the Great North Road, one was at Retford (see chap. 10, n. 38), another at Welwyn.

35. "the poor's-rate was reduced to a meer trifle": Because of the prosperity of the inhabitants, fewer needed the proceeds of the local tax assessed to relieve and support the poor, which varied from parish to parish. The Old Poor Law was based upon Elizabethan statutes, especially the Act for the Relief of the Poor (1598); see Paul Slack, *The English Poor Law: 1531–1782* (London: Macmillan, 1990), 18.

36. "golden age": A mythic time of health, happiness, and simplicity said by classical poets to have been the world's first and best age. The ideal animates pastoral poetry.

37. "Temple": Two Inns of Court (see n. 38, below), comprising the Inner and Middle Temples; so called from its original function as the dwelling of the Knights Templar. See Jowitt and Walsh.

38. "Inns of Court": The two courts constituting the Temple (see n. 37, above). Gray's Inn and Lincoln's Inn together functioned as collegiate houses with "the exclusive privilege of conferring the rank or degree of barrister" (i.e., "calling to the bar"). See Jowitt and Walsh.

39. "Serjeant's Inn": A serjeant at law is the highest degree in the common law. Until 1758 the serjeants held a house on Fleet Street, which continued to be called Serjeants' Inn. Their other premises, located in Chancery Lane from 1416 to 1854, were known as Old Serjeants' Inn. See Jowitt and Walsh, "Serjeants-at-law."

40. "as good a wit and a critick as any Templar": The law students, called Templars for the buildings they occupied (see n. 37, above), were commonly perceived as critical theatergoers. Will Honeycomb in Joseph Addison and Richard Steele's *Spectator* (1709–11) set the fictional pattern for the Templar as theater critic (see Evans, 217).

41. "*the Town*": Originally a geographical designation for the fashionable part of London (as opposed to the City, the business district), the term came to identify the fashionable and witty young men of London. Bonnell Thorton and George Col-

man wrote *The Connoisseur* (1754–56) using the persona "Mr. Town, critic and censor-general."

42. "Butcher-row": Close to the Temple and the other Inns of Court, the butchers provided cheap cooked meals as well as meat for purchase. An eighteenth-century engraving of the street with Temple Bar at the end and the unglazed windows of the shops along the sides is reproduced in Richard B. Schwartz, *Daily Life in Johnson's London* (Madison: University of Wisconsin Press, 1983), 101. The engraver, not mentioned in the book, is Anthony Walker, who illustrated *Sir Launcelot Greaves.*

43. "regulated the diversions of the theatre": By published drama criticism, word of mouth, and loudly "damning" performances, the young gentlemen affected the fortunes of plays, or thought they did so. James Boswell's *London Journal* (1762–63) records typical behavior of such "regulators" of the theater; Boswell himself wrote *Critical Strictures on the New Tragedy of Elvira* (1763) with his friends George Dempster and Andrew Erskine.

44. "Darnel": Paul-Gabriel Boucé suggests the biblical "tare" as a synonym for Anthony Darnel's name (*The Novels of Tobias Smollett* [London: Longman, 1976], 181); Peter Wagner adds "damn" (*Sir Launcelot Greaves*, ed. Wagner [London: Penguin, 1988], 18). Neither is convincing for a name that the villain shares with the heroine. Hambridge identifies a village named Darnall near Aston in Yorkshire (24).

45. "the borough of Ashenton": Hambridge disputes Kahrl's identification of Ashenton as an actual place "in the hundred of Stafford, West Riding, Yorkshire" (Kahrl, 57); he insists that Kahrl must mean "Aston, in the hundred of Strafforth and Tickhill" (23).

46. "*pactum familiæ*": Family agreement. Such arrangements between leading families were common in the eighteenth century to avoid the high cost of contesting elections.

47. "in *propria persona*": In his own person.

48. "Greavesbury-hall": Kahrl notes that in the same hundred as Ashenton (or Aston; see n. 45, above) "was a Gravesburgh or Greasburg . . . which supplied the name at least of the hero" (19; see also 57–58). Hambridge thinks the name may have come "from a Greaves Hall located near the parliamentary borough of Pontefract" in Yorkshire (24). Smollett might have remarked these places during his travels through Yorkshire in 1750 or 1753.

49. "his own dark hair flowed about his ears in natural curls": To "wear one's own hair" instead of a wig might suggest unconventionality or eccentricity.

50. "when the celebrated Garrick . . . any other top character": Smollett's opinion at this time of David Garrick (1709–79) corresponded to the general English view: "The exhibitions of the stage were improved to the most exquisite entertainment, by the talents and management of Garrick, who greatly surpassed all his predecessors of this, and perhaps every other nation, in his genius for acting" (*Continuation,*

4:126). Garrick played Richard III seven times from 1756 to 1760 and Lear ten times from 1755 to 1760. In *Roderick Random* (chapters 62–63) and in the first edition of *Peregrine Pickle* (chapters 55 and 102), Smollett had satirized Garrick, whom he thought had kept his tragedy *The Regicide* from reaching the stage. Favorable reviews by Smollett of Garrick in the *Critical Review* and Garrick's production of Smollett's farce *The Reprisal* (1757) led to a friendship (*Letters*, 52–54, 97–98, 103–4). The second edition of *Peregrine Pickle* (1758) omitted the attacks on Garrick. Lewis M. Knapp examines their relationship in "Smollett and Garrick" (*Elizabethan Studies and Other Essays in Honor of George F. Reynolds*, University of Colorado Studies 2 [1945], 233–43). See also chap. 5, n. 14.

51. "a Pitt, an Egmont, or a Murray": William Pitt (1708–78), later first earl of Chatham; William Murray (1705–93), first earl of Mansfield; and John Perceval (1711–70), second earl of Egmont, regarded as the greatest parliamentary speakers of the period. Smollett dedicated the *Complete History* and the *British Magazine* to Pitt, for his mutable opinion of whom see Introduction, xl–xlii; and see Lewis M. Knapp, "Smollett and the Elder Pitt," *Modern Language Notes* 59 (1944): 250–57. Egmont and Murray were Scots associated with the Prince of Wales, soon to be George III. According to Smollett, Egmont "possessed a species of eloquence rather plausible than powerful: he spoke with fluency and fire: his spirit was bold and enterprising, his apprehension quick, and his repartee severe" (*Continuation*, 1:9). Mansfield displayed "an irresistible stream of eloquence, that flowed pure and classical, strong and copious, reflecting, in the most conspicuous point of view, the subjects over which it rolled, and sweeping before it all the slime of formal hesitation, and all the intangling weeds of chicanery" (*Continuation*, 1:11). Ironically, Mansfield sentenced Smollett to jail during the writing of *Sir Launcelot Greaves;* the author's later, less flattering portrait of Mansfield, as Muri-clami, appears in *Adventures of an Atom*, 38.

52. "corporation": The municipal corporation; "the civic authorities of a borough or incorporated town or city" (*OED*).

53. "harangue": Oration, speech. The word had no negative overtones at the time.

54. "Aurelia": Typically, for Smollett's heroines, Aurelia (based on the Latin for "gold") bears a romance name. It had been used by, among others, George Farquhar in *The Twin Rivals* (1703).

55. "limner": Painter.

56. "O! she is all that . . . poets fancy when they love!": Nicholas Rowe, *The Fair Penitent* (1703), 3.1.244–45. The first line of Rowe's popular domestic tragedy, spoken by Altamont of the tragic heroine Calista, is actually a rhetorical question which begins, "Is she not more than painting can express? . . ."

57. "your Venus de Medicis": This statue, discovered at the end of the sixteenth century, was highly regarded through the eighteenth century. Smollett would come under attack for his criticism of the statue in *Travels through France and Italy* (Letter 28). Hambridge (26) notes that Joseph Wilton (see n. 59, below) made a copy in

1751 for Lord Rockingham that Smollett could have seen; the statue, however, was widely copied. The introduction of Sophia Western in *Tom Jones* (bk. 4, chap. 2) also begins with a comparison to the Venus de' Medici.

58. "your Dianas, your Nymphs, and Galateas": The most famous statue of Diana, huntress goddess of the moon, was *Diane Chasseresse* in the Louvre, copied for Charles I by Hubert Le Sueur in 1634 and widely copied in the second half of the eighteenth century (see Francis Haskell and Nicholas Penny, *Taste and the Antique: The Lure of Classical Sculpture, 1500–1900* [New Haven: Yale University Press, 1982], 196–98). Such statues as *Nymph with a Shell* and *Nymph Adjusting Her Sandal* were common in the period (see Haskell and Penny, *Taste and the Antique*, 281–82, 186, 206). Given the aesthetic context of the comparisons, Galatea is probably not just a sea nymph, or Nereid (Evans, 218) or "the sea-nymph whose tragic love affair with Acis was the subject of Handel's *Acis and Galatea*" (Hambridge, 27) but the statue that Pygmalion sculpted and loved.

59. "Praxiteles, and Roubillac, and Wilton": Praxiteles (c. 390–332 B.C.), the greatest of the Classical Greek sculptors and possibly creator of the original from which the Venus de' Medici derived; Louis François Roubilliac (1695–1762), the best eighteenth-century sculptor in England, who immigrated from France after 1730; and Joseph Wilton (1722–1803), the best native-born sculptor of the century. Smollett praises Roubilliac and Wilton in *Continuation* (4:131).

60. "*parva componere magnis*": "To compare great things with small" (Virgil *Georgics* 4.176).

61. "at the York-assembly, during the races": Horse races were held annually at York during the August sessions of court ("the York-assembly").

62. "Bishoprick": "The province of a bishop; a diocese" (*OED*).

63. "*Scipio*": Scipio Africanus Major (c. 234–183 B.C.) and his son Scipio Africanus Minor (c. 185–129 B.C.), famous Roman generals. Horses were often named for military leaders.

64. "Miss *Cowslip*": "Cowslip" is Dolly's surname ("Mrs.," subsequently, does not comment on her marital status). The cowslip is the fragrant yellow wildflower Paigle (*Trimula veris*), mentioned by Clarke in the preceding paragraph.

65. "*Muley*": Muley-Moluch (spelled variously) was emperor of Barbary at the end of the sixteenth century. He, like Mustapha (see n. 66, below), is a character in John Dryden's historic tragedy *Don Sebastian* (1690) and in other plays.

66. "*Mustapha*": A common name for Ottoman sultans during the period.

67. "Odd's heartlikins": "God's little heart."

68. "running tackle": That part of the ship's tackle (pulleys and ropes) not fixed to one of the blocks.

69. "'Noint my block": "Anoint (i.e., beat) my head." Probably the literal meaning of "block" here is "pulley in a casing," the nautical usage, rather than "a large solid piece of wood" or "a wooden head for a wig." See *OED*, which does not make the distinction.

70. "a rope's end": A flogging.
71. "Discord seemed to clap her sooty wings": Smollett uses this image in chapter 33 of *Roderick Random*, but the personification is not original to him. See John Harvey, *The Life of Sir Robert Bruce* (Edinburgh, 1729): "Discord, with hideous Grin and livid Eyes, / Swift, thro' the Host, on sooty Pinions flies" (1.249–50). The phrase "sooty Wings" appears in Joseph Trapp's translation *The Aeneis of Virgil* (London, 1718), 7.537.
72. "denunciation of war": Announcement of war.

Chapter 4

1. "Pallas": Pallas Athena was the Greek goddess of wisdom and of war; here wisdom ("Discretion") prevails.
2. "Merry-Andrew, or Jack-Pudding": In chapter 10, Ferret prides himself on not being accompanied by "a foolish fellow in motley" (p. 77), the jester or clown who accompanies a mountebank or provides various sorts of entertainment. Here he is himself taken for one.
3. "salt-box": A box, generally for keeping salt, used in popular music.
4. "sonnata on the tongs and gridiron": English popular music. In *Adventures of an Atom*, Peacock is accused of liking only "a sonata on the salt-box" or similar low music (95; and see n. 3, above). In *A Midsummer Night's Dream*, Bottom tells Titania, "I have a reasonable good ear in music. Let's have the tongs and the bones" (4.1.28–29).
5. "shield of Achilles": Described at length in Homer *Iliad* 18.558–719 (Robert Fagles translation). For Discord, Athena, and Achilles, see 20.49–64.
6. "the emblem of good old English fare . . . the *Beef-stake Club*": The nationalistic association of England with beef was strong. Smollett refers to the Sublime Society of Beefsteaks; here, the brandishing of the gridiron (the club's emblem, which bore the motto "Beef and Liberty") becomes the mock-heroic occasion for celebrating a club that Smollett suggests he had visited. He accurately describes the regalia of the president and some of the club's practices. Founded in 1735, its members included William Hogarth, John Wilkes, and William Huggins, a close friend of Smollett around the time of the publication of *Sir Launcelot Greaves* (see chap. 5, n. 18). See Walter Arnold, *The Life and Death of the Sublime Society of Beefsteaks* (London: Bradbury, Evans, 1871); and Louis Clark Jones, *The Clubs of the Georgian Rakes* (New York: Columbia University Press, 1942), 142–55. Hambridge (28) suggests plausibly that Smollett attended as Huggins's guest, but it seems more probable that his host was Wilkes, who may have invited him in 1759 (*Letters*, 77), or one of the men to whom he alludes in this paragraph (see n. 8, below).
7. "Come cut me—come cut me": Echoes *Don Quixote*: "Come, eat me: come, eat

me" (2:374–75); see also *Adventures of an Atom*, 57–58. This is a variant on a proverb; see Tilley, P315.

8. "the obliging and humorous Jemmy B——t, the gentle Billy H——d . . . the generous Johnny B——d": The actors James Bencraft (d. 1765), William Havard (d. 1789), and John Beard (1716?–91), all elected to the Sublime Society of Beefsteaks in the 1740s. The names are spelled out in Dublin editions of *Sir Launcelot Greaves* (1762). Havard had spoken the Prologue at the opening night of Smollett's *The Reprisal*, on which occasion Beard had appeared as Haulyard (see *Poems, Plays, and "The Briton,"* 175, 176). Given Smollett's characterization of Beard as "generous," that actor seems the likeliest of the three to have been Smollett's host, if Wilkes was not (see n. 6, above). But for the reference in the Dublin editions, "Billy H——d" might be taken as William Howard (d. 1785), another actor and member of the Society.

9. "card": A compass card, a circular piece of stiff paper marked with the thirty-two points of the compass (see chap. 13, n. 7). "Since I knew a card from a compass" may be a sailor's proverb, though it is not in Taylor, Tilley, or *ODEP*.

10. "bowlings": Bowlines, ropes fastened near the middle of the perpendicular edge of the square sails to keep the sails steady when winds are unfavorable (Falconer). The word is the source of Lieutenant Bowling's name in *Roderick Random*.

11. "athwart thy hawser": Across the forepart of your ship. The hawser is a large rope, but in this sense it is a small distance ahead of a ship with reference to the cables before the ship's stern when at anchor. "Hawser" is Commodore Trunnion's given name in *Peregrine Pickle*.

12. "a-driving under thy bare poles": With the sails furled owing to the severity of a storm.

13. "hurried over a precipice": This beginning of Aurelia's love for Sir Launcelot recalls the love of Sophia Western for Tom Jones after he saves her from a rearing horse. See *Tom Jones*, bk. 4, chap. 13.

14. "longe": The earliest *OED* example for any spelling of "lunge" as a substantive comes from chapter 12 of *Roderick Random*.

15. "convicted of murder": The notion that the circumstances would make a difference is inaccurate in point of law. When a duelist was killed, his opponent was guilty of murder regardless of questions concerning transgression or behavior (see *NLD*, "*Duel*"). Smollett criticizes dueling in *Travels through France and Italy* (Letter 15).

16. "tartan": A small, large-sailed, single-masted Mediterranean vessel (Falconer).

17. "gravel": A disease characterized by the presence of painful urinary crystals.

18. "rupture": Hernia.

19. "*vi et armis*": By force and arms. "Vis is any kind of Force, Violence or Disturbance, relating to a Man's Person, or his Goods, Right in Lands, &c." (*NLD*).

20. "he would settle it with the parish": The father of a bastard might save the mother

from financial assessments and imprisonment by agreeing to pay for the child's upkeep. In *Humphry Clinker*, Jery Melford agrees to "pay the penalty" to the parish if a bastard child is sworn as his by the mother (Jery Melford to Sir Watkin Phillips, Bath, April 24, p. 29).

21. "cracked pitcher": A woman who has lost her virginity. Jery Melford uses this common metaphor in *Humphry Clinker* (Jery Melford to Sir Watkin Phillips, Bath, May 6).

22. "publish the banns": To read a proclamation in church, generally on three successive Sundays, of an intended marriage.

23. "the statute of barretry": The statute mentioned, 34 Edw. 3, c. 1 (1360), was intended to discourage wanton litigiousness, though later laws, such as the Frivolous Arrests Act of 1725, also pertain. Clarke's description of the offense follows *NLD*, "*Barrator.*"

24. "*Communis . . . litium*": Quoted from the indictment for barratry: "a common evildoer, calumniator, and sower of quarrels" (*NLD*, "*Barrator*").

25. "a coif in the court of common pleas": A serjeant-at-law or serjeant of the coif, from the linen skullcap (later a patch on the wig) worn when receiving the degree. Only serjeants-at-law were allowed to plead at the bar of the Court of Common Pleas, the superior court of civil actions (Jowitt and Walsh, "Serjeants-at-law," "Coif").

Chapter 5

1. "a certain utensil, that shall be nameless": A chamber pot. In chapter 1 of *Ferdinand Count Fathom*, Smollett objected to readers who "stop their noses with all the signs of loathing and abhorrence, at a bare mention of the china chamber-pot" (ed. Jerry C. Beasley [Athens: University of Georgia Press, 1988], 10). But in chapter 14 of the second edition of *Peregrine Pickle*, Smollett deleted an episode in which Peregrine drills holes in the chamber pot of Trunnion and his bride.

2. "actual fire would have been produced . . . substances": Smollett derives the notion from Peter Kolb (*The Present State of the Cape of Good Hope*, 2 vols., trans. Guido Medley [London, 1731], 2:xii), whom he mentions in chapter 19 of *Peregrine Pickle* when relating the fate of Tom Pipes. Charles Dickens may have had Smollett's passages in mind when he had his character Krook die of spontaneous combustion in *Bleak House* (1852).

3. "running a-head": "A-head" is the space in front of the bow of a ship; therefore, to run a-head is to sail recklessly forward. The word was used figuratively, as here, from the seventeenth century on (see *OED*).

4. "Wounds!": "God's wounds," a mild oath.

5. "Newgate": The prison, built in the fifteenth century near the Old Bailey criminal

courts in east-central London, was rebuilt after the Great Fire of 1666. Prisoners were held there for trial, as were debtors and convicted felons awaiting transportation or hanging.

6. "Jack Ketch": The generic term for the public hangman. The actual Jack Ketch (d. 1686?) served as executioner under Charles II and James II and beheaded as well as hanged the condemned.

7. "clerk of the assize": A court employee who wrote down everything done by the justices in their court sessions, held in a range of locations or "circuits" (*NLD*).

8. "the grand jury": The grand jury consisted of property owners (freeholders of £20 or more); see *OED*.

9. "great tythes": The great (chief) tithes are of corn, hay, wood, fruit, and other crops. For the small tithes, personal to the vicar of the parish, see chap. 17, n. 35.

10. "*compos mentis*": Of sound mind.

11. "the eve of the festival of St. George": 22 April.

12. "joint stool": "A stool made of parts joined or fitted together; a stool made by a joiner" (*OED*).

13. "St. Michael, and St. George": The biblical archangel Michael is a warrior-prince; Saint George is the patron saint of England. They are the patron saints of knights-errant.

14. "the idea of the ghost in Hamlet . . . acted in Drury-lane": For other references to old Hamlet's ghost in the novel, see chap. 2, n. 4 and chap. 18, n. 9. Drury Lane Theatre, managed by Garrick, was the subject of almost all the drama reviews published in the *British Magazine*, for which Garrick himself probably wrote "The Difficulty of Managing a Theater" (1 [1760]: 266; see Basker, 284). See also chap. 3, n. 50.

15. "lacquered black . . . first quarter": The first reference to the color of Sir Launcelot's armor and the crescent moon on his shield, both depicted in Walker's engraving for chapter 2, which appeared in the February number of the *British Magazine*. See Introduction, xx–xxi, for the implications of the composition of the novel in this respect; and see chap. 2, n. 12.

16. "*impleat orbem*": "Let it fill the world." This motto may appear on the shield in Walker's first illustration, though the lettering is not clear (see plate 3).

17. "Bronzomarte": "Bronzo" is Italian for "brass" or "bell-metal." "Marte" is Italian for "Mars."

18. "Bayardo, Brigliadoro": In *Don Quixote*, a song by an academician in praise of Quixote's horse concludes: "Ev'n Rozinante wears the bay; / Let Brilladore and Bayard bray" (1:402). A footnote in the second edition of Smollett's translation reads: "The horse of Orlando Furioso was called Brigliadoro; as Bayardo was the name of the steed belonging to Ruggiero, the second, if not the first hero in Ariosto's incomparable poem" (4 vols. [London, 1761], 2:313, n.). The footnote errs: Bayardo is Rinaldo's horse, as is mentioned later in the translation (2:244). Smollett had read *Orlando Furioso* in Italian, reviewed the translation of his friend Wil-

liam Huggins in 1757 (see *Letters*, 50–51), and in this novel quotes and translates a line from the original (see chap. 15, n. 1).

19. "whipper-in to Sir Everhard": See Introduction, xxxviii, for Crabshaw and his model Sancho Panza. A whipper-in keeps the hounds in the pack during a hunt.

20. "bantlings": Small children, frequently derogatory; brats.

21. "Greenland canoe": A kayak; "the Groenland canoe . . . is about three fathoms in length, pointed at both ends, three quarters of a yard in breadth, composed of thin rafts fastened together with the sinews of animals, covered with dressed seal-skins, both below and above, in such a manner, that a circular hole is left in the middle, large enough to admit the body of one man" (*Present State*, 1:47). The illustration of a "Kaiak" appears earlier in *Present State* (opposite p. 40). It is possible that this detail was meant to stimulate interest in "Igluka and Sibbersik, A Greenland Tale," which appeared in the same issue of the *British Magazine* as the present chapter did.

22. "as common as duck-weed": This phrase has the form of a proverb, though it is not listed in Tilley or *ODEP*.

23. "quickset-hedge": A hedge formed of living plants; the source of Sir Valentine Quickset's name (see chap. 9, n. 16).

24. "old king Stephen, from the horse armoury, in the tower": The corporal pretends to mistake Sir Launcelot for King Stephen (1097–1154), as portrayed in the armory next to the White Tower in the Tower of London. William Maitland noted that "the Figures of Fifteen Kings of *England*" were represented there; see *The History of London* (London, 1739), 496.

25. "the fellow that rides armed at my lord mayor's shew": The Company of Armourers was represented by a man in armor on Lord Mayor's Day (9 November), when the lord mayor paraded to Westminster Abbey (the show, or "shew").

26. "curvettings and caprioles": Equestrian maneuvers. A curvet is a leap in which the forelegs of the horse are raised together and advanced equally; the hind legs spring before the forelegs reach the ground. The capriole, as its name implies, is a goatlike leap of the hind legs. Smollett presumably uses the terms to suggest high-spirited but less exact motions.

27. "halbert": Or halberd, "a kind of combination of spear and battle-ax, consisting of a sharp-edged blade ending in a point, and a spear-head, mounted on a handle five to seven feet long" (*OED*).

28. "pettifogger": A lawyer of inferior status; the type was often satirized in the period.

29. "mittimus": A warrant named for its first word (Latin: "we send"), by which means a justice of the peace can commit someone directly to prison.

30. "a good action . . . either by information or indictment": An information is an oral declaration by a prosecutor, plaintiff, or informer; an indictment is a written declaration. Both are complaints against a person for some criminal offense. The indictment is generally lodged by a grand jury; see *NLD*, "*Information.*" Distinguishing indictable from unindictable injuries, *NLD* specifies that "where a Person is

beaten, he may proceed for this Trespass by *Indictment*, or Information, as well as Action" (*NLD*, "*Indictment*").

31. "rib-roasted": Beaten, cudgeled. The first citation of this form of the verb in *OED* is from Smollett's translation of *Don Quixote*.

32. "Ferry-bridge": Hambridge points out that this small town in Yorkshire's West Riding on the river Are is about two miles from a Greaves (or Grove) Hall. See Hambridge, 35; and see chap. 3, n. 48.

33. "the distance . . . fourscore or ninety miles": Noting Kahrl's estimate that ninety miles is the distance from Weston to Greasburg through Sheffield and Ferrybridge (Kahrl, 58), Hambridge claims that Greaves or Grove Hall would be approximately eighty miles from Weston (35).

Chapter 6

1. "chain-shot": Cannon shot made of two linked balls or half balls, designed to destroy masts and rigging.

2. "taffrel": Taffril. See chap. 2, n. 50.

3. "fire-breathing chimæra": The divine monster of Greek mythology—part lion, part she-goat, part serpent—slain by Bellerophon. See Homer *Iliad* 6.212 (Fagles translation).

4. "rated": A nautical term meaning classed or ranked. See *OED*; see also chap. 7, n. 5.

5. "tip me the traveller": "To tell wonderful stories, to romance" (Francis Grose, *A Classical Dictionary of the Vulgar Tongue* [London, 1785]). See *OED*, "tip."

6. "compos": A shortened, or interrupted, form of "compos mentis," of sound mind.

7. "box my compass": Not only to repeat the names of the thirty-two points in order and backwards, but also to be able to answer any questions respecting its division.

8. "tackle": Gear.

9. "long pole headed with iron": Lance.

10. "target": Shield.

11. "*Mufti*": An official, often important, who gives opinions on Muslim law.

12. "Sheffield": City in the West Riding of Yorkshire, known for metal work.

13. "wake": Keep vigil over. In the medieval period, for example, after "ritual washing," the aspirant knights of the Order of Bath would spread their armor in a chapel before the altar for the night; see David Piper, *London* (New York: Holt, Rinehart and Winston, 1971), 16. Don Quixote keeps wake in *Don Quixote*, pt. 1, bk. 1, chap. 3.

14. "Don Quixote was dubbed by his landlord": See *Don Quixote*, pt. 1, bk. 1, chap. 3.

15. "St. Martin . . . proper patron to a noviciate": Saint Martin (c. 316–97) served as a Roman soldier before becoming a Christian and bishop of Tours. The eve of Saint Martin's Day is 10 November. Several commentators have noticed the con-

tradiction to the narrator's earlier statement that the novel opens "about the beginning of the month October" (3).

16. "flip": A hot, sweetened mixture of beer and spirits often drunk by seamen.

17. "Hilloa! . . . hip": Expressions of greeting, the first often indicating surprise. See
also chap. 7, n. 1.

18. "whistling black joke": "Coal Black Joke," a popular air to which a number of
songs, generally indecent, were set. "Black joke" refers to the vagina; see, for example, Grose, *A Classical Dictionary*. In plate 3 of Hogarth's *A Rake's Progress*
(1735), a woman in a brothel prepares to entertain customers with a copy of the
song (*Hogarth's Graphic Works*, 305). A soldier whistles and hums this song in chapter 53 of *Roderick Random*.

19. "black-ey'd Susan": John Gay's "Sweet William's Farewell to Black-ey'd Susan"
(1720), also published as "Black ey'd Susan's Lamentation for the Departure of her
Sweet William," was set to music by Richard Leveridge and others. See John Gay,
Poetry and Prose, ed. Vinton A. Dearing with Charles E. Beckwith, 2 vols. (Oxford:
Clarendon Press, 1974), 1:249–51. Humphry Clinker claims he can sing the song
(Jery Melford to Sir Watkin Phillips, London, 24 May). See also Smollett's poem
about a constant man separated from his love: "A Declaration of Love. Ode to
Blue-Ey'd Ann" (*British Magazine* 1 [1760]: 213; *Poems, Plays, and "The Briton,"*
52–53).

20. "sea-mew": Seagull.

21. "larboard watch": Though "larboard" is the left side of a ship, the "larboard
watch" is that part of "a ship's company on duty, while the other is relieved from
it" (Falconer).

22. "a cast of his office": A "cast" is "a stroke; a touch" (Johnson, *Dictionary*); the form
is obsolete. The expression thus has the force of "a bit of his business."

23. "If we can't go large, we must haul upon a wind": If we cannot take advantage of a
favorable wind, we must sail nearer to it. See Falconer, "Large," and "To Haul the
wind."

Chapter 7

1. "Hilloah": Adapted to nautical slang, indicates "an exclamation of answer, to any
person, who calls to another" (Falconer, "Holloa!"). See also chap. 6, n. 17.

2. "b——s": "Bitches" and its singular are sometimes spelled out by Smollett (e.g.,
Peregrine Pickle, chap. 95), sometimes not.

3. "by the lead": The lead and line were used to measure the water's depth.

4. "hawse-holes": "Cylindrical holes cut through the bows of a ship . . . through
which the [anchor] cables pass" (Falconer).

5. "disrated": Removed a ship from its rate or class, or reduced an officer to a lower

rank; see *OED*, which has no illustration of either meaning as early as this metaphorical usage. See also chap. 6, n. 4.

6. "clap hard aweather": Sail quickly toward the windward side.

7. "had recourse to his Pater-noster": Recited the Lord's Prayer (Matthew 6:9–13).

8. "forelights": The farthest forward lanterns on a ship.

9. "truckle-bed": Trundle bed.

10. "peddling": Piddling, petty.

11. "dishabillé": Literally, undress; in common usage, informal dress.

12. "Bartlemey-tide": Saint Bartholomew's Day, 24 August.

13. "reins": Kidneys.

14. "harslet": Haslet; the edible organs of a hog or other animals. See also chap. 2, n. 8.

15. "crazy-peated": Crazy-pated; mentally unstable.

16. "Papishes": Papists, Roman Catholics.

17. "cast a figure": To draw up and interpret a horoscope.

18. "measured his length on the ground": A mock-epic formula favored by Fielding; see, for example, *Joseph Andrews* (London, 1742), bk. 3, chap. 6.

19. "a friendly warrant": Hambridge, noting the term's absence from law dictionaries of the period, suggests that "it may be synonymous with an 'information'" (38). Richard L. Lettis suggests that such a warrant might not require arrest; see "A Study of Smollett's *Sir Launcelot Greaves*" (Ph.D. diss., Yale University, 1957), 209. See also chap. 5, n. 30.

20. "*furtum*": Legal Latin for "Theft, or Robbery of any Kind" (*NLD*).

21. "*in alta . . . terrorem, &c.*": The Latin phrases are close to the wording of the "old Form of Proceedings" of an indictment for robbery; those not translated by Smollett mean "and feloniously captured and carried off with great terror." See *NLD*, "*Robbery*."

22. "will not be ousted of his clergy": Will not lose his right to the plea of "clergy" to a felony (familiarly known as "benefit of clergy"), the original presumption being that those who could read were clergymen and as such exempt from the secular court's punishment for a first offense, typically hanging for theft. See *NLD*, "*Clergy*."

23. "Davy Jones in the shape of a blue flame": In *Peregrine Pickle* (chapter 15), Smollett wrote, "Davy Jones, according to the mythology of sailors, is the fiend that presides over all the evil spirits of the deep, and is often seen in various shapes, perching among the rigging on the eve of hurricanes, shipwrecks, and other disasters, to which a sea-faring life is exposed; *warning the devoted wretch of death and woe*" (p. 72). "Jones" may be a corruption of Jonah. The phenomenon described is known as Saint Elmo's fire, an electrical discharge frequently observed on masts and other pointed objects during a storm.

24. "Jacks o'the Lanthorn, and Wills o'the Wisp": Equivalent terms. The illusive light was likened to a night watchman with his lantern. See chap. 10, n. 10; and see the superstitious Partridge in *Tom Jones*, bk. 12, chap. 12.

25. "A knight-errant ought to understand the sciences": Don Quixote asserts that "Knights-errant . . . ever had, and ought to have, some knowledge of every thing" (1:7).

26. "casuist": One who can determine right and wrong in complicated cases of conscience.

27. "I know plain sailing and mercator": Plane sailing is the art of locating a ship by assuming that the earth's surface is a plane. Mercator, named for the geographer whose projection maps were used at sea, trigonometrically determined location on the earth's surface. See Nathan Bailey, *An Universal Etymological English Dictionary* (London, 1761), "Mercator's sailing."

28. "the viol block or the geer capstan": The viol is a large rope used to raise an anchor. On the fore part of a ship, it requires a block that leads to the geer (or jear) capstan to haul it up. See Falconer, "Voyol." Crowe compares himself to large, senseless things.

29. "St. Catherine's": Saint Catherine's by the Tower is a parish in Wapping "inhabited chiefly by sea-faring people, or such as deal in naval stores" (*Present State*, 3: 209).

Chapter 8

1. "proceeded in a southerly direction": Hambridge, who finds that "the movements of Greaves and Crabshaw in this chapter can be traced fairly accurately," says that Sir Launcelot sets out from Scarthing Moor, near Weston (40).

2. "wage a teaster": Wager a tester, that is, a sixpence.

3. "dispossess": Drive out evil spirits.

4. "a mortal good hand at giving a flap with a fox's tail": Skilled at giving "a lenient or pretended reproof" (*OED*); but Ray defines "to give one a *flap* with a fox's tail" as "to . . . defraud" (245), and the proverb is often used to indicate trickery. See Tilley, F344; *ODEP*, 266.

5. "with a murrain to 'un": A plague upon him.

6. "it becomes him as a sow doth a cart-saddle": It ill becomes him. See Tilley, s672; *ODEP*, 757.

7. "leame of the same leg": Suffer from the same infirmity. See Tilley, L185; *ODEP*, 710.

8. "your honour's face is made of a fiddle; every one that looks on you loves you": See Ray, 243; Tilley, F11; *ODEP*, 237.

9. "a horse that was foaled of an acorn": A wooden horse; figuratively, the gallows. See Ray, 253; Tilley, H708; *ODEP*, 387.

10. "a market-town": Newark-upon-Trent.

11. "had lost his wits . . . to secure him": "By a late statute, *Lunaticks*, or Madmen wandering may be apprehended by a Justice's Warrant, and locked up and chained

if necessary; or be sent to their last legal Settlement" (*NLD*, "*Lunatick*"). The beadle, as an inferior court officer, a kind of under-bailiff or watchman, would be empowered to apprehend Crabshaw.

12. "you may pound me into a peaste, as the saying is": The proverb is not listed in Taylor, Tilley, or *ODEP*.

13. "the following salutation": Evans (221) notes the similarity to Sancho Panza's speech in *Don Quixote* (pt. 2, bk. 4, chap. 3) upon recovering Dapple, his stolen horse, who cares for him as little as Gilbert cares for Crabshaw.

14. "a pize upon thee!": An oath of uncertain origin, probably incorporating a form of "a pox" or "a pest" (see *OED*). Old Bellair uses it habitually in Etherege, *The Man of Mode*.

15. "unsocial animal . . . even with Bronzomarte": Evans (221) notes that Gilbert's behavior in this respect is different from Sancho's ass, which in *Don Quixote* (pt. 2, bk. 1, chap. 12) is friendly with Rozinante.

Chapter 9

1. "blue cockades": Blue was the Tory color; cockades (see chap. 3, n. 33) in this case are insignia identifying party affiliation.

2. "LIBERTY AND THE LANDED INTEREST": The most common version of this Tory slogan, "Liberty and Property," appears in Hogarth's engraving *An Election Entertainment* (1755), the first of the *Four Prints of an Election* (see *Hogarth's Graphic Works*, 2:215–21). For these prints and *Sir Launcelot Greaves*, see Introduction, xxxiv–xxxv. Smollett had recently reviewed a pamphlet on the prints; see "A Poetical Description of Mr. Hogarth's Election Prints," *Critical Review* 7 (1759): 274–75. The "landed interest" identifies the Tories as country gentlemen rather than courtiers, the stereotype of the Whig.

3. "No FOREIGN CONNECTIONS,—OLD-ENGLAND FOR EVER": Tory slogans against England's support of Hanover, German birthplace of George I and George II. "Old England" identifies a mythopoetic ideal of England before the Revolution of 1688, which brought William III to the throne and initiated a long period of barely interrupted Whig supremacy.

4. "No SLAVERY,—No POPISH PRETENDER": Whig slogans expressing fear of Catholicism and of the exiled Stuart monarchy, identified with divine-right kingship. The Young Pretender, Charles Edward Stuart, was rumored to be planning an invasion, a follow-up to his unsuccessful attempt in 1745. Shebbeare represented slogans like these as covers for increases in taxation and in the national debt (*Third Letter*, 27, see also 16–18). Shebbeare is represented in *The Polling* (1758), Hogarth's third engraving from *Four Prints of an Election*; see *Hogarth's Graphic Works*, 2:220.

5. "dead cats": Throwing dead cats was a standard form of unruliness. César de Saussure, in letters home to Switzerland (1725–29), claimed that on Lord Mayor's Day the well-dressed risked having "dead dogs and cats" thrown at them (qtd. in Schwartz, *Daily Life in Johnson's London*, 169).

6. "surtouts": Overcoats.

7. "orange ribbons": The Whig color derives from William of Orange, the Protestant who, as William III, replaced the Catholic James II on the throne of England in 1689.

8. "*God save great George our king*": Written earlier in the century, perhaps to a tune by Henry Carey; with some changes, it remains the British national anthem. The tune was also adapted for "America" ("My Country 'tis of Thee"). It may derive from a German original.

9. "a thin, swarthy personage . . . though his address was aukward": This description consists of typical anti-Semitic stereotypes. Hogarth's representation of a Jew in the second plate of the *Harlot's Progress* (1732) embodies a number of the same characteristics; see *Hogarth's Graphic Works*, 2 : 128. The stereotypes correspond to those identified by Frank Felsenstein in *Anti-Semitic Stereotypes: A Paradigm of Otherness in English Popular Culture, 1660–1830* (Baltimore: Johns Hopkins University Press, 1995), for example, 50, 86, 87, 280, n. 80. See also n. 11 below.

10. "LIBERTY OF CONCIENCE AND THE PROTESTANT SUCCESSION": The Whig slogan trades on fears of Catholicism and of the restoration of the heirs of James II; see also n. 4 above.

11. "ingratiated himself with the good women, who . . . sent forth many ejaculatory petitions in his favour": The portrayal draws on stereotypes of Jewish lasciviousness, suggested by the candidate's "goggling eyes"; see Felsenstein, *Anti-Semitic Stereotypes*, 118, for the typical charge. Medical opinion held that women ejaculated during intercourse.

12. "the schoolman's ass between two bundles of hay": The scholastic philosophers' example, frequently employed in considering problems of free will, had become proverbial.

13. "before the peacock and the ladies": In a footnote to his translation of *Don Quixote*, Smollett illustrates his claim that "ridiculous oaths or vows are not confined to romances" by quoting the vow of Philip the Good, duke of Burgundy, "to God, the holy virgin, the peacock and the ladies, that he would declare war against the infidels" (1 : 50, n.).

14. "by the peacock": An obsolete oath (Evans, 222), though it may simply repeat the silliness of the previous oath.

15. "bastinado": Corporal punishment inflicted with a stick, usually upon the soles of the feet.

16. "sir Valentine Quickset and Mr. Isaac Vanderpelft; the first a meer fox-hunter": Quickset's name comes from an English boundary marker of rural land, the quick-

set hedge (see chap. 5, n. 23). Smollett thought poorly of foxhunters: "Their whole lives are spent in following the hounds, riding, leaping, and hollowing, as if they were mad, and after the chace, in carousing and riot; so that they are become as savage as the beasts they pursue" (*Present State*, 2:217). For Vanderpelft, see Introduction, xliii–xliv.

17. "stock-jobber": Stockbroker who buys and sells for his own account. Johnson's *Dictionary* conveys Smollett's animus: "A low wretch who gets money by buying and selling shares in the funds." In the *Continuation*, Smollett speaks of the profits from the war "by the practice of stock-jobbing in England" (2:399); earlier in that work he describes the financial interest as "Jews and jobbers" (1:418).

18. "contractor": See chap. 2, n. 9.

19. "his grace of ———": Newcastle; Thomas Pelham-Holles (1693–1768), duke of Newcastle, the Whig leader whom Smollett consistently opposed. He served as first minister in the 1750s. Shebbeare attacked him in *Second Letter*, 19–20, 26–28; and *Third Letter*, 30.

20. "copyholders": An anachronism, or perhaps an indication that the election is modeled on that of 1754. After June 1758, copy-holders, those whose claim to property consisted in having their names enrolled in the "copy," or manorial court-roll, were prohibited from voting. Smollett approved of the bill; see *Continuation*, 2:218.

21. "dissenters": Protestants who dissented from the Church of England suffered political disabilities by law. They tended to support the Whigs, and Whig governments in turn often advocated toleration of dissent.

22. "weavers": They were poor and thought to be politically disaffected and possibly radical.

23. "hustings": The platform on which those who stand for Parliament give their speeches.

24. "since the revolution": See n. 3 above.

25. "three skips of a louse": Proverbial expression for worthlessness. See Tilley, L472, S512; *ODEP*, 817.

26. "hanged as high as Haman": See Esther 7:9–10. Haman, enemy of Mordecai and the Jews generally, was hanged on a gallows "fifty cubits high"—roughly seventy-five feet—designed for Mordecai. Taylor (89) lists this phrase as proverbial.

27. "H——r": Hanover. See n. 3 above.

28. "vour shillings in the pound": Before decimalization, the pound sterling consisted of twenty shillings, each worth twelve pence. The land tax, therefore, equaled 20 percent of the land's "ancient value." The Tories, as landholders, opposed the tax.

29. "the ould interest": The Tories; see *Continuation*: "the strength and influence of what they called the old and new interest, or, to speak more intelligibly, of the Tories and Whigs" (1:236–37). More covertly, the term referred to Jacobites, against whom Vanderpelft inveighs. Boswell uses the term in this way when de-

scribing his and Johnson's visit with Scottish Jacobites in 1773: "Mr. Johnson and I were both visibly of the *old interest* (to use the Oxford expression), kindly affectioned at least, and perhaps too openly so" (James Boswell, *Journal of a Tour to the Hebrides*, ed. Frederick A. Pottle and Charles H. Bennett [New York: Viking, 1936], 162).

30. "an abjured, and outlawed pretender": The Stuart claimant to the throne at this time was James Francis Edward (1688–1766). After the defeat of his son, Charles Edward, in the rebellion of 1745, Jacobitism was moribund, though it was invoked during elections, and there was some fear of another invasion during this period; see n. 4 above and chap. 17, n. 2. Persons standing for Parliament (and holding certain other positions) were required to take an oath of abjuration, renouncing James II and his heirs.

31. "puncheon": A large cask.

32. "stole away!": Said of a fox that leaves its den unobserved by hunters (*OED*).

33. "freemen of England": Sir Valentine's "vreehoulders"; owners of freeholds worth forty shillings, who had the franchise to vote.

34. "all patriotism . . . administration": In the late 1730s and afterward, a group of Whig "patriots" joined forces with some opposition Tories. "Patriotism" remained a byword for opposition politics, in which sense it was attacked by Smollett; see *Complete History*, 4:619–20. And see Johnson's famous claim, "Patriotism is the last refuge of a scoundrel" (*Boswell's Life of Johnson*, ed. George Birbeck Hill and L. F. Powell, 6 vols. [Oxford: Clarendon Press, 1934–50], 2:348).

35. "sordid knave": For Smollett's use of this phrase and its association with Newcastle, see Introduction, xxxix–xli.

36. "no God but mammon": The slur was often directed at believing Jews. For Mammon, whose name means "riches" and who was represented as the chief of the lowest order of demons, see Matthew 6:24 and the influential depiction in *Paradise Lost* 1.679–92.

37. "usury": One of the most virulent of the anti-Semitic stereotypes cast Jews as usurers. See Felsenstein, *Anti-Semitic Stereotypes*, 200–201, for the eighteenth-century context.

38. "hoicksed the speaker": The call "hoicks" was used to incite hounds to hunt.

39. "Jowler . . . Whitefoot": All standard names for hunting dogs.

40. "like the devil": Jews were frequently compared to the devil. See Felsenstein, *Anti-Semitic Stereotypes*, 27–39.

41. "an utter stranger": Vanderpelft, unlike Sir Valentine, is not from the county that he hopes to represent, but the stereotype of the Jew as alien lies behind the locution.

42. "independency": This was one of Smollett's assertions about his own political position. See Introduction, xxxviii–xxxix.

43. "set up for himself": Evans (223) notes that in Fielding's *Don Quixote in England*

(1734, 2.3), Quixote is encouraged to stand for office in a county election "to ensure opposition and promote bribery." Fielding's play probably provided the impetus for this chapter.

44. *"a posteriori"*: Smollett plays on the literal meaning: reasoning "from behind" (that is, inductively).

45. "a pillory, of mud": Those confined to the pillory were often pelted by passers-by.

Chapter 10

1. *"he who plays at bowls, will sometimes meet with rubbers"*: A "rubber" is the decisive contest in a tied match, but a "rub" is an "Inequality of ground, that hinders the motion of a bowl" (Johnson, *Dictionary*); this word frequently appears in the proverb. O'Clabber mangles the proverb in *The Reprisal* (2.3); Jery Melford uses it in *Humphry Clinker* (Jery Melford to Sir Watkin Phillips, October 3). See also Tilley, B569; *ODEP*, 630.

2. "one of the gates of the town": Identifying the town as Newark, Hambridge deduces that since Ferret, followed by Sir Launcelot, is led away from the gate "measuring back the ground he [Sir Launcelot] had traveled the day before," the reference appears to be to the North Gate (45).

3. "Mr. Ferret, mounted upon a stool . . . very vehement strain of elocution": Ferret's appearance and behavior are typical of the mountebank. For such a vial as Ferret's in an eighteenth-century engraving, see Grete de Francesco, *The Power of the Charlatan*, trans. M. Beard (New Haven: Yale University Press, 1939), 25.

4. "tye-periwig": A man's wig, tied behind, fashionable earlier in the eighteenth century.

5. "a foolish fellow in motley": A Merry-Andrew. Smollett sometimes links politicians to such figures; see, for example, *Continuation*: "The management of a mighty kingdom was consigned into the hands of a motley administration" (4:114).

6. *"ad captandum vulgus"*: To capture the vulgar.

7. "high German doctor": A hit at the Hanoverian king and his minister.

8. "empirics . . . quacks in government": In medicine or science, an empiric "relies solely upon observation and experiment" (*OED*). The harangue is indebted to Ben Jonson's *Volpone* (1607, 2.2). It hits at Shebbeare, whom Smollett called a "political quack" in his review of Shebbeare's *A Fifth Letter to the People of England on the Subversion of the Constitution* (London, 1757); see *Critical Review* 5 (1758): 274; and see Smollett on Shebbeare as "a quack in politics" in *Critical Review* 4 (1757): 552. Lettis suggests that Smollett may have drawn on the anonymous *Yorick's Meditations* (London, 1760), which Smollett probably reviewed (*Critical Review* 10 [1760]: 71) and which asserts that "in every profession there are quacks. There are quacks in the law, quacks in divinity, and scribbling quacks" (32; see Lettis, "A Study of Smollett's *Sir Launcelot Greaves*," 141).

9. "like the people of Nineveh . . . her right hand from her left": See Jonah 4:11.

10. "an *ignis fatuus*, a Will o' the wisp": Latin and common forms for the "false fire" of a phosphorescent glow caused by the "exhalation" mentioned in the text; hence, an illusion, pursued to no avail. See also chap. 7, n. 24.

11. "through Westphalian bogs . . . H——n pit": Westphalia was often used as a code word for nearby Hanover. Shebbeare refers to "Dutch Bogs" in *Sixth Letter*, 7.

12. "Elixir of Long Life": The claim to possess such a substance was characteristic of quacks. G. S. Rousseau notes that the "Count Saint-Germain" claimed to have the elixir in the 1740s; see "Quackery and Charlatanry in Some Eighteenth-Century Novels, Especially in Smollett," in *Tobias Smollett: Essays of Two Decades*, ed. Rousseau (Edinburgh: T. and T. Clark, 1982), 124–37.

13. "Aristotle's four principles of generation, unformed matter, privation, efficient and final causes": Aristotle was still admired for his physics and for the medical implications of his writings. Although Ferret ridicules Aristotle's "principles," he draws on them later in this speech when referring to the sun and the moon (the two principles of generation in the macrocosm) and man (who with woman constitutes the corresponding principles in the microcosm). For Aristotle, form and matter make substance. "Privation" is matter without form, and "unformed matter" is a condition necessary for change. The "efficient" and "final" causes were the causes concerned in the generation of the works of nature. Ferret also borrows the idea of the "first . . . mover," Aristotle's name for the organizing force of the universe (see n. 31 below).

14. "Dioscorides, with his faculties of simples, his seminal, specific, and principal virtues": Dioscorides Pedanius (fl. first century A.D.), whose *De materia medica* was for centuries the standard work on medical remedies. Simples are pure medicinal substances. The "virtues" of such substances were the beneficial effects expected from using them. Dioscorides is mentioned several times in *Don Quixote*, for example, pt. 1, bk. 3, chap. 4.

15. "Galen, with his four elements, elementary qualities, his eight complexions, his harmonies, and discords": The Greek physician Galen of Pergamon (c. 129–99), retained his position as the classical source of medical theory. In fact, however, the conception of the "elements" of water, earth, fire, and air was Aristotelian, though followed by Galen. The "elementary qualities"—hot, cold, moist, and dry—gave rise through paired combinations to the "eight complexions"; a balance of all four, the ideal for health, was a ninth. These were familiar in the English Renaissance and after as the "humors." Harmonies and discords refer to the balance or imbalance of elementary qualities in the body. Galenic medicine sought to cure by opposites, introducing, for example, cold and dry remedies to counteract hot and moist maladies.

16. "the alkahest of that mad scoundrel Paracelsus . . . flints into salt": Paracelsus (1493–1541) expounded a chemical philosophy that influenced medicine and alchemy. Ironically, given his position in Ferret's list, he attacked Aristotle and Ga-

len. In a review that Smollett may have written, Shebbeare is criticized for relying upon Paracelsus, who appears therein as Bombastus Parcelsus, from his real name, Phillippus Aureolus Theophrastus Bombastus von Hohenheim; see *Critical Review* 5 (1758): 370–71. In the later eighteenth century, Paracelsus was in disrepute. Alkahest (or alcahest) was "coined by Paracelsus to signify a most pure and universal *menstruum*, or dissolvent," that is, a universal solvent that would "reduce all things into water" (Ephraim Chambers, *Cyclopædia* [1791]). The process putatively turns its subject into salt before turning it into water. Paracelsus and alkahest are mentioned in *Adventures of an Atom* (60).

17. "the *archæus* or *spiritus rector* of that visionary Van Helmont, his simple, elementary water, his *gas*, ferments, and transmutations": Jean Baptiste Van Helmont (1577–1644), mentioned in *Adventures of an Atom* (60), adapted the Paracelsean idea of the archaeus to mean "an Invisible Species, vague and separating itself from Bodies, the Physician's Power, and Nature's Virtue"; he believed that the archaeus "consists in a Connection of the vital Air, as Matter, with the seminal Form, which is the Interior spiritual Nucleus" (James, "Archeus"). "Spiritus Rector" was the "Ruling Spirit of Vegetables [that imparts] that Smell and Taste to every individual Plant" (James, "Spiritus Rector"). For Smollett's skepticism about spiritus rector, see *An Essay on the External Use of Water* (London, 1752, 53). Van Helmont thought water more "simple" than earth and believed with Paracelsus that all matter could be reduced to it. Van Helmont coined the term "gas" for "a spirit incapable of coagulation" (James, "Gas"). He used "ferments" to indicate gastric "gas" but regarded a "ferment" as "an indwelling formative energy" (qtd. in Hans H. Simmer, "The Beginnings of Endocrinology," in *Medicine in Seventeenth-Century England: A Symposium Held at UCLA in Honor of C. D. O'Malley*, ed. Allen G. Debus [Berkeley: University of California Press, 1974], 229). Like his predecessors, Van Helmont was interested in the transmutation of substances.

18. "the salt . . . *acidum vagum* . . . volatilized vitriol of other modern chymists": Ingredients central to chemical and alchemical writings in the Paracelsian tradition. "*Acidum vagum*" is sulphuric acid. Shebbeare uses the term in *A New Analysis of the Bristol Waters* (1740), which Smollett, who later wrote on medical uses of water, probably read. See also G. S. Rousseau, "Smollett's *Acidum Vagum*," *Isis* 58 (1967): 244–45. "Volatilized vitriol" was of several sorts and was put to different uses; for example, boiled white copperas was used as an emetic; see James, "Vitriolum."

19. "a Germanized m——r": Newcastle; see chap. 9, n. 19.

20. "juggler": The phrase is also used to describe Newcastle (the Cuboy of Fika-kaka) in *Adventures of an Atom* (44–45), where he is also called a "mountebank in patriotism."

21. "dazzles your eyes": Discussing the opening remarks for the 1758 parliamentary session, Smollett said that "the protestant religion" was introduced "into messages and speeches from the throne in order to dazzle the eyes of the populace" (*Continuation*, 2:197).

22. "balance of power is a meer chimera": Shebbeare wrote of the "Balance of Power"

that "No Chimera can be more visionary than this Idea of fearing Universal Empire, and balancing the States of *Europe*" (*Second Letter*, 53).

23. "protestant religion . . . allies on the continent": Shebbeare depicted the Germans as growing great by the money England paid for mercenaries and added, sarcastically, "These are the friends and allies of *England*" (*Second Letter*, 27).

24. "a felonious dry-salter returned from exile": Joshua Ward (1685–1761), whose pills contained antimony and other ingredients. He fled to France to avoid repercussions of an election scandal; George II became his patron after his return.

25. "an hospital stump-turner": Unidentified. A stump-turner made wooden legs for amputees.

26. "a decayed stay-maker": Sir William Read (d. 1715), a tailor who became Queen Anne's oculist and was knighted in 1705.

27. "a bankrupt-printer": Unidentified. Many printers were associated with the nostrums they advertised in their publications.

28. "insolvent debtor, released by act of parliament": Unidentified. Since such bills were enacted in the reign of George II, the quack is recent. Smollett's ridicule masks his support for this sort of legislation (see *Continuation*, 3:58–59). See also chap. 11, n. 9.

29. "led-captains": Sycophants.

30. "*chrusion pepuromenon ek puros*": "Gold tried in the fire"; see Revelation 13:18. In a review of Shebbeare's *Fifth Letter*, Smollett wrote, "Like all other quacks, he loves to be mysterious and therefore addresses us in *Greek*" (*Critical Review* 4 [1757]: 274–75). Shebbeare's *Sixth Letter* takes its epigraph from Revelation.

31. "first created mover": The prime mover is Aristotle's key conception of the force that gives form to the universe. See n. 13 above.

32. "counselled in the Revelations": See Revelation 13:17–18: "Because thou sayest, I am rich, and increased with goods, and have need of nothing; and knowest not that thou art wretched and miserable, I counsel thee to buy of me gold tried in the fire, that thou may'st be rich." See also n. 30 above.

33. "pure fire": Probably electricity. "Of the reality of fire," in Shebbeare's *Practice of Physic*, 2 vols. (1755), 1:27–51, discusses electricity at length. Smollett ridiculed Shebbeare's theory in *Critical Review* 1 (1756): 321.

34. "calcined to a *caput mortuum*": Reduced by heat to a "death's head," the worthless remainder in alchemy and chemistry.

35. "menstruum": An agent, such as alkahest, that dissolves a solid substance (see n. 16 above).

36. "the woman may be cloathed with the sun": Revelation 12:1.

37. "the catholicon": "The Whole, universal, a boasting Epithet of some medicines, pretended to cure all Distempers, and most liberally bestow'd by the Chymists on their Nostrums" (James, "Catholicus").

38. "another small borough": Probably Retford, a parliamentary borough on the Great North Road.

39. "'The Life and Adventures of Valentine and Orson'": Probably a popular chap-

book, often reprinted in the eighteenth century, based on a fifteenth-century French romance about two princes, one of whom, Orson, is raised by bears. It is one of the romances that Toby Shandy bought at school; see Laurence Sterne, vol. 6 of *Tristram Shandy* (London, 1762), chap. 32.

40. "Adds bobs!": A mild oath, probably meaning "by God's blows." Compare "adad," chap. 2, n. 20, and "adds-bunt-lines," chap. 13, n. 9.

41. "patience is a good stream-anchor, and will hold": Proverbial; not listed by Tilley or *ODEP*. A stream anchor is lighter than the main anchor.

42. "boltsprit": Bowsprit, "a large boom or mast, which projects over the stem, to carry sail forward"; "the principal support of the fore-mast" (Falconer).

43. "athwart hawse": "The situation of a ship when she is driven . . . across the fore-part of another" (Falconer).

44. "down came the round-top—up with the dead lights": A top is "a sort of platform, surrounding the lower mast-head" (Falconer); deadlights are shutters that replaced the glass in cabin windows when storms threatened (Falconer).

45. "seven senses": The idea that in addition to the five external senses there are two internal senses (the moral sense and the sense of beauty) dates to the seventeenth century but was given fullest form by Francis Hutcheson in *An Inquiry into the Original of Our Ideas of Beauty and Virtue* (1725).

46. "broached upon my broadside": A windward incline caused the ship (or Crowe's body) to lurch over (see Falconer, "Broach-To," "Broadside").

47. "*non compos*": Non compos mentis, "not of sound Mind, Memory, and Under-standing" (*NLD*), a legal definition of madness.

48. "trespass . . . *falsum imprisonamentum*": "False imprisonment (*falsum imprisonamen-tum*) is a Trespass committed against a Person, by Arresting and Imprisoning him without just Cause, contrary to Law." If an action is brought successfully, "consid-erable damages are recoverable" (*NLD*).

49. "*auditâ querela*": "*Audita Querela* is a Writ that lies where a Man hath any Thing to plead, but hath not a Day in Court to plead it" (*NLD*).

50. "wandering lunatics by the statute . . . legal settlement": See chap. 8, n. 11.

51. "to constitute robbery . . . a thing stolen": The description contains verbatim lan-guage from *NLD*, "Robbery."

52. "*vi et armis*": See chap. 4, n. 19.

53. "Words, which may be taken . . . ambiguous words——": Clarke is quoting ver-batim from *NLD*, "*Words,*" when Sir Launcelot cuts him off. He would have gone on to say that ambiguous words "are to be construed so as to make them stand with Law and Equity; and not to be wrested to do Wrong."

54. "as you brew you must drink": Proverbial; see Tilley, b654; *ODEP*, 85.

55. "this shall be a dear day's work": This shall cost you dearly; a proverbial phrase not in Taylor, Tilley, or *ODEP*.

56. "the braying ass . . . to lie upon litter": Taylor calls the first of these proverbs "rare" (85). For the first two, see Tilley, a359, b70; *ODEP*, 22, 29. Neither the third nor the fourth appears in Tilley or *ODEP*.

57. "There's no cake . . . clear weather": Three proverbial phrases; see Tilley c14, c412, c442; *ODEP*, 97, 562, 6. Crabshaw's multiplication of proverbs recalls Sancho Panza; see, for example, *Don Quixote*, pt. 1, bk. 3, chap. 11.

58. "look to'un jailor, there's a frog in the stocks": The proverb, listed but not defined by Ray (72), probably means to get what one does not expect. See Tilley, j31; *ODEP*, 483; and see Evans, 225; Hambridge, 305.

59. "three ordinary men could scarce have lifted from the ground": A formula of Homeric epic, for example, "Not two strong Men th'enormous Weight could raise, / Such Men as live in these degen'rate Days" (*Iliad* 5.371–72, 7.284–85, Alexander Pope translation). For another mock-heroic adaptation, see Fielding, *Joseph Andrews*, bk. 3, chap. 9.

60. "cast in a swinging sum": "Defeat[ed] in an action at law" (*OED*) for a large amount.

Chapter 11

1. "Crabshaw was put in the stocks, as an idle stroller": See chap. 2, n. 35. This detail may echo the stocking of King Lear's follower the earl of Kent (2.4) in Shakespeare's representation of another mad hero.

2. "justice Gobble": Frank Donoghue argues that Gobble is meant to satirize Smollett's rival Ralph Griffiths, editor of the *Monthly Review*. Both are bad judges (a "critic," etymologically, is a judge); both are former tradesmen with wives whom Smollett perceived as mixing in their business. See Donoghue, *The Fame Machine: Book Reviewing and Eighteenth-Century Literary Careers* (Stanford: Stanford University Press, 1996), 148. Smollett introduces a Squire Gobble in passing in chapter 12 of *Roderick Random*.

3. "a certain peer": Identified in the following chapter as Lord Sharpington, Justice Gobble's patron.

4. "Lammas-market": Annual market held in conjunction with the harvest festival, 1 August.

5. "vestry-clerk": The clerk for parish meetings. See n. 17 below.

6. "not only abused him . . . violent hands upon his person": "If one make an Assault upon a *Justice of Peace*, he may apprehend the Offender, and send him to Gaol. . . . if a *Justice* be abused in the Execution of his Office, the Offender may be also indicted and fined" (*NLD*, "*Justices of the Peace*").

7. "a statute of bankruptcy": *NLD* describes the various statutes of bankruptcy. The affidavit of the creditor swears to a debt of £100 or more and swears that the debtor has become a bankrupt under one or more of the statutes. See *NLD*, "*Bankrupt*."

8. "certificate": The certificate of the commissioners assigned to the case that the creditors sign to indicate their consent to a prisoner's discharge. See *NLD*, "Bankrupt."

9. "parliament . . . insolvent debtors": In the *Continuation*, Smollett comments on the

treatment of insolvent debtors, giving a brief history of the bankruptcy laws and of the conflicting claims of "the liberty of the subject, and the security of the land-holder" (3:57). He concludes, "It might . . . deserve the consideration of parliament, whether, in extending their clemency to the poor, it should not be equally diffused to bankrupts and other insolvents; whether proper distinction ought not to be made between the innocent bankrupt, who fails through misfortunes in trade, and him who becomes insolvent from fraud or profligacy; and finally, whether the enquiry and trial of all such cases would not properly fall within the province of chancery, a tribunal instituted for the mitigation of common law" (3: 58–59). See also *NLD*, *"Prisoners Discharged."*

10. "skittle-ground": An area for the playing of skittles, or ninepins.

11. "deprived of his licence": The justice of the peace licensed alehouses and fined those operating without a license; see *NLD*, *"Justices of the Peace."* Smollett agreed with the purposes of the acts that gave the justices this power but was wary of the oppression to which he saw it leading in practice; see his representation of a bill to enable "the more easy conviction of persons selling ale and strong liquors without licence" as "an act which impowered the justices of peace to tyrannize over their fellow subjects" (*Continuation*, 1:141). More generally, comments in the *Continuation* on a 1752 act extending the authority of the justices provide the background for his portrait of Gobble: "Many of those who exercised this species of magistracy . . . were, to the reproach of government, men of profligate lives, needy, mean, ignorant, and rapacious, and often acted from the most scandalous principles of selfish avarice" (*Continuation*, 1:122).

12. "bantlings": See chap. 5, n. 20.

13. "settlement": The wife and children would be treated as vagrants and returned to the husband's last legal place of habitation or place of birth, where they would come under the parish poor laws. See *NLD*, *"Vagrants"*; see also Slack, *The English Poor Law*, 36–39.

14. "young Oakely, was pressed for a soldier": The name Oakely, with its evocation of the English oak, was often used in newspapers as a generic name for a sailor or soldier. To be pressed is to be apprehended by a press-gang, which rounded up men for military service.

15. "nourished me with her milk": Better-off families put their infants out to wet nurses; later in the century there was a vogue for the nursing of one's own children.

16. "Habeas Corpus": Literally, "you should have the body," the first words of "the great Writ of *English Liberty*" (*NLD*, *"Habeas Corpus"*). Clarke's warning follows *NLD*.

17. "vestry and quarter-sessions": The parish meeting, usually held in the vestry of the church, and the quarterly general court held by the justices of the peace in each county.

18. *"socius criminis"*: Partner in crime.

19. "I'd . . . ferk you with a primineery": To "firk" is to whip, in the sense of correction (Johnson, *Dictionary*). The writ of praemunire (literally, "to be forewarned") was originally used "against one charged with introducing a foreign power into the land" (Evans, 225) but had long been put to various purposes. Here, Mrs. Gobble means, "I'd put you in a legal predicament." Smollett uses the term in a general rather than legal sense in chapter 49 of *Peregrine Pickle* and in chapters 38 and 55 of *Ferdinand Count Fathom*.

Chapter 12

1. *"more ways to kill a dog than hanging"*: Proverbial; see Ray, 127; Tilley, w156; *ODEP*, 872. Compare to the familiar "more than one way to skin a cat."
2. "in the stays": "Said of a ship when her head is being turned to windward for the purpose of tacking" (*OED*, "in stays").
3. "weather the point": To sail to the windward side of a point of land; hence, to manage or survive.
4. "fore-foot": "A piece of timber which terminates the keel at the fore-end" (Falconer).
5. "taken all a-back": The sails of a ship flattened against the masts "by a sudden change of the wind, or by an alternation in the ship's course" (Falconer, "Aback").
6. "the same unsavoury effects . . . done in the Dutch stile": The justice has befouled himself in fear; the allusion is to Hogarth's self-parody (and parody of Rembrandt) *Paul before Felix Burlesqued* (1751; *Hogarth's Graphic Works*, 379), in which Paul's speech has such an effect upon Felix. For Paul before Felix, see Acts 24:24–25. The "Dutch stile" echoes Hogarth's claim that his engraving was "Design'd and scratch'd in the true Dutch taste," in opposition to this dignified Italianate painting *Paul before Felix*, based upon Raphael, for which the burlesque served as a subscription ticket. For another allusion to this engraving, see *Adventures of an Atom*, 34.
7. "without bail or main-prize": Without need for someone to take legal responsibility to appear in his place before the court.
8. "say black is the white of your eye": Proverbial, meaning to accuse one of a crime; see Tilley, e252; *ODEP*, 64. Jery Melford uses the expression in *Humphry Clinker* (Jery Melford to Sir Watkin Phillips, London, June 5).
9. "tag, rag, and bobtail": The rabble. Bobtail, from the cut-off tail of a horse or dog, came to mean a "contemptible" man (*OED*). See Tilley, t10; *ODEP*, 797.
10. "Marry come up": Expresses indignant contempt. "Marry" is a mild oath: by (Saint) Mary.
11. "quotha": Says he.
12. "a taylor that was made a knight": See chap. 10, n. 26.
13. "the form of proceeding . . . *coram non judice*, and void": Verbatim from *NLD*,

"*Justices of the Peace.*" "*Coram non Judice* [literally, before one not a judge] is when a Cause is brought and determined in a Court whereof the Judges have not any Jurisdiction," which voids it (*NLD*).

14. "he shall be fined": the ensuing legal discussion paraphrases *NLD*, "*Justices of the Peace.*"

15. "information": See chap. 5, n. 30.

16. "*Banco Regis*": king's bench, that is, the Court of King's Bench.

17. "fined a thousand marks": The mark equaled 160 pence, two thirds of a pound sterling.

18. "to dinner with what appetite you may": Smollett used the quotation again in *Humphry Clinker* (Jery Melford to Sir Watkin Phillips, London, May 24); the source is *Henry VIII:* "to breakfast with / What appetite you may" (3.2.202–3). The first folio reading, preferred by modern editors, is "What appetite you have," but Smollett's reading follows editions of Shakespeare from Nicholas Rowe's (1709) to Samuel Johnson's (1765).

19. "fish a man's yard-arm . . . slings": A fish is "a long piece of oak, convex on one side, and concave on other," used to support or strengthen a mast. Yard-arms are the extremities of the yards, "long piece[s] of timber suspended upon the masts." Hence, this nautical language is exact for the occurrence of an arm broken by the ropes used to hoist heavy weights, or slings: "their form, application and utility are exactly like those of the [splints] applied to a broken limb" (Falconer, "Fish," "Yard," "Slings").

20. "prize-money": Money from the sale of a captured ship, shared by all captors.

21. "the spirit of the young farmer": In *Tom Jones* (bk. 7, chap. 14), Tom is taken for his own ghost when he appears with a bloody wound.

22. "dues": Expenses owed to jailors, who were unsalaried, for the room, supplies, and food.

23. "admiral P——'s ship": Vice-Admiral Sir George Pococke returned on 22 September 1760. This chapter appeared on 1 December 1760; Smollett could not have written these words more than two months in advance. Barbara Laning Fitzpatrick regards this reference as the most topical in the novel; see "The Text of Tobias Smollett's *Life and Adventures of Sir Launcelot Greaves*, the First Serialized Novel" (Ph.D. diss., Duke University, 1987), 79–80. Hambridge suggests that Smollett may simply have added a fortuitous detail (64).

Chapter 13

1. "the end of the chapter": Laurence Sterne employs this euphemism for death in, for example, volume 1 of *Tristram Shandy* (London, 1760); see chap. 10.

2. "a commission of lunacy": "A commission out of [the Court of] *Chancery* to inquire whether a Person represented to be Lunatick be so or not, that if Lunatick, the

King may have Care of his Estate" (qtd. from 17 Edw. 2, c. 10 [1328], in *NLD*, "*Commission of Lunacy*").

3. "crazy bark": A shattered or broken ship.

4. "spank it away": Sail away quickly.

5. "'ware timbers": Beware of sinking. Timbers are the ship's ribs.

6. "rotten ratline": Ratlings are ropes that form ladders aloft for sailors, valueless if rotten.

7. "five points of the wind": Mariners divide the horizon into thirty-two points called "winds" and four quadrants of eight points, each named for a direction (see Falconer, "Wind").

8. "a-pize": See chap. 8, n. 14.

9. "adds-bunt-lines": A nonce oath; compare chap. 2, n. 20 and chap. 10, n. 40. Bunt-lines are "ropes fastened to the bottoms of the square sails, to draw them up" (Falconer).

10. "hawse-holes": See chap. 7, n. 4.

11. "knows not a cat from a capstan": Proverbial, though Taylor (85) gives this as the sole example. A "cat" is "a contrivance for raising an anchor." See Tilley (c171) for "know a cat from a . . . cowlstaff," of which Smollett may have devised a nautical variant.

12. "started a hoop in rolling": The phrase, suggesting mere flirtation, is not known to be proverbial.

13. "tight as a nut-shell": Virginal; a proverbial phrase, though not in Tilley or *ODEP*.

14. "sail upon a parallel": Hold to a parallel of latitude, that is, hold a steady course.

15. "as well as e'er a frigate . . . northward of fifty": As well as any Englishwoman. England lies somewhat above fifty degrees north latitude.

16. "pork-slush": "Refuse fat or grease" from the pork boiled on a ship (*OED*).

17. "stockfish": "Cod or other gadoid fish cured without salt by splitting open and drying hard in the air" (*OED*).

18. "they would confine him to his cage": In *Don Quixote* (pt. 1, bk. 4, chap. 19) Quixote is trapped in a cage by the barber and the curate.

19. "Dulcinea": Don Quixote exalts a "hale, buxom country wench" (1:6) into his imaginary mistress, Dulcinea del Toboso. *OED* cites chapter 8 of *Roderick Random* as the first source to use the term in English. In fact, the term appears in Christian Davies, *The Life of Mrs. Christian Davies, Commonly Call'd Mother Ross* (London, 1740, 84); but Smollett may have popularized it as a signifier of "sweetheart." See also *Ferdinand Count Fathom*, chapter 13; and *Peregrine Pickle*, chapters 18, 34, 40, 44, 63.

20. "trim tram, like master, like man": Proverbial. The nonsense words exist for the rhyme. See Tilley, M723, T525; *ODEP*, 839.

21. "a Rowland for their Oliver": These warriors from the French epic *Chanson de Roland* became proverbial. The two were closely matched, though Roland was the greater hero. See Tilley, R195; *ODEP*, 682.

22. "let every cuckold wear his own horns": Proverbial; a man with an unfaithful wife was thought to grow horns. See Ray, 6; Tilley, c882; *ODEP*, 159.
23. "Hectors": See chap. 2, n. 39.
24. "Bethlem": Saint Mary of Bethlehem Hospital ("Bedlam"), which confined the insane.
25. "as mad as e'er . . . in Moor-fields": Hambridge suggests an allusion to Hogarth's mad king in plate 8 of *A Rake's Progress, Tom Rakewell in Bedlam*, though, he notes, "the notion of madmen thinking themselves king was commonplace" (65). Saint Mary of Bethlehem was located in Moorfields in northeast London (see n. 24 above).
26. "stockholder at Jonathan's when the rebels were at Derby": Stockbrokers frequently conducted business at Jonathan's Coffee House in Exchange Alley, Cornhill. When Charles Edward Stuart, the Young Pretender, pressed as far south as Derby during the rebellion of 1745, the financial interests, Smollett wrote, "exhibited the plainest marks of horror and despair" (*Complete History*, 4:667). For Smollett's detestation of stockbrokers, see chap. 9, n. 17; see also his satire *Reproof* for "the vile tribes of usurers . . . who sneak at *Jonathan*'s" (ll. 145–46; *Poems, Plays, and "The Briton,"* 42, 43).
27. "Yorkshire hug": A wrestling hold; compare "Cornish hugg" in Grose, *A Classical Dictionary*.
28. "joseph": A long cloak with a small cape, usually worn for riding by women. Its name alludes to the garb left behind by Joseph while eluding Potiphar's wife; see Genesis 39:12.
29. "masqued": The practice of women wearing masks to preserve the complexion or to move about incognito dates from the Renaissance.

Chapter 14

1. "*a man cannot always sip, When the cup is at his lip*": Proverbial; not listed in Taylor, Tilley, or *ODEP*. For variations on "There's many a slip twixt the cup and the lip," see *ODEP*, 160.
2. "dropped her pocket-book": Compare *Tom Jones* (bk. 12, chap. 4), where Tom retrieves Sophia's purse.
3. "led-captains": See chap. 10, n. 29.
4. "a charge of lunacy . . . heir apparent": See chap. 13, n. 2, for the commission of lunacy. As trustee for the estate, Darnel could accomplish his designs, though nominally acting in behalf of the "lunatic." A lunatic could not marry, so he would maintain his status as heir.
5. "myrmidons": Literally, the warlike tribe that followed Achilles, but frequently used by Smollett to indicate any group of forceful followers. Commonly used in the period to identify bailiffs.

6. "changeling": Probably here meaning "half-wit" rather than "turncoat" or "child exchanged for another."

Chapter 15

1. "*Natura il fece . . .* the dye destroy'd": Lodovico Ariosto, *Orlando Furioso* (1516, 10.84.6). Zerbino is a love-mad Scottish prince in this epic. The translation appears to be by Smollett.
2. "interesting": Moving, affecting (Johnson, *Dictionary*).
3. "I 'aive yeaten hool-cheese": "I have eaten Hull-cheese," a Yorkshire expression indicating intoxication. Francis Grose notes that "Hull is famous for strong ale" (*A Provincial Glossary* [London, 1790], "Yorkshire").
4. "bit his nether lip, rolled his eyes around": See *Othello*, 5.2.37–38, 43.
5. "hero of romance mounted upon a winged steed": In *Don Quixote* (pt. 2, bk. 3, chaps. 8–9) the countess Trifaldi tricks Quixote into believing that he is on a flying horse.
6. "there's a salve for every sore": Proverbial; see Tilley, s84; *ODEP*, 698. Hambridge notes that "this is the first proverb spoken by Sir Launcelot, and Smollett may be imitating Cervantes' use of role reversal indicating the increasingly intimate relationship shared by Don Quixote and his squire" (68).
7. "for every zow there's a zirreverence": For every sow there's a sir-reverence (i.e., a "save your reverence," or turd). The mock-proverb has a proverbial precursor in Robert Greene, *A Quip for an Upstart Courtier* (1592): "As far as a hungry sow can smell a sir reuerence" (*OED*).
8. "Thatch your house with t——d . . . more teachers than reachers": Proverbial; if you have a disagreeable undertaking, more will be willing to advise than help. The missing word is "turd." See Ray, 209; Tilley, H761; *ODEP*, 809.
9. "Venetian masques": Masks, often grotesque, covering the upper part of the face, worn publicly in Venice.

Chapter 16

1. "the whole family": The entire household, including servants.
2. "Marry hap, worse ware may have a better chap": To be sure, come what may, worse goods may have a better customer. Taylor finds no other examples of this sexually suggestive proverb. Evans (227) notes the similarity of Dolly's letter to those of Win Jenkins in *Humphry Clinker*; Hambridge (69) notes the similarity to the epistolary style of Deborah Hornbeck in chapter 45 of *Peregrine Pickle*. For "Marry," see chap. 12, n. 10.
3. "most interesting information": See chap. 15, n. 2.
4. "inflammation of the *pia mater*": The pia mater is the innermost of the three membranes covering the brain and spinal cord. George S. Rousseau claims that the

diagnosis recalls Dr. William Battie (1704–76); see "Doctors and Medicine in the Novels of Tobias Smollett" (Ph.D. diss., Princeton University, 1966), 146–47. See also chap. 23, n. 23.

5. "a doctor in the village, an odd sort of a humourist": A humourist is an eccentric, led by his humors; see chap. 10, n. 15. Relations between doctors and apothecaries were often strained. Some doctors, including Smollett (see *Essay on the External Use of Water*), objected to the increased use of drugs, which apothecaries, "chemists," and "druggists" provided.

6. "atrabilious": Characterized by black bile or melancholy as a predominant humor (see James, "bilis").

7. "borborygmata": "A rumbling Noise [in the bowels] excited by Wind" (James, "Borborygmus").

8. "venæsection": The cutting or opening of a vein, colloquially known as bleeding, widely practiced as a remedy for a range of complaints.

9. "vesicatory . . . *inter scapulas*": "A sharp, irritating ointment, plaster or other application" causing blisters on the skin (*OED*), applied between the shoulder blades. Colloquially known as a blister.

10. "cathartic apozem": A strong laxative "decoction or infusion"; see *OED*, which quotes *Ferdinand Count Fathom* (chapter 19, a mistake for chapter 6).

11. "alexipharmic boluses and neutral draughts": A bolus is "an internal Medicine, soft, coherent, a little thicker than honey, and whose quantity is a little Morsal or Mouthful" (James); "alexipharmic" means used as an antidote. In the cathartic liquid medicine, neither acid nor alkaline is to predominate.

12. "harateen": "A kind of linen fabric formerly used for curtains, bed-furniture, and the like" (*OED*, "harrateen").

13. "obstropolous": *OED* cites chapter 8 of *Roderick Random* for this comic variant of "obstreperous."

14. "seven senses": See chap. 10, n. 45.

15. "fauces": The cavity at the rear of the mouth.

16. "eat a horse behind the saddle": Proverbial; see Ray, 253; Tilley, H654; *ODEP*, 393.

17. "bumboat": Usually a scavenger boat, but Smollett's footnote in chapter 24 of *Roderick Random* clarifies his usage: "A bum-boat-woman, is one who sells bread, cheese, greens, liquor, and fresh provision to the sailors, in a small boat that lies along-side of the ship" (ed. Paul-Gabriel Boucé [Oxford: Oxford University Press, 1979], 139, n.).

18. "caps used by the light horse": Black leather helmets.

19. "hop-pole": A support for growing hops in a garden.

20. "a basket-hilt broad sword, like that of Hudibras": "His puissant *Sword* unto his Side / Near his undaunted Heart was ty'd; / With Basket-hilt, that would hold Broth, / And serve for Fight and Dinner both" (Butler, *Hudibras*, ed. Zachary Grey, 2 vols. [Cambridge, 1744], 1.1.351–54).

Chapter 17

1. "St. George of Cappadocia encountering the dragon": As the patron saint of England, Saint George appeared on many inn signs. His slaying of the dragon freed the Libyans of Selena and led to their conversion to Christianity.

2. "French invasion": England was at war with France from 1756 to 1763 (the Seven Years' War), and rumors of an invasion were persistent. The Jacobites, too, may have been planning an attempt from that country; see Claude Nordmann, "Choiseul and the Last Jacobite Attempt of 1759," in *Ideology and Conspiracy: Aspects of Jacobitism, 1689–1759*, ed. Eveline Cruickshanks (Edinburgh: John Donald, 1982), 201–17.

3. "grog": Rum or brandy and water. This sailor's slang probably derives from a nickname for Adm. Edward Vernon ("Old Grogam"), who in 1740 ordered that his sailors be given a daily ration of this drink. *OED* has no illustration as early as Smollett's use here.

4. "bread-room": Sailor's slang for "stomach"; the bread-room literally was "a place parted off below the lower deck," where bread was stored in a ship (*OED*).

5. "hawse-holes": See chap. 7, n. 4.

6. "noggin": A cup or mug.

7. "a quartern": A quarter of something, in this case, a pint.

8. "afterhold": The hold of a ship is the cavity containing cargo and provisions. The afterhold is located below deck at the stern of the ship (Falconer) and is therefore at the farthest remove from the forecastle, which is above and forward.

9. "the Gordian-knot was cut": The difficulty was solved by force. Confronted with King Gordius's famous knot, Alexander the Great cut it rather than trying to untie it.

10. "*secundum artem*": According to the rules of art.

11. "steering his course to Birmingham": Kahrl, who places Gobble at a post stop in West Retford, Nottinghamshire, observes that "from West Retford, Captain Crowe could easily make a short excursion in the direction of Birmingham and return to the main London road in time to be rescued from the angry farmers by Sir Launcelot and Tom Clarke" (58).

12. "journal": "A day's travel; a journey" (*OED*). Also "a daily register of the ship's course, the distance traversed, the winds and weather, etc." (*OED*); it measures the day from one noon to the next (Falconer).

13. "bring-to": Bring a ship to a stop (Falconer).

14. "clew up their corses": Truss up their chief sails. See Falconer, "Clue-Garnets," "Courses."

15. "foul of their quarters": Entangled in the ropes of the yardarms; see chap. 12, n. 19.

16. "luffed": Turned (a ship) away from the wind.

17. "Besselia Mizzen": Compare Don Quixote on his preferred treatment of Dulcinea del Toboso in *Don Quixote* (pt. 1, bk. 1, chap. 4).

18. "the broad pendant": The usual pennant, or swallow-tailed flag on a ship, was narrow. The broad pennant flew from the commodore's ship, hence called the "flagship."

19. "clapped on all their sails": Literally, arranged to sail closer to the wind (*OED*); here, prepared briskly to engage.

20. "athwart his forefoot": See chap. 12, n. 4.

21. "tacked about": Changed direction.

22. "on the lee-quarter": From behind; on the side away from the wind.

23. "upper works": The upper-work is all of a ship above water when balanced for a voyage (Falconer); metaphorically, here, it means Crowe's head.

24. "broached-to": Keeled over. In chapter 85 of *Peregrine Pickle*, "broach'd to" (p. 422), on Commodore Trunnion's tombstone, means "died"; see also chap. 22, n. 27.

25. "hand-spike": A wooden bar used as a lever.

26. "a mosqueto fleet": A mosquito fleet consists of "small, light vessels adapted for rapid manoeuvering" (*OED*).

27. "made prize": Captured the ship. See chap. 12, n. 20.

28. "pooped with a sea": Literally, what happens when waves cover "the highest and aftmost deck" (Falconer, "Poop").

29. "crowd away with all the cloth they could carry": To crowd is to accelerate quickly, accomplished by carrying "an extraordinary force of sail" (Falconer).

30. "enlargement of the prisoners": In *Don Quixote* (pt. 1, bk. 3, chap. 8) Quixote frees prisoners who, he delusionally believes, have been improperly detained.

31. "tag, rag, and bob-tail": See chap. 12, n. 9.

32. "'size": Assize; session of court.

33. "*affray . . . dignity*": Prickle's complaint follows closely *NLD*, "*Affray*"; see chap. 2, n. 36. The statute concerned is 2 Edw. III (1328).

34. "false imprisonment": See chap. 10, n. 48.

35. "the vicar . . . small tythes": The vicar would sue in the ecclesiastical court to receive his small, or predial, tithes, as distinct from the great tithes, for which see chap. 5, n. 9.

36. "scot and lot": "A customary Contribution laid upon all Subjects, according to their Ability" (*NLD*).

37. "I should ill vindicate the dignity . . . imprison you for contempt": See *NLD*, "*Justices of the Peace*."

38. "mittimus": See chap. 5, n. 29.

39. "Joseph": See chap. 13, n. 28.

40. "sack-whey": Medicinal beverage made of sherry or white wine and the watery part of milk, usually drunk warm.

Chapter 18

1. *"en cavalier"*: Cavalierly; in an arrogant or offhand manner.
2. "in imitation of the batchelor Sampson Carrasco . . . injunctions of the victor": In pt. 2, bk. 1, chap. 12 of *Don Quixote*, Sampson (Sansón) Carrasco, in disguise, loses his first challenge to Don Quixote; in pt. 2, bk. 4, chap. 13 Carrasco bests him and commands him to return home.
3. "Z——s!": "Zounds"; by His wounds, a mild oath.
4. "the Knight of the Crescent": See chap. 2, n. 12; chap. 5, n. 15.
5. "Griffin": The villain Sycamore styles himself Knight of the Griffin; in *Don Quixote*, Quixote explains that he "should assume some appellation, by the example of former knights," and instances among others "the Griffin" (1:112).
6. "POLYDORE": Almost certainly from Thomas Otway's popular play *The Orphan* (1680), which had been performed most recently in April 1760. Otway's Polydore is one of twin brothers in love with Monimia. He takes the place in bed of his brother, who has secretly married Monimia; the villain of Smollett's love triangle chooses as his pseudonym Polydore. Smollett used "Monimia" as a pseudonym for the heroine in chapter 43 of *Ferdinand Count Fathom*, where he set up a number of parallels between the play and his novel (see *Ferdinand Count Fathom*, 419, n. 2).
7. "larboard watch": See chap. 6, n. 21.
8. "lie board and board for a few glasses": Fight side by side for an hour. Sand glasses were used to measure time at sea, often, as here, in half-hour increments.
9. "Angels and ministers . . . to bend his eye on vacancy": Conflates two passages from *Hamlet*: "Angels and ministers of grace defend us! / Be thou a spirit of health, or goblin damn'd" (Hamlet to the ghost; 1.4.39–40) and "you do bend your eye on vacancy" (Gertrude to Hamlet; 3.4.117). See also chap. 2, n. 4 and chap. 5, n. 14.
10. "sheet-anchor": See chap. 2, n. 19.
11. "What man dare . . . tremble": *Macbeth* 3.4.98–102, on the appearance of Banquo's ghost.
12. "Jack": Often "Jack Tar," a generic name for a sailor.
13. "rig yourself": Probably "ready yourself" rather than "dress yourself."
14. "into the offing": Out to sea.
15. "in the turning of a capstan": Quickly. The capstan, a massive timber column, enables sailors to do heavy tasks easily by means of levers. See Falconer, "Capstern."
16. "raw head and bloody bones": The names of two nursery specters.
17. "brought to": Stopped.
18. "the bear and ragged staff": Evans notes that this is a public house sign based on the crest of the earls of Warwick (229).
19. "the lists": The place of combat, originally marked by barriers, hence such persisting phrases as "entered the lists."

20. "black patch": An invention of the late Renaissance to cover blemishes. It could be used to hide the effects of syphilis, though it also served as a beauty mark.
21. "vaulted into the saddle like a winged Mercury": Echoes the description of Prince Hal in *1 Henry IV* 4.1.104–8.

Chapter 19

1. "armed capapie": See chap. 2, n. 1.
2. "the regulations of the combat": The following battle recalls that of Quixote and the disguised Sampson Carrasco. See chap. 18, n. 2 and *Don Quixote*, pt. 2, bk. 1, chap. 14.
3. "trumpeter . . . charge to battle": In both their battles, Sampson Carrasco and Quixote joust "without waiting for sound of trumpet, or other signal" (*Don Quixote*, 2:80).
4. "poltroon": Coward.
5. "his armour crashed around him as he fell": Another adaptation of an epic formula; see, for example, Homer *Iliad* 5.7 (Fagles translation).
6. "blown bladder . . . pebbles were inclosed": A variant of the trick played on Quixote and Sancho Panza in *Don Quixote* (pt. 2, bk. 1, chap. 11).
7. "*spolia opima*": Honorable spoils; the armor of the vanquished leader. Smollett uses the expression in *The Reprisal* (1.2) and in chapter 68 of *Peregrine Pickle*; see also Jery Melford's use of "*opima spolia*" in *Humphry Clinker* (Jery Melford to Sir Watkin Phillips, November 8, p. 331).
8. "calves": Stupid or foolish people.
9. "I'se make yaw knaw your churning days": Proverbial. See Tilley, D117; *ODEP*, 124. Crabshaw plays on the turns taken making butter to let Sycamore's servant know that it is his turn to be whipped.
10. "crow-trodden": Treated ignominiously; see *OED*, "crow-tread."
11. "I mun gee thee back the pig . . . poke": I must give you back the pig; based on the proverbial phrase "to buy a pig in a poke (bag)." See Tilley, P304; *ODEP*, 95.
12. "Crown-office": "An office belonging to the Court of *King's Bench*" that dealt with crimes and misdemeanors (*Student's Law-Dictionary*).
13. "steerage way": The "degree of progressive motion communicated to a ship, by which she becomes susceptible of the effects of the helm to govern her course" (Falconer).
14. "binnacle": The case on a stand in which a compass and other items were kept.
15. "sea room": Room enough to maneuver a ship at sea.
16. "commission of lunacy": See chap. 13, n. 2.
17. "*Banco Regis*": See chap. 12, n. 16.
18. "stink-pots": In war at sea, hand missiles used prior to boarding to divert the enemy by the sound of their explosion and by their suffocating smell.

19. "Bugden": Buckden, in Huntingdonshire, a coach stop on the Great North Road.

20. "May-fair": Mayfair, a fashionable part of London developed earlier in the century.

21. "joseph": See chap. 13, n. 28.

22. "Caffre or Æthiopian": Caffre, or kaffir, derives from the Arab word for infidel and was applied derogatorily to South Africans, especially Bantus. Its use with "Æthiopian" suggests that Smollett was not overly troubled by distinctions between African peoples, whom he racially stereotypes. Smollett was a slaveowner.

23. "Hatfield": A stage stop on the Great North Road, north of London in Hertfordshire.

24. "the Bull and Gate inn in Holborn": The name is a corruption of "Boulogne Gate," probably commemorating an English victory over the French. Its location as the first London coach stop on the Great North Road made it popular. Tom Jones stays there when he arrives in London; see *Tom Jones*, bk. 13, chap. 2.

Chapter 20

1. "*Hero descends into the Mansions of the Damned*": The descent to the underworld was a convention of epic poetry, adapted, for example, by Alexander Pope in canto 4 of *The Rape of the Lock* (1714).

2. "the neighbourhood of Golden-square": East of modern Regent Street above Piccadilly Circus. Smollett lived on Chapel Street, not far from Golden Square, from 1746 to 1748 (Knapp, 42); in July 1765 he lived on Brewer Street off Golden Square (*Letters*, 125). The travelers in *Humphry Clinker* stay in Golden Square (Jery Melford to Sir Watkin Phillips, London, May 24).

3. "upper-deck": The highest deck that extends throughout the ship. Crowe recommends an apartment in the uppermost storey.

4. "St. Catherine's": See chap. 7, n. 29.

5. "alderman Parsons' great brewhouse": Humphrey Parsons (1676–1741) began as a brewer and became alderman and, twice, lord mayor of London.

6. "Rotherhithe": This parish east of Southwark and London Bridge on the right bank of the Thames "consists chiefly of one street of a vast length, running along the shore, and winding with the great bend of the river" (Pennant, *Some Account of London*, 58).

7. "hackney-coach": Coach for hire.

8. "spunging-house": Sponging-house, a private house, usually belonging to a bailiff or another officer, where those arrested were confined. The name derives from the practice of squeezing money from prisoners who boarded there.

9. "the Gate-house, Fleet, and Marshalsea": London prisons where many prisoners were held for debt, a commonly trumped-up charge. See also *Roderick Random*, chapters 61–62, 64; *Peregrine Pickle*, chapters 97–104; and *Ferdinand Count Fathom*, chapters 38–42.

10. "the King's-bench": In this section, Smollett draws from his own experience in the King's Bench prison; see Knapp, 230–36; and Introduction, xviii, xix.

11. "the Borough": The borough of Southwark.

12. "St. George's-fields": Location of King's Bench prison from 1758, about a mile south of Westminster Bridge.

13. "state-rooms": Ironic adaptation of term for rooms in palaces where visitors are received.

14. "dunghills": Cowards; a dunghill cock is one that refuses to fight.

15. "split into factions": See Fielding's *Jonathan Wild*, bk. 3, chap. 4, for such a split.

16. "*divide et impera*": "Divide and rule."

17. "I have been detained . . . sign my certificate": See chap. 11, n. 8.

18. "taken in execution": "Execution . . . signifies the last Performance of an Act, as of a Judgment, &c." (*NLD*).

19. "atrabiliarious": Atrabilious; see chap. 16, n. 6.

20. "the Acroceraunian promontory": Projecting from the Adriatic coast in southern Albania, then part of the Ottoman Empire.

21. "a cross-buttock": A wrestling throw.

Chapter 21

1. "Captain Clewlin": The name comes from "clew-line," a rope to the corner, or clue, of a square sail (Falconer). Evans (230) and Hambridge (330–31) plausibly suggest that Clewlin is modeled on Captain George Walker (d. 1777); Smollett knew Walker in the King's Bench prison, and he characterized him as a courageous captain whose bankruptcy case contained some "extraordinary allegations" (*Continuation*, 3:54).

2. "Bridewell": See chap. 2, n. 31. Inmates of the prison were subjected to physical punishment, frequently for prostitution, hence the threat.

3. "active war": The Seven Years' War (1756–63).

4. "rib": Wife; see Genesis 2:21–22.

5. "taken in stays": See chap. 12, n. 2.

6. "he'd never make a weft in his ensign": He would not fold up his flag to hang as a signal.

7 "bays": Baize, presumably under the carpets.

8. "jointure": The guaranteed annual income paid a wife who survived her husband, if contracted in marriage settlement or at another time during the marriage. The jointure stated here is high, even among the wealthier classes.

9. "duns": Harassing creditors or their agents.

10. "circular letters": Letters directed to a number of people (a circle) who share an interest (*OED*).

11. "his sole creditor, a quaker, who refused to sign his certificate": Fielding also de-

picted Quakers as unfeeling or mercenary; see *Tom Jones*, bk. 7, chap. 10. Any creditor could by law refuse to sign the certificate needed to effect a prisoner's release; see *Continuation*, 3:58. See also chap. 11, n. 8.

Chapter 22

1. "*sublimed*": Raised "to an elevated sphere or exalted state" (*OED*).
2. "the fields by the Foundling Hospital": Lamb's Conduit Fields in Bloomsbury, London, in which still stand the remains of the Hospital for the Maintenance and Education of Exposed and Deserted Young Children, or "Foundling Hospital," founded by Thomas Coram and opened in 1741.
3. "bottoms": Resources.
4. "God's revenge against murder": Echoes John Reynolds, *The Triumphs of God's Revenge against Murder* (1621), a classic of providence literature.
5. "discuss": Jocularly, "to investigate or try the quality of (food or drink)" (*OED*).
6. "cunning man": A clairvoyant, such as Grubble claims to be. See n. 8 below.
7. "the right sow by the ear": Proverbial. See Tilley, s684; *ODEP*, 756. It is more common as "the sow by the right ear," although Henry VIII (speaking of Thomas Cranmer, archbishop of Canterbury) and, more recently, Sir Robert Walpole (speaking of Queen Caroline) had used the form employed by Smollett crudely to indicate the successful application of political influence.
8. "Dr. Grubble": Louis L. Martz notes that Grubble's role recalls Cadwallader Crabtree's activities as mock astrologer in chapters 90–92 of *Peregrine Pickle*; see *The Later Career of Tobias Smollett* (New Haven: Yale University Press, 1942), 14.
9. "Grubble . . . sent to Bridewell": Under various statutes, those who "pretend . . . to tell fortunes" could be arrested and imprisoned. The Vagrant Act of 1744 stiffened the penalties. See *NLD*, "*Vagrant*." For Bridewell, see chap. 2, n. 31.
10. "sybil": A prophetess in the ancient world, known in some traditions as old and ugly. The word was extended generically to female fortune-tellers and witches.
11. "like a bear to the stake": The metaphor, drawn from bearbaiting, a popular entertainment in which dogs were set upon a chained bear, also appears in chapter 9 of *Peregrine Pickle*. See also *Adventures of an Atom*, 43.
12. "black bays": A funereal wreath of laurel leaves.
13. "down't go to baind me oover to the Red Sea like": In Exodus 10:19, the plague of locusts is "cast" into the Red Sea, and in Exodus 14 the Egyptians are drowned there. Evans plausibly speculates that the beard of the astrologer "reminds Crabshaw of Moses" (231). Grose claims that "what a Ghost likes least, is the Red Sea; it being related, in many instances, that Ghosts have most earnestly besought the exorcists not to confine them in that place" (*Provincial Glossary*, "Popular Superstitions"). Crabshaw seems to share the ghosts' fear. In *Peregrine Pickle* Trunnion tells of a parson who "conjured the spirits into the Red Sea" (chapter 2, p. 6).

Joseph Addison's play *The Drummer; or, The Haunted House* (1716, 1.2) may have provided the impetus for this scene.

14. "Yorkshire tyke": A native of Yorkshire; see Tilley, Y34. Compare chap. 1, n. 24.

15. "a must be a good hand at *trapping* . . . starns a *napping*": Not listed by Taylor, Tilley, or *ODEP*, though Tilley (N35–37) has "to take one napping," and *ODEP* (111) has "Now night growes old; yet walks here in his trappinge Till Daye come catch him . . . nappinge." "Starns" is a northern and Scottish form of "stars."

16. "cast a figure": See chap. 7, n. 17.

17. "houses . . . trines, and trigons": Astrological terms. A "house" is a "station of a planet in the heavens, astrologically considered" (Johnson, *Dictionary*). A "trigon" is a "set of three signs of the zodiac" that in effect form an equilateral triangle; synonymous with "trine," "the aspect of two planets distant 120 degrees from each other" (*OED*).

18. "Tyburn tree": The gallows where criminals were hanged publicly until 1783; the site of the modern Marble Arch.

19. "the first fact": The first "act," meaning "crime."

20. "cast at the Old Baily": Found guilty of felony at the central court of London, the Old Bailey.

21. "nosegay . . . the Whole Duty of Man": *The Practice of Christian Graces, or the Whole Duty of Man* (1658), possibly by Richard Allestree (1619–81), was popular throughout the late seventeenth and eighteenth centuries. Evans (231) suggests that Grubble's exhortation to carry the book and a nosegay on the way to be hanged evokes Hogarth's *The Idle 'Prentice Executed at Tyburn*, plate 11 of *Industry and Idleness* (1747), but a Bible and a nosegay were conventional attributes of the condemned.

22. "the staggers": A disease of sheep and other animals that causes them to stagger.

23. "Tisiphone": One of the Erinyes (Furies) in Greek mythology who avenged crimes, especially against kinship.

24. "heave your eye into the binnacle, and box your compass": For "binnacle," see chap. 19, n. 14; for the boxing of the compass, see chap. 6, n. 7.

25. "fowls of a feather": Proverbial; see "birds of a feather flock together," Tilley, B393; *ODEP*, 60.

26. "slipped his cable . . . and has lost company": Quit his anchorage and been separated from the rest of the fleet.

27. "broach'd to": See chap. 17, n. 24.

28. "pawwawing": Powwowing; practicing sorcery.

Chapter 23

1. "his prison was no other than the house of a messenger": Messengers worked for the secretary of state and were permitted to confine state prisoners in their houses prior to their commitment to jail. See *NLD*, "*Warrant*" and "*Messenger*."

2. "*habeas corpus* . . . not suspended at this juncture": *Habeas corpus* (see chap. 11, n. 16), which could have been used to procure Sir Launcelot's release, was suspended in 1723 by Sir Robert Walpole, perennially anxious about Jacobite insurrection. William Pitt opted against suspension, though the country was at war. See *Complete History*, 2:34, 108, 306.

3. "His ears . . . against the wainscot": George S. Rousseau plausibly suggests that Smollett was influenced by Tom Rakewell in Bedlam, in plate 8 of Hogarth's *A Rake's Progress*, for some of the mad characters in this chapter ("Doctors and Medicine," 118–22; and see *Hogarth's Graphic Works*, 97–98, 316–17). Compare chap. 13, n. 25.

4. "hoarse voice": Frederick II of Prussia (1712–86), Frederick the Great. Smollett opposed involvement in the German theater and objected to the subsidies that ensured Frederick's loyalty. The depiction of Frederick is consistent with charges of brutality recorded in the press in the late 1750s; see Robert Donald Spector, *English Literary Periodicals and the Seven Years' War* (The Hague: Mouton, 1966), chap. 1. Readers of the novel in serial form could have encountered repeated references to Frederick in the *History of the Present War*, a continuing feature since the inception of the *British Magazine*.

5. "Brutandorf's brigade": The proper name in German means "brood on village," but "brute on village" is probably nearer to what Smollett wants to suggest.

6. "black hussars": Hungarian light cavalry who wore black uniforms.

7. "Lusatia": A region of Germany east of Dresden, extending north from the Lusatian Mountains and west from the Oder, now partly in Poland. Frederick is reported as "directing [his army] through Lusatia" in the *British Magazine* for July 1760 (1:441).

8. "the suburbs of Pera": Pirna, on the Elbe, southeast of Dresden. The torching of Pirna in November 1758 is mentioned in *British Magazine* 1 (1760): 48; see *Continuation*, 2:363, for Smollett's indignant response to the event.

9. "my brother Henry": Friedrich Heinrich Ludwig (1726–1802), Prussian prince. In the *British Magazine* for May 1760 he is said to have just met with Frederick at Meissen (1:145).

10. "pass the Elbe at Meissen": The *British Magazine* for May 1760 mentions Frederick's plan to cross the Elbe at Meissen, northwest of Dresden, on 16 April 1760 (1:146).

11. "parallel": A trench parallel to the works under siege.

12. "Schittenbach": Roughly translatable as "stream of rubbish," although the scatalogical overtones are no doubt intentional. See also Smollett's use of the name Donder, or "thunder," earlier in the sentence.

13. "works": Fortifications.

14. "saved by works . . . I abhor good works": An attack on some of the main tenets of Methodism. Like Fielding, Smollett mistrusted the "enthusiasm" of the Methodists and their preference for faith over works. See *Continuation*, 4:121, on the "su-

perstition stiled Methodism"; Matthew Bramble, often a mouthpiece for Smollett, attacks Methodism in *Humphry Clinker* (Jery Melford to Sir Watkin Phillips, London, June 10).

15. "communication": A pun melding religious and sexual meanings. *Humphry Clinker* provides the earliest illustration of the sexual meaning in *OED* (see Jery Melford to Sir Watkin Phillips, Hot Well, April 18, p. 20).

16. "sister Jolly": Methodists, like many Protestant sects, often referred to female members as "sisters." The term also suggests a prostitute; see, for example, *Roderick Random*, chapter 23; and *Peregrine Pickle*, chapter 59. "Jolly" can mean "wanton" and "lustful" (*OED*). Religious zeal was often satirized as sexual in origin; see, for example, Jonathan Swift, *A Tale of a Tub* (London, 1704), chap. 8.

17. "the Marche": The Mark of Brandenburg, Prussia. The term refers to a border province.

18. "finding the longitude": In 1714 a prize of £20,000 was offered to the discoverer of a method for determining longitude at sea. Forty-six years later, the first number of the *British Magazine* ran a piece on the continuing problem (16–17); see also *Continuation*, on the "many mathematical heads [that] have been disordered" in the pursuit of the solution (3:424). The full award for the solution was granted to John Harrison only in 1773. For Hogarth's depiction of a similar madman, see Tom Rakewell in Bedlam, n. 3 above.

19. "moment of de proshection": In alchemy, when the powder of the philosopher's stone (the "powder of projection") transmutes base metal into gold (*OED*). The speaker satirized is French.

20. "St. Peter's keys": Symbols of papal power; see Matthew 16:19.

21. "*waistcoat*": Strait waistcoat or straitjacket, an eighteenth-century invention.

22. "P——": Prussia.

23. "a weakness of the nerves . . . sensation": Follows William Battie, *A Treatise on Madness* (London, 1758), 17, perhaps to suggest that the character is based on Battie, perhaps to satirize Battie's position on this topic. Richard A. Hunter and Ida Macalpine claim that Smollett reviewed Battie's book in *Critical Review* 4 (1757): 509–16; see "Smollett's Reading in Psychiatry," *Modern Language Review* 51 (1956): 409–11. The review is mostly positive but singles out the passage in question as incomprehensible. The idea of "a weakness of the nerves" was common. See also chap. 16, n. 4.

24. "Dick Distich": The satirist Charles Churchill (1731–64). The joke depends in part on the transformation of the stocky and unattractive Churchill, Hogarth's "Bruiser" (see *Hogarth's Graphic Works*, 415), into the "tall, thin" (and unattractive) Distich, who, like Churchill, was thirty in 1761. See Alan D. McKillop, "Notes on Smollett," *Philological Quarterly* 7 (1928): 371–74. "Distich," or couplet, is an appropriate name for Churchill, who, like Pope (whom he quotes), wrote in rhymed couplets. Pope had used the name "Dick Distich" as an autobiographical figure in his description of the Club of Little Men; see *Guardian*, 26 June 1713.

25. "Ben Bullock": Churchill's friend Robert Lloyd, the beginning of whose surname appears in the middle of Bullock's. See also nn. 26–30 below.

26. "his ode to me beginning with 'Fair blooming youth'": Lloyd nowhere uses this exact phrase (the notion of the huge Churchill as a "blooming youth" is comic), but the cliché "blooming youth" appears in the chorus and at the conclusion of his *Arcadia; or, The Shepherd's Wedding* (London, 1761), 19–20. In 1761 Lloyd wrote an "Epistle to C. Churchill: Author of the Rosciad" and "The Poet: An Epistle to C. Churchill."

27. "We were sworn brothers . . . and quoted each other": Churchill's poem *Night*, addressed to Lloyd, appeared in October 1761; volume 2, number 10 of the *British Magazine*, in which this chapter first appeared, was published 2 November 1761. "Rural Happiness: An Ode to R—— L——, Esq" (1751) has been attributed to Churchill. Lloyd would express his admiration for Churchill in *The Whim* (1764 [?], ll. 127, 171–72). See also n. 26 above.

28. "we denounced war against all the world, actors, authors, and critics": "Denounced" means "announced" (*OED*). The main references are to Churchill's *The Rosciad* (1761), which attacked Garrick and other actors; Churchill's *The Apology: Addressed to the Critical Reviewers* (1761), which attacked Smollett and his journalists; Lloyd's "The Actor" (1760); and Lloyd's and George Colman's *Two Odes* (1760): "To Oblivion," a parody of William Mason, and "To Obscurity," a parody of Thomas Gray.

29. "the Bœotian band of Thebes": The Boeotian League, formed c. fifth century B.C., was located in "a country of so gross and heavy an air, as to render the extreme stupidity of its inhabitants proverbial" ("Pindar," in *A New and General Biographical Dictionary* [London, 1762]). Churchill and Lloyd were affiliated with a group called the Nonsense Club.

30. "kennel": Gutter; an open sewer or drain. This may be an allusion to Arthur Murphy's *An Ode to the Naiads of Fleet Ditch* (1761), a satire on Churchill and to a lesser extent Lloyd, to which Lloyd responded. Murphy's poem echoes Pope's *Dunciad* (1728; 1744), which Distich quotes immediately below.

31. "He vig'rous rose . . . stunk along": See *The Dunciad* (1728), 2.97–98.

32. "when I was drunk": Churchill, though a clergyman, was well known for his dissipation.

33. "*Qui me commorit . . . cantabitur urbe*": "But if one stir me up ('Better not touch me!' I shout), he shall smart for it and have his name sung up and down the town" (Horace *Satires* 2.1.45–46, H. Rushton Fairclough translation).

34. "reviled as ignorant dunces several persons . . . allowed to have genius": See, for example, Churchill's attack on Smollett's critical skills in *The Apology* (ll. 298–99, 302–5).

35. "those whom Pope lashed . . . personal attack": Pope's own reiterated belief, which Smollett probably endorsed. Smollett thought himself in a position like Pope's; his early satires *Advice* and *Reproof* (1748) are Popean in form and conception. In *Pres-*

ent State, Smollett asserted that "the satire and epistles of Pope as yet are unequalled" (2:227).

36. "his French pattern Boileau": Nicholas Boileau-Despréaux (1636–1711); his *Le
Lutrin* (1674–83) influenced Pope's *Rape of the Lock*; his *L'Art poétique* (1674) influenced Pope's *Essay on Criticism* (1711).

37. "Quinault, Perrault, and the celebrated Lulli": Frequent objects of Boileau's satire:
Philippe Quinault (1635–88), poet, satirist, dramatist, and librettist for Jean-
Baptiste Lully (Giovanni Battista Lulli, 1632–87), an Italian who became the foremost composer of French Baroque opera; Charles Perrault (1628–1703), poet,
critic, and author of fairy tales.

38. "apply for a committee": Apply for a commission of lunacy; see chap. 13, n. 2.

39. "Bastile in France . . . Inquisition in Portugal": The French prison was notoriously
a repository for people incarcerated at the behest of the nobility; for the British,
the inquisition in Portugal and Spain exemplified Catholic religious intransigence.

40. "a private mad-house in England": Such establishments operated in the homes of
doctors who cared for the insane; for early criticism, see Daniel Defoe, *Augusta
Triumphans* (London, 1728), and Alexander Cruden, *The London-Citizen Exceedingly Injured; or a British Inquisition Display'd* (London, 1739). In 1763 Charles
Townshend became chair of a parliamentary committee to investigate them, particularly with respect to their incarceration of the sane, Sir Launcelot's concern
here. The Act for Regulating Madhouses was passed in 1774. See Ida Macalpine
and Richard Hunter, *George III and the Mad-Business* (New York: Pantheon, 1979),
chap. 23.

41. "party-wall": "A wall between two buildings or pieces of land intended for distinct
occupation, in the use of which each of the occupiers has a partial right" (*OED*).

42. "turtle's": Turtledove's.

43. "Philomel's love-warbled song": The song of the nightingale. See, for example,
Ovid, *Metamorphoses* 6, for the rape of Philomela and her transformation into this
bird.

44. "Lychas, whom Hercules in his frenzy destroyed": Poisoned by the cloak of the
centaur Nessus, Hercules threw his servant Lichas, who had brought it to him,
into the sea. See, for example, Ovid, *Metamorphoses* 9.

Chapter 24

1. "no person has a right to treat me as a lunatic": See chap. 8, n. 11. Sir Launcelot,
however, has not been legally apprehended.

2. "I have a right . . . to be tried by a jury": Sir Launcelot has in mind the provisions
of habeas corpus; see chap. 11, n. 16. The lord chancellor had "the King's absolute
Power to moderate the written Law, governing his Judgment by the Law of Nature
and Conscience" (*NLD*, "*Chancellor*"). See also n. 18, below.

3. "Golden-square": See chap. 20, n. 2.

4. "Upper Brook-street": Off Grosvenor Square in Mayfair (see chap. 19, n. 20).

5. "Queen-street": East of Saint Paul's in east-central London, extending south of Cheapside, a major shopping district where porters would be found easily, to Southwark Bridge.

6. "Daily Advertiser": Founded in 1730, the newspaper published a range of such notices.

7. "a Sallee Rover on the coast of Barbary": A Moroccan pirate ship on the North African coast; the Salee Rovers issued from the harbor of the city of Salé.

8. "two glasses ago": An hour ago. See chap. 18, n. 8.

9. "started": Poured, as from one vessel into another (*OED*).

10. "Mrs. Kawdle": The character and her husband, Dr. Kawdle, introduced in the subsequent paragraph, are named for "caudle," a medicinal drink of thin gruel and wine or ale.

11. "undress": Informal dress.

12. "writ of conspiracy": "Writ available, upon acquittal, to a person conspired against with the intention of procuring false indictment; if conspiracy is proved, the perpetrators may be punished accordingly." See *NLD*, "*Conspiracy*." Sir Launcelot has not been indicted falsely.

13. "dishabille": See chap. 7, n. 11.

14. "bays": Possibly "baize," but it suggests a crown of laurel leaves, signaling superior poetic accomplishment.

15. "cordwainer": Shoemaker.

16. "keen iambicks": Harsh satire, from the foot preferred in Greek and Latin satiric verse.

17. "genever": Gin; from juniper, the berry from which it is made.

18. "protection of the lord-chancellor": The lord chancellor is de facto guardian of a child from the death of a father until the election of a guardian. See *NLD*, "Guardian"; and see n. 20 below.

19. "the dead palsy": A stroke producing complete insensibility or immobility.

20. "choose another guardian . . . minority": The form for "an *Election of a Guardian* by a Minor" requires the minor to be about eighteen years old and to choose a guardian to serve until she turns twenty-one; see *NLD*, "*Guardian*." Aurelia is twenty years old.

21. "*pro tempore*": For the time; temporarily.

Chapter the Last

1. "A judicial writ *ad inquirendum*": "A Judicial Writ, commanding Enquiry to be made of any Thing relating to a Cause depending in the King's Courts. It is granted upon many Occasions for the better Execution of Justice" (*NLD*, "Ad Inquirendum").

2. "writs of *capias, alias, & pluries* . . . outlawry": These writs are pursued successively

if a party summoned before the court on an original writ fails to appear. Each allowed fifteen days; if the third were not returned, the defendant was outlawed. In effect, this means that all goods and chattels were forfeited to the king and that the sheriff could kill the felon on sight. See *NLD*, *"Alias," "Capias," "Pluries," "Outlaw," "Outlawry."*

3. "the Seven Dials": Seven streets radiating from what is now the intersection of Monmouth and Mercer Streets in west-central London. Seven sundials were located there on a column; a reconstruction now stands.

4. "the devil and the deep sea": Taylor (88) lists this phrase as proverbial. He notes that Smollett's usage "suggests an allusion to a familiar story or scene" and adds that "the parallels do not ordinarily refer to a man in this situation." See also Tilley, D222; *ODEP*, 179.

5. "negromancer": Necromancer, one who communicates with the dead.

6. "Albumazar": Abu-Mashar Jafar ibn Mohammed (805?–85), Arabian astronomer, protagonist of the comedy *Albumazar* by Thomas Tomkis (1615), adapted by James Ralph (1744) and Garrick (1747). The name is used generically for an astrologer in, for example, William Congreve, *Love for Love* (1695, 2.5); and chapter 91 of *Peregrine Pickle*.

7. "bring you up by the head . . . abaft the beam": Bring you to a stop (to anchor) alongside the forepart of my ship, despite the strength of a wind from behind the stern.

8. "bilboes": Bolts and shackles from steel made in Bilbao, used by the Spanish to confine prisoners' legs.

9. "a state of nature . . . devouring one another": In part 1, chapter 13 of *Leviathan* (1651), Thomas Hobbes (1588–1679) presented the "state of nature" as a condition in which "every man is enemy to every man" (ed. Michael Oakeshott [Oxford: Basil Blackwell, 1946], 82). The villainous Ferdinand Count Fathom subscribes to the idea that "the sons of men preyed upon one another, and such was the end and condition of their being" (chapter 10, p. 42). In chapter 22 of *Roderick Random*, Miss Williams becomes a prostitute after reading various philosophers, including Hobbes.

10. "sent to Bridewell as an impostor": See chap. 2, n. 31 and chap. 22, n. 9.

11. "fish my topmasts! . . . reeved": A reeved rope has been passed through a pulley; the action described concerns attaching a piece of wood to the masts to form a makeshift gallows.

12. "Hobby-hole in Yorkshire": Hambridge (99) notes the similarity of the names of several estates listed in Thomas Langdale, *Topographical Dictionary of Yorkshire* (Northallerton: J. Langdale, 1809), for example, Helaby-Hall, Hobberley-House, and Holley-Hall. But "Hobby-hole," which suggests a small and mean place fit for farm horses, need have no original.

13. "clandestine marriage": Shebbeare had written a novel, *The Marriage Act* (1754), against the Act of 1753, designed to prevent clandestine marriages. Although

Smollett supported the Act, he thought its terms harsh and to some extent "ineffectual" (*Complete History*, 2 : 471).

14. "a *covert femme*": A married woman who required her husband's consent for any such transaction; see *NLD*, "*Coverture*."

15. "alienation": The "Transferring the Property of a Thing to another: It chiefly relates to Lands and Tenements" (*NLD*).

16. "intail": See chap. 1, n. 27.

17. "negligee": See chap. 3, n. 15.

18. "Golconda": A deserted city of Hyderabad, India, proverbial for the wealth it had attained through diamond mining and cutting.

19. "a white coat and blue sattin vest": White and blue were British colors, in some contexts associated with Tories. See chap. 9, n. 1.

20. "bag-wig *a la pigeon*": A bagwig was a "man's wig in which the tail or queue was enclosed in a bag of black satin or silk. . . . The open end of the bag was enclosed around the top of the queue by a drawstring that was concealed beneath a stiff black decorative bow." A pigeon's wing periwig was "a man's wig dressed with two horizontal rolls above the ears." See J. Stevens Cox, *Illustrated History of Hairdressing and Wigmaking* (London: Hairdressers' Technical Council, 1966), 21, 118.

21. "lutestring": Or "lustring," a silk taffeta dress with a glossy sheen.

22. "turned methodists": Another similarity to *Tom Jones*, in which the villain Blifil converts to Methodism at the conclusion (bk. 18, chap. 13).

23. "match with her own brother": Compare Joseph and Fanny in *Joseph Andrews* (bk. 4, chap. 15). The threat of incest has a long history in comedy.

24. "corporation": See chap. 3, n. 52.

25. "marriage-favours": "Knots of white ribbons or bunches of white flowers worn at weddings" (*OED*).

26. "epithalamium": A lyric poem in celebration of a wedding, originally intended to be sung outside the bridal chamber.

TEXTUAL COMMENTARY

PUBLICATION HISTORY

Early advertisements for the first number of the *British Magazine; or, Monthly Repository for Gentlemen and Ladies* began to run in the *London Chronicle* for 18–20 December 1759 and continued in the issues for 20–22, 22–25, and 25–27 December. Similar notices appeared in the *Whitehall Evening-Post, Lloyd's Evening Post*, the *Universal Chronicle*, the *Daily Advertiser*, and *Jackson's Oxford Journal*. The *Daily Advertiser* noted that the first sixpenny number of the magazine, "for January 1760," was published on 1 January 1760 by James Rivington and James Fletcher Jr. at the Oxford Theatre and Henry Payne at Dryden's Head; both establishments were in Paternoster Row, London. Contrary to the norms of periodical publishing, the editor rather than the booksellers controlled the contents and probably owned a majority interest in the copyright. Smollett's proprietary role in the *British Magazine* is clear from a royal license of 18 January 1760, which cost him at least £6 7s. 6d. and prevented anyone else from reprinting, abridging, or publishing the contents for fourteen years.[1] The license also publicly declared Smollett the editor; reprinting its text on the outer blue wrappers of the second, third, fifth, and sixth numbers of the magazine was intended to boost sales as much as to intimidate potential plagiarists.

Although he controlled the *British Magazine*, Smollett evidently was not sole owner of its copyright; however, details of the business arrangements behind the periodical's production remain unknown, except for one record of partial ownership by a bookseller. A trade sale catalog of 1764 shows that George Kearsly offered at his bankruptcy auction all or part of his copyright shares in the *British Magazine*. These were split into two lots, one of one-sixteenth share and the other of one-forty-eighth share. There are no marginal notes in the catalog to indicate that either lot found a buyer, and it is not known when Kearsly purchased his shares.[2] His fractional shares in 1764 do suggest that there could have been as few as four shares offered originally in the *British Magazine* or possibly as many as eight or even sixteen. Smollett, of course, probably controlled a sufficient number of shares to give him a majority voice in the periodical's governance. Other probable partners in the magazine were the printer Archibald Hamilton Sr., and the booksellers James Rivington and James Fletcher Jr.; Henry Payne and William Cropley; John Coote; John

Newbery; and Richard Baldwin Jr. Among the booksellers, Kearsly, Coote, Newbery, and Baldwin were not named in the magazine's imprint; but along with Fletcher, Payne, and Cropley, they advertised their publications on the outer wrappers of the monthly numbers of the *British Magazine*, a practice indicative of their connection with the periodical.[3] Three of the probable partners—Rivington, Fletcher, and Hamilton—had worked together with Smollett on other endeavors, most notably, his immensely successful *Complete History of England*. The second edition of that work, revised by Smollett and published in sixpenny numbers in 1758, brought Rivington and Fletcher over £10,000 in gross profits.[4]

After such a triumph it would have been surprising if the booksellers had not been eager to collaborate with Smollett in his new periodical. According to a rebus in the April 1760 number of the *British Magazine*, Archibald Hamilton Sr. was the printer, and he served in that capacity at least through December 1761, as demonstrated by the rows of ornamental type flowers that recur in successive monthly numbers of the magazine during that period.[5] Rivington and Fletcher, on the other hand, having launched the *British Magazine* along with Henry Payne on 1 January 1760, were bankrupt by 3 January.[6] Immediately, Payne took over as sole publisher, according to a change of names in the magazine's imprint in the advertisement carried by the *Daily Advertiser* for 3 January. Payne, joined by his partner, William Cropley, in July 1760, published the *British Magazine* until July 1761, when James Fletcher Jr. returned to business in partnership with his father, a well-known Oxford bookseller who remained in that city while his son opened a new shop at the Oxford Theatre in St. Paul's Churchyard. The younger Fletcher took over publication of the *British Magazine* from Payne and Cropley, and his name appeared on the title page of each succeeding volume until the magazine's demise in 1767.[7]

Physically, the first number of the *British Magazine* reflects the difficulties that beset Smollett and his booksellers in January 1760. Originally, Rivington and Fletcher and Payne included with the first number an engraved title page with their three names in the imprint.[8] Subsequently, however, Payne had a replacement title page engraved, bearing his name alone. The January number also exists in two settings, designated *a* and *b*, *a* being the earlier.[9]

The only number of the first two volumes of the *British Magazine* ever reprinted was the first. Evidently, Payne ordered the February 1760 number and subsequent numbers printed in large enough quantities to meet the demands of readers. It is not known how many copies of the *British Magazine* were printed monthly through 1761, but in 1758 William Strahan printed five thousand copies of the *Grand Magazine* each month, and in the following two years the figures fluctuated monthly from a high of six thousand to a low of three thousand just before that periodical's demise in 1760.[10] Monthly press runs of the *British Magazine* may also have reached five thousand copies.

Readers may have complained about the schedule of publication followed by Smollett's miscellany. Most magazines came out at the end of the month, but each of the first four numbers of the *British Magazine* was published at the beginning of the month for which it was designated. Such a plan went against convention and meant that the foreign and domestic news or "intelligence" reported in the *British Magazine* was always one month older than readers would expect. Bowing to demand, Smollett and his booksellers "added" an extra number—designated "No. V"—between the numbers for April and May 1760. According to the *Daily Advertiser*, this number was published on 1 May 1760, and all later numbers then fell into place at or near the beginning of the month. Consequently, the first volume of the *British Magazine* comprised thirteen numbers, and the second volume, twelve. See page 301.

The Life and Adventures of Sir Launcelot Greaves was first offered to the public in the *British Magazine* in twenty-five monthly installments, each a chapter in length, from January 1760 through December 1761 (the last chapter appearing on 1 January 1762, according to the *Daily Advertiser*). Little is known of the circumstances surrounding Smollett's composition of the novel, but it has long been assumed that he wrote it piecemeal over the two-year period during which it first appeared.[11]

Soon after *Sir Launcelot Greaves* had finished running serially, at least two of the probable shareholders in the *British Magazine*, and possibly Smollett as well, decided to have the novel produced in book form for its second edition. Beginning on 11 March 1762, less than three months after the final chapter appeared in the magazine, advertisements in the *London Chronicle* announced the forthcoming publication of the novel in two duodecimo volumes.[12] On 31 March the book appeared, and the advertisement was updated:

> This Day was published, In Two Volumes in Twelves. Price 5s. sewed, or 6s. bound THE ADVENTURES of Sir LAUNCELOT GREAVES. By the Author of RODERICK RANDOM. Printed for J. Coote in Pater-noster-row; and G. Kearsly in Ludgate-Street.[13]

The publishers of this edition were John Coote and George Kearsly; although both names were included in the *London Chronicle* notices, Coote's alone appeared on the title page of the book, probably because he held a major share of the copyright.[14] Details of any transfer of copyright from Smollett and possibly other partners in the *British Magazine* to these two men, who themselves were involved in ownership of the periodical, are unknown.[15] It is doubtful whether Smollett retained any part of the property; his concern seems to have been restricted to publishing the novel serially, although he was responsible for at least one of the revisions in the second London edition.

Despite the optimism of Coote and Kearsly that a two-volume edition of *Sir Launcelot Greaves* would attract buyers, the second edition was not popular; it was, in fact, the only London edition in book form published during Smollett's lifetime. By 1769 Coote and Kearsly apparently had sold the copyright, along with all remaining copies of the second edition, to George Robinson and John Roberts, who advertised the novel in the *London Chronicle* beginning in late February of that year.[16] Robinson also brought out a third edition of *Sir Launcelot Greaves*; dated 1774 on the title page, it was in fact first advertised in the *London Chronicle* for 25–28 February 1775.[17] There is no clear reason for any delay in publication, unless perhaps the unnamed editor had been unexpectedly slow in revising the text. Smollett had died in September 1771, but he himself may earlier have had opportunity to edit it: as Robinson had probably purchased the copyright by 1769 and subsequently designated the third edition "a new edition, corrected," he could have asked the author to revise the novel. However, Smollett was not the editor who undertook the work; the edition is, in the words of Albert Smith, "nothing more than a reprint, in which little is corrected and a fairly large number of errors are introduced."[18] It is likely that Robinson paid an unidentified corrector; the surviving documents in the George Robinson Archive prove that he often paid for revisions of later editions of the works he published.[19]

Three Irish editions of the novel were published during Smollett's lifetime, but none of their texts is demonstrably authoritative. James Hoey Jr. brought out two one-volume Dublin editions, one appearing in late January 1762 and the other, despite a date of 1763 on the title page of the few extant copies, probably in June 1762. A third Irish edition was published at Cork in 1767.[20]

EDITORIAL PRINCIPLES

The autograph manuscript for *Sir Launcelot Greaves* no longer exists. In fact, no printer's copy for any of Smollett's works has survived. The nature of the manuscript can only be deduced from letters, never intended for publication, and from an examination of the manuscript revisions that the author made in a copy of the 1766 first edition of *Travels through France and Italy* for a new edition of that work that did not appear.[21] The revisions for the *Travels* include additions, translations of passages in foreign languages, and corrections to the printed text. It might be argued that Smollett, by the mid-1760s largely free from his numerous editorial tasks, had new leisure to correct the *Travels;* but an examination of other works he saw through the press shows much the same care, for he left uncorrected only the kinds of errors that none but the most exacting proofreaders might have caught.[22]

The revisions to the *Travels* are written in Smollett's neat hand, which, after more than two centuries, can be read with ease. A compositor, then, would have had no difficulty reading the author's manuscript of *Sir Launcelot Greaves*, but in the process of setting the type an overlay of normalization no doubt occurred. As John Smith notes in *The Printer's Grammar* (1755), "By the Laws of Printing, indeed, a Compositor should abide by his Copy, and not vary from it. . . . But this good Law is now looked upon as obsolete, and most Authors expect the Printer to spell, point, and digest their Copy, that it may be intelligible and significant to the Reader; which is what a Compositor and the Corrector jointly have regard to, in Works of their own language." The compositor peruses his copy, but, before beginning to compose, "should be informed, either by the Author, or Master, after what manner our work is to be done; whether the old way, with Capitals to Substantives, and Italic to Proper names; or after the more neat practice, all in Roman, and Capitals to proper Names and Emphatical words," and nothing "in Italic but what is underscored in our Copy." When composing from printed copy and "such Manuscripts as are written fair," Smith continued, "[we] employ our eyes with the same agility as we do our hands; for we cast our eyes upon every letter we aim at, at the same moment we move our hands to take it up; neither do we lose our time in looking at our Copy for every word we compose; but take as many words into our memory as we can retain."[23] Since *Sir Launcelot Greaves* and the *Travels* are printed in the new way, numerous changes must have occurred between each manuscript and its respective printed magazine serial or book, including some normalization of spelling.

In the lengthy manuscript additions to Letter 11 of the *Travels*—the English translation of a Latin letter to Antoine Fizes and of the professor's reply in French—Smollett followed the old practice, though somewhat inconsistently, of capitalizing nouns and some adjectives. Schooled to capitalize substantives, he continued in his habitual way.[24] But he certainly knew that his capitalization and his use of the ampersand for "and" would be brought into conformity with the rest of the book. He seems to have accepted this styling by the printer, or at least to have acquiesced in it. In the printed text of the

Travels, he corrected such small matters as a transposed letter, "muscels" (the bivalve mollusk) to "muscles," and "affords" to "afford." At the same time he allowed to stand variant spellings such as "paltry" and "paultry," "ake" and "ach," and so on. Smollett was not consistent in his spelling, although he did have a preferred spelling for some words; but the compositors, having taken as many words into their memories as they could retain, sometimes introduced their own preferences. Smollett appears to have been content with compositorial changes in spelling as long as they were correct, and he did not attempt to restore his own capitalization and punctuation.

The first edition of *Sir Launcelot Greaves*, the magazine serial, probably printed from Smollett's lost autograph manuscript and perhaps at least in part seen through the press by the author, is the only authoritative text and has been chosen as copy-text for this edition. The first edition contains relatively few errors, indicating that Smollett may have corrected proof; evidence from the publication histories of his earlier works shows that Smollett habitually read proof as his works were going through first printings.[25] He was in London during much of the time that the serial was running in the *British Magazine* and so would have had opportunity to make corrections. However, he also traveled to Scotland in the summer of 1760 and possibly to Ireland in the summer of the following year; his movements from July to October 1761 have not been documented.[26] Exactly how many chapters of the serial he saw through the press cannot be known. No solid evidence exists that Smollett knew or communicated with the Irish printer and bookseller James Hoey Jr., who was responsible for the two Dublin editions of *Sir Launcelot Greaves* in 1762. The January edition was set from the first edition, and the June edition was set from the January edition. The first of the two Dublin editions corrects some errors and introduces others; it also provides full names for the three members of the Sublime Society of Beefsteaks praised by Smollett in chapter 4. However, evidence that these editions are authoritative is inadequate, and readings from them have not been included in the textual apparatus. An Irish edition published in Cork in 1767 was based on Hoey's second Dublin edition.

The author's role in preparing the second London edition for the press seems to have been minimal. Smollett, typically, was toiling at a number of projects during 1761 and 1762: he edited part of Voltaire's *Works;* contributed to the *Critical Review;* edited the *British Magazine;* worked on his *Continuation of the Complete History;* and, of course, during 1761 continued to provide installments of *Sir Launcelot Greaves.*[27] After the serial was completed in December 1761, he may have had an opportunity to consider revising the novel, but by early 1762 his health had begun to decline. In January of that year he apologized to David Garrick for the "inconveniencies arising from ill-health"; and in late March, just as the second edition of *Sir Launcelot Greaves* was being published, he wrote to John Wilkes: "I have been ill these three months."[28] Thus reasons for limiting his revision of the novel could be traced to the pressure of his other labors or to his poor health, or both.

Compositors, paid according to the amount of type they set, in general were not interested in emendation and improvement. They normally followed their copy with some care since they knew they would be penalized for failing to do so. Hence, the normal assumption is that substantive revisions are authorial. An alert compositor or proofreader might have corrected typographical errors such as "Enlishman" to "Englishman" (chapter 9, 71.36), "engagment" to "engagement" (chapter 19, 146.3), or "strenously" to "strenuously" (chapter 22, 172.10). On the other hand, revisions such as "unextinguished" to "undistinguished" (chapter 1, 4.16), "cased in" to "eased with" (chapter 2, 13.20), or "hairs" to "ears" (chapter 25, 196.16) appear to be more than compositorial. Their respective contexts make plain, however, that they are not authorial. Indeed, these clumsy alterations to the text, coupled with the failure to correct such obvious errors from the first edition as "seamen" for "seaman" (chapter 7, 61.2) and "you . . . my kiss my——" (chapter 19, 151.19–20) argue that Smollett was not responsible for revisions in the second edition.

One emendation, however, does appear to be authorial. The heading to chapter 19, which in the first edition is "*Discomfiture of the Knight of the Griffin,*" has been revised in the second to "*The atchievements of the knights of the Griffin and Crescent.*" The original heading destroyed suspense concerning the outcome of the chapter; the later one restores it. Smollett had been concerned with the maintenance of suspense in all the other chapter headings to the novel. Apparently, sometime before the publication of the second edition, he realized that this heading was anomalous and so modified it.[29]

In the present edition no attempt has been made to achieve a general consistency in spelling, punctuation, or capitalization, because in the absence of the manuscript one cannot determine whether Smollett or the compositor was responsible for their variations. Hence the spelling, punctuation, and capitalization of the 1760–61 first edition have been retained except when they are clearly in error, or when they obscure meaning or distract the attention of the reader. All emendations to the copy-text have been made on the authority of the textual editor. Hyphenated words at a line-end have been adjusted according to the usual practice of the first edition insofar as that practice could be ascertained from other appearances or parallels. Only the following changes have been made silently: all turned letters or wrong fonts have been corrected, the long *s* has been replaced by the modern letter *s*, the abbreviation "Chap." has been expanded to "Chapter" in headings, and the display capitals that begin the first paragraph in each chapter have not been exactly reproduced. Conventions reminding readers that the work was originally a serial have been omitted; these include repetition of the novel's full title that opens each chapter through chapter 5; the abbreviated title "SIR LAUNCELOT GREAVES. [*Continued.*]" that heads chapters 6 through 24; the closing announcement "SIR LAUNCE-LOT GREAVES. [*Concluded.*]" that heads the final chapter; and the recurrent promise "[To be continued.]" that immediately follows most chapters. Quotations have been indicated according to modern practice, and the punctuation in relation to the quotation marks has been normalized. The length of dashes and the space around them have also been normalized.

APPARATUS

A basic note in the list of emendations provides the page-line reference and the emended reading in the present text. Except for the silent alterations described above, every editorial change in the first edition copy-text has been recorded. Following the square bracket is the earliest source of emendation and the history of the copy-text reading up to the point of emendation. The historical collation follows the same form, except that after the square bracket is given the subsequent history of the substantive variants in the texts examined. This historical collation is confined to substantive variants in the first and second editions, whether these are emended first-edition readings or rejected unauthoritative readings. Emendations not found in the first two editions are marked "W" and are the responsibility of the present edition, whether they originated here or with a previous editor. A wavy dash (~) is substituted for a repeated word associated with pointing, and an inferior caret (ᴧ) indicates pointing absent in the present text or in one of the editions from which the variant was drawn. The form of the reading both to the right and the left of the bracket conforms to the system of silent alterations, and there is no record of any variations except for the instance being recorded. When the matter in question is pointing, for example, the wavy dash to the right of the bracket signifies only the substantive form of the variant, and any variation in spelling or capitalization has been ignored. Emendations from catchwords are indicated as *cw*. A (*c*) indicates the reading in the corrected state of the form and (*u*) the uncorrected state. A vertical stroke (|) indicates a line-end.

Some emendations and decisions to retain the copy-text reading are discussed in textual notes. All hyphenated compounds or possible compounds appearing at line-ends in the copy-text are recorded in the word-division list. The reader should assume that any word hyphenated at a line-end in the present text, but not appearing in this list, was broken by the modern typesetter.

COLLATION

The present edition, with the exception of chapter 1, has been printed from the copy of the first two volumes of the *British Magazine* in the Howard-Tilton Memorial Library, Tulane University (PR1134 .B75 Rare). Because the Tulane copy contains the *b* setting of the first chapter, which is the later, apparently unauthoritative setting, chapter 1 has been printed from the copy of the *British Magazine* in the Boston Public Library (PER. *7227.19 v.1 1760), which contains the *a* setting. The Boston Public Library copy was sight-collated against chapter 1 of the copies belonging to the Beinecke Library, Yale University (z17.297d/1); the Sterling Library, Yale University (Franklin 111 B77 1); and James G. Basker. The Basker copy was compared on the Lindstrand Comparator with the copy at the University of Texas at Austin (O52 B7776 Rare Books Col). No press variants were discovered. A photocopy of the Tulane University copy of setting *b* of chapter 1 was sight-collated against the copy at the Bodleian Library, Oxford University (Hope Adds 1158). No press variants were found. The Tulane University copy of chapters 2 and following was compared on the Lindstrand Comparator with the copies belonging to James G. Basker and the University of Texas at Austin, and a photocopy was sight-collated with the copies held by the Boston Public Library and the Beinecke Library, Yale University (microfilm). Eight press variants were found.[30] A copy of the 1762 second edition in the University of Illinois Library (X823 Sm7a) was compared on the Lindstrand Comparator with copies belonging to the University of Texas at Austin (Jerome Kern PR3694 L3 1762) and the University of Iowa (xPR3694 S5 1762). No press variants were found. The copy of the first edition at Tulane University was sight-collated against the copy of the second edition held by the University of Illinois.

Notes

1. See Lewis M. Knapp, *Tobias Smollett: Doctor of Men and Manners* (Princeton: Princeton University Press, 1949), 221, n. 3.
2. See British Library, Longman, "Booksellers' Trade Sale Catalogues, 1718–1768," No. 136, 16 October 1764, Lots 17, 18.

3. John Newbery in particular has long been associated with the establishment of Smollett's *British Magazine*, but beyond the wrapper advertisements there is no concrete evidence that he was a partner in it. The one-seventh share he reputedly owned in Smollett's periodical was actually a share in an earlier *British Magazine*, published from 1746 to 1751. The error occurs in Charles Welsh's 1885 account of Newbery. Welsh found evidence of a share in a "*British Magazine*" in a schedule of assets that Newbery had drawn up around 1746 or 1747 when he was settling with his creditors; however, when he consulted this schedule as an aid in compiling his appended "List of the Books Published by the Newberys from 1740 to 1800," Welsh confused the earlier magazine with the later and so was mistaken in reporting that "Newbery's seventh share in [Smollett's *British Magazine*] was worth £10, 10*s*. in the schedule of assets, when he made an arrangement with his creditors" (*A Bookseller of the Last Century* [London: Griffith, Farran, Okeden & Welsh, 1885], 33, 177).

4. William Strahan to David Hall, 7 January 1760, David Hall Papers, American Philosophical Society Library. For details indicating that gross profits from the sale of the *Complete History* did not necessarily translate into substantial profits for the booksellers, see Patricia Hernlund, "Three Bankruptcies in the London Book Trade, 1746–61: Rivington, Knapton, and Osborn," in *Writers, Books, and Trade: An Eighteenth-Century English Miscellany for William B. Todd*, ed. O M Brack Jr. (New York: AMS Press, 1994), 91, 117, n. 38.

5. See James G. Basker, *Tobias Smollett: Critic and Journalist* (Newark: University of Delaware Press, 1988), 189; Barbara Laning Fitzpatrick, "The Text of Tobias Smollett's *Life and Adventures of Sir Launcelot Greaves*, the First Serialized Novel" (Ph.D. diss., Duke University, 1987), 51, 55–56.

6. See Public Record Office, B4/16, f. 18.

7. See *London Chronicle*, 30 July–1 August 1761. An Irish agent, Peter Wilson, began advertising the *British Magazine* in the *Dublin Journal* for 8–11 March 1760; his name was not included in the London advertisements until the magazine's fifth number came out in late April (*Whitehall Evening-Post*, 29 April–1 May 1760). Wilson apparently knew little about the editorship of the *British Magazine:* the Dublin advertisement credited the periodical to "Thomas Smollett, M.D. and Others."

8. According to the advertisement in the *London Chronicle* for 18–20 December 1759, the first number of the *British Magazine* included the frontispiece; the title page is conjugate with the frontispiece and thus must have accompanied the January number.

9. The change in imprints and the two January settings were first noted by Albert Smith, who examined five copies of the first volume of the *British Magazine;* see "*Sir Launcelot Greaves:* A Bibliographical Survey of Eighteenth-Century Editions," *Library*, 5th ser., 32 (1977): 222–23, 235. Four of his copies displayed the Rivington and Fletcher and Payne title page and contained the *a* setting; one copy

included the Payne title page and contained the *b* setting. Given this evidence, Smith tentatively pronounced the *a* setting the earlier of the two, surmising that "presumably after the bankruptcy of Rivington and Fletcher, and possibly as late as the end of 1760, Payne discovered that not enough copies of the first number were available and made arrangements for a new edition" (225). Examination of fifteen copies of the January 1760 number (including the five seen by Smith) confirms that the *a* setting did indeed precede the *b* setting; furthermore, the date for the printing of the second edition of the January number can be narrowed down more precisely. Seven of the fifteen copies (University of London; Trinity College, Cambridge [1]; Trinity College, Cambridge [2]; National Library of Canada/Bibliothèque nationale du Canada [1]; Yale University [1], at the Beinecke Library; University of Texas at Austin; and James G. Basker) include the Rivington and Fletcher and Payne title page. Seven (British Library; Bodleian Library; National Library of Canada [2]; Yale University [2], at the Sterling Library; Folger Shakespeare Library; Tulane University; and Boston Public Library) include the Payne title page. One (National Library of Ireland) includes both. Twelve of the copies contain the *a* setting, and three (Bodleian, Folger, Tulane) contain the *b* setting. Since five of the *a* copies and all three of the *b* copies include the Payne title page, Payne must have substituted his title page for the original one while he still had copies of the *a* setting available. Internal evidence in the form of recurring rows of ornamental type flowers shows that the *b* setting could have been imposed as early as January 1760 but no later than April 1760 (Fitzpatrick, "The Text of Tobias Smollett's *Life and Adventures of Sir Launcelot Greaves*," 48–50). Perhaps by late January, Payne realized that the demand for the January number was exceeding his supply, and he had Hamilton reprint it; this second press run was probably one fourth the size of the first, based on the relative numbers of surviving copies of the two settings.

10. See Robert D. Harlan, "The Publishing of 'The Grand Magazine of Universal Intelligence and Monthly Chronicle of Our Own Times,'" *Papers of the Bibliographical Society of America* 59 (1965): 434.

11. For an account of the composition of the novel, see Introduction, xix–xxi.

12. *London Chronicle*, 9–11, 18–20 March 1762.

13. *London Chronicle*, 30 March–1 April 1762. The advertisement was repeated in the issues for 3–6 and 8–10 April.

14. No record of Coote's share of the copyright survives, but his probable ownership may be inferred. The appearance of his name following the words "printed for" in the book's imprint is the strongest evidence. Coote seldom if ever acted as a "trade publisher"; when an imprint claimed that a work was printed for him, this meant that Coote held some share of the property and was not merely lending his name to the property of another bookseller who wished to remain anonymous. For details of Coote's bookselling practices, see Barbara Laning Fitzpatrick, "J. Coote," in *The British Literary Book Trade, 1700–1820*, ed. James K. Bracken and Joel Silver,

Dictionary of Literary Biography, vol. 154 (Detroit: Gale Research, 1995), 57–65. George Kearsly offered for sale a one-third share of the second edition of *Sir Launcelot Greaves* at his bankruptcy auction on 16 October 1764 (Longman No. 136); presumably he already possessed this share when his name appeared in the newspaper advertisements in 1762. Coote, whose name preceded Kearsly's in the imprint carried in the advertisements and who thus may have held a majority interest in the property, owned either two thirds of the copyright or, possibly, one third, as Smollett himself could have retained a one-third share in the novel. However, Smollett usually sold the rights to all his novels except *Peregrine Pickle*. For payments that Smollett received for copyrights, see O M Brack Jr., Textual Commentary, *The Expedition of Humphry Clinker*, ed. Thomas R. Preston (Athens: University of Georgia Press, 1990), 450–51, n. 2.

15. Because surviving records are so scarce, little is known about ownership of magazine contents and about whether or not individual pieces could be considered as separate from property in the magazine as a whole.

16. *London Chronicle*, 28 February–2 March, 4–7, 11–14 March 1769. In the advertisement, for three new and six previously published books, Robinson and Roberts were apparently offering the second edition rather than a new edition of *Sir Launcelot Greaves*. As part of the terms for the purchase of the copyright, they probably would have received from Coote and Kearsly any remaining stock of the 1762 edition. Such had been the conditions for their purchase of a translation of Mme de Sévigné's *Letters*, one of the other old titles listed in the advertisement: according to a receipt in the George Robinson Archive, on 26 August 1767 Coote sold to Robinson and Roberts, for £100, three fourths of the copyright and 320 sets of the second edition of the *Letters*. No receipt for *Sir Launcelot Greaves* seems to have survived. The contents of the extant fragment of the Robinson archive are summarized in G. E. Bentley Jr., "Copyright Documents in the George Robinson Archive: William Godwin and Others 1713–1820," *Studies in Bibliography* 35 (1982): 67–110.

17. This advertisement was repeated in the issues for 4–7 and 11–14 March 1775.

18. Smith, "*Sir Launcelot Greaves:* A Bibliographical Survey," 232.

19. See Bentley, "Copyright Documents," 70.

20. Advertisements for the first Dublin edition commenced in the *Dublin Journal* for 26–30 January 1762 and appeared in five consecutive issues of the paper. Hoey promised a second edition in an advertisement in the *Dublin Journal* for 18–22 May 1762 and announced its publication in a series of advertisements that appeared consecutively in the same newspaper from 26 June to 24 July 1762. For a full discussion of the Irish editions published before 1800, see Fitzpatrick, "The Text of Tobias Smollett's *Life and Adventures of Sir Launcelot Greaves*," chap. 5.

21. This copy of the *Travels* is in the British Library, shelf mark C.45.d.20, 21. Apart from the manuscript revisions of the *Travels* and a relatively small number of ho-

lograph letters, little survives in Smollett's hand; see *The Letters of Tobias Smollett*, ed. Lewis M. Knapp (Oxford: Clarendon Press, 1970), xvi–xvii.

22. Smollett was content to make small changes because the *Travels*, written at a relatively slow pace, did not require the extensive stylistic revisions of the earlier works. In the works of his later career, revision seems to have been carried out before publication; by this time he was a more experienced writer. For discussion of the composition of the *Travels*, see Frank Felsenstein, Introduction, *Travels through France and Italy*, ed. Frank Felsenstein (Oxford: Oxford University Press, 1979), xxxv–xli.

23. John Smith, *The Printer's Grammar* (London, 1755), 199, 201–2, 209.

24. See Bertrand H. Bronson, *Printing as an Index of Taste in Eighteenth Century England* (New York: New York Public Library, 1958), 17.

25. See O M Brack Jr., "Toward a Critical Edition of Smollett's *Peregrine Pickle*," *Studies in the Novel* 7 (1975): 364, n. 12. There is no clear proof that Smollett was responsible for the numerous minor changes introduced to chapter 1 of *Sir Launcelot Greaves* when the January 1760 number of the *British Magazine* was reset. The only substantive change, the correction of "seamen" to "seaman" (3.27), could have been made by an attentive compositor. Following is a list of the differences between the two settings of chapter 1; readings from the *a* setting (Boston Public Library, Yale [1], Yale [2], Texas, Basker) appear on the left; readings from the *b* setting (Tulane, Bodleian) appear on the right. A wavy dash (~) is substituted for a repeated word associated with pointing, and an inferior caret (ᴧ) indicates pointing absent in the *b* setting but present in the *a* setting. A vertical stroke (|) indicates a line-end:

Mediterranean-trade	Mediterranean trade
seamen	seaman
fellow,	~ᴧ
Captain	captain
bottom-planks	bottom planks
Captain's	captain's
Captain	captain
bilander.—	~ᴧ—
to be a—ship	to be—a ship
lee-shore	lee shore
headland	head land
blood,	~ᴧ
whirligig.—	~ᴧ—
brotherᴧ—	~,—
a|year	a-|year
shore.—	~ᴧ—

a year	a- year
conveyancing-way	conveyancing way
in *tail*	*in tail*
foundering.—	~ ∧ —
government;	~,
party-writer	party writer
mouth,	~ ∧
cellar;	~:

26. See Knapp, *Tobias Smollett*, 228–30, 243. Smollett also spent three months— 28 November 1760 to about 23 February 1761—in the King's Bench Prison, but he could have read proofsheets while confined (Knapp, *Tobias Smollett*, 236).

27. See Knapp, *Tobias Smollett*, 244.

28. *Letters*, 103, 104.

29. For further discussion of this heading, see Barbara Laning Fitzpatrick, "The Revision of a Chapter Heading in Smollett's *Sir Launcelot Greaves:* Evidence from an Irish Edition," *Notes and Queries* 233 (1988): 184–87.

30. Chapters 19 and 23 (*British Magazine* 2 [June 1761] and 2 [October 1761]) exhibit press variants. Five copies of chapter 19 were textually collated (Tulane, Boston Public Library, Yale [1], Texas, Basker). Ten copies of chapter 23 were textually collated (Tulane, Boston Public Library, Yale [1], Texas, Massachusetts Historical Society [lacks sig. 3S1], Bodleian, University of London, Cambridge [1], Cambridge [2], Basker). Press variants are as follow: vol. 2, sig. 2Q3^r, p. 309.A.45 (chapter 19, 150.25) *uncorrected:* "Drama" (Tulane, Boston Public Library, Basker); *corrected:* "drama" (Texas, Yale [1]). Vol. 2, sig. 2Q3^r, p. 309.B.43 (chapter 19, 151.6) *uncorrected:* "demonstrete" (Boston Public Library, Yale [1]); *corrected:* "demonstrate" (Tulane, Texas, Basker). Vol. 2, sig. 3S1^v, p. 506.B.3 (chapter 23, 175.31–32) *uncorrected:* "hapily" (London, Texas); *corrected:* "happily" (Tulane, Boston Public Library, Cambridge [1], Cambridge [2], Bodleian, Yale [1], Basker). Vol. 2, sig. 3S1^v, p. 506.B.3 (chapter 23, 175.32) *uncorrected:* "juncture" (London, Texas); *corrected:* "time" (Tulane, Boston Public Library, Cambridge [1], Cambridge [2], Bodleian, Yale [1], Basker). Vol. 2, sig. 3S2^v, p. 508.B.23 (chapter 23, 180.4) *uncorrected:* "me ∧" (Tulane, Boston Public Library, Massachusetts Historical Society); *corrected:* "me," (London, Texas, Cambridge [1], Cambridge [2], Bodleian, Yale [1], Basker). Vol. 2, 3S3^r, p. 509.B.9 (chapter 23, 179.17) *uncorrected:* "who ask want" (Tulane, Boston Public Library, Massachusetts Historical Society); *corrected:* "those that ask" (London, Texas, Cambridge [1], Cambridge [2], Bodleian, Yale [1], Basker). Vol. 2, sig. 3S3^r, p. 509.B.12–13 (chapter 23, 179.18) *uncorrected:* "situa-|ation" (Tulane, Boston Public Library, Massachusetts Historical Society); *corrected:* "situa-|tion" (London, Texas, Cambridge [1], Cambridge [2], Bodleian, Yale [1], Basker). Vol. 2, sig. 3S3^v, p. 510.B.15 (chapter 23, 180.24) *uncorrected:* "instant" (Tulane, Boston Public Library, Massachusetts Historical

Society, London, Texas); *corrected:* "instantly" (Cambridge [1], Cambridge [2], Bodleian, Yale [1], Basker).

The textual editing of *Sir Launcelot Greaves* dates back over ten years, during which time I have relied on the help and encouragement of many people. Jerry C. Beasley, O M Brack Jr., Alexander Pettit, and Robert Folkenflik deserve notice in this regard, as do Richard Flanagan, Mignon Fahr, Stephanie Womble, and Jacquelyn Abby. Of the archivists and rare book librarians who aided me, I am grateful in particular to Elaine Smyth, Head, Rare Book Collections, Hill Memorial Library, Louisiana State University, who enabled me to collate at her institution rare volumes lent by the University of Illinois, the University of Iowa, the University of Texas at Austin, Tulane University, and James G. Basker. I wish also to express my gratitude to Sylvia V. Metzinger, Rare Books Librarian, Howard-Tilton Memorial Library, Tulane University; Joyce A. Banks, Rare Books and Conservation Librarian, National Library of Canada/Bibliothèque nationale du Canada; Charlotte A. Stewart, Director of Archives and Research Collections, Mills Memorial Library, McMaster University; and A. Katherine Swift, Keeper of Early Printed Books, Trinity College Library, Dublin. Further thanks are due the considerate archivists and librarians at the American Philosophical Society Library; the Beinecke Rare Book and Manuscript Library and the Sterling Library, Yale University; the Bodleian Library, Oxford; the Boston Public Library; the British Library; the Folger Library; the Free Library of Philadelphia; the Lilly Library, Indiana University; the University of London Library; the National Library of Ireland; the Public Record Office, London; and Trinity College Library, Cambridge. I wish to extend my deep appreciation to the reference and interlibrary loan staffs at the Perkins Library, Duke University, and the Long Library, University of New Orleans, and to acknowledge the careful work and cheerful attitude of my graduate research assistants at the University of New Orleans, Rosary Fazende and Dale Massey. Part of my research for this edition was supported by grants from the University of New Orleans Research Council and College of Liberal Arts Organized Research Fund; my thanks go to Dean Philip B. Coulter of the College of Liberal Arts and to Linda L. Blanton and John W. Cooke of the Department of English, University of New Orleans. For their encouragement, mentoring, and friendship, I am continuously grateful to George Walton Williams and Robin Myers. I owe my deepest gratitude to J. F. Fitzpatrick Jr., who has always patiently supported and sustained me.

LIST OF EMENDATIONS

[The following sigla appear in the textual apparatus of the Georgia Edition: 1 (the first edition; *British Magazine*, London, 1760–61; a [January 1760, setting 1, J. Rivington and J. Fletcher, and H. Payne]; b [January 1760, setting 2, H. Payne]), 2 (the second edition; London, J. Coote, 1762); W (the present edition).]

3.27	seaman] 1b seamen 1a
5.5	Captain):] W ~:) 1–2
6.22	before?] W ~. 1–2
6.32	cried] W cries 1–2
7.19	avast":] W ~:" 1–2
7.27	Christ's] W Christis 1–2
16.38	other).] W ~.) 1–2
20.12	tautology] 2 tautalogy 1
23.20	jolly,] W ~; 1–2
26.34	his father] 2 father 1
38.27	Sunday] 2 sunday 1
41.9	sir,] 2 ~ₐ 1
42.16	Ferret] 2 Ferrett 1
50.6	Rare] 2 rare 1
50.14	doctor,] W ~ₐ 1–2
50.16	mayn't] 2 may'nt 1
50.19	like,] 2 ~ₐ 1
50.36	saying,] 2 ~ₐ 1
51.27	church, towards] W ~. Towards 1–2
52.12	Maker] 2 maker 1

52.31   began] 2 begun 1

53.4   sexton,] 2 ~ₐ 1

53.14   brother,] W ~ₐ 1–2

59.7   itₐ] W ~, 1–2

59.21   &c.,] W ~.ₐ 1–2

60.22   conversable] 2 conversible 1

60.27   perils.] 2 ~: 1

61.2   seaman] W seamen 1–2

62.8   muleₐ] W ~, 1–2

62.9   knight);] W ~;) 1–2

62.15   knight);] W ~;) 1–2

62.18   Launcelot).] W ~.) 1–2

67.31   horses'] W ~ₐ 1–2

69.14   Pretender, an] W Pretender. An 1–2

71.36   Englishman] 2 Enlishman 1

77.33   *archæus*] W *archoeus* 1–2

79.35   captainₐ] 2 ~, 1

81.20   emotion).] W ~.) 1–2

81.24   wordsₐ——"] W ~".—— 1; ~"ₐ —— 2

81.26   layingₐ] W ~, 1–2

84.4   attorneys'] W ~ₐ 1–2

90.30   fellowₐ] W ~, 1–2

90.30   justice).] W ~.) 1–2

94.36   Oakely] W Oakley 1–2

98.15   restored.] 2 ~, 1

100.34   transport):] W ~:) 1–2

103.20	dogs'] W ~_∧ 1–2
104.12	ladies'] W ~_∧ 1–2
105.9	highway?] W ~. 1–2
105.31–32	cowardice.] 2 ~, 1
113.21	was inter- | mitted] 1(*cw*) was mitted 1(*text*)
115.23	emotion).] W ~.) 1–2
116.9	justice_∧] W ~, 1–2
116.9-10	replied):] W ~:) 1–2
116.22	madam_∧] W ~, 1–2
116.23	adventurer).] W ~.) 1–2
120.7	conveyance_∧] W ~, 1–2
120.7	Launcelot).] W ~.) 1–2
122.4	like_∧] W ~, 1–2
122.4-5	room-door).] W ~.) 1–2
127.12	borborygmata_∧] W ~, 1–2
127.13	physician).] W ~.) 1–2
127.16	alexipharmic] 2 alexipharmci 1
127.17	indeed_∧] W ~, 1–2
127.17	doctor);] W ~;) 1–2
128.1	sensibly. _∧ _∧Have] W sensibly." "Have 1–2
128.2	heart_∧] W ~, 1–2
128.2	physician).] W ~.) 1–2
128.8-9	fauces_∧] W ~, 1–2
128.9	apothecary):] W ~:) 1–2
134.25	farmers] W farmer 1–2
138.7	He] 2 he 1

139.24   very idea‸] W ~~. 1–2

139.25   Sycamore).] W ~.) 1–2

139.25   Your idea,] 2 ~‸ 1

139.37   Nay,] 2 ~‸ 1

139.39   you,] 2 ~‸ 1

140.4   Here,] 2 ~‸ 1

140.6   notes?] W ~. 1–2

140.6   Nay,] 2 ~‸ 1

140.7   All] W all 1–2

140.8   Come,] 2 ~‸ 1

140.38   words:] 2 ~. 1

141.6   however] 2 how- | wever 1

142.14   May-hap,] 2 ~‸ 1

142.16   stowage;] 2 ~, 1

142.26   Damn'd,] 2 ~‸ 1

142.26   goblins,] 2 ~‸ 1

142.35   names,] 2 ~‸ 1

143.4   When] W when 1–2

144.19   nay,] 2 ~‸ 1

145.2–3   *Containing the atchievements of the knights of the Griffin and
                Crescent.*] 2 *Discomfiture of the Knight of the Griffin.* 1

145.12   trumpeter] 2 trum- | puter 1

146.3   engagement] 2 engagment 1

149.11   what,] W ~‸ 1–2

150.15   mayn't] W may'nt 1–2

150.25   drama] 1(*c*) Drama 1(*u*)

151.10	Crowe] 2 Crow 1
151.18	couldn't] W coudn't 1–2
151.19	may kiss] W my kiss 1–2
155.21	resolved] 2 re- | solving 1
157.20	phlegmatic] 2 phegmatic 1
157.29	Crabclaw's] 2 Crabclaws's 1
158.17	be] W be be 1–2
161.25	uttered] 2 ut- | terred 1
162.37	Clarke's] W Clark's 1–2
163.3	For] 2 for 1
170.4	accent:] W ~; 1–2
170.29-30	be so bauld] 2 be bauld 1
172.1	fate?] W ~. 1–2
172.10	strenuously] 2 strenously 1
172.34	case,] 2 ~∧ 1
173.2	he∧)] 2 ~,) 1
175.32	juncture] 1(*u*) time 1(*c*), 2
178.14	youth'?] W ~.' 1–2
179.17	who ask and want it] W who ask want it 1(*u*); those that ask it 1(*c*); those who ask it 2
179.18	situation] 1(*c*) situa- | ation 1(*u*)
179.37	with∧] 2 ~, 1
182.31	for] W or 1–2
183.2	was] W was was 1–2
186.11	sigh∧)] 2 ~,) 1
186.33	he∧)] 2 ~,) 1

186.35   she_∧)] 2 ~,) 1

187.24   duration.—] 2 ~,—1

191.25   brother";] W ~;" 1–2

191.28   Crowe] 2 Crow 1

194.4   other extraneous] 2 extraneous 1

195.27   blush,] W ~_∧ 1–2

195.27   besides_∧] 2 ~, 1

196.31   instant,] 2 ~_∧ 1

196.39   kinswoman).] W ~.) 1–2

197.25   Oakely] W Oakley 1–2

94.36   Oakely] The spelling of "Oakely" has been regularized. The name appears only twice as "Oakley" (here and in Chapter the Last, 197.25); it appears thirteen times as "Oakely," indicating that Smollett preferred the latter spelling. Smollett also clearly preferred "Ferret" and "Clarke"; therefore, the single appearances of "Ferrett" (chap. 5, 42.16) and "Clark" (chap. 21, 162.37) have been emended. Names that appear infrequently and are variously spelled, such as "Bess Mizen" or "Mizzen," have not been regularized.

128.1   sensibly. Have] In the first two editions, during a scene in which Greaves, Crabshaw, a cynical physician, an ignorant apothecary, and a drunken nurse are all present in Crabshaw's sickroom, the line "Oh, he begins to talk sensibly" follows Crabshaw's announcement that he wishes the knight would throw the nurse and apothecary out of the room. It is not clear, however, who makes this comment. Immediately following it, the physician tells Crabshaw, "Have a good heart"; since he is contemptuous of Crabshaw's two inept attendants, the physician is likely the speaker of the unassigned sentence.

134.25 farmers] Five farmers lodge a complaint against Crowe. Four are identified by name as Prickle, Stake, Dolt, and Bumpkin. Presumably, Muggins is the fifth, in which case "farmer" should be plural. The singular form of the noun could have been a result of compositorial error or of Smollett's haste as he wrote.

145.2–3 *Containing the atchievements of the knights of the Griffin and Crescent.*] See Textual Commentary, 261.

175.32 juncture] Although the word "time" is in the corrected state, it is clear that Smollett intended the uncorrected word "juncture" to stand. In uncorrected copies of the *British Magazine*, the line containing "juncture" reads "hapily not suspended at this juncture." The words are crowded together, and the sentence period is placed at the right margin. When a compositor found it necessary to correct the spelling of "hapily," he saw that there was insufficient space to add the missing *p*. In order to make room in the line, he merely substituted a short synonym for "juncture" and so, he thought, solved his problem.

179.17   who ask and want it] When first printed, chapter 23 (gathering 3s, imposed for work and turn, in the October 1761 number of the *British Magazine*) contained an unusually high number of errors. Besides misspelling "happily" (175.32), the compositor who originally set the type failed to indent the paragraph beginning "Our adventurer . . ." (176.33), misread Smollett's manuscript so as to produce the nonsensical "who ask want it" (179.17), misspelled "situation" (179.18), and inserted a comma after the preposition "with" as though it were part of the series that follows it (179.37). This compositor was indeed muddled, but the man who corrected his errors introduced new problems. Early in the print-run he substituted "time" for "juncture" (175.32), and later he changed Smollett's poetic "instant" to the prosaic "instantly" (180.24). He also made his own sense of "who ask want it," dropping the second verb and altering the clause to "those that ask it." Lacking sensitivity to Smollett's text, he apparently perceived no connection between "pardon" and "ask," and "counsel" and "want," and he disregarded the plural pronoun "them" in the following line that clearly refers to both "your pardon and your counsel." As a result, he destroyed the balance Smollett had set up between asking pardon and wanting counsel.

WORD-DIVISION

I. LINE-END HYPHENATION IN THE GEORGIA EDITION

[The following compounds, hyphenated at a line-end in the Georgia Edition, are hyphenated within the line in the 1760–61 first edition.]

22.37	silk- | hose	103.18	knight- | errant
24.39	May- | day	109.20	good- | sense
26.36	wild- | fire	117.38	hool- | cheese
30.22	chimney- | corner	127.20	window- | shutters
33.13	Greavesbury- | hall	130.29	bread- | room
34.5	tender- | hearted	131.36	post- | boys
35.21	sea- | faring	137.9	good- | will
40.1	pre- | engaged	151.34	May- | fair
42.36	hour- | glass	154.31	fellow- | creatures
49.21	Ferry- | bridge	162.9	dram- | drinker
54.26	hawse- | holes	163.12	tea- | things
57.24	crazy- | peated	170.37	horse- | stealing
59.12,		175.5	iron- | gate
108.16	knight- | errantry	176.11	new- | light
60.7	glow- | worm's	180.18	fellow- | creatures
79.32	night- | cap	180.34	well- | nigh
80.17	public- | house	183.4	Golden- | square
98.20	new- | married	193.5	Hobby- | hole

2. LINE-END HYPHENATION IN THE
1760–61 FIRST EDITION

[The following compounds or possible compounds are hyphenated at a line-end in the first edition. The form in which each has been given in the Georgia Edition, as listed below, represents the usual practice of the 1760–61 first edition insofar as it may be ascertained from other appearances or parallels.]

4.30	market-town	26.37	bon-fires
6.3	day-light	29.31	headlong
7.15,		29.31	stone-quarry
28.1	overcast	30.10	horsewhip
7.34	pennyworth	31.3	gridiron
12.32	a-says	31.8	Merry-Andrew
13.9	tennis-ball	35.21	good-humour
13.12	sharp-pointed	36.8,	
16.32	blunderbusses	115.15,	
16.36,		164.2	overwhelmed
50.16,		40.39	landlords
134.10,		44.10	Drury-lane
145.8	highway	44.37	knight-errantry
19.10	feather-bed	45.23	grey-hound
19.17	snatch-block	45.27,	
19.32	chicken-hearted	50.10	forehead
23.1	churn-staff	45.38	day-break
23.3	hog-butcher	46.32	huntsman's
23.7	ploughmen	48.15,	
24.37	kissing-strings	80.27	highwaymen
25.6	holiday-garments	49.20	rib-roasted

50.5	sea-laugh	69.16	horsewhips
51.1	scull-cap	71.2	tradesman
51.16	god-father	71.9	copyholders
51.34,		71.31	parliament-men
154.31,		72.22	outlawed
192.4,		73.10	birth-right
198.3	fellow-creature	76.7	free-born
51.35	undertook	76.15	furze-bush
52.23	prayer-book	79.9	nostrum-monger
56.11	stair-case	80.6	hearkye
56.11	truckle-bed	80.10	round-top
56.12	bed-chamber	84.35	overstocked
56.29	midnight	85.23	ale-houses
62.14	cart-saddle	85.26	ill-qualified
62.17,		86.35	shop-keeper
163.3,		86.37,	
168.14	sea-faring	124.7	gentlewoman
62.33	fiddle-stick	87.14	ill-manners
64.4	wherefore	88.17	forthcoming
64.8	aspen-leaf	89.9	over-clean
66.1	undergone	89.24	upheld
66.16	curry-combed	93.14	moreover
66.30	outshone	93.38	low-bred
69.1	church-tower	95.5,	
69.11	market-place	97.4	landlady

98.7	ever-honoured	128.18	heart-whole
101.21	thoroughbred	129.9	pitch-forks
101.28	adds-bunt-lines	131.24	afterhold
101.31	knight-errant	131.26	clasp-knife
101.34	a-don't	131.33	tin-cap
102.5,		132.32	hand-spike
132.23	sweet-heart	133.7	look-out
102.11	northward	137.9	good-will
105.12	Moor-fields	143.14	wry-nose
108.21	pocket-book	146.33	eye-sight
108.32	post-boy	147.1	overthrown
112.36,		154.35	St. George's-fields
124.26	overtaken	155.5	chandlers-shops
117.9	overwhelm	157.3	outlived
117.13	downcast	157.20	short-winded
118.15	brother-in-law	157.37	well-nigh
118.33	overcharged	162.17	fellow-prisoners
118.39	gunpowder	167.16	newspapers
120.25	askance	167.29	public-house
121.11,		168.4	overcome
126.22,		168.30	fortune-teller
178.23	landlord	169.15	a-head
122.4	room-door	173.31	pawwawing
124.16	bare-heir	174.30	hackney-coach
126.37	a-year	175.15	to-morrow

175.18	double-lock	185.25	search-warrant
176.36,		186.38	over-rate
188.25	mad-house	192.25	weak-minded
177.10	breakfast	193.5	Hobby-hole
181.5	head-ach	194.24	marriage-bed
182.2	overpowered	194.24	bride-groom's
183.4	Golden-square	194.32	post-chariot
183.16	coachman	194.35	horsemen
183.19	master-coachman	195.12	mankind
184.8	brimfull	196.12	overjoyed
185.16	well-bred	197.20	fancy-knots

3. SPECIAL CASES

[The following compounds or possible compounds are hyphenated at a line-end in both the Georgia Edition and in the 1760–61 first edition.]

23.3	hog- | butcher	122.4	room- | door
23.7	plough- | men	137.9	good- | will
48.15	highway- | men	154.31	fellow- | creatures
56.11	truckle- | bed	183.4	Golden- | square
84.35	over- | stocked	193.5	Hobby- | hole

HISTORICAL COLLATION

3.27	seaman] seamen 2
4.4-5	and the orphan] and orphan 2
4.16	unextinguished] undistinguished 2
5.5	Captain):] ~:) 1–2
5.7	alow] allow 2
5.15	about with him] about him 2
5.33	upon] on 2
5.35	on] upon 2
6.21	2, 13] 2.13 2
6.21	I.] *omit* 2
6.22	before?] ~. 1–2
6.32	cried] cries 1–2
6.32	Ferret] Ferrett 2
6.38	after possibility] after a possibility 2
7.6-7	in *tail*] *in tail* 1
7.19	avast":] ~:" 1–2
7.27	Christ's] Christis 1–2
13.2	strutted out] strutted 2
13.9	contractor] contracter 2
13.17-18	by the marines] by marines 2
13.20	cased in] eased with 2
13.27	rolled his eyes] rolled about his eyes 2
15.23	extravagances] extravagancies 2

15.26　　　　traytor] trai- | tor 2

16.10　　　　complection] complexion 2

16.38　　　　other).] ~.) 1–2

17.28　　　　meer] mere 2

18.36　　　　compleat] complete 2

20.4　　　　*secundum artem*] *secundem artem* 2

20.12　　　　tautology] tautalogy 1

21.2　　　　Snug's] Snugg's 2

22.17　　　　increase] encrease 2

22.39　　　　milching] milking 2

23.20　　　　jolly,] ~; 1–2

25.15　　　　pretty,] ~ₐ 2

26.34　　　　his father] father 1

28.5　　　　should but barely] should barely 2

29.7　　　　who was hasty as] who was as hasty as 2

31.5　　　　reflection] reflexion 2

31.38　　　　hemms] hems 2

34.22　　　　your own father] your father 2

34.24　　　　dispensations] dispen- | sation 2

35.5-6　　　making further] making any further 2

35.14　　　　began to think] thought 2

35.18　　　　domestics] domesticks 2

35.28　　　　restrain] restain 2

35.33　　　　without taking effect] without any effect 2

35.36　　　　in the air] into the air 2

36.27　　　　of health] of his health 2

38.14	county] country 2
38.27	Sunday] sunday 1
38.36	on the grass] in the grass 2
39.6	tho'] though 2
39.15	fullness] fulness 2
40.12	*et*] *&* 2
40.33-34	this warning] the warning 2
40.34-35	this judge] his judge 2
41.9	sir,] ~∧ 1
41.20	naturally] naaturally 2
42.7	had not he] had he not 2
42.16	Ferret] Ferrett 1
43.28	saowl] saoul 2
43.29	soomething] something 2
44.23	chivalry!] ~? 2
44.24	lance] launce 2
44.27	it is not] is not 2
45.7	dismally.] ~? 2
45.29	got into] got in 2
46.31	encircled] incircled 2
46.35	with hardly any] hardly with any 2
47.10	tower] Tower 2
48.11	carcase] carcass 2
50.6	Rare] rare 1
50.14	doctor,] ~∧ 1-2
50.15	or a what] or what 2

50.16   mayn't] may'nt 2

50.19   like,] ~∧ 1

50.28   keeping reckoning] keeping a reckoning 2

50.36   saying,] ~∧ 1

51.12   chapel] chappel 2

51.21   fingers] fingres 2

51.27   should be keeping] should keep 2

51.27   church, towards] ~. Towards 1–2

51.31   seemed to have acquired] had acquired 2

51.34   meerly] merely 2

52.12   Maker] maker 1

52.17   on the top of the steeple] on the stee- | ple [cw] 2

52.19   still∧] ~, 2

52.19   had not power] had no power 2

52.31   began] begun 1

52.37   but that if] but if 2

53.4   sexton,] ~∧ 1

53.14   brother,] ~∧ 1–2

53.15   whistling black] whistling the black 2

53.20   noviciate] novitiate 2

53.24   can't] cannot 2

54.29   t'other] th'other 2

56.6   of the] in the 2

56.20   an] and 2

56.30   rencounter] en- | counter 2

57.2   dishabillé] dishabille 2

58.1	company conveyed] company had conveyed 2
58.8	lance] launce 2
59.7	it∧] ~, 1–2
59.21	&c.,] ~·∧ 1–2
59.36	disagreable] disagreeable 2
60.19	compleat] complete 2
60.22	conversable] conversible 1
60.27	perils.] ~: 1
61.2	seaman] seamen 1–2
61.16	exhorted] exorted 1
61.30	Crabshaw] Crrbshaw 2
62.8	mule∧] ~, 1–2
62.9	knight);] ~;) 1–2
62.15	knight);] ~;) 1–2
62.18	Launcelot).] ~.) 1–2
62.30	master] measter 2
65.16	peaste] peast 2
65.17	and an't] an't 2
65.36	had lodged] lodged 2
66.16	comfortable] confortable 2
67.31	horses'] ~∧ 1–2
69.14	PRETENDER, an] ~. An 1–2
69.36	ceiling] cieling 2
70.22	understand] un- | sterstand 2
71.4	meer] mere 2
71.17	Quickset] Quicket 2

71.30   all] All 2

71.31   ne'er] ne'r 1

71.36   Englishman] Enlishman 1

71.38   oun] own 2

72.5-6   vreehoulder] vreeholder 2

75.9   rewards of venality] rewards venality 2

76.25   harrangued] harangued 2

77.19   rock] rocks 2

77.33   *archæus*] *archoeus* 1–2

78.4   meer] mere 2

78.5   religion] rellgion 2

78.5   no body] nobody 2

78.16   harrangue] ha- | rangue 2

78.22   meer] mere 2

79.19   intreaties] entreaties 2

79.32   woolen] woollen 2

79.35   captain∧] ~, 1

81.6   or be] or to be 2

81.13-14   steal nothing, but to steal ourselves away—] steal ourselves
               away— 2

81.20   emotion).] ~.) 1–2

81.23   law in a general] a law in general 2

81.24   words∧——"] ~".—— 1; ~"∧—— 2

81.26   laying∧] ~, 1–2

82.9   eats little] eats a little 2

84.4   attorneys'] ~∧ 1–2

84.13	a large sum in the way] in the large way 2
86.39	Oakely] Oakley 2
87.6	a fair prospect] a prospect 2
87.17	Oakely] Oakley 2
88.5	her] the 2
89.3	croud] crowd 2
89.31	dealt] delt 2
89.37	accessory] accessary 2
90.9	a notorious criminal] no-	torious criminal 2
90.27	you are all in a gang] you are in a gang 2
90.28	one day all in a cord] one day in a cord 2
90.30	fellow∧] ~, 1–2
90.30	justice).] ~.) 1–2
91.23	groveling] grovelling 2
92.16	privilegs] privileges 2
92.25	and void.] void. 2
92.37	of peace] of the peace 2
93.14	intitled] entitled 2
93.20	tranquillity] tranquility 2
93.36	attone] atone 2
93.39	of your power] of power 2
94.7	Justice] justice 2
94.11	jailer] jailor 2
94.21	compleat] complete 2
94.36	Oakely] Oakley 1–2
95.13	Oakely] Oakley 2

95.17   Oakely] Oakley 2

95.28   Oakely] Oakley 2

95.29   Oakely] Oak- | ley 2

95.36   come home too late] come too late 2

95.37   Oakely's] Oakley's 2

96.8   Fillet] Mr. Fil- | let 2

96.12   attonement] atonement 2

96.22   Oakely] Oakley 2

96.34   Oakely's] Oakley's 2

97.2   Oakely] Oakley 2

97.20   comliest] comeliest 2

98.7   not the strain] not in the strain 2

98.9   Oakely's] Oakley's 2

98.12   Sedgemoor] Sedgemore 2

98.15   restored.] ∼, 1

98.19   Oakely] Oakley 2

100.32   What!] ∼; 1–2

100.34   transport):] ∼:) 1–2

102.2   meer] mere 2

102.16   mackarel's] mackerel's 2

102.17   Hearkye] Harkye 2

103.20   dogs'] ∼∧ 1–2

103.23   nicompoop] nincom- | poop 2

104.12   ladies'] ∼∧ 1–2

104.38   duty it is] duty is it 2

105.9   highway?] ∼. 1–2

105.23	motionless] mo- | tianless 2
105.25	pannic] panic 2
105.27	had done] done 2
105.31-32	cowardice.] ~, 1
107.17	sequestered] sequestred 2
108.13	being] bein 2
108.23	Oakely] Oakley 2
110.9	which] whlch 2
110.36	operate] opetate 2
112.21	thro'] through 2
113.8	situation.] ~; 2
113.13	extraordinary] axtraordinary 2
113.18	rhetorick] rhetoric 2
114.24	at sight] at the sight 2
115.23	emotion).] ~.) 1-2
116.9	justice_∧] ~, 1-2
116.9-10	replied):] ~:) 1-2
116.22	madam_∧] ~, 1-2
116.23	adventurer).] ~.) 1-2
116.32	know] nkow 2
117.30	eulogium] elogium 2
118.26	sweetest, gentlest,] sweetest, and gent- | lest, 2
120.7	conveyance_∧] ~, 1-2
120.7	Launcelot).] ~.) 1-2
120.15	hoondred] houndred 2
120.16	oan't] oon't 2

120.29   ejaculations] ajacu- | lations 2

122.4   like∧] ~, 1–2

122.4-5   room-door).] ~.) 1–2

124.18   servant] servannt 2

126.4   inquired] enquired 2

127.12   borborygmata∧] ~, 1–2

127.13   physician).] ~.) 1–2

127.16   alexipharmic] alexipharmci 1

127.17   indeed∧] ~, 1–2

127.17   doctor);] ~;) 1–2

127.39   many a score] many score 2

128.1   sensibly.∧ ∧Have] sensibly." "Have 1–2

128.2   heart∧] ~, 1–2

128.2   physician).] ~.) 1–2

128.8-9   fauces∧] ~, 1–2

128.9   apothecary):] ~:) 1–2

129.1   antient] an- | cient 2

129.20   musquets] muskets 2

129.38   perceived that some] perceived some 2

130.18   heralds] haralds 2

132.19   that, when] when 2

134.25   farmers] farmer 1–2

135.35   with a paroxysm] with paroxysm 2

137.34   ten or dozen] ten or a dozen 2

138.7   He] he 1

138.28   hoping,] ~∧ 2

138.28	that$_\wedge$] ~, 2
139.5	sphere] spere 2
139.24	very idea$_\wedge$] ~~. 1–2
139.25	Sycamore).] ~.) 1–2
139.25	Your idea,] ~~$_\wedge$ 1
139.26	conception?"] ~." 1
139.37	Nay,] ~$_\wedge$ 1
139.39	you,] ~$_\wedge$ 1
140.4	he's] he is 2
140.4	Here,] ~$_\wedge$ 1
140.6	notes?] ~. 1–2
140.6	Nay,] ~$_\wedge$ 1
140.7	All] all 1–2
140.8	Come,] ~$_\wedge$ 1
140.38	words:] ~. 1
141.6	however] how-	wever 1
142.14	May-hap,] ~$_\wedge$ 1
142.16	stowage;] ~, 1
142.26	Damn'd,] ~$_\wedge$ 1
142.26	goblins,] ~$_\wedge$ 1
142.35	names,] ~$_\wedge$ 1
143.4	When] when 1–2
143.6	errand] errant 2
143.8	surprise] surprize 2
143.13	an hobgoblin] a hobgoblin 2
144.19	nay,] ~$_\wedge$ 1

145.23   *Containing the atchievements of the Knights of the Griffin and*
                Crescent.] *Discomfiture of the Knight of the Griffin.* 1

145.5   gryphon] griffin 2

145.12   trumpeter] trum- | puter 1

145.29   intreaties] entreaties 2

146.3   engagement] engagment 1

147.19   to the head] on the head 2

147.20   signal to battle] signal of battle 2

149.11   what,] ~∧ 1–2

150.15   mayn't] may'nt 1–2

151.10   Crowe] Crow 1

151.18   couldn't] coudn't 1–2

151.19   may kiss] my kiss 1–2

153.29   landschape] land- | scape 2

153.35   convey'd] con- | veyed 2

154.30   of the jailor] of jailor 2

155.21   resolved] re- | solving 1

155.30   cure] care 2

157.11   sequestred] sequestered 2

157.18   atrabiliarious] atrabilarious 2

157.20   phlegmatic] phegmatic 1

157.29   Crabclaw's] Crabclaws's 1

158.17   be] be be 1–2

159.1   CHAPTER XXI.] CHAP. XX . 2

159.8   committment] commitment 2

161.4-5   inconceivable] inconceiveable 2

161.25	uttered] ut- | terred 1
161.26	acquainted] aquainted 2
161.33	pappa] papa 2
162.26	he's] he is 2
162.37	Clarke's] Clark's 1–2
163.3	For] for 1
163.6	he'd] he would 2
163.34	length] lenght 2
164.5	gaol] goal 2
166.1	tho'] though 2
167.5	employed] emyloyed 2
168.6	being again brought] being brought 2
168.36	thro'] through 2
170.3	conjuror] conjurer 2
170.4	accent:] ~; 1–2
170.4	conjuror's] conjurer's 2
170.12	East Riding] East Raiding 2
170.29-30	be so bauld] be bauld 1
172.9	on a Thursday] on Thursday 2
172.10	strenuously] strenously 1
172.34	case,] ~ᴧ 1
172.38	propitious] more propitious 2
173.2	heᴧ)] ~,) 1
173.27	didn't] did not 2
173.37	inquiries] enquiries 2
175.2	frequented] unfrequented 2

175.11   chear;] cheer, 2

175.11   assured] assuring 2

175.32   juncture] time 1(c), 2

177.35   and so tractable] and tracta- | ble 2

178.14   youth'?] ~.' 1–2

179.17   who ask and want it] who ask want it 1(u); those that ask it
                1(c); those who ask it 2

179.37   escape!] ~; 2

179.37   with∧] ~, 1

180.4   hath] has 2

180.24   instant] instantly 1(c), 2

180.37   profitting] profiting 2

181.2   paroxism] paroxysm 2

182.31   for] or 1–2

182.33   begone] be gone 2

183.2   was] was was 1–2

184.1   tho'] though 2

184.8   brimfull] brimful 2

184.30   emotion] emotions 2

184.33   repaired] retired 2

185.8   delay; nothing] ~. Nothing 2

186.11   sigh∧] ~,) 1

186.33   he∧] ~,) 1

186.35   she∧] ~,) 1

186.36   obligations] obligatious 1

187.24   duration.—] ~,— 1

187.27	genever] geneva 2
189.9	This] The 2
190.4	at her proper] at a proper 2
191.25	brother";] ~;" 1–2
191.28	Crowe] Crow 1
191.37	empirical] empyrical 2
193.30	centre] center 2
193.38	in presence] in the presence 2
194.4	other extraneous] extraneous 1
194.25-26	Virtue's] virtue's 2
194.37	Tho'] Though 2
195.23	if] If 2
195.27	blush,] ~ₐ 1–2
195.27	besidesₐ] ~, 1
195.39	if he do not prove] if he prove not 2
196.16	hairs] ears 2
196.18	surprise] surprize 2
196.31	instant,] ~ₐ 1
196.39	kinswoman).] ~.) 1–2
197.17	Mattocks] Mattox 2
197.19	well as] well sa 2
197.25	Oakely] Oakley 1–2

PUBLICATION DATES

THE BRITISH MAGAZINE: OR, MONTHLY REPOSITORY FOR GENTLEMEN AND LADIES (1760–61)

VOL. I

No. 1 (for January 1760). Published 1 January 1760 (*Daily Advertiser*, 1 January 1760).
Sir Launcelot Greaves, Chapter 1.

No. 2 (for February 1760). Published 1 February 1760 (*Daily Advertiser*, 1 February 1760).
Sir Launcelot Greaves, Chapter 2.

No. 3 (for March 1760). Published 1 March 1760 (*Daily Advertiser*, 1 March 1760).
Sir Launcelot Greaves, Chapter 3.

No. 4 (for April 1760). Published 1 April 1760 (*Daily Advertiser*, 1 April 1760).
Sir Launcelot Greaves, Chapter 4.

No. 5 ("No. V"). Published 1 May 1760 (*Daily Advertiser*, 1 May 1760).
Sir Launcelot Greaves, Chapter 5.

No. 6 (for May 1760). Published 3 June 1760 (*Daily Advertiser*, 3 June 1760).
Sir Launcelot Greaves, Chapter 6.

No. 7 (for June 1760). Published 1 July 1760 (*London Chronicle*, 28 June–1 July 1760).
Sir Launcelot Greaves, Chapter 7.

No. 8 (for July 1760). Published 2 August 1760 (*Daily Advertiser*, 2 August 1760).
Sir Launcelot Greaves, Chapter 8.

No. 9 (for August 1760). Published 1 September 1760 (*Daily Advertiser*, 1 September 1760).
Sir Launcelot Greaves, Chapter 9.

No. 10 (for September 1760). Published 1 October 1760 (*Daily Advertiser*, 1 October 1760).
Sir Launcelot Greaves, Chapter 10.

No. 11 (for October 1760). Published 1 November 1760 (*Daily Advertiser*, 1 November 1760).
Sir Launcelot Greaves, Chapter 11.

No. 12 (for November 1760). Published 1 December 1760 (*Daily Advertiser*,

1 December 1760).
Sir Launcelot Greaves, Chapter 12.

No. 13 (for December 1760). Published 1 January 1761 (*Daily Advertiser*, 1 January 1761).
Sir Launcelot Greaves, Chapter 13.

VOL. 2

No. 1 (for January 1761). Published 3 February 1761 (*Daily Advertiser*, 3 February 1761).
Sir Launcelot Greaves, Chapter 14.

No. 2 (for February 1761). Published 2 March 1761 (*London Chronicle*, 28 February–3 March 1761).
Sir Launcelot Greaves, Chapter 15.

No. 3 (for March 1761). Published 1 April 1761 (*London Chronicle*, 31 March–2 April 1761).
Sir Launcelot Greaves, Chapter 16.

No. 4 (for April 1761). Published 2 May 1761 (*Daily Advertiser*, 2 May 1761).
Sir Launcelot Greaves, Chapter 17.

No. 5 (for May 1761). Published 1 June 1761 (*London Chronicle*, 30 May–2 June 1761).
Sir Launcelot Greaves, Chapter 18.

No. 6 (for June 1761). Published 2 July 1761 (*Daily Advertiser*, 2 July 1761).
Sir Launcelot Greaves, Chapter 19.

No. 7 (for July 1761). Published 1 August 1761 (*Daily Advertiser*, 1 August 1761).
Sir Launcelot Greaves, Chapter 20.

No. 8 (for August 1761). Published 1 September 1761 (*Daily Advertiser*, 1 September 1761).
Sir Launcelot Greaves, Chapter 21.

No. 9 (for September 1761). Published 1 October 1761 (*Daily Advertiser*, 1 October 1761).
Sir Launcelot Greaves, Chapter 22.

No. 10 (for October 1761). Published 2 November 1761 (*Daily Advertiser*, 2 November 1761).
Sir Launcelot Greaves, Chapter 23.

No. 11 (for November 1761). Published 1 December 1761 (*Daily Advertiser*, 1 December 1761).
Sir Launcelot Greaves, Chapter 24.

No. 12 (for December 1761). Published 1 January 1762 (*Daily Advertiser*, 1 January 1762).
Sir Launcelot Greaves, Chapter the Last.

BIBLIOGRAPHICAL DESCRIPTIONS

Sir Launcelot Greaves was initially published serially in twenty-five parts in the *British Magazine*, volumes 1–2 (1760–61).

1. THE FIRST EDITION

THE | **British Magazine** | OR | *Monthly Repository* | FOR | **Gentlemen** & **Ladies**. | VOL. I. | [device] | LONDON. | *Printed for* James Rivington & James Fletcher, *at the* | *Oxford Theatre;* & H. Payne, *at Dryden's Head, in* | PATER NOSTER ROW.
Head-title: [row of printer's flowers] | THE | LIFE AND ADVENTURES | OF | SIR LAUNCELOT GREAVES.

Volume 2: THE | **British Magazine** | OR | *Monthly Repository* | For | **Gentlemen** *and* **Ladies**. | VOL. II ᵈ. | [device] | London. | *Printed for H. Payne, & Wm. Cropley, at Dryden's Head, in* | *Pater Noster Row.*
Collation: 8° in 4s, half-sheet imposition (209 x 128 mm). Volume 1: engraved title+B–5A⁴. Pp. engraved title page, [i]–ii dedication to William Pitt, 3–56 *British Magazine* number for January 1760, 9–14 chapter 1 of *Sir Launcelot Greaves;* 57–112 February, 57–64 chapter 2; 113–168 March, 124–133 chapter 3; 169–224 April, 169–178 chapter 4; 225–280 Number V, 225–232 chapter 5; 97[281]–152[336] May, 97[281]–101[285] chapter 6; 337–392 June, 338–344 chapter 7; 393–448 July, 393–398 chapter 8; 449–504 August, 449–455 chapter 9; 505–560 September, 513–518 chapter 10; 561–616 October, 570–576 chapter 11; 617–672 November, 618–624 chapter 12; *673–728* December, 690–696 chapter 13; [1–8] Index.
Volume 2: engraved title+A–4P⁴ 4Q⁴ (–4Q⁴). Pp. engraved title page, [i]–ii Advertisement, 3–56 January 1761, 3–9 chapter 14; *57–112* February, 57–64 chapter 15; *113–168* March, *113–120* chapter 16; *169–224* April, 185–192 chapter 17; 225–280 May, 252–257 chapter 18; *281–336* June, 305–311 chapter 19; *337–392* July, 355–360 chapter 20; *393–448* August, 427–434 chapter 21; *449–504* September, 461–467 chapter 22; *505–560* October, *505–511* chapter 23; 561–616 November, 593–601 chapter 24; *617–672* December, 625–632 "Chapter the Last"; [1–6] Index.

Press figures: Volume 1: 4-8 *or* 8-1 15-3 22-6 *or* 23-4 26-5 *or* 27-3 34-1 *or* 37-3 42-1 *or* 44-4 50-3 *or* 53-5 62-1 72-1 74-2 85-3 91-2 103-4 108-1 116-4

122-7 130-7 143-5 146-6 158-1 162-2 175-5 182-5 192-1 196-7 205-1 210-2 220-5 228-7 238-6 242-6 253-1 260-1 271-3 278-2 103-2 108-3 114-6 126-4 135-6 141-3 149-2 344-3 351-3 359-4 365-1 370-1 383-3 389-6 398-5 407-3 414-5 421-3 428-3 440-1 444-5 450-4 466-4 474-5 486-1 504-4 509-2 520-1 527-2 535-1 542-5 546-2(?) 559-3 562-4 570-5 584-3 597-5 604-1 612-2 628-2 640-5 663-2 666-1 676-2 694-1 702-5 706-2(?) 722-1. Volume 2: 4-5 23-4 26-2 36-1 45-5 52-1 77-5 85-5 96-4 101-1 114-5 126-5 132-6 141-3 151-1 158-4 162-6 173-6 184-4 189-6 197-5 202-3 215-6 221-4 229-3 237-3 248-1 255-6 262-5 268-3 276-1 287-6 295-3 302-1 309-1 316-3 326-2 332-3 344-3 350-2 354-3 366-5 372-3 383-1 388-2 394-5 405-5 415-5 418-2 430-3 434-2 447-3 456-3 464-5 472-2 479-2 485-3 498-2 509-2 *or* 509-5 524-3 535-3 544-3 551-3 567-2 574-2 580-5 590-3 596-2 604-3 614-3 623-2 631-2 637-3 648-2 656-2 664-5.

Typography: Volume 1: 161–168 in some copies = 153–160, 281–336 = 97–152, 485 in some copies = 548, 543 = 54, 616 in some copies = 16, 727 = 723. R2 unsigned, Y in some copies signed X, 2E in some copies signed 2F, 2O–2U⁴ signed O–U⁴, 4K2 signed 4H2. Catchwords (*Sir Launcelot Greaves*): 62 he] the 340 mey] mey-ʌ 451 speech,] ~ʌ. Volume 2: 175 = 179, 333 = 233, 597–598 = 497–498. N2, 2G2, in some copies 2I2, 3Z2 unsigned, T2 in some copies signed M2. Catchwords: 8 inter-] mitted.

Plates: Volume 1: 35 plates, including frontispiece; plate facing p. 57 "Sir Launcelot Greaves, & his Squire, Timothy Crabshaw.—" signed A. Walker; plate facing p. 449, "Sr. L. Greaver and his Squire T. Crabshaw at a Country Election.—." Volume 2: 26 plates, including frontispiece.

Note: The title page of volume 1 is in two states: (1) with the imprint as above and vignette of the Sheldonian Theatre, Oxford; (2) with only H. Payne in the imprint and a portrait of Dryden replacing the vignette. The engraved titles are conjugate with the frontispieces. The January 1760 number exists in two settings, *a* and *b*. A note to the binder appears on p. [8] of the index to volume 1: "After the magazine for April, and before that for May, place Number V. The page of the first sheet of the magazine for May, instead of 97, should be marked 281, and the signature of that sheet instead of O, should be Oo."

Copies: Textually collated (*Sir Launcelot Greaves*) Boston Public Library (PER. *7227. 19), James G. Basker (private collection), Massachusetts

Historical Society October 1761, Tulane University (PR1133 .B7 Rare), University of Texas at Austin (052 B7776 Rare Books Col), Yale University, Beinecke Library (Z17 2297d/1–2). Bibliographically collated (*British Magazine*) Folger Shakespeare Library (AP 3 B7 cage), vol. 1, Yale University, Sterling Library (Franklin 111 B77 1), vol. 1, London University Library (Periodicals), National Library of Canada/Bibliothèque nationale du Canada ("Oxford Theatre"), vol. 1 ("Dryden's Head"), January–May 1760, National Library of Ireland (J 05), University of Oxford, Bodleian Library (Hope Adds 1158–9).

2. THE SECOND EDITION
THE | ADVENTURES | OF | Sir Launcelot Greaves. | By the Author of RODERICK RANDOM. | In TWO VOLUMES. | VOL. I. | [printer's ornaments] | LONDON: | Printed for J. COOTE, in Pater-Noster-Row. | M DCC LXII. |

Volume 2: Title page as in volume 1 except "VOL. II." substituted for "VOL. I."
    Collation: 12° (163 x 95 mm). Volume 1: [A]² B–M¹². Title page, verso *blank*, iii–iv contents, *1–264* text. Volume 2: [A]² B–M¹² N¹⁰. Title page, verso *blank*, iii–iv contents, *1–283* text, *284 blank*.

Press figures: Volume 1: 2-2 12-5 46-3 48-6 69-3 84-5 93-5 120-5 124-5 130-3 158-6 165-2 182-6 216-2 239-3 261-5 263-3.
Volume 2: 2-3 60-2 62-3 95-2 144-5 159-6 183-6 192-5 220-5 238-2 253-4 262-5 281-2.

Typography: Volume 1: B6 unsigned. Catchwords 6 What] With 69 the] least 82 pro-] cured 172 ∧ for] (~ 177 know] in. Volume 2: Catchwords 54 coul] could 146 ea y] easy 204 horses:] ~;.

Copies: Textually collated University of Illinois (X823 Sm7a), University of Texas at Austin, Harry Ransom Humanities Research Center (Jerome Kern PR3694 L3 1762), and University of Iowa (xPR3694 S5 1762). Additional copies bibliographically examined Indiana University, Lilly Library (PR3694 .L3 1762), Yale University, Beinecke Library (Im Sm79 762A), British Library (12614. d. 30).

INDEX

NAMES, PLACES, AND TOPICS IN INTRODUCTION, TEXT,
NOTES TO THE TEXT, AND TEXTUAL COMMENTARY

(Reference to topics is necessarily selective. Location of some places is indicated according to eighteenth-century geography.)

Act for Regulating Madhouses (1774), 180 (n. 40)
Addison, Joseph: *Drummer*, 170 (n. 13); *Spectator*, 25 (n. 40)
Allen, Brian, liii (n. 88)
Allestree, Richard, 172 (n. 21)
Amadis de Gaul, xxviii, 15 (n. 30)
Amherst, Jeffrey, xl
Amhurst, Nicholas. See *Craftsman*
Anderson, Robert: "Life of Smollett," xxv, l (n. 33)
Angelica; or, Quixote in Petticoats, xxxvii
Angeloni, Batista [pseud.], 9 (n. 48)
Ariosto, Ludovico: *Orlando Furioso*, 44 (n. 18), 115 (n. 1)
Aristotle, 77 (nn. 13, 16), 78 (n. 31)
Aston (Yorkshire), 26 (nn. 44, 45, 48)

Baldwin, Richard, Jr., 256
Bannerman, Alexander, xlvii
Barbauld, Anna Laetitia, xxv
Basker, James G., xviii, xxiii, xlvii, xlviii (nn. 2, 6), xlix (n. 14), li (n. 55), liv (n. 98), 264 (n. 5)
Bastille (prison), 180 (n. 39)
Battestin, Martin C., li–lii (n. 59)
Battie, William, 126 (n. 4); *Treatise on Madness*, xxxi, 177 (n. 23)
Battle of the Reviews, xxii
Beard, John, 31 (n. 8)
Beasley, Jerry C., xxv
Beattie, James: "Essay on Laughter," xxiv, l (n. 26); "On Fable and Romance," xxiv

Bedlam. *See* St. Mary of Bethlehem Hospital
Bee. *See* Garden, Francis, Lord Gardenstone
Bencraft, James, 31 (n. 8)
Bentley, G. E., Jr., 266 (n. 16)
Bible, 26 (n. 44); Acts, 91 (n. 6); Esther, 71 (n. 26); Exodus, 170 (n. 13); Jonah, 77 (n. 9); Matthew, 54 (n. 7), 176 (n. 20); Revelation, 78 (nn. 32, 36)
Black Lion Inn (Nottinghamshire), 3 (n. 2)
Blake, William, xlviii
Boege, Fred W., xxi
Boeotian League, 178 (n. 29)
Boileau-Despréaux, Nicholas, 179 (nn. 36, 37); *Art poétique*, 179 (n. 36); *Lutrin*, 179 (n. 36)
Bolingbroke, Henry St. John, viscount. See *Craftsman*
Boswell, James: *Critical Strictures*, 26 (n. 43); *Journal of a Tour to the Hebrides*, 72 (n. 29); *London Journal*, 26 (n. 43)
Boucé, Paul-Gabriel, xxv, xxxi, xlviii (n. 1), 26 (n. 44)
Boulogne Gate (inn), 152 (n. 24)
Brack, O M, Jr., xlix (n. 12), lii (nn. 69, 75), liii (n. 77), 266 (n. 14), 267 (n. 25)
Brandenburg (Prussia), 176 (n. 17)
Brewer Street (London), 153 (n. 2)
Bridewell (prison), 16 (n. 31), 159 (n. 2), 168 (n. 9), 192 (n. 10)
British Magazine. *See* Smollett, Tobias George: works; journalism

Briton. See Smollett, Tobias George:
    works; journalism
Bronson, Bertrand H., 267 (n. 24)
Browning, Reed, lii (n. 72), liii (n. 86)
Brutus, Lucius Junius, 15 (n. 26)
Buckden (Huntingdonshire), 151 (n. 19)
Bull and Gate Inn. *See* Boulogne Gate
    (inn)
Burton, Robert: *Anatomy of Melancholy*,
    xxxi
Bute, John Stuart, earl of, xviii, xl, xliv
Butler, Samuel: *Hudibras*, xxxvi, xlvi, li
    (n. 41), liv (n. 94), 13 (n. 7), 129 (n. 20)

Campbell, Alexander Hume, 4 (n. 7)
Cantrell, Pamela, li (n. 55)
Carey, Henry, 69 (n. 8)
Cervantes Saavedra, Miguel de: *Don
    Quixote*, xxiv, xxviii, xxx, xxxi, xxxv,
    xxxvi, xxxvii, xxxviii, xlvi, 13 (nn. 7, 18),
    15 (nn. 24, 25, 27, 29, 30), 19 (n. 53),
    31 (n. 7), 44 (n. 18), 51 (nn. 13, 14), 60
    (n. 25), 66 (nn. 13, 15), 77 (n. 14), 82
    (n. 57), 103 (nn. 18, 19), 119 (n. 5),
    120 (n. 6), 132 (n. 17), 133 (n. 30), 139
    (n. 2), 141 (n. 5), 145 (nn. 2, 3), 147
    (n. 6)
Challe, Robert: *Continuation de l'histoire
    de l'admirable Don Quichotte*, xxxvi
Chalmers, Alexander, xxv
Chanson de Roland, 103 (n. 21)
Chapel Street (London), 153 (n. 2)
Charlton, Sir Job Stanton, xliii
Churchill, Charles, 178 (nn. 24, 26, 27,
    29, 30, 32); *Apology*, 178 (nn. 28, 34);
    Night, 178 (n. 27); *Rosciad*, 178 (n. 28)
Clennell, Luke, xlviii
Clive, Robert, xl
Clowes, Butler, xlvii
"Coal Black Joke," 53 (n. 18)
Cole, Richard Cargill, xlix (n. 18), l
    (n. 25)
Colman, George: *Connoisseur*, 26 (n. 41);
    Two Odes, 178 (n. 28)
Congreve, William: *Love for Love*, 191
    (n. 6)

Coote, John, xxii, 255–56, 257–58, 265–
    66 (n. 14), 266 (n. 16)
Corbauld, Richard, xlviii
Craftsman, xl, 17 (n. 40)
Critical Review. See Smollett, Tobias
    George: works; journalism
Cropley, William, 255–56
Cruden, Alexander: *London Citizen
    Exceedingly Injured*, 180 (n. 40)
Cruikshank, George, xlviii
Cumberland, William Augustus, duke
    of, xl

Daily Advertiser, 183 (n. 6), 255, 257
Darnall (Yorkshire), 26 (n. 44)
Davies, Christian: *Life*, 103 (n. 19)
Day, Robert Adams, lii (n. 66), liv (n. 97)
Defoe, Daniel, xvii; *Augusta Triumphans*,
    180 (n. 40); *Jonathan Wild*, 17 (n. 38)
Dickens, Charles: *Bleak House*, 42 (n. 2)
Dioscorides Pedanius, 77 (n. 14)
Donoghue, Frank, 83 (n. 2)
Drury Lane Theatre, 44 (n. 14)
Dryden, John: *Don Sebastian*, 30 (n. 65)
Dublin Journal, xxii, xxiv, 264 (n. 7), 266
    (n. 20)

Edgerton, Judy, liii (n. 90)
Essick, Robert N., liv (n. 96)
Etherege, George: *Man of Mode*, 14
    (n. 20), 66 (n. 14)
Evans, David, xix–xx, xxv, li (n. 57), liii
    (n. 85), 28 (n. 58), 66 (n. 15), 75
    (n. 43), 124 (n. 2), 143 (n. 18), 159
    (n. 1), 170 (n. 13)

Fabel, Robin, lii (n. 66)
Farquhar, George: *Twin Rivals*, 28
    (n. 54)
Felsenstein, Frank, 69 (nn. 9, 11), 75
    (nn. 37, 40)
Fénelon, François de Salignac de la
    Mothe-: *Aventures de Télémaque*, xix
Ferdinand, duke of Brunswick, xl
Fielding, Henry, xvii, xxxvii; *Don Quixote
    in England*, xxxiv, xxxvi, 75 (n. 43);

Jonathan Wild, 17 (n. 38), 156 (n. 15);
Joseph Andrews, xxxii, 58 (n. 18), 196
(n. 23); *Tom Jones*, xx, xxxiii–xxxiv, 12
(n. 4), 28 (n. 57), 32 (n. 13), 60 (n. 24),
96 (n. 21), 108 (n. 2), 152 (n. 24), 165
(n. 11), 196 (n. 22)
Fitzpatrick, Barbara Laning, xviii, l
(nn. 29, 30), 97 (n. 23), 264 (n. 5), 265
(nn. 9, 14), 266 (n. 20), 268 (n. 29)
Fizes, Antoine, 259
Fleet (prison), 154 (n. 9)
Fletcher, James, Jr., 255–56, 264–65
(n. 9)
Foord, Archibald S., xli
Foster, James R., 4 (n. 11), 9 (n. 47)
Foundling Hospital. *See* Hospital for
the Maintenance and Education of
Exposed and Deserted Young
Children
Frederick II, king of Prussia ("the
Great"), xl, 175 (nn. 4, 7), 176 (n. 9)
Friedman, Arthur, xlix (n. 13)
Friedrich Heinrich Ludwig, prince of
Prussia, 176 (n. 9)

Galen, 77 (n. 15)
Garden, Francis, Lord Gardenstone: *Bee*,
xxiv–xxv; *Miscellanies in Prose and Verse*,
xxiv–xxv
Garrick, David, 27 (n. 50), 44 (n. 14),
178 (n. 28), 261; "Difficulty of
Managing a Theatre," 44 (n. 14),
191 (n. 6)
Gatehouse (prison), 154 (n. 9)
Gay, John: "Sweet William's Farewell,"
53 (n. 19)
Geber. *See* Ibn Haiyan, Abu Musa Jabir
George II, king of England, xxxix, xliv
George III, king of England, xliv
George, Saint, 130 (n. 1)
Gideon, Samson, xliii, xliv
Golconda (India), 194 (n. 18)
Golden Square (London), 153 (n. 2), 183
(n. 3)
Goldsmith, Oliver: *Good-Natur'd Man*, 6
(n. 36); *Public Ledger*, xlix (n. 13)

Grand Magazine, 257
Graves, Richard: *Spiritual Quixote*, xxxvii
Gray, Thomas: *Elegy Written in a
Country Churchyard*, xxvii
Gray's Inn. *See* Inns of Court
Great North Road, 3 (n. 1), 25 (n. 34), 79
(n. 38), 151 (n. 19), 152 (nn. 23, 24)
Greaves Hall (Yorkshire), 49 (nn. 32, 33)
Greene, Donald J., lii (n. 66)
Greene, Robert: *Quip for an Upstart
Courtier*, 120 (n. 7)
Grey, Zachary, xlvi, li (n. 41), liv (n. 94)
Griffiths, Ralph, 83 (n. 2)
Grignion, Charles, xlvi, xlviii
Grove Hall. *See* Greaves Hall
Guillen, Claudio, xxxi

Hall, David, 264 (n. 4)
Hambridge, Roger A., xliii, lii (n. 66), 4
(n. 11), 6 (n. 28), 26 (n. 45), 28 (nn. 57,
58), 31 (n. 6), 49 (nn. 32, 33), 59
(n. 19), 61 (n. 1), 76 (n. 2), 97 (n. 23),
120 (n. 6), 124 (n. 2), 159 (n. 1), 192
(n. 12)
Hamilton, Archibald, Sr., 255–56
Hammelmann, Hanns, xliv, xlv
Handel, George Frederick: *Acis and
Galatea*, 28 (n. 58)
Harlan, Robert D., 265 (n. 10)
Harrison, James, xxiv
Harrison, John, 176 (n. 18)
Hartau, Johannes, liv (n. 93)
Harvey, John: *Life of Sir Robert Bruce*, 30
(n. 71)
Hatfield (Hertfordshire), 152 (n. 23)
Havard, William, 31 (n. 8)
Hawkins, William, xlviii
Hayman, Francis, xlv, xlvi
Henry VIII, king of England, 168 (n. 7)
Hernlund, Patricia, 264 (n. 4)
His Majesty's Declaration of War, lii–liii
(n. 75)
Hobbes, Thomas: *Leviathan*, 192 (n. 9)
Hoey, James, Jr., xxii, xlvi, xlvii, 260
Hogarth, William, xxxiv, li (n. 55), liv
(n. 94), 31 (n. 6), 178 (n. 24); *Four*

Hogarth, William (*cont'd*)
  Prints of an Election, xxxiv, 69 (nn. 2, 4);
  Harlot's Progress, 69 (n. 9); *Industry and
  Idleness*, xxxv, 172 (n. 21); *Paul before
  Felix Burlesqued*, 91 (n. 6); *Rake's
  Progress*, xxxv, 53 (n. 18), 105 (n. 25),
  175 (n. 3), 176 (n. 18)
Homer: *Iliad*, 17 (n. 39), 31 (n. 5), 50
  (n. 3), 82 (n. 59), 147 (n. 5)
Horace (Quintus Horatius Flaccus):
  Satires, 178 (n. 33)
Hospital for the Maintenance and
  Education of Exposed and Deserted
  Young Children, 166 (n. 2)
Howard, William, 31 (n. 8)
Huggins, William, 31 (n. 6), 44 (n. 18)
Hunter, Richard A., li (n. 46), 177 (n. 23)
Hutcheson, Francis: *Inquiry into the
  Original of Our Ideas of Beauty*, 80 (n. 45)

Ibn Haiyan, Abu Musa Jabir ("Geber"), 6
  (n. 33)
Ibn Mohammed, Abu-Mashar Jafar, 191
  (n. 6)
"Igluka and Sibbersik," 45 (n. 21)
Inns of Court, 25 (nn. 37, 38)
Insanity. *See* Madness

Jackson's Oxford Journal, 255
Jacobitism, 7 (n. 45), 72 (nn. 29, 30), 130
  (n. 2), 175 (n. 2)
Jarvis, Charles, xxxv
Jeffrey, David K., xlix (n. 9)
Jephson, Robert, l (n. 25)
Jewish Naturalization Bill (1753), xliii–xliv
Johnson, Samuel, 94 (n. 18); *Rasselas*, xxxi
Jonathan's Coffee House, 105 (n. 26)
Jones, Davy, 60 (n. 23)
Jonson, Ben, xxxiii; *Volpone*, 77 (n. 8)
Journal encyclopédique, xxii

Kahrl, George M., 26 (nn. 45, 48), 49
  (n. 33), 132 (n. 11)
Kearsly, George, 255–56, 257–58, 266
  (n. 14)
Kelly, George, xxxv

King's Bench (court), 92 (n. 16), 150 (n. 12)
King's Bench (prison), xviii, xxiv, 154
  (n. 10), 159 (n. 1)
Kirkwood, John, xlviii
Kitchen, Thomas: *English Atlas*, xlv
Knapp, Lewis Mansfield, xix, xxv, xlviii
  (nn. 1, 5, 6), xlix (n. 8), l (n. 24), 27
  (n. 50), 154 (n. 10), 263 (n. 1), 268
  (n. 26)
Knowles, Charles, xviii, xli
Kolb, Peter: *Present State of the Cape of
  Good Hope*, 42 (n. 2)

Lackington, James, xxiv
Lamb's Conduit Fields (London), 166
  (n. 2)
Langford, Paul, xxxviii
Lascelles, Henry, xliv
Lennox, Charlotte: *Female Quixote*,
  xxxvi–xxxvii
Le Sage, Alain René: *Diable boiteux*, xvii,
  xxxiii; *Gil Blas*, xvii
Le Sueur, Hubert, 28 (n. 58)
Lettis, Richard L., 59 (n. 19), 77 (n. 8)
Levin, Harry, li (n. 43), 19 (n. 53)
Library, xxiii
"Life and Adventures of Valentine and
  Orson," 79 (n. 39)
Lincoln's Inn. *See* Inns of Court
Linsalata, Carmine R., lii (n. 59)
Lloyd, Robert, 178 (nn. 25, 29); "Actor,"
  178 (n. 28); *Arcadia*, 178 (n. 26);
  "Epistle to C. Churchill," 178 (n. 26);
  "Poet," 178 (n. 26); *Two Odes*, 178
  (n. 28); *Whim*, 178 (n. 27)
Lloyd's Evening Post, 255
London Chronicle, 255, 257, 264 (nn. 7, 8)
Longitude, 176 (n. 18)
Lully, Jean-Baptiste, 179 (n. 37)
Lusatia (Germany), 175 (n. 7)

Macalpine, Ida, li (n. 46), 177 (n. 23)
Madness, xxvii, xxx–xxxi, xxxv, 177
  (n. 23)
Maitland, William: *History of London*, 47
  (n. 24)

Malory, Sir Thomas, li (n. 42)
Manners, Lord William, xliii
Marivaux, Pierre Carlet de Chamblain
    de: *Pharsamond*, xxxvi
Marriage Act (1753), 193 (n. 13)
Marshalsea (prison), 154 (n. 9)
Martin, Saint, 51 (n. 15)
Martz, Louis L., 168 (n. 8)
Mauduit, Israel: *Considerations on the
    Present German War*, liii (n. 81)
Mayfair (London), 151 (n. 20)
Mayo, Robert D., xx, xxv, xxviii
McKillop, Alan D., 178 (n. 24)
Middleton, Richard, lii (n. 73)
Militia Bill (1757), 7 (n. 44)
Monro, John: *Remarks on Dr. Battie's
    Treatise on Madness*, xxxi
Montcalm, Louis Joseph de, xl
Monthly Review, xxiii, xxxvi
Moore, John, xxxix
Motteux, Peter, xxxv
Mudford, William, xxv
Muley-Moluch, emperor of Barbary, 30
    (n. 65)
Murphy, Arthur: *Ode to the Naiads of Fleet
    Ditch*, 178 (n. 30)
Murray, William, first earl of Mansfield,
    xviii, 27 (n. 51)
Mynde, J., xlvi, liv (n. 94)

Newark, 64 (n. 10), 76 (n. 2)
Newbery, John, 255–56, 264 (n. 3)
Newcastle, Thomas Pelham-Holles,
    duke of, xxxix–xli, xlii, xliii–xliv, 71
    (n. 19), 75 (n. 35)
Newgate (prison), 42 (n. 5)
Nonsense Club, 178 (n. 29)
Novelist's Magazine, xxiv

Old Bailey (court), 172 (n. 20)
"Old England," 69 (n. 3)
Oliver, Isaac: *Edward Herbert*, xlv
Otway, Thomas: *Orphan*, 141 (n. 6)
Ovid (Publius Ovidius Naso):
    Metamorphoses, 180 (n. 43), 181 (n. 44)
Ozell, John, xxxv

Paracelsus, 77 (n. 16)
Parsons, Humphrey, 153 (n. 5)
Paulson, Ronald, xxv, li (nn. 55, 56)
Payne, Henry, 255–56, 264–65 (n. 9)
Perceval, John, second earl of Egmont,
    27 (n. 51)
Perrault, Charles, 179 (n. 37)
Pirna (Germany), 176 (n. 8)
Pitt, William, first earl of Chatham, xl,
    xli, xlii, lii (n. 70), 7 (n. 44), 27 (n. 51),
    175 (n. 2)
Pococke, George, 97 (n. 23)
Poor Laws, 25 (n. 35), 86 (n. 13)
Pope, Alexander, 179 (n. 35); *Dunciad*,
    178 (n. 31); *First Satire of the Second
    Book of Horace*, xxxii; *Guardian*, 178
    (n. 24); *Rape of the Lock*, 153 (n. 1)
Praxiteles, 28 (n. 59)
Prussia, 175 (n. 7), 176 (nn. 8, 17)
Public Ledger, xxi

Queen Street (London), 183 (n. 5)
Quinault, Philippe, 179 (n. 37)

Ralph, James, 191 (n. 6)
Raven, James, xlviii (n. 3)
Ravenet, Simon Francis (the elder), xlvi
Read, William, 78 (n. 26)
Retford (Nottinghamshire), 79 (n. 38).
    See also West Retford
Reynolds, John: *Triumphs of God's
    Revenge against Murder*, 167 (n. 4)
Richardson, Samuel, xvii, xlix (n. 14)
Rider, William: *Historical and Critical
    Account*, xxiii
Rivington, James, 255–56, 264–65 (n. 9)
Roberts, John, 258, 266 (n. 16)
Robinson, George, 258, 266 (n. 16)
Rockingham, Charles Watson-
    Wentworth, second marquess of,
    28 (n. 57)
Ross, Ian Campbell, liii (n. 83)
Rotherhithe (London), 153 (n. 6)
Roubilliac, Louis Françoise de, 28 (n. 59)
Rousseau, G. S., xliii, lii (n. 66), 4 (n. 11),
    77 (n. 12), 126 (n. 4), 175 (n. 3)

Rowe, Nicholas, 94 (n. 18); *Fair Penitent*, 28 (n. 56)

Rowlandson, Thomas, xlviii

"Rural Happiness" (Churchill?), 178 (n. 27)

St. Catherine's by the Tower (London), 61 (n. 29), 153 (n. 4)

St. George's Fields (London), 154 (n. 12)

Saint-Martin, Françoise Filleau de: *Histoire de l'admirable Don Quichotte*, xxxvi

St. Mary of Bethlehem Hospital, 105 (n. 24)

Saintsbury, George, xxv

Saunders, Joseph, xlviii

Saussure, César de, 69 (n. 5)

Scarthing Moor (Nottinghamshire), 3 (n. 2), 61 (n. 1)

Scipio Africanus Major, 29 (n. 63)

Scipio Africanus Minor, 29 (n. 63)

Scott, Sir Walter, xix, xxv

Sekora, John, 22 (n. 14)

Serjeant's Inn, 25 (n. 39)

Seven Dials (London), 191 (n. 3)

Seven Years' War, xl–xli, 130 (n. 2), 160 (n. 3), 175 (nn. 4, 7), 176 (n. 9)

Shakespeare, William, 94 (n. 18); *As You Like It*, xxxii, 12 (n. 2); *Hamlet*, xix, xxviii, 12 (nn. 1, 4), 16 (n. 33), 44 (n. 14), 142 (n. 9); *I Henry IV*, 144 (n. 21); *Henry VIII*, 94 (n. 18); *King Lear*, 83 (n. 1); *Macbeth*, 142 (n. 11); *Midsummer Night's Dream*, 31 (n. 4); *Othello*, xxix, 118 (n. 4)

Shebbeare, John, xxi, xliv, 6 (n. 33), 9 (n. 47); and Hogarth, xxxiv, 69 (n. 4); *Letters on the English Nation*, 9 (n. 48); *Letters to the People of England*, xlii–xliii, 7 (nn. 43, 45), 9 (nn. 47, 48), 17 (nn. 41, 44, 45), 18 (n. 46), 69 (n. 4), 71 (n. 19), 77 (nn. 8, 11), 78 (nn. 22, 23, 30); *Marriage Act*, 193 (n. 13); *New Analysis of the Bristol Waters*, 77 (n. 18); *Occasional Critic*, xxxvi; *Practice of Physic*, 78 (n. 33); and Smollett, xxii,

xxxvi, xlii–xliii, 4 (n. 11), 17 (n. 41), 77 (nn. 8, 16, 18), 78 (nn. 30, 33)

Sheridan, Richard Brinsley: *Rivals*, xxxii

Skinner, John, li (n. 42)

Slack, Paul, 25 (n. 35)

Smith, Albert, xlviii (n. 6), liii (n. 92), 258, 264 (n. 9)

Smith, John: *Printer's Grammar*, 259

Smith, John (poet), li (n. 56)

Smith, Richard, xxiii

Smollett, Anne (wife), xviii

Smollett, Tobias George: career as doctor, 126 (n. 5); career as writer and editor, xvii–xviii; and Churchill, 178 (nn. 24, 26, 27, 28, 29, 30, 32, 34); death, xix; health, xviii–xix; and Garrick, 27 (n. 50); in Italy, xviii–xix; legal problems, xviii, xlviii (n. 5), 4 (n. 7), 27 (n. 51), 159 (n. 1); in London, 153 (n. 2); miscellaneous opinions, 36 (n. 15), 71 (nn. 16, 17), 176 (n. 14); political opinions, xxxix–xli, xlii, xliii–xliv, liii (n. 81), 13 (n. 9), 17 (n. 41), 71 (nn. 19, 20), 72 (n. 29), 73 (n. 34), 75 (n. 35), 77 (n. 5), 78 (nn. 21, 28), 85 (nn. 9, 11), 105 (n. 26), 176 (n. 8), 193 (n. 13); and Shebbeare, xxii, xxxvi, xlii–xliii, 4 (n. 11), 17 (n. 41), 77 (nn. 8, 16, 18), 78 (nn. 30, 33); slaveowner, 152 (n. 22); and Sublime Society of Beefsteaks, 31 (nn. 6, 8); theory of the novel, xxv–xxvi; travels, xviii, 26 (n. 48)

WORKS:

—*Sir Launcelot Greaves:* advertised, xxii, 257, 266 (nn. 16, 20); autograph manuscript, 258, 260; in *British Magazine* (first edition), xvii–xviii, xix–xxii, 13 (n. 12), 44 (nn. 15, 16), 45 (n. 21), 257; book-editions, xvii, xxii–xxiii, xxiv, 31 (n. 8), 257–58, 260–61, 266 (nn. 16, 20), 267 (n. 25); chivalry in, xxxvi, xxxvii; color black in, xx–xxi, xlvi; composition, xix–xxi, 27 (n. 51), 97 (n. 23); copyright, 258, 266 (n. 14); form of, xxv–xxvi, xxxi–xxxii;

geography of, 3 (nn. 1, 2), 12 (n. 3), 25 (n. 34), 26 (nn. 44, 45, 48), 49 (nn. 32, 33), 61 (nn. 1, 29), 64 (n. 10), 76 (n. 2), 79 (n. 38), 132 (n. 11), 151 (n. 19), 152 (nn. 23, 24), 153 (nn. 2, 4), 154 (nn. 11, 12), 192 (n. 12); illustrations, xx–xxi, xlv–xlviii, 13 (n. 12), 44 (nn. 15, 16); influences, xx, xxviii–xxix, xxxii, xxxiii–xxxviii, li (nn. 41, 42); Jews in, xliii–xliv, liii (n. 85), 69 (nn. 9, 11), 75 (nn. 36, 37, 40, 41); justice in, xxxvii; knight-errantry in, xxvii, xxxi; language, xxxii–xxxiii; madness in, xxvii, xxx–xxxi, 177 (n. 23), 180 (n. 40); main character, xxvi–xxvii, xxvii, xxviii, xxix, xxxvii–xxxviii, xlvi–xlvii; Methodists in, 176 (nn. 14, 16), 196 (n. 22); politics in, xxxiv–xxxv, xxxviii–xliv; practical jokes in, xxxvii; printing, xvii, xxii–xxiii, xlix (n. 18); Quakers in, 165 (n. 11); racial stereotyping in, 152 (n. 22); reception (eighteenth-century), xxi–xxv; reception (nineteenth- and twentieth-century), xxv; satire in, xxxii; Sublime Society of Beefsteaks in, 260; textual commentary, 255–69
—Other Prose Fiction: *Adventures of an Atom*, xviii, xlviii, liii (nn. 81, 83), 6 (n. 33), 12 (n. 4), 27 (n. 51), 31 (nn. 4, 7), 77 (n. 17), 78 (n. 20), 91 (n. 6), 169 (n. 11); *Ferdinand Count Fathom*, xvii, xxi, xxiv, xxv–xxvi, xlviii, 4 (n. 11), 12 (n. 2), 90 (n. 19), 103 (n. 19), 127 (n. 10), 141 (n. 6), 154 (n. 9), 192 (n. 9); *Humphry Clinker*, xvii, xix, xxiv, xxxi, xxxii, 12 (n. 4), 13 (n. 9), 19 (n. 53), 22 (n. 14), 40 (nn. 20, 21), 53 (n. 19), 76 (n. 1), 91 (n. 8), 94 (n. 18), 124 (n. 2), 149 (n. 7), 153 (n. 2), 176 (nn. 14, 15); *Peregrine Pickle*, xvii, xxiii, xxxii, 3 (n. 5), 12 (n. 1), 20 (n. 7), 27 (n. 50), 31 (n. 11), 42 (n. 1), 54 (n. 2), 60 (n. 23), 90 (n. 19), 103 (n. 19), 124 (n. 2), 132 (n. 24), 149 (n. 7), 154 (n. 9), 169 (n. 11), 170 (n. 13), 176

(n. 16), 191 (n. 6); *Roderick Random*, xvii, xxiv, xxxii, xxxv, xlvii, 5 (n. 14), 27 (n. 50), 30 (n. 71), 31 (n. 10), 36 (n. 14), 53 (n. 18), 103 (n. 19), 127 (n. 13), 129 (n. 17), 154 (n. 9), 176 (n. 16), 192 (n. 9)
—Plays: *Regicide*, 27 (n. 50); *Reprisal*, 27 (n. 50), 76 (n. 1), 149 (n. 7)
—Poetry: *Advice*, 179 (n. 35); "Declaration of Love," 53 (n. 19); *Ode to Independence*, xix, xxxviii; *Reproof*, xliv, 105 (n. 26), 179 (n. 35)
—Journalism: *British Magazine*, xvii–xviii, xl, xlvi–xlviii, 27 (n. 51), 44 (n. 14), 45 (n. 21), 175 (nn. 4, 7), 176 (nn. 8, 9, 10, 18), 178 (n. 27), 255–58, 260, 264 (nn. 3, 7, 8); *Briton*, xviii, xliv; *Critical Review*, xvii, xviii, xxiii, xxxiv, xxxvi, xlii, xlviii, xlviii (n. 5), 6 (n. 33), 9 (nn. 46, 48), 17 (n. 44), 27 (n. 50), 69 (n. 2), 77 (n. 8), 78 (n. 33), 177 (n. 23), 178 (n. 28), 260
—Translations: *Adventures of Telemachus*, xix; *Devil upon Crutches*, xvii, xxxiii; *Don Quixote*, xvii, xix, xxxv, 12 (n. 1), 44 (n. 18), 49 (n. 31), 70 (n. 13); *Gil Blas*, xvii
—Other Prose: *Complete History*, xxxix, xlv, lii (n. 70), 16 (n. 37), 17 (n. 42), 27 (n. 51), 73 (n. 34), 105 (n. 26), 175 (n. 2), 193 (n. 13), 256; *Continuation of the Complete History*, xvii, xviii, xxxix, xl, xli, xlii, xliii, liii (nn. 81, 83), 17 (n. 40, 41), 27 (nn. 50, 51), 71 (nn. 17, 20), 72 (n. 29), 77 (n. 5), 78 (nn. 21, 28), 85 (nn. 9, 11), 159 (n. 1), 165 (n. 11), 176 (nn. 8, 14, 18), 260; *Habbakkuk Hilding*, li (n. 53); "Life of Cervantes," xxxv–xxxvi; *Present State*, xviii, 45 (n. 21), 61 (n. 29), 71 (n. 16), 179 (n. 35); *Travels*, xviii, 28 (n. 57), 36 (n. 15), 258–59, 266–67 (n. 21)
—Miscellaneous: *Essay on the External Use of Water*, 77 (nn. 17, 18), 126 (n. 5); *Letters*, lii (nn. 67, 68, 69), 4 (n. 7), 27 (n. 50), 44 (n. 18), 153 (n. 2), 267 (n. 21), 268 (n. 28); *Works* (Voltaire), xviii, 260

Somervile, William: *Chace*, xlv; *Hobbinol*, xlv–xlvi
Sorrel, Charles: *Berger extravagant*, xxxvi
Southwark (London), 154 (n. 11)
Spector, Robert Donald, 175 (n. 4)
Spitsbergen (Norway), 4 (n. 12)
Steele, Richard: *Spectator*, 25 (n. 40)
Sterne, Laurence: *Tristram Shandy*, xxxi, xlvii, 79 (n. 39), 100 (n. 1)
Stothard, Thomas, xlviii
Strahan, William, 256–57, 264 (n. 4)
Stuart, Charles Edward ("The Young Pretender"), 69 (n. 4), 105 (n. 26)
Stuart, James Francis ("The Old Pretender"), 72 (n. 30)
Sublime Society of Beefsteaks, 31 (nn. 6, 8), 260
Sutherland, Guilland, liv (nn. 93, 94, 96)
Swift, Jonathan: *Examiner*, 17 (n. 40); *Gulliver's Travels*, 17 (n. 44); *Tale of a Tub*, 176 (n. 16)

Temple. *See* Inns of Court
Thicknesse, Philip, xxiv, l (n. 24)
Thorton, Bonnell: *Connoisseur*, 26 (n. 41)
Tinney, John, xliv
Tomkis, Thomas: *Albumazar*, 191 (n. 6)
Tories, xxxviii–xl, xliii, 69 (nn. 1, 2, 3), 72 (n. 28), 73 (n. 34), 194 (n. 19)
Townshend, Charles, 180 (n. 40)
Trapp, Joseph: *Aeneis of Virgil*, 30 (n. 71)
Trent (river), 12 (n. 3)
Tyburn (London), 172 (n. 18)

Universal Chronicle, 255
Upper Brook Street (London), 183 (n. 4)

Vagrant Act (1744), 168 (n. 9)
Vandeput, George, liii (n. 85)
Van Helmont, Jean Baptiste, 77 (n. 17)

Vanneck, Sir Joshua, xliv
Vernon, Edward, 130 (n. 3)
Vernon, Francis, Lord Orwell: *Letter to the Right Honourable Lord Orwell*, xxiii–xxiv
Virgil (Publius Vergilius Maro): *Georgics*, 28 (n. 60)

Wagner, Peter, 26 (n. 44)
Wagstaffe, Jeoffry (pseud.), xxiv
Walker, Anthony, xx, xliv–xlviii, l (n. 26), 13 (n. 12), 26 (n. 42), 44 (nn. 15, 16), 304
Walker, George, 159 (n. 1)
Walker, William, xlvii–xlviii
Walpole, Horace, xlv, liii (n. 89)
Walpole, Sir Robert, xl, 168 (n. 7), 175 (n. 2)
Ward, Joshua, 78 (n. 24)
Welsh, Alexander, xxxvii
Welsh, Charles, 264 (n. 3)
Wenman, Joseph, xxiv
Westminster Magazine, xix, xlix (n. 8)
West Retford (Nottinghamshire), 132 (n. 11). *See also* Retford
Whigs, xxxviii–xxxix, xliii, 69 (nn. 4, 7, 10), 71 (n. 21), 72 (n. 29), 73 (n. 34)
Whitehall Evening-Post, 255, 264 (n. 7)
Whole Duty of Man (Allestree?), 172 (n. 21)
Wilkes, John, 31 (n. 6), 261
Wilmot, Charles Henry, xxxv
Wilson, Peter, 264 (n. 7)
Wilton, Joseph, 28 (nn. 57, 59)
Wolfe, James, xl
Wright, Joseph, xlv
Wright of Derby. *See* Wright, Joseph

Yorick's Meditations, 77 (n. 8)
York, 29 (n. 61)